IN THE FOOTSTEPS OF ROME

IS THE UNITED STATES FOLLOWING THE HISTORY OF THE ROMAN EMPIRE?

Philip J. Tarnoff

Strategic Book Publishing and Rights Co.

Strategic Book Publishing and Rights Co., LLC
USA I Singapore

For information about special discounts for bulk purchases, please contact Strategic Book Publishing and Rights Co. Special Sales, at bookorder@sbpra.net.

ISBN: 978-1-68181-446-9

Book Design: Suzanne Kelly

ACKNOWLEDGMENTS

Creating a book of fiction is a major undertaking that can take as much as a year for its completion. It is a year of considerable effort that requires more than the outline of a story. The transition from ideas to reality includes the creation of believable characters, filling in the details of the story, and identifying memorable conclusions. During the year that this work occurred, the author relied on the patience of his family as well as inspiration from others. For these reasons, the acknowledgments of this book may be its most important section, since without such support the book might not exist.

First and most important, I would like to express my appreciation to my wife, Nancy, for her support and patience while the book was being written. She exhibited commendable patience with my many hours at the computer and additional hours of daydreaming required to develop the complex tale contained in the following pages.

Writing is not a social occupation. It is necessary to live in the story as it develops, rather than associating actively with those around you. *In the Footsteps of Rome* is a particularly complex story with action that is global in nature. As a result, it was necessary to research and describe the environments of seven countries on four continents. More than seventy characters are introduced and described here. Truly a daunting task to develop credible details describing the places and people that you will meet as you read the book. Thus the need for daydreaming and research to support the writing.

Many book clubs are social gatherings where members gather to share refreshments and casual conversation about their latest selection. Depending on the makeup of the group, the books being discussed may be mysteries, love stories, war stories, or historical fiction. The book club that was the source of inspiration for this book is different. Its focus is on more thoughtful novels that address historical trends, philosophy, human nature, and political science. The club includes Robert Long, Chester Wagstaff, Lynn Russell, David Rowland, Jeff Davis, and myself. Together, our discussions have been thought-provoking and educational. Without realizing it, the discussions of this club have served as a source of inspiration for the story-line and conclusions of this book.

Selections of the club relevant to this book have included: *The Cave and the Light*, by Arthur Herman; *Why Niebuhr Matters*, by Charles Lemert; *Plain, Honest Men—the Making of the American Constitution*, by Richard Beeman; and *From Dawn to Decadence—1500 to the Present*, by Jacques Barzun. In one way or another, these resources describe the evolution of civilization through the eyes of Plato, Socrates, and many other philosophers, political scientists, artists, and scientists who influenced the development of civilization and its govern-ments. They also described the process, philosophies, debates, and theories that underlie the United States Constitution. The reader is encouraged to scan these texts to extract the wisdom they contain. Pertinent sections of these texts are quoted in the following pages.

Although the story focuses on the conflicts between the United States and the terrorist organizations of the Middle East, it hints of some parallels between this conflict and the invaders of the Roman Empire. However, the readings of the club made it clear that modern governments, as we know them today, began with the experiments of the Greeks with various forms of gov-ernment. One of the conclusions of the club as well as the fol-lowing story is the fact that external forces such as the uprisings in the Middle East will ultimately lead to drastic changes in our current form of government. The current turmoil in Washington, DC, supports this conclusion. This was the nature of the subjects discussed by the book club. I am indebted to its members for their assistance in understanding the forces at work as well as the likely outcomes.

TABLE OF CONTENTS

PREFACE

The Roman Empire

According to legend, the City of Rome was founded in 753 BC by Romulus, the son of the gods Rhea and Mars. The city's initial location was the Palatine Hill, one of the well-known Seven Hills of Rome. Although there are several versions of the story, it is generally believed that Remus, Romulus's twin, was killed by his brother during a dispute over the initial location of the city.

From that ancient time until the conquest of the last state of its Eastern Empire by the Ottomans in AD 1461, the Roman Empire experienced successes and failures unmatched in the history of the world. During 2,200 years of existence, the empire was ruled by more than 160 emperors. For more than 700 years prior to that, Rome's government underwent many changes, from monarchy, to military rule, to a republic. As a republic, the city was governed by the senate, which in turn reported to a variety of magistrates and consuls. In fact, Julius Caesar's leadership was as a military leader rather than as an emperor or an elected official.

In its later days, the Empire was divided into an Eastern Empire with Rome as its capital and a Western Empire with Byzantium as its capital. The Eastern Empire, which is known as the Byzantine Empire, survived for a thousand years after the fall of the Western Empire. This preface and the following book refer only to the Western Empire, although many of its conclusions are also applicable to the Eastern Empire.

Many historians consider AD 410, the year that the Western Empire was overrun and sacked by the Visigoths, as the date of its downfall. Others consider AD 476 to have been the final year of the Western Empire. This was the year that the Odoacer, a German leader, led an uprising that deposed Emperor Romulus Augustulus. Whatever the date, the lifespan of the Western Empire was impressive, with a duration of approximately 1,200 years.

The lifespan and accomplishments of the Roman Empire are remarkable, considering its many struggles. The Empire's longevity in the absence of a well-defined system of governance is also noteworthy. Its single most impressive accomplishment was the establishment of an Empire whose rule controlled the peoples and lands of three continents. This achievement was the product of an army whose superiority was unquestioned, not because it possessed better technology, but because of its unsurpassed resources, leadership, and tactics.

The Romans' military successes were accompanied by the construction of buildings, aqueducts, amphitheaters, roads, walls, cities, and palaces. Many of their buildings and civil works exist to this day. The infrastructure of aqueducts and roads remains visible throughout Europe. Consider the fact that the Romans constructed more than 40,000 miles of stone-paved roads and a total of 250,000 miles of all types of roads. These roads enabled the effective rule of their expansive empire. It is interesting to note that the 47,000-mile US Interstate Highway System is comparable to the extent of the Roman construction of paved roads. The justification for this system, like that of the Romans, was the efficient movement of military equipment and troops. In 1956, when President Eisenhower announced the legislation that established the Interstate System, he also justified it on the basis of the movement of military equipment and troops. For that reason, it was known as The National Defense Highway System.

The Romans' intellectual contributions are equally impressive. They are responsible for the introduction of Latin throughout Europe, a language that has influenced many of our existing languages. They also introduced the Roman alphabet that is in use in most of the Western world. Their system of laws, including the Justinian Code, forms the basis for our modern legal system.

Comparison of the United States with the Roman Empire

There are many differences between the Roman Empire and the United States, not the least of which are their relative appetites for empire building. During the nineteenth century, the United States was a relatively isolated country whose populace was inwardly focused toward the expansion of the seemingly limitless continent. Our initial experience with foreign conquests occurred as a result of the Spanish-American war of 1898, during which America's resounding defeat of the Spanish led to the country's graduation from that of a second-tier world power to that of a significant force within the community of nations. When the war ended, US troops occupied Cuba, Puerto Rico, Guam, and the Philippines, all of which could potentially have been absorbed as US possessions representing the beginnings of a US empire. Instead, only Puerto Rico and Guam became US Territories, while Cuba was granted independence. A great debate raged over the status of the Philippines. Some favored returning the islands to Spain, others wanted to retain strategic regions of the Philippines as military outposts, while others favored adopting the archipelago as a colony. After fifty years of arguments and conflict, the Philippines became independent, with the US retaining several regions for military installations.

Comparison of the US Empire with that of the Romans, British, and French reveals significant differences in priorities. At the end of the Spanish-American War, the United States occupied 162,000 square miles of land that was home to 1.8 percent of the world's population. This so-called empire was short-lived in that the United States granted Cuba its independence and was continuously plagued by Philippine uprisings until also granting that country its independence fifty years later. By comparison, the British Empire dwarfed that of the US. It covered thirteen million square miles of land that was home to twenty percent of the world's population.

In 150 AD, the Roman Empire included two million square miles occupied by thirty-five percent of the world's population. Comparisons between the Roman and British empires can be misleading, since the known world was significantly smaller in 150 AD than it was in 1900. However, it goes without saying that empire building was a central element of the British and Roman civilizations, whereas the questionable American empire was merely the indirect by-product of the country's wars.

There are other significant differences between the US and Roman civilizations. On June 21st, 1788, the US Constitution was ratified and has defined this country's government since that time. Unlike the Romans, the United States has been consistently structured as a tricameral democracy that has been adjusted from time to time to reflect the circumstances of the times. In spite of these adjustments, our system of government remains fundamentally unchanged. Before one becomes too smug over the long-term success of government within the United States when compared with the chaotic Roman government, it should be acknowledged that the United States has been in existence for a mere 240 years, while Rome's Western Empire existed in various forms for approximately 1,200 years—more than five times longer.

With the benefit of the Constitution's guidance, US leadership transitions have generally been peaceful. Eight of the country's forty-three presidents have died in office, either through assassination or disease. In all cases, the transfer of power has been smooth, proceeding along the lines defined by the Constitution. By contrast, fifty-five of the 160 Roman emperors died of natural causes. The remaining 105 died in office. The majority of these were assassinated or died in battle. In all cases, the death of an emperor was followed by significant turmoil and major changes in governance.

There are many other obvious differences between the US modern society and the Roman Empire. Some are the result of technological progress, others from the continuous restructuring of the political boundaries of the world. In spite of these relatively superficial changes, the underlying characteristics of human nature that influence a country's actions and decisions have not changed much during the intervening 1,000 years.

Human behavior is, to a great extent, governed by emotions. Some theorists have described human emotions as "discrete and consistent responses to internal or external events . . ." This definition is a useful way to understand the behavior of nations as well as individuals. Recent research into human emotions has established that mankind suffers from the basic emotions of happiness, sadness, fear, anger, surprise, and disgust. Since these emotions influence both individual and group behavior, their continued existence as a fundamental human trait suggests that the behavior of groups as well as supergroups (i.e., nations) will remain consistent and predictable throughout the generations. This is the fundamental relationship on which George Santayana's maxim is based: *Those who cannot remember the past are condemned to repeat it.*

Repeating the Past

Santayana's maxim serves as the basic theme for this book. While the superficial differences between the United States and the Roman Empire are significant, there are startling similarities between the two, which are a result of the consistency of human emotions and behaviors. The following list of similarities is a demonstration of consistent human nature. Scholars studying the Roman Empire have concluded that these items are the fundamental weaknesses that caused its collapse. The fact that these weaknesses are shared by the United States is cause for concern. For convenience, the comparisons are written in the past tense, although obviously, the description of the United States should be in the present and future tenses.

- Both were ruled by tricameral governments that included a president or emperor, a legislative body, and courts.
- The balance of power among their three branches of government tended to shift with time, primarily depending on the inclinations of the president/emperor. It should be noted that the potential for shifting power was a concern of the framers of the US Constitution.

- In their prime, both countries were leading world powers with the ability to influence the actions and well-being of the other parts of the world.
- In both Rome, and recently the United States, Christianity was less tolerant of other religions. An example from Rome was Emperor Theodosius, who ended the Olympic Games because they honored Zeus rather than Christ. Many examples exist in the United States of politicians, who in the name of Christianity and fear of outsiders, have proposed discriminatory actions against Muslims.
- As their citizens became more secure, and their quality of life improved, attention shifted from their occupations, participation in governance and religion, to diversions such as sports, games, and theater. The majority of the populace was content to go about their daily affairs and let their governments take care of them.
- The defense of both was supported by mercenary armies whose loyalty and effectiveness depended on their salaries and quality of life.
- High taxes led to unrest among the general population. Taxes to support their military activities accounted for much of their budgets. As military spending increased, civil infrastructure was allowed to fall into disrepair.
- Public distrust of their government resulting from the incompetence of the senate and congress, as well as the excesses of their emperor and president.
- Perhaps most significantly, both the United States and the Roman Empire were attacked by multiple enemies whose home countries were difficult to identify. The nature of the enemy attacks shifted with time, making it difficult to defend against the next onslaught.

Neither the Western nor the Eastern branches of the Roman Empire were attacked by a single well-defined enemy. Nor were their enemies the simple barbarians often described by legend. Rather the Roman Empire was beset by multiple heterogeneous groups in uncoordinated attacks that were staged to take advantage of some perceived weakness.

The barbarians from the north were quick to recognize the decay of the Western Empire. One after another they launched attacks on various parts of the crumbling empire. Attackers included the Visigoths, Vandals, Angles, Saxons, Franks, Ostrogoths, and Lombards. As the invading hordes succeeded in their attacks, they laid claim to their captured lands. For example, the Angles and Saxons overran the British Isles, while the Franks settled in France.

In 476, Romulus, the last Roman Emperor of the Western Empire, was deposed by Odoacer, a Germanic leader. He was the first barbarian to rule in Rome. His rule represented the end of a single unified government in Europe.

The attacks of the barbarians were motivated by a desire to be free from the despotic rule of the Romans. They also wanted land for farming and some degree of hegemony over their lives. They achieved their goals with their successful attacks. But the price they paid was a chaotic existence in a troubled land.

It should be noted that the term barbarian was not intended as a pejorative term as it is today. The word has its roots in the Greek word *barbaroi*, referring to someone who was not Greek. In their case it was a reference to the Medes and Persians. The Romans could be considered barbaroi to the Greeks. The Romans repurposed the word to mean someone who was not Roman, such as the barbarians.

Like the Romans, the United States is confronted by many hostile groups seeking to weaken it or end its existence. While the complete disintegration of a country as large and powerful as the United States would undoubtedly require years if not centuries to occur, the process by which it takes place is insidious. The initial cracks in the country's veneer initially go unnoticed. Gradually they enlarge until both friends and enemies alike recognize that deterioration has begun. While friends might politely criticize, enemies will undoubtedly develop strategies that take advantage of its weakened condition.

The list of those who are overtly hostile to the United States is long. It includes the many warring factions of the Middle East as well as rogue states such as North Korea, Libya, and Iran. As the conflicts in the Middle East progress, many of the so-called warring factions are likely to become full-fledged rogue states in their own right. But as the Roman's experience with the barbarians demonstrates, a hostile faction does not require the trappings of a nation to be a legitimate enemy. It can be a tribe or a sect or an ethnic group and still inflict significant damage. In spite of their stateless status, organizations such as ISIS and al-Qaeda are well funded and run by clever people. They have demonstrated their ability to organize and effectively challenge the best armies in the world.

The similarities between the Roman Empire and the United States demonstrate that chinks are appearing in the US armor. They are significant chinks, but it is not too late to repair them. If action is not taken soon, the United States could well follow in the footsteps of the Roman Empire, and it could conceivably occur within our children's lifetimes. Nothing in the tale related by this book is science fiction. The events it describes could occur tomorrow or next week. It's time to begin repairing the chinks

CAST OF CHARACTERS

Members of ISIS (Iraq and Syria):

Aabis	Ali's close friend from infantry training. In Arabic, Aabis means lucky
Ali	ISIS soldier and representative to Bis Saif. In Arabic, Ali means greatest
Gen. Hussain	ISIS general to whom Mohammed reports
Mohammed	Ali's platoon commander
Moiz	Ali's close friend from infantry training. In Arabic, means he is a protector

Members of Boko Haram (Nigeria):

Abalunam (Aba)	Udo's best friend in Baga. In Nigerian, means don't argue with me
Fela	Mayor of Baga. In Nigerian, means warlike
Gen. Modukuri	Leader of Boko Haram, with headquarters in Maiduguri
Ibiba	Udo's younger brother. In Nigerian, means it will be good
Maduka	Major in the Nigerian Army
Udo	Second male son of his family and Boko Haram representative to Bis Saif
Ugo	Udo's driver from airport. In Nigerian, means eagle, strength, and royalty

Members of Hamas (Palestine):

Abdul Nasser	Engineer in the missile laboratory
Gen. Murtaja	Hamas commander and sponsor of Hasan
Hasan Jouda	Hamas representative to Bis Saif, developer of missile guidance system
Ossama	Director of the missile lab and Hasan's immediate superior
Shadi	Hasan's predecessor at the lab and currently a Hamas web designer

Members of Bis Saif (Worldwide, headquarters in Jakarta, Indonesia):

Abu Ahmed-al Kuwaiti	Adam's close friend and supporter in Bis Saif
Adam al-Zhihri	Leader of Bis Saif
Leroy Williamson	Adam's African-American friend and Bis Saif's technical expert
John Smith	Bis Saif's contact with the British MI-6, aka Cecil Breathwaite

Members of MI-6:

Cecil Breathwaite	Bis Saif spy, aka John Smith
Stan Comstock	Breathwaite's supervisor

JCN employees and their relatives:

Bill Jaski	JCN President
Jack Vermeer	JCN Security Officer
Jahmir Al Saadi	Computer developer, JCN employee, Iraqi heritage, nicknamed James
Jane Smith	Bill Jaski's administrative assistant
Joan Toner	JCN Contracts Manager
Kelly Jaffari	Jahmir's girlfriend and employee of JCN

Lilliane Jaffari	Kelly Jaffari's mother
Marylou Sachler	JCN chief scientist
Rick Stringer	Jahmir's friend, co-developer at JCN
Sami Jaffari	Kelly Jaffari's father, whose home is in Timonium, MD
Sean Casey	JCN Corporate Attorney

Members of the United States Government and Their Relatives:

Adm. Arnold DeForce	Director—National Security Agency
Al Kaplan	Lead analyst—Central Intelligence Agency
Brad Nelson	Majority Leader—US House of Representatives—Democrat
Christopher Jeffers	President of the United States—Republican
Donald Squlo	Junior member of the House, from Orange Co., California—Republican
Gen. Elliott Drake	Chairman of the US Joint Chiefs of Staff—US Department of Defense
George Wilson	Director of National Intelligence (DNI)
Glenn Jeffers	Christopher Jeffers' father
Jan Adams	The president's administrative assistant
James Proctor	Director—Federal Bureau of Investigation
Janice DeBeers	Director—Department of Homeland Security
Kevin Goldberg	Program Manager—Defense Advanced Research Projects Agency
Lee Sanders	Special Agent in Charge—Federal Bureau of Investigation
Loren Sanderson	Governor of the State of Minnesota
Mary Lou Jeffers	Christopher Jeffers' mother
Matthew O'Brien	Director—Central Intelligence Agency
Melissa Jeffers	Christopher Jeffers' wife and first lady of the United States

Philip J. Tarnoff

Paul Greenburg	Minority Leader—US Senate—Democrat
Paul Lynd	President's press secretary
Robert McIntyre	Majority Leader—US Senate—Republican
Sam Papas	Department of Justice and expert on Constitutional law
Thomas McAllen	Director—Defense Advanced Projects Agency
Wayne Zyder	Minority Leader—US House of Representatives—Republican

US Citizens:

Bear	Leader—First Baptist Church anti-Muslim group
Bill Solenski	Cyber security expert—Google
Brian Klenger	Youngest member—First Baptist Church anti-Muslim group
Charles Ardley	Beekeeper—University of Maryland
Damian Johnson	African-American member—First Baptist Church anti-Muslim group
Dave Crain	Analyst—National Highway Transportation Safety Admin. FBI informer
David Powers	Chief Executive Officer—PJM Interconnections
Earl	Member—First Baptist Church anti-Muslim group
Gus Waters	Anti-Muslim activist
Joanna Crain	David Crain's wife
Megan Crain	Crain family eleven-year-old daughter
Steve Crain	Crain family eight-year -old son
Tex	Member—Hadad-Mahmood Mosque Muslim terrorist group

Foreign Leaders:

Moshe Tamer	Prime Minister—Israel
Paul Akerman	Ambassador—Israel
Sutanto	President—Indonesia

Groups

The Leadership Group:

Brad Nelson	Majority Leader—US House of Representatives—Democrat
Paul Greenburg	Minority Leader—US Senate—Democrat
Robert McIntyre	Majority Leader—US Senate—Republican
Wayne Zyder	Minority Leader—US House of Representatives—Republican

President's War Cabinet:

Adm. Arnold DeForce	NSA
Gen. Elliott Drake	DOD
George Wilson	DNI
James Proctor	FBI
Janice DeBeers	DHS
Matthew O'Brien	CIA

BOOK 1
CAN THINE ENEMIES BE LOVED?

The history of religion is for Gibbon intimately connected to the decline and fall of the Roman Empire, but religion is hardly his only theme. We encounter also "Barbarians" (a term loosely applied to those outside the empire, who often coveted the riches they saw); mercenary militarism (without efficiency, bravery, or patriotism); oppressive taxes (levied unfairly and exacted most mercilessly from those least able to pay;, corrupt politicians, tyrannical government, and endless warfare against the enemies of the Roman order, both at home and abroad. These themes are not without resonance today.

Critical forward by Hans-Friedrich Mueller to
Edward Gibbon's classic,
The Decline and Fall of the Roman Empire.

CHAPTER 1
THE BARBARIANS

Kirkuk, Iran

Ali was crouching behind a rock on a hillside overlooking Kirkuk when the mortar shell exploded. Even after months of a rigorous training program provided by the Islamic State in Iraq and Syria, or ISIS, as it was popularly known, he was not prepared for the concussion. It sucked the air out of his lungs and deafened him. He had no idea how long he lay on the ground trying to regain his breath. He knew the fight was necessary if they were ever going to rid the continent of the United States and its allies, or the great white Satan, as it was popularly known. But he was scared.

As a high school student in Raqqa, Syria, with an abiding interest in the unlikely combination of computer programming and American-style baseball, Ali was as well-suited for the ISIS battleground as Winston Churchill would have been for life as a ballet dancer. Although he had an athletic build and the dark complexion characteristic of Syrian Arabs, his interests were far from military pursuits. Life was difficult in Raqqa. However, if one ignored the intermittent electric power, wildly fluctuating prices, and constant sounds of mortar and gunfire, it was generally bearable. But Ali was looking for a better life and had joined the ISIS movement over the objections of his parents shortly after President Assad's Syrian troops had raided his house and stolen his most precious possession—his computer. This occurred shortly before Raqqa fell to the Islamic State, which had claimed it for their headquarters. The vandalism of the Syrian troops, the omnipresence of ISIS, combined with pressure from his peers, and the appeal of a better life with

3

regular meals, clothing, and a small weekly stipend had made his decision an easy one.

His initial experience in the ISIS boot camp had included both indoctrination into the Sunni version of the Muslim religion and combat training. Ali's admission into the training program as well as his continued existence on this earth required a satisfactory answer to four questions: (1) What is your name? (2) Where do you live? (3) How do you pray? (4) What music do you listen to? The subtle differences between the responses to these questions would determine whether one was a Sunni or Shia Muslim and whether one would experience the reward of admission into the ISIS army or torture and death.

During the indoctrination that accompanied the training program, Ali learned that the overall objective of the ISIS movement was the establishment of a caliphate that would eventually oversee all of the Muslim world. A desirable by-product of the fight to establish the caliphate would be the defeat or weakening of the West, specifically North America and Europe. As he listened to the lectures, Ali concluded that ISIS was staging a historical reenactment of the past glories, with the intent of recreating the golden years of the caliphs that ruled from AD 632 to 661, during which the caliphate controlled the entire Muslim world. Ali left boot camp for the hazards of the battlefield with many doubts about the jihad's ability to succeed with such a grand plan. However, he wisely kept his thoughts to himself, not even sharing them with the two close friends he had made in the camp: Moiz, who had been appropriately named with the Arab word meaning gives protection, and Aabis, who, it turned out, was inappropriately named using the Arab word for lucky. Neither of his new friends shared his dual love of computers and baseball, preferring the game of soccer, which they played endlessly with other recruits during their few free moments from the rigorous ISIS training regimen.

Dazed from the concussion of the mortar shell explosion, Ali sat up and began looking for his AK-47 rifle, which had been blown out of his hands. He saw it lying a few yards away and stood up to retrieve it, an action that brought an immedi-

4

ately shouted reprimand from Sergeant Mohammed, his platoon commander. "Get down! Are you crazy? Do you want to get killed?" The reprimand was accentuated by a burst of gunfire from the nearby suburbs of Kirkuk. The combination of the gunfire and reprimand elicited a rapid response from Ali, who dove to the ground behind the rock that had been his shelter, fortunately suffering nothing more serious than a scraped knee. He looked across the rocky field that separated the troops of the Islamic State from the peshmerga, as the Kurdish troops defending Kirkuk were known. At the far side of the field was a large grove of small hardwood trees and underbrush, and beyond that were the southern suburbs of Kirkuk.

Ali once again began his efforts to retrieve his rifle and to look for his two good friends, Moiz and Aabis. He saw Moiz slowly regaining consciousness from the explosion. Moiz waved weakly to indicate he was OK. In spite of his name, Aabis was not the lucky one. He was lying on his back with his eyes wide open, staring at the sky—lifeless. Suddenly Ali wished he was safely back in his room at home with his computer rather than crawling on a battlefield strewn with bodies and wounded fighters who had fallen attempting to revive the distant memory of the caliphate.

His musings were cut short by a loud command from Mohammed. "Check your rifles and get ready to attack on my signal." He saw Mohammed talking on the radio and realized that his platoon was part of the regiment that was going to be the backbone of the attack. Mohammed then raised his arm and quickly lowered it, shouting "Allahu Akbar!" ("God is great!"). Using his shout as inspiration, the troops took up the cry, left their cover, and charged the hidden Kurdish troops defending the Kirkuk suburbs, screaming "Allahu Akbar" as they ran. The noise and confusion was overwhelming. Machine-gun fire from the Kurdish lines mowed down many of the ISIS troops. Their return fire and the explosions from the grenades being launched by both sides added to the chaos. Above the noise of the weapons fire came the screams of the wounded as they lay bleeding on the battlefield. Most would die from the lack of adequate medical attention, a deficiency of the ISIS army in the field.

This was not the first time the ISIS had attacked Kirkuk. A similar attack had been staged in 2015, which was beaten back by the combination of Kurdish and Iraqi forces. This time their attack was from a different location, trying again to overwhelm this Kurdish peshmerga army position in the southern suburbs in order to capture Kirkuk. Once that was completed, it would be on to Baba Gurgur, eight miles to the north, where the second largest oil fields in the world were located. If ISIS could capture the Baba Gurgur fields, they could influence worldwide oil prices and establish a virtually unlimited source of income for themselves. The oilfields were an elusive prize that was too tempting for ISIS to ignore.

It was equally important for the Kurds to prevent ISIS from succeeding. The Kurds had long claimed the Kirkuk region as their ancestral home and were determined to continue its governance. With the support of Iraqi troops, they had successfully defended the city against the ISIS attacks in the past, even though ISIS was well equipped with armored vehicles and accompanied by many willing suicide bombers.

The current attack did not appear to be succeeding any better than the previous 2015 attack until a distant dust cloud and the sound of diesel engines signaled the arrival of a brigade of ISIS armored vehicles along with a few tanks that had been captured during previous battles. A cheer went up from the ISIS ground troops when they realized that they would soon be receiving armored support. The ISIS mechanized company formed a battle line that slowly advanced on the suburbs. As they moved along, the troops took up positions behind the vehicles, using them as shelter from the incoming machine gun and mortar fire. Ali was relieved to realize that with the support and the sheltering vehicles, he might actually survive this battle.

But the peshmerga were not without their own resources. In addition to their scattered machine gun and mortar positions, they had the support of Iraqi tanks as well as the air forces of the allied countries from the West. The elation of the ISIS troops began to fade when a shot from an Iraqi tank destroyed one of their armored vehicles, killing most of the ground troops that had been using it for cover. In spite of their losses, the ISIS troops continued to advance until they were within 100 yards of the Kurdish positions.

At that point the situation began to deteriorate. The sound of jet aircraft and helicopter blades could suddenly be heard over the noise of the diesel engines and explosions. Everyone in the ISIS army knew that this meant the arrival of allied air support, with missiles and rapid-fire guns. The Apaches were first to arrive, making a low, high-speed pass over the battlefield while the troops vainly fired their rifles at them. This first pass was presumably made to assess the situation, although the veterans among the troops knew that the assessment had already been made by drones that overflew the area while they were focused on the ground-level fighting. The first pass was followed by two additional helicopters, which fired their Hellfire missiles and M230 chain guns at the armored vehicles, with devastating effect. Four Hellfire missiles were fired. One missed its target while each of the remaining three hit a vehicle, which disintegrated in a ball of fire, killing their crew and most of the nearby troops. Additional vehicles were disabled by the chain guns firing their 30 mm armor-piercing ammunition at a rate of 300 rounds per minute. Suddenly, standing close to an armored vehicle didn't seem as if it was a very good idea.

Ali made a zigzag dash across the 100 yards separating the ISIS lines from the grove of trees on the outskirts of the suburbs they were attacking. Although he heard the impact of bullets around him as he ran, Allah must have been protecting him because he arrived in the grove unscathed. Many of the ISIS fighters who had remained in the open did not fare as well. Ali watched with horror as the Apaches were replaced by a pair of F-16 fighters armed with M-61 Gatling guns firing at a rate of 6,000 rounds per minute, which produced a virtual curtain of bullets. The jet fighters appeared and systematically raked the field in which the remaining troops were exposed. He heard an authoritative voice sounding the retreat and watched the remnants of the ISIS force along with its supporting armored company leave the battlefield. He knew he should join them, but was afraid to recross the open space between the grove and the retreating troops. He thought he could wait until nightfall and return to camp under cover of darkness.

His wait in the grove seemed an eternity. He was closer to the Kurdish lines than he was to his own army. When the ISIS troops retreated, Ali heard cheers erupting from the Kurds. He heard them talking softly and then assembling for what was presumably a midday meal. He spent his time improving the quality of his hiding place while trying to ignore his empty stomach. By the time he had finished covering himself with mud and branches, he was all but invisible.

The afternoon crept by until late in the day when he heard groups of Kurds walking through the grove looking for wounded or dead ISIS troops. When they found a dead soldier, they searched him for valuables, took his rifle and ammunition, and added them to a growing pile in the back of a battered pickup truck. If the soldier was not dead, they shot him, and then repeated the process. Watching this activity did not calm Ali's already frayed nerves.

The soldiers with the pickup truck picked their way through the grove, gradually coming closer to Ali's hiding place. He lay under his pile of brush, scarcely daring to breathe. As the Kurds shuffled past him, they were distracted by an unexploded rocket lying on the ground and stopped to examine it. Eventually they tossed it into the pile of bodies in the back of the pickup and then drove on, continuing their ghoulish activity. After they drove off, silence enveloped Ali's grove. He could hear the sounds of the soldiers in the camp on the outskirts of Kirkuk, but he was alone.

His solitude didn't last long. He heard the sounds of a motor again, which could have been the same pickup truck or its decrepit twin. Ali briefly wondered whether the Toyota factory produced a line of pre-worn pickups with dirt, dents, and at least one cracked window, as these were the only types of trucks he had seen either in Kirkuk or while he was at the ISIS training camp.

This pickup was being used for a different purpose. The soldiers with this truck were burying land mines or improvised explosive devices (IEDs) throughout the grove. Obviously they were expecting another ISIS attack, and IEDs would be an effective defense against the first wave of infantry. Ali forgot his discomfort as he watched the activity with great interest, trying to memorize the location of each device. He momentarily forgot that technically he was a deserter, an offense that was punishable by execution in most armies, including the ISIS. His focus had shifted to that of discovering a way in which he could warn his fellow soldiers about the location of the IEDs.

Ali did not have much time to develop a plan. He suddenly heard shouts of "Allahu Akbar!" from the ISIS lines. The ISIS commanders recognized the importance of attacking a second time shortly after the allied planes and helicopters had left since they had to return to their base to refuel. The limitations on flying time was a major handicap of the allied forces, and one that was well recognized both by the allies and their enemies.

Ali tore off his black shirt and, with the help of his field knife, began cutting it into squares. Each square he attached to a stick that he stuck in the ground next to an IED. He finished his labor with multiple scratches on his exposed upper body, mud from his hiding place, and bleeding hands from burying the sticks. As he marked the last IED, he heard the sounds of a radio and an advanced platoon coming through the grove. He rushed to meet them and was almost shot by his comrades, who thought he was a remaining Kurd. He raised his hands and shouted, "I am Ali. I am one of you. I am in Mohammed's platoon." Two of the ISIS soldiers grabbed him, threw him to the ground, and searched him. When they saw his AK-47 with the ISIS markings and realized that he was speaking Syrian, the advanced guard relaxed and let him sit up. Without explaining why he was there, Ali immediately began telling them about the IEDs and the manner in which he had marked their location. He showed them the nearest IED and his marking. Members of the platoon complimented him on his ingenuity and began questioning whether he had marked all of the IEDs that had been buried. Ali felt that the ones he had marked constituted a safe lane through the grove, and that if the approaching ISIS troops stayed within the boundaries defined by the marked sticks that had been within his field of vision from his hiding place, they would be safe.

Ali's discussion led to a long radio conversation between the platoon commander and the ISIS headquarters. Ali would be responsible for working with the platoon to disable all of the marked IEDs. They had a total of fifteen minutes to complete the work, at which time, the army would begin to move through the safe passage they had established. Ten minutes after the conversation, the ISIS army appeared, dashing quietly through the space between their encampment and the grove. They moved quietly and, without any urging, funneled themselves into the lane containing the disabled IEDs. As they left the grove, they quietly spread out and lay in the shrubbery at the edge of the suburbs.

The Kurds had relaxed following their earlier victory over the ISIS troops. They were standing in small groups talking, cleaning their rifles, or rebuilding fortifications. The first shot from the ISIS troops quickly changed the atmosphere. The battle took place in the close quarters of the Kurds' camp, with small arms firing responsible for most of the deaths and injuries. ISIS brought their armored vehicles through Ali's lane, as it was now called, and began destroying the Kurdish camp. It was a short battle, which ended with the Kurds fleeing into the heart of Kirkuk.

Ali, still shirtless, but with his unfired AK-47, stood mutely witnessing the battle. "So what happened?" Mohammed said as he walked up to him. "I thought you had been killed in the first battle since you weren't with us after the retreat."

Mohammed was a big man with a square frame and a black beard. With his black ISIS uniform, he was an imposing figure. Behind his back, the troops called him The Tank. Ali was intimidated by Mohammed, realizing that he had the power of life and death over friends and foes alike. Thinking quickly, Ali replied, "I hurt my leg and fell while we were retreating. I ended up hiding in the woods, and from there witnessed the burying of the IEDs. I couldn't let my friends be slaughtered by these devices, so I took a chance and marked them." He made it a point to limp as he edged away from Mohammed.

10

"Ali, you're a hero with the troops. I'm not sure whether you're a hero or a coward, but it's easier to give you credit for the good you've done and ignore the doubt. That's what I intend to do. But one more act of cowardice and desertion, and I will personally see to it that you are shot."

The ISIS troops paused on the outskirts of Kirkuk to consolidate their position and wait for reinforcements while they dug in and buried their dead. During the ensuing battles for the city itself, Ali was accompanied by his close friend Moiz. The two had become close since the death of Aabis, and on many occasions the two had covered each other during assaults on Kurdish strongholds.

At the end of each day of battle, Mohammed would lead them in their evening prayers, which included the recital of prayers to Allah, thanking him for their victories of the day and acknowledging his greatness while they performed the traditional ceremonies of bowing, prostrating themselves, and sitting while the prayers were recited.

Two days later, when additional troops arrived, ISIS continued its progress toward the goal of capturing the entire city. They realized this would be a slow process involving house-to-house fighting with significant losses incurred by both sides. But ISIS had encountered similar circumstances many times in the past and was prepared to patiently execute their plans while they wore down the enemy. After several weeks, the Kurdish troops retreated, leaving the city under ISIS control. Now all that separated them from the Baba Gurgur oil fields was eight miles of desert, an environment in which they excelled.

As they advanced toward the oil fields, they were continually harassed by air attacks. The attacks slowed their progress until they were forced to retreat to the relative shelter of the city and the protection of its civilian population. They remained in this position, cursing the effectiveness of the Western air forces. Perhaps, in time, Allah would provide them with an effective defense against these aerial weapons.

Kirkuk was a city of less than 400,000 inhabitants. Before the battle, its broad streets had been well lit and clean. Land was inexpensive, which resulted in a city that was spread out, with few high-rise buildings. Many of its citizens worked in the nearby oil fields. These features favored ISIS governance, since surveillance of the general public was simplified.

Although they had not been able to capture the Baba Gurgur fields, ISIS occupation of Kirkuk was not without benefit. ISIS had developed effective procedures for governing defeated provinces that involved imposition of strict Sunni Muslim law while levying heavy taxes on their citizens. Kirkuk was destined to feel the heavy hand of ISIS rule.

But the ISIS troops had not abandoned the idea of capturing the oil fields. In the evenings, the generals would gather to discuss various alternatives for making the hazardous eight-mile march while avoiding the punishing allied air attacks. On many occasions the discussions would continue into the early hours of the morning, but invariably failed to produce a plan for a successful assault on the oil fields.

Ali had successfully been reintegrated into his battalion and avoided contact with Mohammed at every opportunity. On one occasion he encountered Mohammed as he walked to his tent in the ISIS camp. As he did at every opportunity, Mohammed reminded Ali that he was being watched, and one false action would result in severe punishment. Ali knew what this meant, but his face remained expressionless. While the threats were being delivered, he silently thanked Allah for saving him from an ugly fate. Little did Ali realize that Mohammed's reprieve would provide him with the opportunity to change the world.

CHAPTER 2
BAGA, BORNO, NIGERIA

Udo lived in one of the small communes that formed the town of Baga. Located in the northeast corner of Nigeria, Baga is part of the State of Borno. Fifty years ago, Baga had been located on the shores of Lake Chad, a large body of water bordered by Nigeria, Chad, Cameroon, and Niger. The lake served as a source of the fish that fed the surrounding areas. But a lengthy drought had dried up the lake to the point that Borno was no longer near the water and relied on agriculture for its sustenance. Because of its isolated location and the poverty of its residents, Baga had been ignored both by the Nigerian government and various terrorist groups. Its people were allowed to live a relatively poor but peaceful existence.

Udo lived in a round mud hut with a cone-shaped thatched roof that was one of several similar dwellings within a walled compound. The inhabitants of the compound made their living farming millet and other grains and some peanuts. It was hard work. They were all related, having a common father and a mother who was one of his father's three wives. Udo's name identified him as the second son of his father's first wife. At nearly six feet tall, thin, and with dark black skin, his looks were similar to those of his eight brothers and sisters.

In spite of their relative isolation, the people of Baga realized that sooner or later they would receive the attention of Boko Haram. The terrorist organization was essentially the Nigerian branch of al-Qaeda. It had been founded in Maiduguri, a city also located in the State of Borno, by Mohammed Yusuf, ostensibly as a school and religious complex for poor Muslim families. In fact, it was an Islamic State school that had been created to recruit potential jihadists. Using a political platform that denounced political corruption and police activities, Mohammed was able to rapidly build the organization that ultimately became known as Boko Haram.

Although Boko Haram had been active throughout Borno, and essentially ran the state's government, Baga had been left alone. Life had continued peacefully there, with the residents tending their farms and educating their children. Udo gave little thought to politics and was content to help support the extended family of which he was a part. Then one hot summer day, while he was hoeing the millet, his younger brother Ibiba suddenly appeared, grabbed his own hoe and began to hack at the weeds while he spoke.

"Udo, you're living a comfortable existence. Enough food on the table and some money for clothing and medicine. Our family is more comfortable than people living in other parts of Borno. Did it ever occur to you how easily and quickly this could all come to an end?"

"Ibiba, I thought your name means *it will be good*. Your words don't sound like optimism to me. But seriously, I think about these things all the time. I'm just not sure what to do about them. What do you think we should do?"

"My friends are assembling a vigilante group that will be armed to repel attacks from Boko Haram. You know their reputation for kidnapping, murder, rape, and ordinary theft. We can't leave ourselves at their mercy. We want you to join us. In fact, we want all the men of your age to join us. Will you do it?"

Udo chewed his lower lip while he considered Ibiba's proposal. "I need to think about it."

Ibiba raised his hands in frustration and then lowered them and slapped his thighs. "I can't believe you need to think about it. While you're thinking, our mothers could be raped and our brothers and sisters kidnapped. We don't have time to waste while you think."

"What will we use for weapons? Are we going to throw rocks at them? And how many of us are there? I'm hoping it isn't just you and me, brother."

"No, we won't have to use rocks. There are a few rifles among us. Mostly single-shot 22s. But our most important weapons are our knives, which we all own and know how to use. We can acquire some rifles from those that we kill. They're armed with automatic weapons, such as the AK-47. There are about fifty of us so far, most of whom you already know. Now will you join us?"

"Do I have a choice?"

"You really don't. Even if you said no, Boko Haram would eventually force you to join us. Either that or you'd be dead. We're meeting tonight with a representative from the Nigerian armed forces. The meeting will be in the grove of trees beyond the old cemetery when the moon is just over the horizon. Be there!"

The remainder of the day passed slowly for Udo as he reflected on the change in his life that this discussion might cause. He loved his peaceful farming existence with his family. Lately he had been seeing a girl from another family and was anxious to continue the courtship. The bride price for his wife-to-be was quite high, so he was hoping that additional income from fishing might help him earn the needed money. He had dreams of buying or building a boat that could be used to renew their fishing heritage on Lake Chad and provide him with the money he needed for his wife-to-be. But all of this would have to wait until the threat from Boko Haram could be neutralized.

That night, Udo quickly ate his simple dinner, and, using the excuse that he was tired from his hoeing, went to his corner of the hut and lay down. He watched the shaft of light coming through the opening in the wall that served as a window travel slowly across the floor. The position and intensity of the light would tell him when the full moon rose over the horizon. As he lay on his sleeping mat, he thought about the other residents of the hut, his mother, whom he loved deeply, his sister, and one brother. His father would join them occasionally, which was a festive occasion since his father was a fun-loving man who often brought simple gifts for the siblings. Eventually the rest of the family retired to their mats, and soon the chorus of heavy breathing and snoring signified that the entire clan was asleep.

The rectangular patch of light on the floor of the hut finally began to brighten and signified that the moonrise was about to occur. He quietly rose from his mat and left the hut. As he walked through the sleeping commune, Udo reflected on its serenity and the ease with which all of this could be lost. He left through the gate of the commune's wall and walked quickly and quietly to the graveyard on the outskirts of the community. He never liked to walk through the graveyard, particularly at night, and took a circuitous route around the outer edge of the cemetery that eventually brought him to the grove where the meeting was to occur.

As he entered the trees, he heard a low whisper from his brother. "Over here, Udo." He followed the sound of Ibiba's voice through the brush and almost collided with him before he saw him. Ibiba was dressed in dark brown clothes, and that, combined with his dark, almost black skin, made him invisible in the shade of the trees. Ibiba, like Udo, was tall and very dark, almost black.

When he recovered from his shock and embarrassment, Udo realized that there were just four of them: his brother, two strangers, and himself. He had expected at least a dozen of the young men from the compounds of Baga. "Where are our vigilantes?" he asked Ibiba in an accusing voice.

"We thought it best not to involve them in this discussion. Let me introduce you to these gentlemen." Turning to the shortest and lightest color of the group, Ibiba said, "I'd like you to meet Major Maduka of the Nigerian army. He's here to coordinate their activities with ours, and to discuss providing needed arms." Ibiba then motioned to the last member of the group and said, "You may already know Fela, our head man."

Udo responded that he was glad to meet both men. He did not pay much attention to politics and had never met Fela. He was awed by the presence of Maduka, who was the highest-ranking soldier he had ever met. He was also elated to realize that the army would provide them with the arms they needed to defend themselves against the Boko Haram. He decided this might be a worthwhile meeting after all.

During the next hour, Maduka explained his ideas about their need for arms. He also described a brief training program that should be conducted to establish some semblance of discipline among the inexperienced mob of vigilantes that Ibiba had assembled. Then he became deadly serious. "I've saved the best for last. Our intelligence says that we have no more than a week to prepare for the arrival of the first Boko Haram hoodlums. Baga is one of the few areas of Borno that they don't control. This is really important symbolically to them. As you know, their movement began in Borno, and they already control most of the state."

He let the bad news sink in before he added a little bit of good news. "While you don't have much time, the hoodlums do not appear to think that you will try to defend yourselves. My intelligence says that they will probably fill two pickup trucks with their so-called soldiers and roar into town firing their guns in the air, thinking that they will intimidate you. If you surrender, they'll spend the rest of the day murdering or conscripting the fighting-age boys and men, raping and kidnapping the women. They will also steal everything that isn't already attached. Since they aren't expecting any resistance, it is within your ability to ensure that they disappear without a trace. This is all that will save you. If word of your resistance gets back to the main Boko Haram force, they will attack you more violently in the future. Remember, they rule by terror."

With the soldier's speech as a prelude, the four of them began planning the resistance. They discussed the positioning of their vigilantes, the armaments needed, and the manner in which they would prevent the escape of any of the Boko Haram hoodlums. In spite of their farming culture, the men of Baga possessed many hunting skills that had been passed on to them by their ancestors. The rifles finally arrived, six days after the meeting in the cemetery. Until their arrival, the potential Baga vigilantes practiced their warfare with sticks and tree branches. They also spent time digging pits, cutting down trees, and arranging rope traps. The rifles were mostly AK-47s in various states of operability. There were also a few single-shot 22 rifles and various other older weapons. Udo and Ibiba were busy during their week of preparation bolstering the courage of their fellow vigilantes and constantly pointing out that they had the advantage of surprise and knowledge of the surrounding area.

The week passed uneventfully. But on the eighth day, they were not disappointed. A runner taking a shortcut through the fields arrived to announce the presence of two small dust clouds in the distance, followed by a much bigger cloud. The vigilantes who had been waiting for the past forty-eight hours quickly took their positions. To outward appearances, everything in the town was normal. Chickens scratched in the paths connecting the compounds, women did their wash by the muddy stream that meandered through the town before emptying into Lake Chad, and small children attended school. As soon as the two pickup trucks causing the smaller dust clouds rounded the last curve in the rough road leading to the center of town, everything changed. Women and children all disappeared from the village and into the surrounding countryside. Anything of value or perceived value had been removed from the compounds and buried in the woods.

The first dust clouds in the form of two pickup trucks arrived with mufflers that had been removed to maximize the noise and terrify the populace of towns being raided. They roared into town with the rabble who were the soldiers firing their guns in the air. Occasionally, one of them would throw a grenade in some arbitrary direction with the intent of further terrifying the local inhabitants. They knew that they were outnumbered, but they were not worried because they knew that they were being followed by the main Boko Haram force, which would arrive shortly. It was the presence of this larger force that Major Maduka had failed to mention, perhaps because he had not known about it, although his motives would never be known.

The vigilantes began firing at the soldiers from their protected positions in the structures of the town. A few soldiers were hit and one was killed, but the Boko Haram return fire and grenades also did considerable damage, setting the thatched roofs of several huts on fire.

The vigilantes had not realized that they would soon be under attack by the main force until their attention was drawn to its presence by machine gun fire erupting from the armored personnel carriers (APCs) that led its advance. Realizing that their small number armed with a few old rifles would be no match for the advancing line of more than 100 soldiers, combined with the withering fire from the APCs, they fled into the brush and open fields that surrounded the town, only to be shot or captured by the pursuing Boko Haram troops. What followed could only be called a massacre. The troops spread out and combed the surrounding countryside until they had rounded up all the citizens of Baga. The young men were herded into the central square, where their hands were tied and they were blindfolded. The women and children were herded into a compound for the later enjoyment of the victorious troops. The elderly were summarily executed because they were of little value.

Udo was one of the few who had escaped. He had been quick to recognize the arrival of the Boko Haram troops and had climbed a large tree within one of the living compounds. The tree had been one of his favorite hiding places when he was a boy, and he had never been discovered due to its thick foliage. The troops searching for the fleeing citizens of Baga had failed to look up, an oversight which saved his life and that of Abalunam, whom he knew as Aba, a boyhood friend who shared his secret. Udo burned with rage at the Nigerian major who had encouraged resistance rather than flight. He felt that the major had been responsible for the massacre of his family and other relatives, whose execution he had watched from his treetop vantage. With a flash of insight, Udo suddenly realized why Nigerians joined the Boko Haram. Was the entire Nigerian government as incompetent and corrupt as its army?

Udo whispered, "Aba, we've got to spend the night here until things settle down below." Abalunam agreed and the two of them spent an uncomfortable and unhappy night in the tree watching the drunken revel below, which included murders and assaults on the citizens of Baga who had been their friends and relatives.

"Udo, what are you going to do after this?"

"Believe it or not, I'm thinking about joining them."

"Are you crazy? They're nothing more than a gang of murderers and rapists. Don't you remember that a few years ago they kidnapped more than two hundred schoolgirls from Chibok, right here in our State of Borno?"

"They may not be that bad. Don't forget, they began as a religious school. Armies are known to pillage the cities of the vanquished and to kidnap in order to raise money. What's happening here is not that unusual and could be considered letting off steam."

"Why would you join them?"

"I think I would like to join anyone who fights the incompetent Nigerian central government, which is the primary objective of Boko Haram."

"I'm not convinced. Soon I'm climbing out of this tree and walking to Maiduguri. It's a short walk, and I have some relatives there who will take me in."

"I wish us both luck. Whatever happens will be the will of Allah."

With that, Abalunam slowly climbed down the tree and disappeared into the dark behind the shed near their hiding place. The problem with escaping notice in Baga is that it is flat, arid, and there are few hiding places. Abalunam followed the fence lines along the boundaries of the family compounds and took cover in sheds and behind abandoned cars.

It was easy to guard Baga, since even in the dark, any movement became obvious, and many Boko Haram soldiers had grown up in similar regions. The soldiers, who were determined to wipe out all traces of the Baga resistance, quickly spotted Abalunam and ended his life before he had walked even a kilometer. Udo heard the shot and correctly interpreted its result. He mourned the loss of his friend, but was numb from mourning the loss of his brother and the rest of his family. He had no more grief to dedicate to those who were special in his life. He decided to remain in the tree until after sunrise.

Around mid-morning, Udo's hunger and his bladder got the best of him. After careful consideration, he took off his shirt and used a small branch to improvise a white flag, thinking it might save his life. He then remained in the tree watching the troops pack their gear and the spoils of their victory. Waiting until the main body of the Boko Haram army had departed, he took his white flag, climbed down from the tree and hid in the brush until he saw a soldier, who was obviously an officer and sober. He held his white flag high and stood in the path being used by the officer, who was startled to see him and who quickly unholstered his pistol. Udo stood perfectly still, knowing he shouldn't move until the officer relaxed from his firing position. After a few minutes of silence, he said in a quiet voice, "I am alone and unarmed. I come to you because I want to join your army."

The surprised officer slowly lowered his pistol as he replied, "If you're sincere, welcome, friend. If you are lying, you will be shot. Come with me."

Udo was led to the center of activity, where a temporary encampment had been established. His new acquaintance introduced him to another officer sitting at a camp table in a command tent, who said curtly, "Follow me. I'll introduce you to your comrades." And with that, Udo joined Boko Haram.

Udo's career with Boko Haram was unremarkable. He was given a rifle and a shirt and subjected to some cursory training. Occasionally he participated in minor skirmishes against the Nigerian army, but most of his time was spent patrolling captured territories in various locations throughout the country.

It would be several months before his reliability and intelligence came to the attention of General Modukuri, who was often frustrated by the lazy and illiterate state of his troops. Udo had been taught to read by his mother, and by his nature was an organized and conscientious individual. These characteristics exhibited themselves during many of his assignments, one of which involved gathering intelligence on the movements of Nigerian army troops as they prepared to counterattack Boko Haram positions near Lake Chad. Udo, who knew the area well, had been able to provide the general with accurate information on the number of troops, their armaments, and their encampments. Most important, while hiding in the brush one day, he overheard two officers discussing plans for an attack on a nearby Boko Haram installation. This information proved invaluable to the general, who repositioned his troops to avoid a major attack by the army.

Because of his good fortune, Udo was soon promoted to work at the general's headquarters in Maiduguri organizing future offensives. Udo enjoyed his work, which allowed him to avoid participation in future field operations, such as the one that he had witnessed in Baga. While he could rationalize the violence that characterized Boko Haram as temporary bloodlust resulting from the adrenaline produced during battle, it contradicted the principles of the Muslim religion that served as his moral foundation.

His interaction with General Modukuri brought the two of them into contact with increasing frequency. As a result of their interaction, Udo gradually realized that the violence characterizing the army's operations was not temporary bloodlust from the heat of battle, but rather the very foundation of the Boko Haram cause. Although he tried to ignore his doubts, they persisted. But Udo was stuck. If he deserted the organization, he had little doubt that they would track him down and kill him.

Little did Udo realize that joining Boko Haram would provide him with the opportunity to change the world in spite of the uncertainties he harbored.

CHAPTER 3
RAFAH, GAZA STRIP, PALESTINE

The laboratory, if you could call it that, was located in the basement of a partially destroyed three-story apartment building in the central district of Rafah. With its mild climate and access to the Mediterranean Sea, Rafah would be considered a resort city, if it hadn't been filled with the misery of refugees from the decades-long war with Israel and the changing relationships with Egypt.

Far from the snooping eyes of the Israeli government, with a climate that would attract talented scientists and engineers and with access to the universities of Egypt, Rafah was the ideal location for the laboratory. The Hamas and their various Palestinian collaborators recognized the need for such a laboratory after their multiple wars with Israel, during which they had been outgunned and defeated by their enemy's superior technology.

The Palestinians were wary of the unreliable assistance they were receiving from their Arab allies, whose friendship and support depended on the political situations in their own countries as well as their desire to appease the West. So at the beginning of the twenty-first century, Hamas decided to marshal their limited funds toward the development of more effective missiles that could be used for both air defense and the destruction of ground targets in Israel. Missile technology had advanced significantly during the late twentieth and early twenty-first centuries, and Hamas wanted to be part of the community of nations with access to that technology. Besides, they realized, if they could develop effective weapons, they might be able to sell them to their Sunni Muslim compatriots throughout the Middle East. The reasoning was unassailable.

Growing up in a middle-class family, Hasan Jouda was one of the lucky Palestinians. His father was a physician and his mother was a nurse. They lived in a comfortable house in Kahn Yunis, a city of approximately 180,000 near the southern end of the Gaza Strip. Because of its location and relatively small size, the city had escaped much of the fighting that had destroyed the City of Gaza and to a lesser extent Rafah. From the day of his birth, Hasan's parents were determined to send him to college. They felt that college was the only way he would escape the grinding poverty and lack of opportunity in the Gaza Strip. Fortunately, Hasan excelled at his studies, which simplified his acceptance at a number of different universities in the Middle East. He selected Alexandria University, in Egypt, both because of its location in historic Alexandria and its strong computer science curriculum, which included graduate work in computer vision—computer interpretation of images—a subject that had always intrigued him.

While a student in Alexandria, Hasan was introduced to the fundamentalist Islam practiced in Egypt, and a powerful political force in that country ever since the Arab Spring. Nearly ninety-five percent of the Egyptian population was Muslim, and the vast majority of these Sunni. Hasan was encouraged to visit the mosque regularly, where he was indoctrinated with the religious and political philosophies of the country. When he completed his education, he returned home as an Islamic radical, much to his parents' consternation, as well as a competent computer engineer, much to his parents' pride in his academic achievements.

***

Not surprisingly, job opportunities in the Gaza Strip for college graduates specializing in computer vision were scarce. Hasan found occasional work as a website developer, and for a brief period he had a full-time position providing software support for the Al-Shifa Hospital in Gaza City. But neither of these activities satisfied his intellect, and none of them allowed him to work toward his stated goal of improving the lives of the Palestinian people. He also viewed the unpleasant one-hour commute from Rafah to Gaza City as an unproductive waste of time.

Hasan's fortunes changed one day when an injured Hamas general was brought to the hospital for treatment. General Murtaja had been working at his office when it was struck by bombs dropped during an Israeli airstrike. The airstrike had been conducted as a reprisal for a recent Palestinian bombing of a school bus in Jerusalem.

General Murtaja's wounds were serious but not life-threatening. Because of his position, he received a private room in the overcrowded hospital, as well as access to the Internet from his personal laptop computer. The room had lime green walls, a single chair, and a hospital bed. It was also unique in that it had a private lavatory, a luxury in the overcrowded hospital.

The general rang for a nurse, expecting an immediate response as he was accustomed to receiving from his troops when he issued a command. By the time that the overworked nurse appeared, Murtaja was in a rage. "Where have you been? I've been pushing this stupid button for fifteen minutes. A man could die in here before receiving the attention he needs."

The nurse was tired and frustrated with the shortage of personnel, medicine, and doctors in a hospital that was overwhelmed with injured from the latest Israeli bombing attack. "General, I know you're important, but you'll have to wait your turn. You're right, many are dying from lack of attention, and spending my time attending to your needs does not help the dying."

Murtaja was taken aback but not intimidated by the aggressive response of the petite nurse in the wrinkled, sweat-stained white uniform. "Is there a computer technician in this hospital that can help me connect to the Internet? I can't get this crappy computer to work. It's important that I be able to communicate with my commanders. If we can't defend this city, there won't be a hospital for your patients."

"There's a new technician here that seems to know what he's doing. His name is Hasan, and I'm sure he can help you."

"Well what are you waiting for? Why don't you get him for me?"

Without another word, the nurse turned on her heel and stalked out of the room, leaving General Murtaja fuming. Murtaja was a big man who looked and acted the part of a high-ranking army officer. His complexion was the color of tanned leather, as you would expect of someone who had spent most of his adult life in the dessert. He spoke in a booming voice that carried up and down the halls, silencing the normal chatter of the hospital.

Hasan appeared about thirty minutes following the general's exchange with the nurse, just in time to prevent another eruption. Hasan looked the part of a computer nerd, with his thin, gangling build and dark-rimmed glasses. He would have been handsome with another fifty pounds on his thin frame, but at his current weight, he seemed almost emaciated. Like the nurse, he was overwhelmed by his workload, impatient to begin his work and get on to the next customer.

As he booted up the general's computer and focused on entering the settings needed for connection with the Internet, Murtaja engaged him in small talk. "Where did you learn to work with computers?"

"I guess I've been doing it all my life. I was fortunate that my parents could afford to buy me a computer. They could also afford to send me to college, where I majored in computer science."

Murtaja was interested in this highly educated citizen of Rafah. He felt that the path to Palestinian success would be a path that included improved education for its citizens. He forgot his impatience with the slow service of the hospital and continued his questioning. "What university did you attend? And what did you learn there?"

As he worked, Hasan warmed to the subject of his educational background. "I attended Alexandria University in Egypt. It was a great school, with many brilliant professors. I received an advanced degree there, specializing in image processing."

Murtaja could not believe his good fortune. Image processing was the one skill that was badly needed for their missile development program. Here was a young engineer with knowledge that was needed to support Hamas's ongoing efforts to develop an improved guided missile that could be used to close the technology gap between the Palestinians and the Israelis. Even better, he discovered that Hasan was a devout Sunni Muslim, with strong antagonism for the West. Murtaja then subjected Hasan to intense questioning, all of which he handled well. At the end of their conversation, Hasan was offered a position with Hamas, which he enthusiastically accepted.

***

After work, following the general's instructions, Hasan rode his bicycle to a partially destroyed apartment building in the southwestern section of the city, within view of the Mediterranean Sea. He found the door hidden behind a pile of rubble and, as Murtaja had directed, rapped quietly three times. The armed soldier at the door asked for his identification and ushered Hasan into the facility, which did not have the luxury of possessing either a reception area or individual offices for the staff. In fact, the entire facility consisted of three large areas separated by cinder blocks, which appeared to have been scavenged from the many destroyed buildings in Rafah. The guard shouted "Nasser" and an engineer emerged from behind a missile positioned on a stand in the middle of the first and largest room.

Nasser had obviously been expecting Hasan's arrival, because he strode up to him with a broad grin and a handshake. Nasser began the tour of the laboratory facilities by showing Hasan the Suquur missile on which he would be working, a missile named in Arabic after the hawk, which swoops out of the sky to kill its prey.

Nasser explained to Hasan that the development of the Suquur was only partially successful. Nasser was tall, thin, and nervous. He was dressed in worn jeans and a nondescript black tee shirt emblazoned in white with the crossed swords of the Hamas logo. He explained that he had worked on the Suquur for three years. His specialty was missile propulsion systems.

Thanks to Nasser's work, their weapon had the range needed to reach the Israeli heartland but not the needed accuracy. During their tests, they had launched the missile west over the Mediterranean Sea, aiming at a barge that had been moored approximately five miles from shore. The missile not only failed to destroy the barge, but seemed to be making a U-turn back toward the launch site, an event that caused no end of consternation on the part of the flight crew and the visitors in the viewing stands. Clearly an improved guidance system was needed, and Hasan was to be given the opportunity to lead its development.

His equipment was barely adequate to satisfy his assignment. It consisted of a high-end PC and printer, along with a lab bench, an assortment of hand tools, integrated circuit chips, and a rat's nest of cables. He concluded that his predecessor had not been terribly neat and wondered what had become of him. His impressions were confirmed by Nasser, who indicated that Shadi was the name of the engineer who had preceded Hasan. Shadi was a computer nerd who knew about developing websites, and had indeed done some impressive work for Hamas. But he did not recognize his own limitations, and as a result, when the opportunity to develop software for a missile guidance system came up, he had immediately volunteered for the job. Because of his failure, he had been returned to web development.

Hasan immediately began work. He emailed his professor at Alexandria University for a copy of the pattern recognition software that he had been given while at the university. He then looked through the engineering drawings left by Shadi to determine the manner in which the computer chip mounted in the missile nose cone would receive video signals from the cameras also mounted in its nose, and send commands to the control surfaces that determine the missile's direction and flight attitude (roll, pitch, and yaw). This combination of equipment was used to change a missile from that of a propelled rock to an intelligent device capable of seeking out and homing in on a predefined target. Hasan understood this and worked for several weeks under continuous pressure from Ossama, the ironically named director of the laboratory.

After several months of twelve-hour days, Hasan believed he had everything working. He had been given access to a prototype Suquur sitting on a test stand in a room adjacent to his laboratory. It took him several days to get the computer chip to move the control surfaces. It took several additional weeks to get the video system to communicate with the same chip. When he tried to load his image-processing software, he discovered that the computer chip did not have either the needed storage capacity or processing power to interpret the video images. As a result, it was necessary to redesign the entire system of electronics that made up the missile's brain, a difficult task to fit additional chips into the cramped space available within the missile's nose cone.

On the day of the test, Hasan joined Nasser, Ossama, and General Murtaja in the small shack at the edge of the launching area. Until that day, Hasan had not realized that Ossama reported to General Murtaja. But their relationship was obvious from Ossama's obsequious attitude toward the general.

The shack was intended as much to shield the observers from the hot sun as it was to protect them from the blast of the missile launch. It was a crude, one-room structure made of cinder blocks and a tin roof, surrounded by discarded oil drums filled with salt water taken from the nearby sea. Inside was a table, which held Hassan's computers, along with simple instrumentation that included a thermometer, an anemometer for measuring wind speed, and several video monitors. Chairs were positioned around the table for the convenience of the observers. The room smelled of a combination of machine oil, cigarette smoke, and the perspiration of the observers.

Hasan was sweating both from the heat and from nervousness about the success of the test. He feared that a failure would jeopardize his position as the primary developer of the missile's guidance system. As if reading his mind, Ossama said, "Well Hassan, we've got a lot of confidence in you. In the name of Allah, I hope this test will be a great success."

Hasan nervously replied, "Sir, I'm optimistic that the missile will hit its target, but please remember that we are in the early stages of development. This is still research. Even the Americans, with their advanced technologies, have experienced many failures of their missiles during their early stages of development. Success is only achieved with great patience."

General Murtaja, anxious to support his protégé, supported Hasan. "Ossama, it would indeed be a blessing if this test succeeded, but sometimes it takes many trials before one achieves one's goal."

Ossama responded, "These missile firings are expensive. We can only afford so many of them." He then lapsed into a sulky silence while Hasan and Nasser nervously busied themselves with their instrumentation.

The test being conducted was a repeat of the test that resulted in the reassignment of Shadi as a website developer. A barge that was to serve as the target had been towed approximately five miles offshore, where it was anchored awaiting the arrival of the unarmed missile. Cameras on the barge were to record the incoming missile's trajectory. The towing vessel had retired to a position several miles from the barge.

Everyone's pulse rate quickened as the launch crew, located in a bunker closer to the launch pad, began their backward countdown. When the count hit zero, there was a flash of light that disabled the cameras nearest to the missile and a roar that seemed to last forever. After a couple of seconds, the Suquur slowly left the ground, accelerating as it roared out over the Mediterranean. As he followed the missile's trajectory, defined by its vapor trail, Hasan quietly mouthed a silent prayer to Allah that the missile would hit the target. To Hasan's initial relief, the arc of the vapor trail was straight and true, heading due west toward the barge as Hasan had programmed the initial phase of the flight, which was controlled by a GPS chip in the missile's nose cone. The cameras on the barge picked up the image of the approaching missile, which then continued its flight, passing over the barge and flying due west until it ran out of fuel and crashed into the ocean, several miles beyond.

Hasan's heart sank with the obvious failure of the Suquur's image-processing system to identify the barge and home in on its target. He had wisely included telemetry equipment in the missile that transmitted the video images being picked up by the cameras in the nose cone. As a result, he had a record of the information being received by the image-processing software that could be analyzed and used for future corrections. He recorded the video stream on one of the computers, which was taken to the basement laboratory for analysis.

There was a palpable silence in the shack. Without saying a word, Ossama stood up and walked out the door to his waiting car. General Murtaja also left, patting Hasan on the shoulder as he walked past him. Nasser began packing up the equipment, saying, "Don't worry, Hasan. It would have been a miracle to have succeeded with so complicated a task on the first try."

"Yes. But it would have been a nice miracle if it had happened. Do you think that Ossama will reassign me? He never liked me, and at times I had the feeling he wanted me to fail," Hasan said.

"That's not true. Ossama is like that with everyone. He's the type of person who expects his people to produce miracles. He's better at scolding for failures than he is for praising good success."

The two packed their equipment in the van and returned to the laboratory.

***

Forgetting about his fear of Ossama, Hasan immediately unpacked his equipment and went to work. His first interest was the video tapes. Had the camera been working? Did it record the presence of the barge? Was it an equipment problem or a software problem?

When he placed the flash drive on which the video telemetry was stored in his computer and began playing it back, he was horrified. He shouted, "How stupid am I?" so loudly that Nasser came running.

"What's wrong?"

"Look at this video picture."

Nasser looked at the screen of the computer on which the video was being played and saw an image of the sky alternating with images of the ocean and then back to the sky. He was puzzled. "What is this?"

Hasan replied, "Don't you see what happened? The missile was rolling as it flew. The camera was mounted on the missile, so as the Suquur rolled, the camera was looking at the sky half the time and at the ground the other half of the time. It never received a continuous image of its target. I don't know why this did not occur to me. Obviously, I took the wrong courses in college."

"You certainly made a beginner's mistake. But how can they expect you to be an expert in the field without any prior experience? They keep firing people because they fail without ever giving them the time to learn anything. I certainly hope they leave you alone long enough for you to succeed."

The two of them stood by the monitor and watched the video as it played for the three minutes of the missile's flight. Nasser was just interested in the rotating image, while Hasan watched to see whether the camera in the missile had picked up any images of the barge as it rotated in its flight. In that respect he was fortunate. The camera was pointed at the sea for a brief period of time as it passed over the barge. The image he saw further discouraged him, since the barge was barely discernable in the glittering waves that surrounded it. The straight lines of the barge's freeboard were not distinguishable within the surrounding waves, which obscured its characteristic shape. He doubted that his software would recognize this object as its target.

He would have to go home, eat some supper, and think about ways to solve the problem.

That night Hasan awoke with a start. His mind was working while he slept and wouldn't let him forget that the missile's GPS system had pointed it on a straight and true course, while the image-processing software had failed. Why hadn't this occurred to him sooner? Why not feed the coordinates of the target into the software and use the GPS for guidance? Because of his background in video image processing, he had automatically assumed that this would be the technology needed for missile guidance. But it was the wrong technology for this application.

Although it was only 4:00 a.m., Hasan was so excited that he got dressed, had an orange for breakfast, and rushed out to the laboratory. Nasser found him that morning bent over the computer keyboard programming a new guidance system that relied exclusively on the coordinates provided by the GPS chip.

It all sounded so simple. But the implementation was not. Nasser and Hasan worked through the day and into the night in order to figure out how the missile should anticipate its arrival at the right coordinates and begin its descent so that it reached the ground at the appropriate location. The two spent hours at the whiteboard in their lab, working on the complex equations that defined the three-dimensional flightpath.

Ossama walked into the lab while they were excitedly working. Not being able to resist taking a dig at Hasan, he said, "Well, my college genius, are we working on another failure?"

Hasan ignored the barb and continued to focus on the translation of the equations on the white board into computer code. But Nasser could not resist a reply. "Why don't you give the kid a break? He's learning on the job without much equipment and no experience. I don't think that pestering him will improve his work. Furthermore, we've figured out what went wrong, and I think we've got a good solution."

Rather than replying to Nasser's defense of Hasan, Ossama asked, "Does this mean we'll be ready for another failure soon? I hope we don't have too many additional failures, since we're running out of test missiles and money."

Nasser did not wait for Hasan to answer, but said, "I think we'll be ready for a test within two weeks. The solution to the problem greatly simplifies the equipment in the missile and will be easy to implement."

"Good, then I'll see to scheduling the test fourteen days from today. General Murtaja is becoming impatient, in spite of his support of Hasan."

Time passed rapidly. Once again Hasan and Nasser spent twelve-hour days reconfiguring the missile hardware and testing the software. Their tests were comprehensive, to the point at which they even mounted the missile electronics on Hasan's jeep, driving it around Rafah to see how it would perform on a moving platform.

They were up all night on the evening of the thirteenth day, getting ready for the second test. During their frantic work to prepare the missile for its test, Hasan said to Nasser, "I wish you had consulted with me before you told Ossama that we only needed two weeks. We could use some more tests, and we need to be certain that the coordinates of the barge's location are correct."

"Don't worry. We'll make it. I spent a few minutes of our valuable time at the Mosque praying to Allah for success."

***

Daylight once again found the two engineers in the shack with Ossama and General Murtaja. As they worked to set up their equipment, their superiors spoke quietly, chain smoked, and drank Turkish coffee. The barge remained anchored as it had been during the previous test. Hasan carefully entered the barge's coordinates of latitude 31° 22' 34.15" N, longitude 34° 10' 25.82' E into the missile guidance system, and with that they were ready to go.

Finally, in the late morning, Hasan radioed the launch crew that they were ready for the test. As before, the backward count-down began. The launch proceeded with the firing of the missile, the destruction of the launchpad camera, and the Suquur soaring into the deep blue Mediterranean sky.

Hasan and Nasser held their breath as they watched it begin its three-minute flight to the barge. As before, it correctly headed due west toward the barge. But unlike the previous test, the missile began an arcing descent as it neared the barge, and, as reported both by the camera on the barge and the observers on the boat monitoring the tests, it splashed down an estimated fifty feet beyond the barge. Hasan and Nasser were elated. They could hardly wait to review the telemetered video data to review the test.

Ossama and Murtaja exhibited restrained elation at the results of the test. Ossama asked Hasan, "That was a lot better, but why did it still miss the barge?"

Ignoring his lack of enthusiasm, Hasan replied, "That was within the kill range of the missile, wasn't it? If we had a real warhead, the barge would have been sunk."

During the next few days, Hasan and Nasser reviewed the video and reviewed all their calculations. After exhaustive work, they uncovered the problem. Their calculations had been based on the weight of an armed missile rather than one with a dummy warhead. That difference could explain the reason for overshooting the target.

They explained the situation to Ossama and the general, both of whom were satisfied that Hasan had succeeded. A few days later, Hasan received the word that the leadership of Hamas had decided to begin mass-producing the Suquur. He was also informed that he would be honored for his work.

Little did Hasan realize that his development of the Hawk guidance system and the honors he had received would provide him with the opportunity to change the world.

CHAPTER 4
EAST JAKARTA, INDONESIA

The six men sitting at the folding aluminum table in the sparsely furnished underground conference room were a polyglot of nationalities, albeit a group with a single focus, that of taking control of the power structure existing in their home countries and replacing it with a Sunni Muslim government loyal to a central caliphate. The room was devoid of decorations and was painted a dull blue except for one of its walls, which had been painted bright yellow, and which Adam had subsequently explained was intended to counteract the absence of sunlight.

Adam surveyed the group from the head of the table. "Let me begin by apologizing for the absence of adequate furnishings," he said, indicating the walls with a single picture of Osama bin Laden, the concrete floors without carpeting, and the table surrounded by folding chairs.

This group had come to Indonesia seeking to acquire the money, arms, and other support that would benefit their movements. They had responded to the invitation from Adam al-Zhihri because their leaders had been intrigued, and had some knowledge of Adam's long association and many successes with al-Qaeda. They were also well aware of the useful time he had spent in America learning the ways of the infidel. They were optimistic that this powerful new organization could benefit their efforts.

Adam continued with his unnecessary explanation of the sparse furnishings, adding a hint of the objectives of his organization. "These facilities will soon be furnished as appropriate for the headquarters of Bis Saif, which is soon to become a major worldwide headquarters for the Sunni Muslim religion.

Bis Saif will soon be replacing al-Qaeda as the most respected and feared organization in the world. It is our hope to be joined soon by the al-Qaeda leadership and many of its talented supporters. It is also our hope to merge our organization with that of Islamic Defenders Front, or the FPI, which as you may already know is the Indonesian fundamentalist Muslim sect. So as you can see, we're gradually integrating all of the Muslim fundamentalists worldwide. In other words, soon a worldwide caliphate will be within our grasp."

Adam al-Zhihri, the self-appointed leader of the organization, had decided to replace the time-worn name al-Qaeda with a new, more inspiring name: Bis Saif, meaning "by the sword" in Arabic. The new name was intended to renew and refresh the image of al-Qaeda.

In addition to his claim of Osama bin Laden as a distant relative, and his access to many of the bin Laden funding sources, Adam had the benefit of a four-year education at Yale University, courtesy of a Fulbright Foreign Student scholarship and a student visa issued by the US State Department. He took great pride in the benefits he had received from the United States—the enemy he was determined to defeat. Adam's credibility was further enhanced by his years of experience fighting the United States and its allies during their invasion of Iraq. In short, Adam was the most dangerous of enemies—a highly educated, brilliant, charismatic, battle hardened individual with a well-defined objective. With the exception of Abu Ahmed, Adam's close friend since childhood in Kuwait, the others in the room were strangers, in awe of Adam's charm and his impressive background.

"I think I know why you are all here," Adam continued. "You hope to receive funding and other forms of support for your causes. I think that is possible, and should be the focus of our conversations. But nothing in life is free. Bis Saif might like something in return for its support of your causes. So please be prepared to give as well as take." As he spoke, Adam thought to himself, *The seed is planted. Now all I have to do is to give it water and food, and I will harvest its fruit.*

Adam then changed the subject to put his visitors at ease. "We have excellent living quarters here, as well as good food, Internet reception, movies, and games. We also have a gymnasium for your exercise and laundry facilities. Undoubtedly some of you will want to take advantage of the laundry since we couldn't help notice that you are all traveling with minimal baggage. Just ask if you need something you cannot find. You will be shown to your rooms to relax and refresh yourselves after your long trips. You will find that the rooms of this facility have been painted many different colors to compensate for our lack of an outdoor view. Most of you are used to spending lengthy periods outdoors. We don't want you to become depressed by the absence of fresh air and sunlight."

Returning to the schedule, Adam added, "Local time here is now 4:00 p.m., and dinner will be served at eight. Feel free to wander around our facility and get to know each other and our staff. Nothing is off limits. There is only one rule: you may not leave the facility until the end of the week when it is time to return home. And when you leave, you will be escorted by one of our security staff to the appropriate exits at the appropriate times. They have been selected to ensure that no one suspects the existence of this facility.

"The exit doors from the facility have all been locked to ensure that this strict rule is not violated. It is for all of our safety," Adam added with a smile of reassurance.

And with that, the initial meeting was concluded. "I'll see you all in the dining room at eight. The staff will show you to your rooms and give you a general idea of the layout here."

With the departure of their guests, Adam and Ahmed were left alone. The contrast between the two was striking. Adam was serious, tall, and good-looking, with striking dark features that were characteristic of many Kuwaiti citizens. By contrast, Ahmed's body resembled that of a fire hydrant. He was short and powerfully built with a face that resembled someone who had been in too many street fights. His nose was flat and off-center, looking as if it had been broken beyond the ability of the doctors to return it to its original position and shape on his face.

He had dark brown eyes that were almost black, which seemed to look through you. His looks disguised a fast mind and a disarming sense of humor.

"Do you think they're beginning to understand why they're here?" asked Adam, who relied on Ahmed's ability to read people.

"I'm not sure. You were pretty cryptic," Ahmed said. "At best you can hope that they're beginning to realize that they are not going to receive any free handouts. Why didn't you make any introductions? They're probably wondering whether they're here to compete with the others for your support."

"A little uncertainty is good for the soul. It will be interesting to see what they tell each other about their mission here. I skipped the introductions, intentionally hoping that they will inquire into each other's backgrounds. Let's go to the security room and monitor their conversations."

Adam and Ahmed then opened the one locked door of the facility, which led to a room that housed banks of closed-circuit TV monitors by which they could keep track of the activities and conversations of their visitors. Cameras were installed in every room of the facility, carefully disguised behind moldings and pictures.

They learned little that they did not already know about their visitors, who were guarded and suspicious of the reasons for the meeting and the motivations of the other guests. One of the visitors, who identified himself by the unimaginative alias of John Smith, was particularly reticent. His origins were misleadingly evident from his British accent. If MI6, the British Intelligence Agency, had checked his ancestry more carefully when they employed him, they would have discovered that his unnamed grandfather was in fact a citizen of Saudi Arabia. Even more significant was the fact that this anonymous relative was a member of the hierarchy of the Wahhabi sect, a particularly virulent Sunni strain of the Muslim religion.

***

The group of six reassembled in the dining room promptly at the appointed hour. None of them were accustomed to luxurious accommodations, and so all were completely satisfied with their living quarters, even though they resembled the basic furnishings of a college dormitory room, the only added luxury being a flat-screen TV.

Sitting in his customary position at the head of the table, Adam first paused to give his guests an opportunity to recite their personal prayer known as the du'a. Each of those present leaned forward prayerfully and quietly said "Bismillah," ("In the name of Allah"). When they had completed their personal prayers, Adam began a longer mealtime prayer, saying, "O Allah! Bless the food you have provided us and save us from the punishment of hellfire. In the name of Allah." After a brief pause, he then began the dinner with a brief welcome, saying, "I hope your accommodations are satisfactory. Unfortunately, we can't provide you with a balcony and a beautiful view since our facility is underground. We have tried to be sensitive to your dietary preferences, but if you are served something you would rather not eat, let us know and we'll find a substitute." To which he received silent nods from his visitors.

Adam continued. "After our meeting this afternoon, I realized I failed to introduce you to each other. I would like to correct that oversight now. Assuming you have not yet introduced yourselves to each other, let me correct my bad manners. To begin with, I am Adam al-Zhihri, a relative of the bin Laden family. I was educated in the United States at the famed Yale University, fought the Iraqi invaders, and have established the Bis Saif organization that is your host."

To his right sat John Smith, the enigmatic one. "My name is John Smith. I was educated in England at Oxford. My degree is in political science. I am a Sunni Muslim, and I am committed to the ascendancy of our culture."

To John Smith's right sat Udo. "My name is Udo. I am Nigerian and a member of the Boko Haram. Our goal is to overthrow the corrupt Nigerian government and replace it with a Muslim government of the people. My brother and many of my relatives have been slaughtered by the corrupt Nigerian army, which is trying to exterminate us."

To Udo's right, and at the foot of the table, sat Ahmed: "My name is Abu Ahmed al-Kuwaiti. As you can tell from my name, I grew up in Kuwait, the son of an oil man. Adam and I are longtime friends. We attended school together in Kuwait. Like Adam, I grew weary of a culture centered on money and governed by an emir whose sole purpose was to pacify the Americans and Europeans. The Koran was ignored, and Muslims were second-class citizens unless they were part of the Kuwaiti elite." To the amusement of the group, he then added, "all the hotels in Kuwait have swimming pools that are used by airline flight attendants in bikinis. I ask you, is that sanctioned by the Koran?"

To Ahmed's right sat Hasan Jouda: "My name is Hasan Jouda. I am a Palestinian. I live in the Gaza Strip, where my people have been impoverished by the Israelis. Unlike the rest of you, I am not a fighting man. I am a computer engineer assigned to the development of missiles that can be rained on Israel."

The last person to introduce himself was Ali. "My name is Ali. I grew up in Aleppo, Syria, a country that is rapidly disintegrating thanks to a corrupt government and meddling by the West. As a result of my disillusionment with the Syrian government, I joined ISIS, where I have seen fighting in many of the cities of Iraq."

Although he did not express his opinion out loud, Adam thought, *These people are all low-level fighters, spies, and engineers. There's not a person in the group capable of making a decision for their organization. It is not surprising that their superiors do not trust us and have sent expendable representatives. We'll have to correct this. But I won't say anything for now since they are not aware of the need for their participation.*

Except for John Smith, the remainder of the meal was spent sharing the experiences of the group, with emphasis on war stories. Udo told of spending the night in a tree trying to ignore the demands of his bladder. Ali regaled the group with his tale of hiding in the woods, watching the IEDs being buried. The group began to appreciate Hasan's mental capabilities when he told of reprogramming the Suquur guidance system. It was a congenial group of like-minded comrades pursuing a common goal. A westerner would have been fascinated by the fact that the congeniality was achieved without resorting to alcoholic beverages.

Dinner was concluded by Adam. "Now you're all undoubtedly tired from your trip. Why don't we end the day with a prayer to Allah for our success and meet again tomorrow? Praise be to Allah, who has fed us and given us drink and made us Muslims."

***

The offices of Bis Saif were an engineering miracle. They were designed by Adam, who was determined to avoid the mistakes of his distant relative Osama bin Laden. Bin Laden had died at the hands of the US Navy Seals on May 2, 2011, in a small residential compound in Abbottabad, Pakistan. Bin Laden had relied on an unreliable ally, the Pakistani security forces. But in spite of this fatal mistake, bin Laden's accomplishments were significant, and they have been admired to this day by assorted groups of Muslim insurgents, many of whom dream of a Sunni caliphate created to establish united leadership of the entire Muslim world. Adam created his offices without the cooperation, or even the knowledge, of the Indonesian government.

The Bis Saif headquarters were located in the bowels of a high-rise office building in East Jakarta, a section of the capital city of Indonesia that housed manufacturing, lower income neighborhoods, and a burgeoning area of new high-rise offices. Adam had selected Indonesia for the location of his headquarters because it was a relatively stable country with a strong economy that supported the largest Muslim population in the world. Among the country's 200 million Muslims, he was able to recruit a loyal cadre of supporters that provided him with the staff needed by the anticipated Bis Saif organization.

Local Muslim supporters had also been tremendously helpful during the time that his facilities were being constructed. These facilities represented a complex undertaking with extensive underground infrastructure as well as long tunnels to be used for access and egress to the compound.

Locating his facilities in East Jakarta placed him near the Indonesia federal government, in a crowded neighborhood with varied professions and income levels that would allow his visitors to come and go without arousing suspicion.

Adam had taken advantage of his relationship with the bin Ladens to obtain financing for a new office building within the new high-rise development. As the owner he was able to influence its construction in a manner that favored the inclusion of subterranean facilities with secure access. Above the street level, the high-rise building appeared to be a normal office complex. Its tenants were a polyglot of businesses that included a major investment firm, which occupied two floors, as well as miscellaneous medical companies, corporate headquarters, and law firms. It featured an impressive lobby entered through double glass doors on which the mythical bird of Vishnu, the crest of Indonesia, was etched. Upon entering the two-story lobby with a large Alexander Calder-like impressionistic mobile suspended over the entryway, the visitor must approach a desk at which two armed guards were seated in front of a row of computer and closed-circuit TV monitors. Anyone without a building pass had to sign in at the guard's desk, where their credentials were checked and a phone call was placed to the individual whom they were visiting. This individual or their representative then had to go to the lobby to sign for their guest and escort them to their meeting destination. Once they were cleared and escorted, they must pass through airport-like security screening on their way to the elevators.

Since the available space in the building was occupied as soon as the building was completed, the bin Laden family was pleased to realize they had made a good investment that would supplement their considerable fortune. Income from the office building more than offset the cost of the Bis Saif offices in the two stories below the lobby.

Employees and visitors to the building's subterranean facilities had to undergo the same process as those visiting the legitimate above-ground offices. The difference was that the individual escorting the visitor had to insert a plastic pass card into a reader slot on the elevator, which activated a unique operation. Upon reading the card, the elevator automatically descended to a designated floor in the subterranean facilities of the building. While descending, the floor displays outside the elevator doors indicated that the elevator was rising rather than descending. It falsely indicated that the elevator had ascended to the top floor of the building, the floor on which the air conditioning, satellite, and radio receiving facilities were located.

The subterranean offices were housed two floors below street level. The first floor housed the conventional facilities of a high-rise building, which typically include the heating plant, backup power, hot water heater, the electrical, and communications distribution systems. This was a clever design since it permitted the outputs of these various systems to be fed upward to the thirty floors of the office tower, and downward to the subterranean offices one floor below. The jumble of pipes, ducts and conduits that snaked through this floor was intentionally designed to confuse any prying eyes regarding their destination.

Visitors to the subterranean floors two levels below the street would be surprised by its lack of ornamentation. The extremely large area, which matched the footprint of the high-rise building, included a small reception area with an armed guard, a half dozen offices, a conference room, a large communications room, sleeping quarters, a kitchen, eating area, and food storage. There was also a utility area that provided filtration for both water and air as well as an emergency generator capable of powering the facility for more than a month. These facilities were designed so that the occupants could survive without support from the outside world for an extended period of time.

Construction of this space was performed by three different subcontractors, none of whom knew its purpose, nor did any single contractor have access to the entire space or its facilities. At the completion of the construction, all construction plans and drawings were destroyed except for one master copy that was kept in a safe in Adam's office.

The Bis Saif leadership could not take the risk of being seen in public with each other, or be seen entering and leaving the same facility. While in theory they could remain in their home countries and communicate electronically, the intensive monitoring by the US National Security Agency (NSA) made this extremely difficult. After much consideration, they decided that cohousing in the same facility was less risky than long distance communication. The invisibility of their facility was maintained by the construction of underground tunnels leading from the subterranean offices into the surrounding neighborhoods. The tunnels had been dug manually by many low-paid laborers, a common sight at Indonesian construction projects. The absence of mechanized tunneling machines minimized the possibility of onlooker curiosity and simplified the process of disposing the excavated material. The tunnels were long. Some of them exceeded a mile in length. Each tunnel ended in a residence or office building in the surrounding neighborhoods. The tunnels were a labyrinth of intertwined passageways that were impossible to traverse without a roadmap. Of course, there were no roadmaps.

The man with the vision to create this facility was Adam al-Zhihri, a brilliant Yale graduate and a devout Sunni Muslim. Adam grew up in Kuwait City, Kuwait, the son of the well-connected owner of a local construction company. He attended public primary and secondary schools, where he excelled at his studies, and became the star of his school's football team, a sport known as soccer in the United States. While in secondary school, Adam began attending the local mosque, where he was a frequent worshipper and participant in the mosque's outreach to the local community. After graduation from the public school system, Adam attended Kuwait University, where he enrolled in a daunting curriculum over the objections of his advisor. He majored in political science, with a minor in Sharia and Islamic

Philip J. Tarnoff

studies. These dual majors, supplemented by courses that provided a detailed education on the history of the Middle East, caused him to wonder at the original supremacy of the empires of the Middle East and the manner in which it was ceded to the West. Why did civilization begin in Egypt and Persia? How did it migrate to Greece and Rome? How did the Arab empire participate in the downfall of Rome, and why did it lose its edge following the establishment of the first caliphate? What opportunities were lost along the way? How could they be recovered?

Adam met Ahmed in high school, where the two became close friends. Ahmed played defense for the football team while Adam was a forward. These roles in which Adam was the leader while Ahmed watched his back were to continue throughout their lives. When they graduated from high school, both men attended university, where Ahmed majored in engineering while Adam pursued his expansive liberal arts curriculum. In spite of their different directions, the two remained close, often debating the meaning of various passages in the Koran or its influence on the history of the region.

Adam wondered whether the answer to the complex questions related to the rise of the West at the expense of the Middle East could be found in a Western university. In his search for answers, he left Ahmed behind and applied for graduate studies at Yale University, which advertised a strong program of world history. He was readily accepted into the graduate program at Yale due to his excellent grades and Yale's desire for a multi-ethnic student body. Adam enjoyed his coursework, which, unusual for a liberal arts degree, included a scattering of technical courses such as computer science and statistics. But his favorites were history, government, and religion. The material covered by these courses provided the foundation for his dream, that of a revolution, not unlike the one that led to the destruction of the Roman Empire, in which the existing power structure was toppled. His studies had convinced him that this was possible because of the many similarities between the weaknesses of the Roman Empire and that of Western civilization. While at Yale he met John Smith, another political science student, and the two soon recognized that they shared a common interest in reversing the decline of the Arab world and the resurrection of the Sunni Muslim religion. They had stayed in contact and together had discussed the feasibility of the Jakarta facility.

With the advantages of the bin Laden family's wealth made available with John Smith as an intermediary, and Adam's innate intelligence, he believed that his dream could be achieved. All that was required was careful planning and the coordinated support of the millions of Muslims throughout the world. The high-rise in East Jakarta was the beginning of the dream.

***

The second day of the gathering in Jakarta began promptly at 8:00 a.m. immediately after a breakfast that catered to the epicurean preferences of each participant. Adam had taken pains to research the dietary habits of his visitors to ensure that the meeting was not disrupted by petty dietary restrictions. He wisely wanted to ensure that the meeting was free of distractions so that his guests would be focused on the business at hand.

"Now let's get down to business," were Adam's opening words. "I thought it would be instructive to begin our meeting with a brief review of the history of our fight against the domination of the West. I apologize in advance if you already know all of this, but I want to be certain that we all have the same level of understanding."

In an attempt to maintain the relaxed atmosphere, Ahmed added, "Adam has always wanted to be a college professor, so let's humor him. When he's finished his tutoring, we can get down to business." His comments drew a polite laugh from the three visitors. John Smith remained unsmiling.

Ignoring Ahmed's comment, Adam forged ahead with his tutorial.

"As you might know, there are 1.1 billion Muslims and 2.1 billion Christians in the world. The Muslim religion accounts for 21.5 percent, and the Christian religion accounts for 32.5 percent of the world's population. What is significant is that

47

the percentages are increasing for Muslims and decreasing for Christians. Based on my experience in the United States, and hopefully backed up by John Smith here, the Muslim worshippers are significantly more dedicated to their religion than the Christians. The latter tend to worship their egos, financial gain, sports, and prestige rather than their God."

The taciturn John Smith nodded in agreement at Adam's reference.

Satisfied with John's silent assent, Adam continued. "Muslims have been responsible for many of the great advances in science, technology, agriculture, and medicine. Examples of advances by Muslims include the development of algebra, the first use of Arabic numerals in the ninth century by Al-Khwarazmi, the treatment of smallpox by Al-Razi in the tenth century, and the invention of a computing machine by Al-Kashani during the fifteenth century. Our people were particularly advanced in the fields of medicine, devising hospitals with separate areas for trauma cases, treatments for cataracts, and certification processes for physicians. They were also responsible for many architectural advances, including the construction of domed edifices and the creation of a variety of well-known architectural styles incorporating geometric shapes. All of this before the fifteenth century."

Pausing to let the facts sink in, Adam continued, "So what has happened since that time? Where has all the talent gone? My theory is that between the sixteenth century and modern times, we have wasted our energies on fighting each other, defending ourselves against the crusades of Christianity and opposing Western colonization. As a result, we have become a third world force engaged in primitive tribal warfare."

His small audience visibly cringed at his reference to the primitive nature of their modern condition. But no one challenged his thesis.

"This is an unacceptable situation," Adam said with his voice rising perceptibly. "You in this room, and others with whom I have yet to speak, have the ability to change the world and put Islam back on its rightful course toward a return to greatness. Now you know why you're here."

His closing remarks sparked a round of spontaneous applause from his audience.

"I have devised a plan. Your organizations offer significant potential for implementing that plan. The first step is to strengthen your operations without alerting the Western powers of our existence. Most important, what I need from you is your commitment to participate with Bis Saif in the rejuvenation of Islam as a powerful world force. Once you have agreed to participate, I need an honest assessment of your organization's objectives as well as the resources you need to accomplish these objectives. I also need your ideas about other organizations similar to yours that would be willing to join us.

"I am assuming that none of you is authorized to enter into a pact with Bis Saif. We have a secure communication link that you can use to discuss this with your superiors and receive their approval. Once that is satisfactorily completed, we can begin discussing your needs and ideas. Anyone who does not want to enter into such a pact will be excused from the remainder of the meeting without prejudice. If that is the case, you will immediately be free to return home. I am hopeful that this will not be necessary. So go and speak to your superiors, and return with your answers."

At that point, the meeting ended with each of the three representatives returning to their rooms. Obtaining the necessary commitments was a lengthy process due to time differences and difficulties contacting their superiors. By the end of the day, they had all returned with the desired commitments, which were readily obtained due to the vague nature of the request and the promise of resources to support their movements. In fact, all of the participating organizations expected the pact to be a toothless agreement that they planned to ignore at will. To further protect themselves, they each indicated that their agreements were contingent on the details of the resources to be provided and the actions to be provided in return. Adam was not surprised by the tone of the responses. After all, this was the Middle East, and one did not enter into an agreement without an appropriate level of haggling as a preamble.

Once the broad agreement to work together had been settled, the remainder of the week was devoted to negotiations related to the specific needs of each participant. As Adam had predicted, the negotiations were not one-sided. Many types of commitments were discussed, including financing, arms, equipment, intelligence, and support from neighboring factions. Each promise of support was accompanied by a reverse commitment of expected results, expanded operations, and the manner in which they would be evaluated. It was made clear that nothing was free. Failure to achieve promised results would lead to changes in leadership, elimination of support, and, worse yet, possible support of opposing factions. Reaching agreements with each of the three organizations required multiple communications with their superiors, who in turn needed the approval of their superiors.

At the end of the week, the delegates except for John Smith looked forward to returning home to a hero's welcome, convinced they had advanced their respective causes. All that would be needed was the electronic signatures of their commanders on the agreements that had been prepared by the Bis Saif clerical staff.

***

"Let's reconvene in the conference room," Adam said as soon as the three guests had departed. In a few minutes, he was joined by John Smith and Ahmed holding cups of steaming strong Arabic coffee. After a brief self-congratulatory discussion, Adam turned to John Smith and asked, "Well John, what do you think? You were part of the group. Did anyone confide anything particularly interesting to you?"

"Actually, they were quite a dull group. I sensed a lot of suspicion, which was not surprising, considering the sudden unveiling of your proposals. Don't forget that they all come from societies in which suspicion is a defense for survival." Almost as an afterthought, John added, "You surprised them with your dissertation on the downfall of the Arab intelligentsia.

50

And by the way, where did you get this information? Are you sure it's correct?"

Ahmed added, "You made us sound like a group of losers. I agree that we do tend to fight among ourselves, but surely Muslims are continuing to make contributions to the advance of civilization." As was his style, Ahmed couldn't resist adding with a grin, "If nothing else, we make great football players."

Adam felt obligated to justify himself, which he could readily do given his phenomenal memory. "If the two of you had read the famous book by Thomas Friedman, *The World is Flat*, you would be ready to accept some of these ideas. Friedman offers one of the best analyses of the Muslim situation I have ever read."

Here it comes, thought Ahmed, who had experienced the results of Adam's ability to retrieve passages from various previously read books and recite them from memory. John, who did not know Adam as well, looked interested as he slouched in his folding chair.

Unaware of the varying degrees of expectation in the room, Adam continued. "In his book, Friedman cited data collected by the Second Arab Human Development Report, which quantified the plight of the Muslim world. He indicated that between 1980 and 1999, Arab countries had been awarded a hundred and seventy-one international patents. During the same period, South Korea alone was awarded more than sixteen thousand patents. Hewlett-Packard files an average of eleven new patent applications a day. If that isn't compelling enough, twenty-five percent of university graduates in the Arab world immigrated to the West. There are eighteen computers per one thousand people in the Arab region today, compared with a global average of seventy-eight per one thousand. While Arabs represent almost five percent of the world population, they produce only one percent of the books published, and a high percentage of these are religious books. The number of religious books produced by Arabs is more than three times the number of books produced by the rest of the world.

Seeing that he had gained the rapt attention of his small audience, Adam continued. "Friedman accurately portrayed the stark contrasts between the Middle East and the rest of the world as *humiliation*. It is a humiliation that we are trying to eliminate our Western enemies through bombing and beheadings. While we may get some temporary satisfaction from these acts, they do not represent a solution to our long-term difficulties. These difficulties arise from the authoritarian governments that control the progress, or lack of progress, of our societies. These problems persist in spite of the guidance provided by the Koran. We should not ignore its brilliance and blame our problems on our religion.

"I have thought about this for a long time and concluded that the violence is a good antidote to the discontent of our people, but the satisfaction it provides is not unlike the satisfaction of a good meal. Shortly after the meal, one is hungry again. For this reason, violence must be supplemented by effective leadership of the Muslim world and a return to the intellectual leadership that it once offered. As you both know, in its prime, the Muslim world was governed by an omnipotent caliphate. Would that be the solution today? Only if the leadership it offers is enlightened. The leadership must emphasize education, technology, medicine, and other intellectual pursuits."

Adam knew he had their attention and continued to reveal his inner thoughts. "Although you have not questioned me about the reasons for my selection of representatives from the Islamic State, Nigeria, and Palestine, I will tell you that it was made with these considerations in my mind. Ali, from the Islamic State, and Udo, from Nigeria, represent the dissatisfied younger generations of the Muslim world in the Middle East and Africa. Hasan was invited as a representative of the college-educated technocrats of the Muslim world. He could prove to be a great asset as our plans evolve. And finally, our friend John Smith here," Adam said, patting John on the knee, "he has been invited as a representative of the Muslim world temporarily stationed in the West. And, not incidentally, for his understanding of the Western intelligence community."

John smiled and nodded at the reference. "You will also notice that none of the three organizations that I invited are currently in conflict with each other. While we share the bond of a common religion, our nationalistic pride often gets in the way of accomplishing our objectives. We must discover a way to deal with this."

As an afterthought, Adam said, "I realize that Ali, Udo, and Hasan are not in the upper echelons of their organizations, but it would have been difficult to convince their senior commanders to attend this conference before they had a complete understanding of our goals. More important, their senior commanders cannot travel easily, since they are probably on the no-fly list at most of the world's airports. It was important for their representatives to see this facility so that they can realize that we are a powerful organization with significant resources. This meeting was just a first step in developing relationships with their organizations. Hopefully the three will return with favorable impressions of our operation. Undoubtedly there will be many follow-up meetings, many of which will occur electronically, which will try the patience of us all. We also know how to deal with any of the organizations that do not want to join us. Now let's get to work."

For the remainder of the day, Adam, Ahmed, and John discussed their next steps. Funds were not a problem as Adam, with John Smith's able assistance, had done well in convincing like-minded wealthy Sunnis of the prospects for Bis Saif's success, particularly the Wahhabi Sunnis in Saudi Arabia. Many details needed to be addressed if they were going to be considered responsive to the organizations that had been represented at the meeting. These included the acquisition of funds and equipment that had been requested. The Islamic State, which was well-funded by their oil revenue, had a need for high-tech equipment, including air-control centers capable of tracking and firing surface-to-air missiles at combat aircraft. Boko Haram had requested funding for small arms and anti-aircraft weapons, such as Stinger missiles. The Palestinians requested technology to improve their guided missiles, as well as long-range drone aircraft with the capability of extended flight times and the ability to fire at ground targets.

Adam recognized the importance of responding to these requests quickly in order to convince his new partners of the resources he had at his command. He recognized that credibility was the path to achieving the respect of his new partners. While some of their requests would be difficult to fulfill, he was confident that the many arms dealers with whom he had contact would be able to meet his requirements.

As dinnertime drew near, John spoke up. "I'd like to end this meeting on a positive note. Adam's information was certainly compelling, but it was also somewhat depressing. The positive side of the story is that the West is also capable of violence of equal magnitude to that which is being wreaked upon our enemies by our Muslim allies.

"Let me quote from a magazine article I read in early 2015." At that point John held up the April 3, 2015, issue of *The Week*, a weekly news magazine that described a piece written by Mathew Lyons, a contributor to *The New Statesman*. "I don't have Adam's memory, so I'll have to read directly from the magazine. It goes as follows:

" 'The English were once as evil as ISIS,' said Mathew Lyons. 'The Islamic State of Iraq and Syria slaughters women and children by the hundreds, beheads people in public to terrify their families, and smashes priceless artifacts to dust. Under Queen Elizabeth I, we did all those things in Ireland. We, too, drank of "the poisonous cocktail of religious self-righteousness and nascent nationalism that so intoxicates ISIS." In a 1569 campaign, for example, the Protestant English troops massacred every Irish Catholic they found, beheaded the corpses and laid the heads in a path to the British commander's tent. Five years later, the Earl of Essex "hunted down and butchered 400 women and children." A few years after that, Lord Grey had 600 Spanish troops who surrendered in Ireland executed, along with all the Irish they were protecting. An approving Elizabeth told Grey, "You have been chosen the instrument of God's glory." Throughout the colonization of Ireland, Catholic churches and*

54

ancient Irish sites were demolished, and all of this was done in the name of God. As we condemn ISIS and fight against it, we must remember that "the human talent for depravity does not belong to one people or one faith or one era."

John concluded his reading of the quote with the observation that, "We should not be ashamed of the excesses of our fellow Muslims. Shia or Sunni, Catholic or Protestant, all believers are driven to commit acts that are justified by the depth of their belief. We are all human beings. But more important, the depth of religious belief is not an excuse for the lagging technical and social development of our Muslim societies. While the British exhibited the same commitment to their religion as the Muslims, their society has continued to advance at the same rate as other Western societies, leaving the Muslim countries in the dust, so to speak. We must look elsewhere for explanations. But enough philosophizing for the time being. We've got all week to continue this discussion. Right now, we need to get back to work."

Ahmed the comedian added, "I agree. My stomach tells me that the next phase of our efforts is a trip to the dining room."

No one disagreed. And the three left their uncomfortable chairs, stretched, and returned to their rooms to get ready for the always delicious dinner they knew would be served at the other end of the hall.

CHAPTER 5
THE HOMECOMING

The three participants in the Jakarta meeting were faced with an arduous return to their organizations. They had said their farewells at the Bis Saif offices realizing they would be leaving the underground facility through different exits and traveling to Jakarta's modern Soekarno-Hatta International Airport using different routes. The duration of their return trips was further increased by the need to travel devious air routes between Jakarta and their destinations. Their tickets had been booked as independent legs, by different travel agents, using different traveler names, making it difficult, if not impossible, for their trips to be traced.

Ali was the first to arrive, landing at the Erbil International Airport, located less than two miles from the outskirts of Erbil, Iraq. As a result of multiple transfers between airlines, he had been traveling for nearly fifteen hours and was exhausted. The chinos and short sleeve sport shirt he had worn to blend in with the other airline passengers reflected the results of a long flight that included sporadic attempts at sleep. By prior agreement, he met his driver at a busy KFC fast food restaurant in Abu Shahab City, a popular entertainment area on the Erbil ring road. His driver was Moiz, his close friend from the training camp and many battlefield trials.

The two embraced, standing in the KFC parking lot, which had ironically been selected by the Islamic State security officers responsible for Ali's safe return to the ISIS camp. There was no need to exchange passwords. Ali and Moiz were almost brothers. Both had aged since they first met, with a scattering of gray showing in Moiz's beard. Ali was clean shaven, one of the precautions he had taken in advance of his air travel to Indonesia.

"I'm anxious to hear all about your trip, but first let's get something to eat for the long drive," Moiz said, breaking the silence following their embrace. With Ali's agreement, the two of them entered the KFC, either in ignorance or ignoring the fact that they were patronizing an establishment that was a product of the "Great White Satan." Carrying their bucket of fried chicken and Cokes, the two returned to Moiz's battered gray Nissan pickup. Ali threw his backpack into the bed of the pickup and climbed into the cab with Moiz to share their lunch.

As they drove through the rundown suburbs of Erbil and into the rolling sandy countryside dotted with occasional scrub growth, Ali began to relate his experiences in Jakarta to Moiz, beginning with a description of the Bis Saif facility.

"They are obviously well-financed. As nearly as I could tell, their facilities are hidden in the subterranean basement of a high-rise office building. I'm not sure where it was, because access is through a maze of underground passageways with entrances that were many kilometers from their facility. Members of the Bis Saif staff met us at the airport and guided us through the passageways. There were four of us, and each arrived through a different passageway. None of us ever emerged aboveground to see the building that stood over their headquarters.

"Their staff is quite small. I'm not sure we met everyone, but they saw to all our needs, including good food, laundry service, and comfortable sleeping quarters. Certainly more comfortable than our quarters at the ISIS camp. For one thing, they had air conditioning."

Although he was interested in the description of the Bis Saif facilities, Moiz was more curious about the nature of the meeting. "Why did they request the Islamic State's presence at the meeting? What did they want? Were they offering anything?"

Ali laughed. "Take it easy, Moiz. I'm getting to that part, which is more complicated to describe than their facilities."

"Bis Saif appears to be a formidable, well-funded organization. But most importantly they have many contacts with our potential friends and some possible enemies. They have very clear goals that are attractive to me because they involve more than just killing and terrorizing our enemies. Although they did not reveal all their plans to me, they seem to be trying to unite the world's Sunni Muslims into a force capable of overthrowing our powerful Western enemies. They seem to be saying that our various fragmented Sunni organizations are not working together, and in some cases they're fighting each other. While each organization has good reasons for its activities, in the view of Bis Saif, this makes no sense. Together we can accomplish much more than any can accomplish independently. So, in a word, they are trying to unite us."

Ali could tell from Moiz's body language that he doubted the wisdom of the Bis Saif goal, a doubt that he expressed with a snort, saying, "Our Sunni brethren are not as stupid as you imply. Each group has its goals, trying to overthrow the entrenched dictatorships of their countries, and for good reason.

"Think about the existing situation. We may be fighting against our respective dictators, but they are all supported by a common enemy—the West! And this is costing us thousands of lives, with very little to show in the way of results," Ali said.

"There is quite a list of local wars underway, in addition to our war in Iraq. The Sunnis are fighting in Syria, Egypt with the Muslim Brotherhood, Tunisia, Libya, and the Wahhabis in Saudi Arabia, not to mention the various sects in Africa. Bis Saif is trying to organize these fragmented movements into a single, effective force. These various conflicts are uniting our enemies against ISIS; both Sunni and Shia alike, including Saudi Arabia, Turkey, Jordan, and, of course, the great Satan itself—the United States."

Rather than arguing, Moiz chose to divert the conversation. "So what do they want us to do?"

"They are offering us support in the form of any military equipment we might need. In return for that, they require that we coordinate our efforts with the fighting of our Sunni brethren. I did not provide them with a list of our needs because that will be up to our commanders. My job was only to evaluate Bis Saif and determine what they wanted."

"Which brings me to my other question," answered Moiz. "Why were you selected for this important mission?"

"I've wondered about that also," Ali said. "My theory is that Mohammed, our old platoon commander, offered my name to the headquarters staff. Mohammed has never liked me ever since the incident during the battle of Kirkuk. He thinks I ran away and hid in the woods as a coward and does not believe that I was injured during the initial attack. No one was sure of this Bis Saif organization and whether or not our representative would survive the visit. Mohammed undoubtedly thought I was expendable."

Their brief discussion was cut short when Ali's exhaustion overtook him, and he slipped into a deep sleep as the dry desert air blew through the open window of Moiz's pickup. He remained asleep for the three-hour drive to the headquarters of the Islamic State.

***

They arrived at the headquarters compound in a cloud of desert sand where Ali was awakened by the squeal of the questionable brakes on the old pickup. Mohammed's bearded face peering into the open side window of the pickup was the first thing he saw as he opened his eyes. Never one to mince words, Mohammed growled, "It's about time you got here. The commander wants to speak with you. Come with me."

As Ali trailed Mohammed through the camp, he was assailed by the familiar sounds and smells of a military encampment inhabited by hundreds of soldiers with limited water and sanitary facilities. As they walked away from the pickup, Moiz shouted, "Don't worry, I'll take care of your things. Do you want any of your papers?" But Ali was already out of earshot.

They walked to the large tent at the center of the camp, which was guarded by two armed sentries and serviced by a portable generator that powered the lights and electric fans that maintained a habitable environment within. Mohammed nodded to the two sentries, unceremoniously pulled the tent flap back, and motioned to Ali to follow him. In the dim musty atmosphere of the tent, Ali could see a decorated soldier seated at a desk with two aides standing by. He assumed that the man at the desk was General Hussain, the supreme commander of the Islamic State's forces in Iraq. Ali and Mohammed saluted and were told to be seated at a camp table in front of the desk.

Their salutes were returned in a perfunctory manner by the commander. Ali was momentarily shaken to be in the presence of the general who had life or death control over every man in the camp. He took a deep breath and steeled himself, realizing that it was important to appear coherent in the presence of this powerful man.

"General Hussain," began Mohammed obsequiously, "it is a pleasure to see you again, as always. As you have requested, I bring the soldier who was assigned to meet with the Bis Saif group in Indonesia. I trust you will like his report." Receiving no response from Hussain, Mohammed nodded to Ali, indicating that he should begin his report.

"General, it is a great honor to be able to deliver this report to you," Ali said.

"Get to the report," growled Hussain. "I don't have time for long speeches." Ali was rattled by the combination of Hussain's surly manner and his imposing figure; he was a big man with a well-trimmed beard and piercing black eyes. Ali felt that the general could see right through him.

Gathering his courage, Ali said, "As you ordered, I traveled to Jakarta to meet with Bis Saif. They appear to be a well-funded and highly organized group. Their headquarters are well-hidden within the city. I doubt that our enemies will be able to discover them. In fact, I doubt that I could locate them again, even though I've been there. I believe you already know that they are Sunnis, like us. Several of their members have had previous experience with al-Qaeda. They are impatient with the progress our brothers are making in the field and feel that the problem is that our various activities are too fragmented.

The meeting, which was also attended by representatives of the Nigerian Boko Haram and the Palestinian Hamas, was intended to be a first step toward coordinating our operations. Bis Saif feels that in order to succeed, we must go to the heart of the evil and ultimately attack the West."

General Hussain listened intently until Ali paused to collect his thoughts. The general then stood up and began to pace. In spite of the desert heat and sand that permeated everything, he was immaculately dressed. With his freshly pressed uniform he looked as if he were preparing to attend a formal dinner. "What do they want us to do? And why should we?"

"I asked them the same questions," Ali said, beginning to realize that the general was genuinely interested in his report. "Their answers were quite specific. They are willing to provide us with any of the armaments we need, and any intelligence information to which they have access."

"And what do they want in return?" asked the general.

Ali hesitated before responding, aware that the answer would not be well-received. "They want us to coordinate our operations with al-Qaeda of the Arabian Peninsula," he said, using AQAP's full name, in spite of the fact that he knew the general was very familiar with that organization. "Bis Saif feels that our objective of a Sunni caliphate will never be achieved as long as our actions are restricted to Iraq and opposed by other Sunnis, such as our enemies in Saudi Arabia. They admire our successes on the battlefield, but think we're being too shortsighted and failing to attack the real enemy. AQAP recognizes the significance of attacking the Great Satan on their own territory to weaken the support of the US public for confrontations in the Middle East."

Mohammed had listened quietly up to that point, but he recognized that Ali's nerves were stretched thin, so he changed the subject away from the charged topic of cooperation with AQAP, asking, "What are they willing to give us?"

Ali was relieved. "We discussed a number of possibilities, including conventional weapons and various types of armored vehicles. But the item that seemed most promising was their offer of drones, surface-to-air missiles, and sophisticated air-traffic control. I told them that I was just a messenger and not authorized to make any requests or offer any promises."

General Hussain, who was fascinated with the use of technology on the battlefield, was momentarily distracted by the possibility of sophisticated weaponry. But his foul mood quickly returned as he contemplated the need to coordinate and cooperate with AQAP. "Our plans and objectives are well-defined. We are making progress. Why should we change direction? Cooperating with AQAP will force us to divert our attention to Yemen, their main battlefield. It will also force us to spend resources attacking targets in the West. None of these will help us with our efforts to take over Iraq and establish a caliphate."

"But enough, I need to think about this and consult with our general staff. Ali, you've done a good job. I may have more questions. I will be meeting with the staff tonight. You will be available to answer any questions they may have."

Ali and Mohammed, realizing that the meeting was over, saluted and left the headquarters tent.

***

Ali paced nervously in front of the two guards at the entrance to the headquarters tent. He had taken advantage of the time between his meeting with the general for some sleep and a quick snack before arriving back at the tent. Armed only with a water canteen, he was grateful that the second meeting had been scheduled for the cooler evening temperatures. As he had done on previous occasions, he passed the time reflecting on his long journey from computer nerd living in a comfortable apartment to a soldier of the Islamic State, which had taken him from his home in Raqqa to this godforsaken desert outpost. He realized that he had made an irreversible decision.

His thoughts were interrupted by a tall, dark-skinned, well-built soldier wearing fatigues with a sidearm strapped to his hip. He recognized the man from his earlier meeting with the general as one of the aides that had stood silently next to the general's desk as Ali had answered questions about his trip.

The aide addressed Ali without preamble. "The general and the committee require your presence. They have some questions about your trip."

Entering the headquarters tent again, Ali found himself standing in front of the general, who had remained at his desk, and four other individuals arrayed around the camp table in front of the desk. The four were dressed in fatigues, and with the exception of the general, all sported the long black beards characteristic of ISIS soldiers. Ali saluted the assembled group. A salute that was not returned. They obviously had other things on their minds.

The general began the discussion, ignoring the formality of introductions. "We think we understand what Bis Saif is asking of us, but we don't have a good idea of the resources they are offering in exchange. What can you tell us about their resources? How generous do you think they will be?"

Ali understood both the question and its implications. He understood that the cooperation being suggested by Bis Saif would have a major impact on the ISIS planning and their allocation of both human and financial resources. More importantly, he understood the natural inclination of Middle Easterners to bargain. One never accepts an initial offer without a counteroffer that is more in the favor of the purchaser. But he also understood something that might not have occurred to the general and his commanders, that Bis Saif was an extremely powerful and well-funded organization with the ability to ignore the ISIS and negotiate with their enemies and competitors if their offer was refused. He did not want to explicitly offer this observation for fear of antagonizing this proud and powerful group of men, particularly since their enmity could negatively affect both his career and possibly his life. So he answered the question very carefully. "I was led to believe that Bis Saif has many resources at their disposal. They made that very clear to me, and it was demonstrated by the elaborate nature of their facilities. Their offices and living quarters are contained in two levels below one of the greatest buildings in Jakarta. It must have been very expensive to build such a facility in secret. I think they also owned the office building that was erected on top of their facilities. In addition to their facilities, they have constructed several miles of underground passages that permit visitors and staff to enter through disguised doorways from dispersed locations. They are able to provide good food, comfortable quarters, high technology equipment, and a large staff without problem. So in answer to your first question, I think that they are well-financed and have connections with the highest levels of government in many countries.

"In answer to your second question, I think they are prepared to be generous. While they implied that our failure to cooperate would require them to deal with other organizations, I believe they understand the significance of our successes in Iraq and Syria. Perhaps they were trying to make me feel important, but on several occasions they implied that I represented the most important of the three organizations attending the meeting." Sensing that he had the full attention of the assembled group, Ali continued with increased assurance. "With the practical considerations of distance and difficulty of secure communications in mind, they made it clear to me that it was not practical to negotiate. In other words, they did not think that it would be possible to haggle over the terms of our agreement. They asked me to be certain that I gave you this message because they feel that a lot of communications with the outside world reduces their security."

"So whatever we decide here will represent our best and final offer to Bis Saif," the general said, summing up Ali's remarks. He then dismissed Ali. "Thank you. We will have a response for Bis Saif by tonight or within a very few days. Be prepared to return to Jakarta by the end of the week."

Ali left the headquarters tent depressed at the thought of another long trip to Jakarta, but curious about his new role as a courier and negotiator. At the same time, he was relieved that in this role he would be able to avoid future battles. He returned to his own tent, which he shared with Moiz, fell onto his camp bed, and was asleep before removing his shoes.

Ali was playing forward in a soccer game in Raqqa. The game had gone well, and he had scored by deflecting a corner kick into the goal. His wonderful dream evaporated as he was rudely awakened by Sergeant Mohammed. "What time is it?" Ali asked, still trying to transition from Raqqa to reality.

"It's five in the morning, and the general wants to see you immediately," Mohammed said. "Get yourself cleaned up and report to his tent in fifteen minutes."

Ali quickly changed to a new uniform, which was not any cleaner than the old one, but less foul smelling and wrinkled. He combed his hair and with a glance in the mirror decided he was ready. Since he was growing a new beard, there was no need to shave. He dashed across the camp, buttoning his shirt as he ran.

Ali was ushered into the general's tent without preamble. Once again, he found the general sitting at his desk looking clean and alert as if it were midday. Ali's salute was interrupted by the general's order to sit down, which was followed by a summary of the previous night's meeting.

"We have decided to accept your friend's offer of assistance in return for our coordination with AQAP. But this is a big step for us because it will divert our troops from our primary targets. We do not take it lightly. So we have prepared these papers." The general motioned to a sheaf of papers held together with a metal clasp lying on his desk. "These papers ask for significant resources from Bis Saif on a basis that is not negotiable. We have also described the way in which coordination with AQAP will occur. It gives us the ability to deny any of their requests if they strain our resources or conflict with our objectives."

General Hussain's next words completely woke up the still sleepy Ali. "Be prepared to remain in Jakarta for an extended period. You will be our representative there. For obvious security reasons, we cannot allow these papers to leave this camp. You are to sit here and memorize their contents. When you arrive in Jakarta, you will orally provide Bis Saif with our terms."

"Are any of these terms negotiable?" asked the nonplussed Ali, wondering how he was going to memorize four pages of material before his departure.

"None are negotiable. But there are some details to be worked out that will require that you use your best judgment.

65

Details such as delivery places and dates, types of coordination and such." Ali's discomfort was further increased by Hussain's concluding statement. "I expect one of two things to occur during your visit. Either our terms will be accepted and you will be asked to remain in Jakarta to consummate the agreement, or our terms will not be accepted and the relationship with Bis Saif will be terminated."

Ali was afraid to inquire about the meaning of termination. Instead he dutifully picked up the proposed agreement, sat at the camp table and began focusing on its contents.

Shortly after the noon mess, Ali was again riding in Moiz's pickup on the way to Erbil airport.

CHAPTER 6
THE ROAD TO NIGERIA

Udo arrived at Kano International Airport in Nigeria several hours after Ali had arrived in Iraq. Like Ali, Udo was exhausted from his longer trip, which included a thirteen-hour, one-stop flight on Qatar Airways from Jakarta to Cairo, followed by a long layover at the inhospitable international transfer terminal in Cairo. This, in turn, was followed by a fifteen-hour flight on EgyptAir to Kano, Nigeria. Udo then faced the prospect of an eight-hour drive from Kano to the Boko Haram headquarters in Maiduguri. The flights had been uneventful, with unremarkable food service that did little to satisfy his hunger during the thirty-hour trip. Although he was able to sleep fitfully on the plane, Udo was exhausted as he traversed one of the few jetways at Kano Airport. After his forged passport received a cursory check at Nigerian customs, he entered the crowded main terminal and was disappointed to discover that there were no restaurants in the airport. Food service was limited to a meager selection of stale sandwiches available from the airport's single bar. As he walked uncertainly through the terminal carrying his overnight bag, Udo decided that his first priority after locating his contact would be to insist on a decent meal before undertaking the long drive to Maiduguri.

Udo spent most of his remaining energy searching for his elusive contact. He finally found him lounging near the only newsstand in the terminal. As he had been informed, his contact was readily identifiable by the New York Yankees baseball cap worn stylishly backward on his shaved head. His dress, which was best described as sloppy Nigerian, consisted of cutoff pants of an indistinguishable color and a matching tank top, an outfit that was in stark contrast with the running shoes, cargo pants, and knit shirt that Udo had been given prior to his trip to Jakarta so that Bis Saif would not think of Boko Haram as a backward organization.

"Ugo, where've you been? I've been searching this stinking airport for the last fifteen minutes looking for you. I thought you would at least meet me at the customs exit."

"Hello Udo. Nice to see you," Ugo said sarcastically. "I'm glad you finally arrived. I'm really tired of this place."

"Let's get out of here and get something to eat. I'm exhausted, hungry, and ready to go home."

"The eating is no problem. Going home is going to take longer. They want to see you at the headquarters as soon as you arrive. We'll stop for food at one of the roadside stands on the way to Maiduguri."

With that, the pair left the airport, climbed into Ugo's dusty pickup truck, and began the long drive to Maiduguri, which was interrupted once by a brief stop to feed Udo. The drive took them through the outskirts of Kano, a sprawling city with a population of more than nine million, featuring miles of one-story shanties. From there they found route A3—Maiduguri Road, which wound through more rundown housing, sand, and scrub growth. Udo eventually got tired of looking at the nondescript scenery and fell into a deep sleep, dreaming about the luxury of the Bis Saif headquarters.

Boko Haram's headquarters were a far cry from those of Bis Saif. Located in a dusty warehouse district of Maiduguri, the unimposing single-story building with its tin roof reflected the Nigerian heat. Udo tried to shake the cobwebs out of his head as he jumped out of the pickup and followed Ugo past the armed guard with the rifle slung over his shoulder and through the steel door that served as the main entrance to the warehouse. The guard knew Ugo and nodded lethargically as the pair pushed through the door and into the dimly lit air-conditioned interior. Maiduguri residents did not question the unmarked building with the armed guard in front, both because they suspected and feared the presence of Boko Haram, and because armed men standing guard outside of businesses were a common sight.

Udo followed Ugo through a facility whose rooms and hall-ways had been defined using two-by-four studs to which cheap wood paneling had been carelessly nailed. Bare incandescent bulbs furnished the glaring lighting. Udo, who had never been to the headquarters before, wondered what was going on in the various offices they passed. There were no computers, and the occupants of these rooms appeared to be immersed in paper-work of various sorts. In one room, several soldiers engaged in heated discussion were bent over a table covered with maps.

The room at the end of the hallway obviously belonged to General Modukuri, the Boko Haram commander of the Borno region. The general was a legend with his troops, having orga-nized many successful attacks, kidnappings, and bombings. He was a target of the Nigerian troops, who were offering a significant reward for information leading to his capture. He had evaded detection for many years by rarely leaving the head-quarters, which were in a neighborhood made up of hundreds, if not thousands, of his followers. It would have been suicidal for someone associated with the Nigerian government to initiate a search in that part of Maiduguri.

General Modukuri looked up from the paperwork on the desk in front of him as Udo and Ugo approached his office. He rose and walked around the desk to greet the two men. The general was a tall, thin Nigerian with bad teeth and hooded eyes. In his ragged fatigues he looked more like a homeless man on the streets of New York than the general of a successful military operation. Udo was very uncomfortable in his presence. As the general walked toward them, he winked at Ugo using a ges-ture commonly used by Yoruba Nigerians with their children. But Ugo understood the significance of the wink and quickly excused himself, leaving Udo alone with the general.

"How is your family?" asked the general, standing close to Udo with his bad breath as he spoke. Udo immediately realized that Modukuri was ignorant of Udo's history with the fighting in Baga.

Udo was momentarily speechless at the insensitive and uninformed question, but finally managed to mutter, "My fam-ily is dead. Killed in the fighting in Borno."

Modukuri was unperturbed. "I'm sorry to hear that," he replied without hesitation. "Now tell me about your experiences in Jakarta."

Udo described what he knew of the Bis Saif facilities and his impressions of their great wealth in the same way that Ali had explained it in Iraq. He also spent some time telling the general of the overall objectives of their organization. Modukuri listened passively, nodding as Udo continued nervously, anxious to leave the presence of this strange man. After a pause, Modukuri dismissed him, saying, "Let me think about this. The story you tell is a strange one and requires significant commitments on our part. We need to call a council meeting and discuss our response to the Bis Saif proposal."

Udo was more than happy to be excused and retired to the temporary quarters he had been assigned.

***

Udo passed the time waiting for an answer from Modukuri, gossiping with his fellow Boko Haram fighters. They discussed past battles, the disposition of hostages, and the future of the organization. He was glad to be able to shed the preppy clothes he had been wearing during his long journey to Jakarta, and once again wear the comfortable loose-fitting khaki fatigues and black tee shirt favored by the Boko Haram fighters. Cigarettes and food were plentiful at the headquarters, and Udo was quite comfortable. But in spite of its relative luxury, he missed his home and remaining relatives. He was also anxious to return to the field and the fight against the Nigerian army.

At last the summons arrived. Udo was once again ushered into Modukuri's intimidating presence, where he waited in silence for the leader to speak. Without preamble, the Boko Haram position was summarized. "We have considered the Bis Saif proposal carefully and decided to turn it down."

Udo was certainly not inclined to debate this decision, but he was shocked. "I thought we had agreed to cooperate with them while I was in Jakarta. May I ask why this is the decision?" he asked timidly.

Modukuri was not inclined to go into details, but he felt that Udo deserved an answer, since he had been through a difficult albeit interesting period. "I will not share the details of our discussion, but you deserve some explanation.

"Think about the situation in Africa," he said in an instructional tone. "We are not the only Muslim group fighting for our independence from repressive governments. There are the Shabab Sunnis from Somalia, who have been attacking various sights in Kenya, such as Garissa University; Al Qaeda in the Islamic Maghreb, who we know as AQIM, fighting in Mali; and the Lord's Resistance Army, a fundamentalist Christian group in Uganda, to name a few. All of the various movements in Africa are relatively independent of each other. Yet we all live in countries with numerous tribes that have many grievances with their governments and with each other. The situation is so complicated that even I as a native Nigerian do not understand it all. It is naïve of Bis Saif to think that they would be able to unite us. It is more naïve to think that Boko Haram, which is attacked by all sides in Nigeria, would be willing to divert its attention to some sort of unified African movement. If we were to become that ambitious it would weaken our current successes and it would be unlikely to lead to a Pan-African movement. Believe me, if I thought there was any prospect of success I would agree with their proposal. But all I can see is failure."

Udo listened, carefully nodding while the general spoke. "Then I guess my work here is done, and I can return to my unit."

Modukuri concluded the meeting with a nod. "Keep up the good work, Udo. We'll send the appropriate message to your friends in Jakarta."

As Udo left his office feeling as if a load had been lifted off his back, the general turned to his aide and began dictating a message to be sent by secret courier to Bis Saif. He knew that it would not be well received and hoped that he would not regret his decision. A decision he would worry about for weeks.

71

CHAPTER 7

DECISIONS IN THE SINAI

Hasan Jouda arrived home before Udo, since the connections between Jakarta and Cairo were superior to those of the flights from Jakarta to Nigeria. In spite of his relative good fortune, he was also exhausted when he arrived at the Hamas offices in Rafah. His air trip from Jakarta to Cairo, and then the long drive to Rafah, had been grueling. Hasan had flown using an assumed name and forged passport on a direct fifteen-hour flight with Saudi Arabian Airlines, which included a two-hour stop in Jeddah, Saudi Arabia, the airlines hub. Hasan also had an advantage over Udo in that the driving distance from Cairo to Rafah was a modest five and a half hours as opposed to Udo's eight-hour drive from Kano to Maiduguri.

Cairo International Airport is a modern albeit crowded facility. Terminal 1, the international arrivals terminal, was renovated in 2002. It featured an impressive promenade with live palm trees bordering its main concourse along with overhanging balconies that housed the restaurants and shops.

Hasan was glad to return to Cairo, where he had spent four years at the university. He knew his way around the city and did not want a chauffeur to drive him to Rafah, preferring instead the private time that the trip would provide. Still wearing the Dockers slacks and button-down shirt he had worn when he left Jakarta, he took the shuttle bus to long-term parking, where he claimed the gray Toyota he had left when he traveled to Jakarta the preceding week. Resisting the temptation for a sentimental visit to the university, he settled in for the long drive through the desert to the Suez Canal at Port Said, and then along the Mediterranean Coast to Rafah.

His welcome in Rafah was similar to the ones experienced by Ali and Udo in Iraq and Nigeria. When he arrived at the decrepit building that housed his laboratory, Hasan was greeted by Ossama, who had been impatiently awaiting his arrival. "It's about time you got here. I've been waiting most of the day. General Murtaja has called me three times so far wondering whether you've shown up."

"I'm sorry, sir, but it was a long trip," was the mumbled reply. "I drove straight from the airport, only stopping briefly once for some food and to relieve myself."

Ossama was not mollified. "Well let's go to see the general. He said he wanted to speak with you at his headquarters in the Aldeira Hotel the moment you return. I'll drive to make sure you don't get lost."

"I could speak more coherently if I could use the restroom before meeting with the general."

"Well make it fast. I don't want to receive another phone call."

***

Hasan used the time in the restroom to splash some of the lukewarm water on his face from the single tap in the washroom sink. When he had finished, he felt somewhat refreshed and ready to meet with the general.

Unlike Ali and Udo, Hasan was not intimidated by General Murtaja. Because of their frequent interactions at the hospital and subsequently during the missile tests, they had developed a relationship similar to that of a father and son. The general had developed an almost religious belief that his Muslim faith had brought Hasan to him at the moment that he needed someone with his particular capabilities. Hasan had begun to appreciate the general's gruff manner as one that was needed to control an army of uneducated and independent volunteers, most of whom had joined for the sole purpose of killing Israelis.

The Aldeira Hotel was one of the best hotels in Rafah. Located with beautiful views of the Mediterranean Sea, it featured large rooms fully equipped with all the amenities of a modern hotel, including backup emergency generators. General Murtaja had established both his living accommodations and the headquarters of the southern command of the Gaza Strip at the hotel since, as an unmarried man, it relieved him of the inconvenience of finding help for cleaning and meal preparation. Hasan had never visited the general at his office and was impressed with the relative luxury of his accommodations. He realized that the elite of Rafah were living better than most of its residents, who in turn had more comfortable lives than those in the rest of Gaza.

He knocked on the door of the first-floor suite housing Murtaja's quarters and was surprised when the general himself answered. "Come on in. You expected an aide to welcome you with a red carpet?"

"I thought a man of your position would have an assistant of some sort," replied Hasan following an embarrassed pause.

"Well we can't afford the luxury of aides to support inflated egos. Now come on in and tell me about your trip."

Hasan quickly summarized his experience in Jakarta, suspecting that the thorough general would have already done his homework and knew more about Bis Saif than he pretended.

When the report was concluded, Murtaja asked, "Did they offer assistance in return for our support?"

"As you would expect, I emphasized our need for improved electronics to support the missile guidance system that we've been developing. Although it seems to work pretty well, some improvements are needed, principally reduced weight and improved protection from jamming of our communications with the missile. But more important, I also requested that we be supplied with drones that could be used for an aerial attack on our neighbors to the north, as you had suggested."

"What was their response?"

"They agreed to my requests without hesitation. In fact, they agreed so readily that I was thinking we should have asked for more."

"You may be correct, but we can always escalate our requests later if the beginning of our relationship goes well."

"So you're prepared to agree to Bis Saif's proposals? Is it necessary to get the permission of the high command?"

"Do you think they can meet our requests? Are they really as powerful as they claim? I need to know this before going higher in our organization to get formal approval."

"If the quality and cost of their facilities is any indication, they are indeed well financed. The fact that ISIS and Boko Haram are willing to speak with them is further proof of their credibility. Beyond that, I can say no more."

"Based on your information and certain other facts that I have been able to gather, I will seek approval. If approval is received, I will contact them directly. No more help is needed from you. Please return to your laboratory and continue your work. You have performed a great service, and I personally appreciate it."

Hasan returned to the missile laboratory to continue his development of the Suquur, the weapon that, in his opinion, would spell the doom of Israel. He was relieved to have completed his assignment in Jakarta because of the length of the trip and the many unknown agendas of Bis Saif. Working with computers had been his dream, and he was enjoying his current position without giving much thought to the future.

CHAPTER 8
NEXT STEPS IN JAKARTA

Adam al-Zhihri, Abu Ahmed, and John Smith were once again seated in the conference room with the yellow wall, which had been dubbed the yellow room. Adam was thoughtfully contemplating the three postcards on the table in front of him.

Finally Ahmed couldn't stand the wait any longer and broke the silence. "Well, Adam, are you going to give us the news?"

"I think the news is mostly good," replied Adam, with his thoughts interrupted. "The postcards from ISIS and Palestine indicate that they agree to our proposal. The postcard from Boko Haram indicates that they do not want to continue with us."

John Smith looked pleased. "This gives us the opportunity we've been waiting for. In Britain we call this a win-win situation. I can further increase my credibility with MI-6 by feeding them some useful information about Boko Haram. When the British use this information to strike, we will be sending a message to other potential partners that refusal to cooperate has its consequences."

In the interest of security, the postcards had followed a torturous route. ISIS had sent their postcard through Turkey. On the front of the card was a photo of the Blue Mosque, one of Istanbul's best known landmarks. The Mosque, which had first opened in 1616, was known as the Blue Mosque because of the blue tiles covering its interior walls. But this card featured the exterior of the mosque with its six spires, central dome, and surrounding smaller domes representing exquisite examples of the possibilities of Muslim architecture of the period. But the three in the yellow room were more interested in the message written on the back, which had been addressed to a fictitious recipient in Indonesia named Nancy Sharkos, presumably the spouse of the sender. The message, written in English, indicated that the sender, whose name was Bill, was having a wonderful time in Istanbul enjoying the landmarks and the good weather. The post-card had been mailed by a young boy on a bicycle, who dropped it in a curbside post box in downtown Istanbul. It had been delivered to the address of a Bis Saif sympathizer in Jakarta. The sympathizer paid another boy on a bicycle, who delivered the postcard to a residence near one of the secret entrances to the Bis Saif facilities. The delivery boys were unrelated to the send-ers or recipients. They had been given a small sum of money to perform their errands. It would have been impossible to trace the source or destination of the postcard.

The other two postcards had followed similar routes. The letter from Boko Haram was delivered from Chad to a second residence in Jakarta. The photo on the postcard featured Lake Chad, a tourist landmark that unfortunately had been drying up. This photo, which featured a beautiful panorama of the lake, had obviously been taken in August when it was at its highest point. The card contained a less positive message, indicating that the trip had been unsuccessful. Bob, the hypothetical tour-ist, had not seen any of the wildlife that famously inhabited the lake, and the fishing had been terrible. As a result, he was end-ing his trip early, and moving on to Kenya to continue his search for interesting wildlife. The message to Bis Saif was clear. The Nigerians were not interested in working with the organization.

The postcard from Hamas had been sent from Cairo. Main-taining the tourist theme of the other two, this card featured the classic photo of pyramids near Cairo with a camel in the foreground. Harry, the sender of the card, indicated that his trip had been exciting and interesting, and that he was well treated by the people of Egypt. He looked forward to continuing his vacation. At the offices of Bis Saif, this card was interpreted as an enthusiastic acceptance of the Bis Saif plans.

Adam had received a second message transmitted through multiple websites and disguised in photographs embedded in the sites. This message from ISIS indicated that Ali would be returning to Jakarta to discuss the specifics of their agreement. Adam was not surprised, as there were many specifics to discuss, but also because he suspected that the ISIS high-level command wanted to assure themselves of the best possible deal.

The combined circuitous routes of the postcards and the innocuous messages they contained were intended to mislead any of the multiple intelligence agencies watching for terrorist correspondence. Future messages would be sent by other means. Bis Saif's security staff had concluded that the safest form of communication would be that which used a variety of media to carry their messages. After all, postcards were safe from the prying electronic wizards of the National Security Agency in the United States, which couldn't possibly monitor all of the world's conventional postal communications.

After an extended discussion of their future activities and the issues to be addressed, Adam concluded the meeting, saying, "Well we've got our work cut out for us. The only way in which we can satisfy the hunger of our new partners and continue moving toward our eventual goal is to divide the tasks to be performed among us. John, why don't you report back to your handlers and feed them the information about Boko Haram. When you've completed that assignment, we will rely on you to work with us to secure the needed additional funding. By the time you return to Jakarta, we will have a better idea of our financial needs."

John agreed. "I expected that would be my role. I look forward to a trip to London for some overdue shopping." With that, he left the meeting and began packing for his trip to London. Like the others, John did not travel on direct flights; he rarely took fewer than three flights from his origin to his destination, each flight under a different assumed name.

"What about me?" asked Ahmed, the impatient one, after John had left the room. "I'm certain I can be of assistance with these tasks."

"I'm coming to that. You can be responsible for fulfilling Hamas's request. Finding military-style drone aircraft should be relatively easy. I hear that the overall drone market in the United States alone is expected to approach the sale of a million drones annually. It should be possible to purchase the devices the Palestinians are requesting without the need to deal with the thieving arms merchants."

"That makes sense. I'll get started on that immediately."

Adam concluded the meeting. "That leaves me with the difficult task of acquiring a modern air-defense system for ISIS. Unfortunately, I'm the one that will have to meet with the arms dealers. I will be anxious to learn whether such a system is even available on the black market, although there is no shortage of potential suppliers from various communist countries.

"I will respond to ISIS and Hamas and invite them for follow-up discussions. There is no need to answer Boko Haram. We also need to provide them with their assignments for coordination with other Sunni groups. Now let's enjoy our midday meal."

***

It would be difficult to recognize the man known as John Smith now that he was wearing a proper dark business suit with white shirt and fashionable blue tie as he walked across the Vauxhall Bridge in London. He was on the way to visit Great Britain's Secret Intelligence Service, also known as SIS, which included the famed Military Intelligence Section 6, or MI-6, as it was known worldwide. This group was responsible for protecting the United Kingdom from outside threats, including unraveling the complex web of terrorism, tribalism, anti-Western feelings, and anti-government sentiment fomenting in the Middle East and threatening the West. John Smith, or Cecil Breathwaite, as he was known to MI-6, was viewed as a contributor to the British efforts to solve the riddles associated with the confused Arab world.

The view of the SIS headquarters from the Vauxhall Bridge was indeed imposing. The building was of the same size as the Blue Mosque shown on the ISIS postcard that had been received in Jakarta on the previous day. But the similarities ended with size. Whereas the Blue Mosque was constructed in the style of Islamic and Ottoman architecture from the 1600s, the style of the SIS building, completed in 1992, on the banks of the Thames River and was quite different. The Blue Mosque has a central dome, eight smaller domes, and six minarets, along with 20,000 handmade tiles covering its walls. The SIS building has two curved facades at either end of the building with a round protuberance at the top that was placed within two structures similar to the Teotihuacan pyramids near Mexico City. In an attempt to capture the style of the building, Deyan Sudjic, the architecture critic of the *Guardian* newspaper, had described it incorrectly as either "a Mayan Temple or clanking art deco machinery." In fact, with its multiple turrets and varying facades, the building defied architectural pigeonholing. The rooms within the interior of the building were not covered with handmade blue tiles, but rather followed the pattern of most government office buildings—plaster walls painted with muted colors to which their occupants attached various posters, photos, and awards related to their careers and families.

Cecil, aka John Smith, entered the building at its river entrance, crossed the impressive lobby, and strode purposefully, flashing his badge without pausing at the guards' desk as he walked to the bank of elevators at the far end of the lobby.

As he exited the elevator on the fourth floor he received an enthusiastic greeting. "Cecil, where have you been? It's been ages since you've stopped by. We're having trouble getting along without you."

With a wave at the attractive secretary who was the source of the greeting, he proceeded to the conference room at the end of the hall, where a group had been assembled for the sole purpose of meeting with him. The gathering was arrayed around a conference table that would be appropriate for any government office. Far from the glamorous exterior and lobby of the SIS building, this table contained the scars and cigarette burns that attested to many years of use. Its occupants were dressed like Cecil, with white shirts and ties, many of whom had their sleeves rolled up in deference to the typical warm and humid atmosphere of British government buildings.

"Breathwaite, it's been a long time," boomed Stan Comstock, Cecil's direct MI-6 supervisor. The others in the room nodded in agreement. Without waiting for a response, Stan continued, "I hope you've brought us some useful information. What rocks have you been turning over this time?"

Cecil had been prepared for this question. "First, let me say that it feels good to be back on British soil dealing with rational human beings. You don't pay me enough to compensate for keeping company with the crazies of this world. I could tell you stories by the hour of the senseless actions I've seen, most being performed without any reason or purpose."

He paused and looked around the room at the four others who had gathered. Cecil had insisted that this meeting be held in a secure conference room without recording devices of any sort, including pads of paper, personal computers, or video cameras. As a result, those present at the meeting had brought nothing more than their cups of tea, which were standard appendages at British meetings of this nature. Cecil realized that without thoroughly sweeping the room and performing a body search of all present, he could not be certain of the absence of microphones. In fact, the primary reason for his request was to impress upon his MI-6 counterparts the sensitive nature of his material, and the need to maintain his own anonymity. He was quite certain that Stan had arranged for the meeting to be surreptitiously recorded for future analysis.

"Now to the business at hand. While for obvious reasons I can't reveal my source, I have been able to locate the headquarters of the Boko Haram." This spectacular news was met with a gasp. Cecil had done what MI-6 had been trying to accomplish for the past three years but were hampered from doing so due to the suspected location of the headquarters in an area of Boko Haram sympathizers in the middle of Maiduguri. His startling pronouncement was met with a flurry of questions.

"Where is it?"

"How did you discover it?"

"Are their leaders working there?"

"How big is the facility?"

"Should we destroy their headquarters or let it continue to exist while we monitor activities around the complex?"

"Are any of their kidnapped victims being held there?"

Stan's loud voice stilled the flow of questions. "Easy does it, lads, slow down. Cecil can only answer one question at a time, and I suspect he won't be able to answer all of them." Turning to Cecil, he added, "Answer what you can. It will probably end up as our responsibility to tackle the unanswered questions."

"Well, first of all, the facility is in Maiduguri, rather than the surrounding countryside. We will need aerial surveillance of some sort to pinpoint its location."

Stan couldn't restrain himself. "Good grief! You mean we've spent all this time searching the jungles for their head-quarters, and they've been in Maiduguri all this time?"

"I'm afraid so," responded Cecil with a modest smile.

"I believe your second question was how I discovered it," Cecil said. He had paid close attention to the questions as well as the questioners. "I have to tell you that I discovered it quite by accident," he lied. "As you know, I've been working in Egypt as a commercial photographer, and I hired an Egyptian model, who had a Nigerian boyfriend. The three of us spent a lot of time together visiting the various tourist sites in Egypt. One day while we were on a photo shoot at the Aswan Dam, her boyfriend mentioned that he wished they had a dam like that in Nigeria because Lake Chad, a lake near his home city, was dry-ing up due to changes in weather patterns. He then continued, as if he were unloading his life's problems, to tell me that he had initially joined the Nigerian army but became disillusioned and then joined Boko Haram. With a little prodding, he bragged that he had visited their headquarters and met the famed General Modukuri. I pretended to doubt his story, and he added that he had actually met the general at the Boko Haram headquarters in Maiduguri."

Those present at the meeting on the fourth floor of SIS head-quarters sat in rapt attention while Cecil related his fabricated story. He was always nervous when piecing together a tale of this nature, fearing that someone would see a flaw in its fabric. But this time he relaxed, realizing he had the audience eating out of the palm of his hand.

As the group digested Cecil's story, Stan asked, "Maiduguri is a big place. Did he say where it was?"

Although Cecil knew the answer to that question, he had decided to provide only a general response, knowing that an incomplete story was more believable than one in which every detail was present. So he provided a vague answer with some clues, saying, "Obviously the boyfriend couldn't or wouldn't provide me with an address. However, he did say that the headquarters were in a warehouse with a metal roof and cinder block walls. Two guards are stationed next to the front door. Apparently it is in the middle of a district that is known to have a large population of Boko Haram supporters. But that's all he told me."

Those present at the meeting forgot their other questions and immediately began debating the best method for finding the headquarters in Maiduguri. They correctly surmised that although it was a big area, it was likely that there were not that many buildings within the town capable of housing a major military headquarters. It was immediately decided that satellite imagery would be the best path to locating this facility. Other questions about next steps could wait until this important question was answered.

At that point, it was clear that Cecil had little additional information to offer. Stan thanked Cecil for his valuable information and suggested he retire to his hotel to relax until their discussions could be concluded. Cecil nodded, left the meeting and, after stopping briefly at the MI-6 personnel offices to complete some overdue paperwork, returned to his hotel as instructed. It had been a good day.

They reconvened the following afternoon. Cecil was briefed by each of the participants. They had been quite busy since their previous meeting double-checking Cecil's information and planning next steps. Cecil was surprised and delighted to learn that MI-6 had shared their information with the CIA. They had done this in order to take advantage of the United States' superior satellite surveillance capabilities, which they felt were needed for a detailed view of the streets of Maiduguri. It didn't take long to identify the location of the headquarters based on traffic patterns and the unique nature of the personnel riding in the pickup trucks arriving and departing from the facility.

The second phase of their work was more complicated. A decision had to be made as to whether to use drones to destroy the headquarters or utilize their newfound knowledge to track the high-level personnel coming and going from the facility. A second decision was whether to involve the United States in the strike if one should be authorized. Once these decisions were made, a memo would be prepared for the necessary authorization from the Prime Minister. Although Cecil, aka John Smith, had hoped for a more immediate strike, he realized that the wheels of bureaucracy turned slowly, leading to a delay of a week or more before punishment could be administered to Boko Haram.

Cecil sat patiently through the lengthy discussion during which the pros and cons of each approach were weighed. He was careful not to offer an opinion that might betray his motives, and for this reason refrained from participating in much of the debate. At around 6:00 p.m., after enduring the long debate and an unknown number of cups of tea, a decision was made. As Cecil had hoped, the MI-6 group decided to enlist the assistance of the Americans in a drone strike of the Boko Haram headquarters with the objective of destroying the facility. It was also agreed that this would only occur after a week of surveillance revealed the work patterns of its occupants. In parallel with the week of watching, the all-important memorandum would be prepared and submitted through channels for the PM's approval. At the same time, contacts would be made with the CIA to establish the feasibility of obtaining American support.

Stan concluded the meeting and the discussion. "Breathwaite, I don't think we need you any longer to participate in the closeout of Boko Haram. You've made a significant contribution to British intelligence, for which we're all grateful. Submit a voucher for your travel expenses to our cashier, and feel free to continue with your ongoing assignment."

Cecil left the meeting elated. Not only had he achieved the dual objectives of enhancing his image with MI-6 and striking at Boko Haram, but the meeting had ended early enough for him to visit his sister before taking a taxi to the airport. Although he didn't feel terribly close to his sister, he felt that it was very important to retain his family ties because his family, including their distant relatives, represented a significant source of income that supported the extensive financial needs of Bis Saif.

***

Back in Jakarta, the planning continued following John Smith's departure for England. The two Kuwaiti friends had moved to the dining room to continue their discussions over a healthy lunch of humus and pita with side salads.

Ahmed began the conversation. "We have quite a list of things to address. Perhaps we should bring in one of your talented associates. Why not involve Leroy Williamson? After all, he should be well informed since he recently attended the Africa Aerospace and Defense Conference."

"You've read my mind as usual," responded Adam. "Do you know whether he's here?"

"I saw him at breakfast this morning. In fact, he was expounding on the capabilities of the drones he saw at the show, and I was thinking of enlisting his help for my part of the assignment."

After thinking for a moment, Adam said, "Why don't we both use him. Let's ask him for his recommendations on both subjects. Then you and I can concentrate on convincing our future partners that this is a good deal for them. When this has been accomplished, we can focus on the second part of our agreement, defining what the partners will bring us in return."

Ahmed nodded in agreement and the two finished their lunch in silence, each thinking about their next steps for ISIS and Hamas. As he got up to leave the table, Adam asked, "Ahmed, if you see Leroy, could you ask him to stop by my office?"

***

When Leroy was an incoming freshman at Yale, he met Adam, who at the time was in his senior year. Leroy lived in the black community of New Haven, Connecticut, and worked at a menial job in the university's cafeteria, busing tables, mopping floors, and washing dishes. In fact, the two had met in the cafeteria while Adam was absorbed in a history textbook and Leroy was cleaning up in preparation for closing. Leroy was attracted by Adam's engaging personality, and the two often grabbed a Coke and discussed many different subjects whenever they were on breaks between their respective cafeteria duties and classes. Adam recognized in Leroy a bright individual who was a victim of his circumstances. Leroy was fascinated by the closely related subjects of religion and the unrest throughout the world that Adam described. Although Bis Saif had not yet been conceived, Adam, always the opportunist, saw benefits in capitalizing on Leroy's discontent, which he actively encouraged. He also spent some time educating Leroy in the ways of Islam, with emphasis on the Sunni interpretation of the faith.

When the facility in Jakarta was nearing completion, Adam had reached out to Leroy, asking whether he would like to join a dynamic and growing organization that offered guarantees of respect and advancement. Leroy jumped at the opportunity. Adam's evaluation of Leroy proved to be accurate, and he quickly became an indispensable member of the Bis Saif headquarters team. The trip to the AAD Conference was both an eye-opening experience for Leroy and a benefit for Adam and Ahmed, who tried to avoid appearing in public spaces as much as possible. Because of his black skin, most of the exhibitors at the conference assumed he was a representative of an African country or terrorist group. This was further reinforced by his natty dress in a gray suit, white shirt, and conservative green tie, which he was clearly not used to wearing as he was constantly adjusting his tie and straightening the matching handkerchief in his breast pocket. But his possible association with a terrorist organization did not discourage the arms sellers at the conference, who were happy to sell their wares to anyone with a checkbook.

Leroy's dress was much more casual as he entered Adam's modest office, which much to Leroy's amusement contained calligraphic quotations from the Koran juxtaposed with Yale University memorabilia. Leroy's greeting to Adam was casual as he slumped, folding his ample frame into one of the stuffed easy chairs in Adam's office. "What can I do for you, my man?"

"Hi Lee," replied Adam, using the unfortunate nickname he had selected for Leroy."

"I wish you'd find another nickname for me. Don't you know that Lee is the name of the southern general that fought to keep my people in slavery? If you insist on deriving nicknames from my name, how about Roy?"

"Roy it is then. Sorry—I didn't mean to insult you. But I didn't ask you here to debate your name. I think you know that we're talking to ISIS about a partnership. And you know how it is in the Arab world. Every deal needs a dowry. In the case of ISIS, they've asked us to buy them an entire air-defense system."

"Wow," was all Leroy could say. "Are you going to do it?"

"The short answer to your question is yes." Then after a brief pause, Adam gathered himself up and quietly added, "Of course, we're asking for a lot in return."

"Well I'll leave the details to you political geniuses. What can I do for you?"

"I was wondering if with your newfound expertise from your trip to the AAD Conference if you could give me some advice. In short, if you were to buy someone an air-defense system, where would you go?"

Much to Adam's surprise, Leroy answered without hesitation. "I'd call the Chinese and order their Sky Dragon Fifty air-defense system. The name isn't much, but the capabilities are awesome. Google it and you'll see what it can do."

Adam swiveled in his chair to face the computer on the credenza behind his desk. In a few seconds he was lost in the text describing the Sky Dragon's capabilities. If it worked as advertised, the system would more than satisfy ISIS's needs. He learned that the system was considered to be a medium-range surface-to-air missile—SAM system—that could intercept both high- and low-altitude targets. The system included a tracking vehicle and up to six launching vehicles, each of which could carry four missiles. The entire system was highly mobile and could be set up in fifteen minutes.

"This is perfect," Adam said, turning back to Leroy. "You've more than justified your exorbitant hotel bills from the conference. How much does it cost?"

"Although I tried pretty hard to get that number, all I would get are generalities. I was told that a complete system with spare missiles would cost in the low eight figures. I assume that means between $10 million and $20 million. I'm sure that there were a number of reasons for their reluctance to answer my question, one of which is that there are some things that vary the cost, such as spare missiles. Or on the other hand, they were just being inscrutable. I've found that's a favorite sport of the Chinese. But they've sold systems to Rwanda and Pakistan. Do you have any contacts in either of those countries that could answer the question?"

"Thanks Roy. That was great. We'll take it from here. The next step is some serious bargaining. My ancestors have taught me well."

Leroy grinned and nodded. "By the way," he added. "I also picked up some information on drones. But more important, the Chinese are nearing the conclusion of an interesting development. They've put together a system called Dragon Fly, which is capable of intercepting drones. I'll bet your ISIS friends would be interested in a little baby like that."

"Good job, Roy. Keep an eye on that development and let me know when it becomes available. In the meantime, I'll use that information to good advantage. Keep up the good work."

After Leroy left his office, Adam began to compose multiple encrypted messages to John Smith and his new "friends" at ISIS. The messages would follow a circuitous path through no less than six different servers before reaching their destination. The messages were buried in the pixels of a photograph of the Grand Canyon. Of particular significance was the message to ISIS, which, although brief, outlined the planned selection of a SAM system as well as Bis Saif's expectations for increased cooperation between ISIS and the Syrian rebels, including a push into the Kurdish areas of northwestern Syria. The message he sent to John Smith was more prosaic, providing him with an estimate of the funding that was needed in order to satisfy the desires of their ISIS and Hamas partners.

***

Ahmed was making similar progress. Hamas had requested drones adequate for an aerial attack on Israel. His discussions with Leroy were as productive as Adam's. Leroy told Ahmed that the Chinese government seemed to have the edge on drone technology, just as it had in SAM technology. He told Ahmed that the Chinese had a series of combat drones that had been assigned the CH designation, an acronym for Cai Hong, which in Chinese meant rainbow. The drones were manufactured by the China Aerospace Science and Technology Corporation, known as CASC.

Ahmed was growing tired of the lecture. "Enough of the background. Let's get to the point of your research. What did you conclude?"

Leroy continued, undiscouraged by Ahmed's rebuff. "China has been exporting the CH series of drones to a number of countries, including most recently the Nigerian army. I have concluded that the one best suited to the needs of our Palestinian friends is the CH-3. This model has a maximum payload of a hundred and seventy pounds and a range of fifteen hundred miles. It can stay in the air for up to twelve hours."

Ahmed was annoyed. "Don't talk to me in American, how many kilograms and kilometers does that equate to?"

The terse reply: "Eighty kilograms and twenty-four hundred kilometers."

Somehow Ahmed and Leroy rarely spoke collegially. Most of their conversations seemed to end in a mini confrontation. Leroy assumed that Ahmed was somehow jealous of his close relationship with Adam. But Leroy was happy at Bis Saif and found it easy to avoid Ahmed when working on his assigned responsibilities.

Ahmed calmed himself and picked up the conversation. "That sounds great. Do they have any other models that I should be aware of?"

"Yes, they have the CH-3A, which is like the CH-3. The difference is that the CH-3A can carry a larger payload of a hundred and eighty kilograms, but with that payload, it can only remain in the air for six hours. The CH-3A can also be controlled using a satellite data link. It seems to me that the CH-3 would be preferable to Bis Saif because it would likely be cheaper. Also, I'm not sure that Hamas could make use of a satellite link. Do you know if they even have those types of facilities?"

Although Ahmed was tempted to chastise Leroy for making decisions for Bis Saif, he was forced to agree with the reasons for selecting the CH-3. As a result, he remained silent and looked down at his notes as if he were studying the best course to take.

After a short pause he concluded the meeting by asking Leroy for contact information at CASC so that they could discuss the terms of a purchase. After Leroy's departure, Ahmed sat down with Adam to discuss next steps. Once again, a coded message was sent to Hamas, with a second message to John Smith. The Hamas message required that in return for the shipment of drones, they would begin to cooperate with the Sunni Muslims of Lebanon, with the aim of overthrowing that government. Successes in both Lebanon and Palestine would place Israel in the awkward position of being sandwiched between two hostile and united Sunni factions. This would certainly keep the Western powers off-balance.

***

Adam retired for the day with a feeling of contentment. His plan to begin the disruption of the Western empire was now underway. He had accelerated activities in Iraq, Syria, Palestine, and Lebanon. His plan would also send a message to other potentially uncooperative groups that Bis Saif was not an organization that could not be ignored. And finally he had secured the funding needed to ensure the continued success of the operation. Surely this had been a productive day. As always, his one nagging doubt had been the possibility of discovery. Now that they had begun to interact with organizations throughout the Middle East, he would have to be very careful.

BOOK 2
THE KEY TO THE KINGDOM

In the ninth century we trace the first dawnings of the restoration of science. After the fanaticism of the Arabs had subsided, the caliphs aspired to conquer the arts (aka sciences) rather than the provinces of the empire: Their liberal curiosity rekindled the emulation of the Greeks, brushed away the dust from their ancient libraries and taught them to know and reward the philosophers, whose labors had been hitherto repaid by the pleasure of study and the pursuit of truth.

From Edward Gibbon's classic,
The Decline and Fall of the Roman Empire.

CHAPTER 9
THE DISCOVERY

At the same time that the Bis Saif meeting was taking place in Jakarta, a second momentous event was occurring in Silver Spring, Maryland. The halls of JCN Technology resounded with shouts that were accompanied by high fives between Rick and Jahmir. After more than three years of intense research, the two had made a breakthrough where others had failed. The two computer scientists had developed a programmable computing device more powerful by many orders of magnitude than any other device on the planet. Little did either realize its future impact on their personal lives and that of Western civilization.

It would be difficult to imagine two more different individuals. Jahmir Al Saadi, with the rest of his family, had emigrated from Iraq nearly twenty years ago, when Jahmir was ten. They had settled in New York City, a haven for new immigrants, where Jahmir, the eldest son of the family, was raised in the crowded quasi-suburban setting of the borough of Queens. Jahmir's father supported his family from a small dry cleaning business established shortly after arriving in New York with funds borrowed from relatives. Arabic was the language of choice at home since the Al Saadi family was anxious for their offspring to retain their cultural ties with the old country.

Recognizing the rapidly emerging discrimination in the West against anyone with a Muslim name, Jahmir, had Americanized his name to James shortly after beginning high school, where his classmates had known him as James throughout his high school and college years. With his thin, almost emaciated build, dark hair, and thick glasses, James looked the part of the nerd that he was. Blessed with a quick mind, he graduated from high school

Philip J. Tarnoff

with exceptional grades and scholastic honors, but little else. He was slow to make friends and did not participate in extracurricular activities except for occasional attendance at the monthly meetings of the school's computer club. But James's grades and admission test scores overcame the absence of outside activities, which are often the basis for entrance at major US universities. Despite his laser-like focus on academics to the exclusion of everything else, James's status as class valedictorian ensured his acceptance at the multiple engineering universities to which he applied. MIT proved to be his school of choice because it offered the computer engineering curriculum that most closely matched his interests. James soon regretted this decision after his first experience with the heavy snows and cold temperatures of the Massachusetts winters. Although he had been raised in New York, which in and of itself had cold winters, his Middle Eastern physiology preferred the hot dry climates found in that part of the world. In fact, he briefly considered transferring to Stanford, with its more hospitable California weather, but he was enjoying his studies and had developed close friendships with a number of his fellow students with interests similar to his, including another freshman named Rick Stringer.

Both freshmen were fascinated by the rapidly evolving world of computers, a world in which the traditional design of the computers of the twentieth and early parts of the twenty-first centuries were being subject to critical scrutiny. James's thoughts of transferring were also discouraged by his first girlfriend, Kelly Jaffari, a Syrian expatriate and fellow MIT student who was ultimately to become his wife. Kelly was an attractive and energetic girl, well-liked by everyone. She also proved to be a talented software developer at JCN.

Rick Stringer's background was quite different from that of Jahmir. Rick was raised in an upper- middle-class family in Scarsdale, a quiet suburb of New York City, where his father, the owner of one of the larger Westchester County auto dealerships, had adequate income to ensure that the family experienced the good life of the New York suburbs. Rick excelled both scholastically and athletically in high school. His blond good

96

looks and success as a wide receiver on the school's football team ensured his popularity with his peers, particularly those of the opposite sex. As is often the case with the teenage crowd, the fact that Rick's grades were borderline genius was a secondary consideration with his peers, who admired his athletic prowess and laid-back attitude rather than his high IQ. The breadth of his achievements ensured his admittance to MIT, the only school to which he applied because of his overwhelming interest in computer architecture, the same subject that had attracted his renamed friend, James.

An advanced degree in computer science would be required to completely understand the technology underlying James and Rick's celebration, let alone appreciate its significance, although the magnitude of their accomplishments was not lost on the majority of JCN employees. They fully understood that Rick and James had solved the problem of harnessing the power of the neural computer that was being studied by many of the leading laboratories throughout the world.

To understand the neural computer, it is necessary to have a basic appreciation of the power of the human brain. The brain is an amazing processor capable of performing the incredible number of functions needed by a human being, all within an organ the size of a small head of cauliflower. The basic building blocks of the brain are nerve cells known as neurons. The typical brain contains approximately 100 billion nerve cells, which together control body functions (temperature, heart rate, blood pressure, breathing, etc.), process the flood of information from an individual's surroundings (vision, hearing, smell, taste, touch, pressure, itch, heat and cold, pain, balance, and many others), control physical movement, and perhaps most importantly, perform the intangible activity known as thinking, including dreaming, reasoning, emotions, and problem solving. All of these functions are performed by 100 billion busy neurons.

The cell bodies of neurons known as soma are similar to the logic gates that make up computers, except that they function through chemical processes rather than electrical impulses. The logic gate of a computer is a very simple device that operates as a valve turning current flow on and off in response to external commands. Neurons are more complex in the sense that their function is electrochemical based on the DNA of the neuron's cell body, which can build protein and produce impulses based on its external stimulation. Thus the activities of the neuron are more sophisticated than that of the single dimensional computer gate.

Communication among neurons is performed using axons which transmit the electromechanical message produced by the soma to their counterparts elsewhere in the brain. The axons are sophisticated "wires" that terminate at the synapse—or connect with other soma.

Thus the human brain is nothing more than 100 billion little electrochemical processors which communicate with each other over multiple pathways that appear and disappear. Truly a remarkable creation. All of this is taking place in parallel as these billions of little processors perform their functions and communicate their results with each other. How is this organized? Who is in charge? And how is it performed by an organ the size of a cauliflower? The answers to these questions have led some to consider this as evidence of the presence of God.

But computer scientists rarely concern themselves with questions of God. They are convinced that with the availability of a computer chip small and fast enough, they can begin to recreate at least some of the functions of the brain. Their challenges are daunting—the interconnection and programming of 100 billion little processors all working in cooperation to achieve a desired function. James, Rick, Kelly, and most of the JCN technical staff had devoted their lives to meeting these challenges, realizing that they were working at the edges of the computer frontier and close to the development of a device thousands of times more powerful than computers found in the early twenty-first century. They recognized the promise of such devices for near-perfect weather forecasting, curing currently incurable diseases, effective control of transportation systems, and yes, greatly improved security systems, including the ability to continuously monitor and analyze *all* electronic communications worldwide.

But in its attempts to recreate the processes of the human brain, mankind had not as yet begun to approach the capabilities of the little cauliflower. At the beginning of the century, IBM was developing a chip called TrueNorth with the goal of 10 billion neurons and 100 trillion synapses. Yes, the number of synapses far exceeds the number of neurons because every neuron is connected with every other neuron in a giant mind-numbing grid. Even these massive numbers represent only one tenth the power of the human brain and less than one tenth of its capabilities.

The high fives occurring that afternoon were the celebration of a JCN breakthrough that would take neural computing to the next level, one that approached the true power of the human brain in a device not much bigger than the little cauliflower. James and Rick had analyzed the workings of the billions of tiny neurons in their little device and recognized that they were not all working equally hard. At any given time, a high percentage of the little guys were loafing along, waiting for inputs from the synapses that connected them with other neurons. They had successfully developed a device that would quickly identify the slackers and put them to work on other tasks while they were waiting for information from other neurons. The device was based on the principle they had discovered that a working neuron has a higher temperature than an idle neuron. When attached to the chip containing the billions of neurons, their device, known as MOM (Mind Over Matter), identified areas of the chip with idle neurons and put them to work on other tasks. They were astounded to discover that this process multiplied the power of the neural computer chip by a factor of ten or more.

MOM put the fledgling R&D company on the map both within their industry and at the Defense Advanced Research Projects Agency (DARPA), the sponsor of their research. Bill Jaski, CEO and founder of JCN, had established the company ten years earlier as Jaski Computer Networks, with the intent of creating an organization that specialized in the development of innovative computer architectures. He was convinced that the popular computer processors manufactured by companies such as Intel, Samsung, and Texas Instruments had reached the limits of their capabilities and that a fresh look at the basic organization of these devices was needed. As the company grew to approximately 300 employees, it was relocated to an office park in Silver Spring, Maryland, a bedroom community northwest of Washington, DC. Bill had briefly considered a relocation to San Jose, California, but decided that proximity to the federal government and his family ties to the suburban Maryland location were more important than a move to the West Coast.

Bill was delighted with the development of MOM, which had borne out his intuition of the potential of new computer architectures as well as his confidence in his star computer engineers. As soon as word of their success reached his office, he prepared an "all hands" email, letting everyone know that work would end early that day, and Happy Hour would begin at four at the Dew Drop Inn, a nearby tavern known by the locals as Dewey's and frequented by JCN employees. Bill assured the staff that the happy hour would be short on speeches and long on refreshments, an assurance that he knew would ensure a good turnout.

Bill's preparations for an early departure to Dewey's were interrupted by Sean Casey, JCN's competent corporate attorney. "Bill, we need to talk ASAP."

"Sean, can't it wait? You can see we've got an important event to celebrate. And I need to be there, since it should be recognized from the top of the organization."

"Bill, that's the reason why we need to talk. MOM needs to be protected carefully if she or it is to remain in the hands of JCN. This thing is too big and needs to be carefully managed."

"What do you mean by that?"

"Bill, we've been together a long time, and you know that I am not into histrionics, but MOM is a potential catastrophe for JCN. Think about its implications. While it's nice to speculate about the benevolent things that can be done with this much computer power, think about the evil for which it could also be used. MOM could probably be used to hack into most of the world's protected websites. It could be used to monitor all electronic communications throughout the world. It could be used to shut down nuclear installations, theirs as well as ours. These capabilities cannot be allowed to fall into the wrong hands. It's something like nuclear energy—it is a force capable of both good and evil that must be carefully controlled."

Bill paced around the office, making a complete circuit before replying. "My God, Sean. Why haven't you mentioned this before? What are we going to do?" Bill glanced around his sparsely decorated office as if the answer would be provided by the awards and diplomas hanging on the walls.

"This is a secure facility, and MOM is a classified project. I would recommend that we allow the celebration to continue this afternoon, but give a speech that reminds everyone of their security responsibilities and points out that anyone discussing MOM outside of JCN will be subject to the harshest repercussions. This would include spouses, boyfriends, girlfriends, and relatives. In short, we've got to lower the proverbial cone of silence on this project. Tomorrow, first thing in the morning, you and I should meet with our director of security, our manager of marketing, and our chief engineer to discuss alternatives."

"OK, I'll set up the meeting for tomorrow at 7:00 a.m. in the corporate board room. The hour should get everyone's attention. As far as the rest of the company, including James and Rick, it will be business as usual until we can develop a plan.

"Now let's go party. I want to be sure everyone is still there when I give my speech. I'm sure it will be a surprise to all."

Sean put on his ever-present gray suitcoat and left for Dewey's. He was followed shortly by a chastened Bill Jaski wearing his signature jeans and blue oxford shirt with a button-down collar.

***

The crowd at Dewey's was noisy and excited. The JCN staff was convinced that MOM would put them on the map as a premier research organization, ensuring their future careers in much the same way as employment at Bell Labs had in the past. James and Rick were the center of attention leaning on the bar, drinking their lite beers and expounding on their research challenges. Both were dressed in jeans, as were most of the staff. If the weather had been warmer, tank tops would have been the dress of the day. James stood with one arm draped possessively around Kelly, who was soon to become his wife.

In another age, Dewey's would have existed in a fog of cigarette smoke, which was now absent, but everything else was typical of an after-work hangout, including the dim lighting and the smell of stale beer and ribs. Happy Hour with half-priced beer and wine began at four and lasted until seven, by which time most customers would be on the way home to their families in the suburbs.

At the relatively early post-work hour of four, the JCN staff dominated the bar crowd. They eventually gravitated to Dewey's back room where they anticipated suffering through one of Bill Jaski's lengthy speeches, which was typically delivered in a monotone. Although Bill was a recognized visionary in the computer world and a leader admired by his staff, he was not an inspiring speaker. The staff fervently hoped that his speech would be mercifully brief, as he had promised. It was a jovial crowd of relatively youthful employees, buoyed by their understanding of the significance of the company's recent success combined with the usual jockeying for the attention of influential coworkers and attempts to attract members of the opposite sex.

Upon the arrival of their CEO and his chief legal counsel, the banter gradually died out to be replaced by a murmur of anticipation as the JCN employees looked forward to the congratulatory words of their leader. Bill took his time getting their attention, slowly taking off his sports jacket and hanging it on the back of a nearby chair. He then mounted the small stage installed in a corner of the room, intended for the various musical groups that provided Dewey's evening entertainment, which could be as varied as jazz, country, or R&B, depending on the evening.

When Bill felt that he had everyone's attention, he asked for those at the rear of the group to close the door to the back room so his comments would not be heard by Dewey's other customers. The sober manner in which he began his speech immediately grabbed everyone's attention as the staff began to recognize that this was not going to be an ordinary pep talk.

"As you all know, today is a momentous day in the life of JCN," Jaski said. "Our research team, led by Rick Stringer and Jahmir Al Saadi, has succeeded in the development of a neural processor that exceeds the capabilities of any other similar device on this planet. Both men are to be congratulated."

Rick, the clown, stepped forward and took a deep bow, which was followed by a round of applause and uplifted beer bottles, many of which were emptied at this excuse. Jahmir, still with his arm around Kelly, turned and spontaneously kissed her, much to the hoots and amusement of his coworkers.

Bill continued. "We've all spent many hours speculating on the market potential of a powerful neural processor, and the many applications that would benefit from its use. We have discussed possible advances in medical research, weather forecasting, traffic control, and agriculture that would result from the availability of unheard of processing power." Many of his employees were nodding in agreement as Bill continued. "We viewed this as a win-win situation in which JCN would become an IT powerhouse, able to attract the best and brightest to its workforce while producing products and software that would benefit all of mankind." He then paused to give emphasis to his following words.

"But there is also a downside to this story. The same device that produces all of these benefits could also be used for evil. And I mean incredible evil. Think about these possibilities introduced by unlimited processing power. It would be possible to monitor and analyze all electronic communications worldwide in real time. It would be possible to hack into any of today's computer systems in the banking, intelligence, and defense industries, both governmental systems as well as those operated by private companies. It would be possible to cripple

103

the nation's power grid. All of these things become possible because of the incredible processing power of the little device we affectionately call MOM."

It was as if the air had been sucked out of the room. No one in the audience uttered a word, and a few gasped as reality dawned on them.

Bill continued. "In some respects, we have created the electronic equivalent of nuclear energy, with the capability of delivering both incredible good and evil. The question is—do we want to unleash this power on the world? An equally significant question is whether our sponsors will permit us to unleash it on the world." And then he ominously added, "It's also important to recognize that we don't have a corner on the ability to imagine MOM's potential for evil. Those that would capitalize on this capability are likely to stop at nothing to acquire this system.

"So now that I have taken you from the heights of euphoria to the depths of depression, let's try to establish some balance. First, we've developed a device that will advance computer technology by several generations. Second, as with most major technological breakthroughs, including nuclear energy, the rest of the world will eventually adapt to its presence, either through the development of competing technology or the creation of defenses against the new technology. Finally, MOM is too significant a development for us to hide it from the rest of civilization. We have an obligation to manage its introduction into society in a positive and productive manner." He paused and then added, "at least to the extent that others will allow us to control its destiny.

"With this as background and speaking as your leader, I am now lowering a veil of silence over this entire project. Effective immediately and until you hear otherwise from me, there is to be no further work on this project. There are to be no contacts with our sponsors in connection with any aspect of the project. No technical papers are to be written and submitted to conferences that describe the project or any of its components. There is to be no discussion with anyone outside of JCN, including friends, relatives, spouses, children, acquaintances, or anyone else. For all intents and purposes, from this day forward, MOM will cease to exist. Any discussions regarding the project inside of JCN are to be limited to subjects associated with its suspension.

"It goes without saying that any violation of the rules I have just outlined will be met with immediate termination of employment with JCN as well as revocation of your security clearance. I realize that these measures seem drastic and hope that they will be temporary. I am imposing them to give us the time we need to work on a plan that addresses the many issues associated with MOM. Now I know you've got dozens of questions, but unfortunately my time is very limited, and I don't have any answers. I would like to meet with our senior managers tomorrow morning at 7:00 a.m. so we can begin to get some of this under control.

"Now remember—no discussion of MOM with anyone." And without another word, Bill departed, leaving a roomful of JCN employees reeling with uncertainty.

***

Kelly, Rick, and James were standing in a corner absorbing the bombshell that had been dropped by their CEO. For a minute none of them spoke, and then Rick said, "Let's go to my place. I'll order pizza." Lacking any better ideas, Kelly and James silently followed him out the door. Other members of the JCN staff watched them leave, wondering what they would do now that the project that had been the focus of their lives was in limbo.

Rick's place was a small, sparsely furnished apartment consisting of a kitchen, multi-purpose living area, two bedrooms, and a bathroom. Travel posters adorned the walls, reflecting Rick's interest in skiing and water sports. The worn furniture reflected its secondhand heritage.

"Hope you guys are OK with pepperoni," Rick said as he unlocked the door for Kelly and James. "I ordered by cell on the way from Dewey's." They both nodded mutely and followed him into the apartment.

"Phew," James said as he fell back onto Rick's well-worn couch. "That sure was an ugly surprise. Who would have thought that a couple of computer nerds were capable of developing the equivalent of the atom bomb?"

"And now we're apparently persona non grata at JCN, to be avoided as if we've got the plague."

Kelly, the optimist, jumped in. "Don't overreact. Mr. Jaski never said that we are to be avoided. In fact, he didn't say much of anything except that our activities are temporarily suspended while he figures out what to do."

James, the activist, responded. "I don't think we should be at the mercy of the JCN management. They will decide what to do based on what is best for JCN and not for us. In the meantime, Rick and I have devoted our working lives to this project and are on the verge of a breakthrough that will make our careers. Why haven't we been included in the meeting tomorrow? Why hasn't anyone asked us what we think?"

At that point the pizza arrived, interrupting the discussion and giving everyone time to consider the situation. Rick said little except, "Maybe we will find some answers in the pepperoni. For myself, I intend to enjoy the paid vacation that Jaski said he was providing." Kelly laughed but James did not.

Rick took a bottle of beer from the refrigerator, saying, "Help yourselves" to the other two. While the beer was opened and everyone dug into the hot slices of pizza, Rick quietly said, "You know there are other alternatives."

"Like what?" James and Kelly asked in unison.

"Well, I've been thinking a lot about MOM during the past few months, and it occurred to me that there's a business opportunity here. Look at all the successful start-ups that have begun with much less than the capabilities that we've developed. We could start a new company called the Braintrust, based on the use of neural technology. Think of the apps we could produce to do all the things we've speculated about: weather forecasting, medical research, and so forth. Right now, MOM is little more than a platform, just like the iPhone is a platform for the thousands of apps it supports. All we would need is one or two winners and the Braintrust would be the next Google."

James said, "That's all very fine, but right now all of the hardware and software we'd need to start the Braintrust is locked away at JCN. It would take a heroic effort to recreate it a second time."

Rick thoughtfully replied, "I guess you're right. It was a dumb idea. That was the beer talking."

The three of them finished the pizza and talked long into the night, until James and Kelly returned to their own apartment down the street from Rick's place.

CHAPTER 10

DECISIONS

The boardroom was the centerpiece of the JCN facilities. Designed both to impress and intimidate visitors, the room was large enough to accommodate nearly two dozen participants at a polished mahogany table flanked by plush executive-style chairs. Straight-backed wooden chairs were arrayed along the walls for observers and other lesser players. The room was entered through glass doors at one end, which were engraved with the JCN lightning-bolt logo. Paintings along the walls were original works of art glorifying old and new technology.

All of this was lost on the individuals clustered at one end of the conference room table. This group included Bill Jaski, the company's CEO; Sean Casey, the corporate attorney; Joan Toner, in charge of JCN contracts; Jack Vermeer, head of security; and Marylou Sachler, who was a JCN vice president and the company's chief scientist. With the exception of Jack Vermeer, who was a relatively new hire, the group had worked together for many years. Sean Casey looked the part of an attorney. He was always dressed in a dark suit and white shirt. His dress stood out from the more casual attire of the other JCN employees. Joan Toner was an introverted individual who rarely spoke up at company meetings. However, she knew contracting and contract law better than anyone Bill had ever met, and her place in the organization was secure. Jack Vermeer was the only African-American on the senior management team. He had a lean athletic build that bespoke his years in the military prior to joining JCN. Although he dressed in casual clothes, they fit him well, giving him a fashion-model appearance. More than anyone else, Marylou Sachler was responsible for the success of

JCN. Although she looked the part of a matronly grandmother, her sharp mind coupled with an eye for talent had developed a research and development team that was unrivalled in the information technology field. The majority of members on this team had seen the company grow from a garage operation to its current staff of more than 300 employees.

While MOM was the centerpiece of the JCN programs, it was only one of many activities underway at the company, most of which were focused on computer-related technology. Jack's recent hire was the result of DARPA's insistence that they strengthen their security procedures in recognition of the sensitivity of their many activities. He oversaw the myriad of security procedures required by the government, including employee security clearances, regular reports, and secure storage for classified documents. He also established a procedure for controlling visitor access. Because of his efficiency and competence, he rapidly established himself as a respected member of the group. He rarely spoke unless he had something intelligent to say.

The group's demeanor reflected the gravity of the situation. They had all been present at the Dew Drop Inn when Bill gave his brief speech, and they had all recognized the need for immediate action.

Jaski's opening remarks set the tone for the morning's meeting. "I think you all know why we're here. I lost sleep over this situation and felt that my performance at Dewey's could have been better. I'm afraid I left our employees confused and scared."

Marylou, a close friend and confidant of Bill's, immediately disagreed. "Bill, your speech was fine. Without it, our employees would have been trumpeting the JCN success all over the Internet. As it was, I think there have still been some leaks."

Jack Vermeer immediately seconded Marylou's thoughts. "My monitoring of the email traffic shows that we've had some leaks in spite of your speech. If you hadn't said something, the leaks would have been replaced by a deluge. The question is what do we do now?"

Jaski's demeanor softened as he resumed his accustomed role as leader of the group. "I've made a list of the items that need our immediate attention. It includes the following: First is to make sure that we've filed for patent protection for MOM. Sean, I believe this is your department.

"Second is ensuring that all equipment, software, and data associated with MOM is secured and made inaccessible to our employees. Marylou, I think you should lead this effort. It is probably the most important of all items on my list.

"Third, we need to notify DARPA, our client, of our progress with MOM and its potential implications. We should meet with them today if possible to determine where we go from here. I've already contacted the DARPA program manager responsible for oversight of our work. He'll be arriving early this afternoon.

"Fourth, Sean, could you also review our contract with DARPA to determine our responsibilities for reporting and protecting any intellectual property that has security implications? Please work with Jack on this, since we might be required to take extraordinary security measures as a result of MOM's powers.

"And finally, Marylou, I know you're already buried with work, but could you please begin to develop a reassignment plan for employees who have been idled by our suspension of MOM research? We'll obviously continue to retain them as full-time employees, and it would be ideal if we could find a way to ensure that they remain productive. I don't think that all these issues will be worked out in a little while, but we don't want our technical success to bankrupt the company in the meantime.

"What have I forgotten?"

No one was anxious to add more items to Jaski's long list, since they were already overwhelmed by their assignments. So the rest of the meeting was spent coordinating activities and preparing a statement to be sent to the staff requesting their patience while the company addressed the many issues associated with MOM.

***

Bill Jaski was at his desk working out the intricacies of reassigning ten percent of his technical staff to other projects. He had spoken with Marylou after the meeting and offered to give her a hand with the staffing changes. He was startled when Jane Smith, his administrative assistant, called to announce his visitors. While he had spoken with his DARPA contact in the morning and expected his arrival that afternoon, he was surprised to learn that his visitors included Kevin Goldberg, the DARPA program manager; Thomas McAllen, the Executive Director of DARPA; and a third person whose affiliation was not identified who introduced himself as George Wilson.

The Defense Advanced Research Projects Agency, or DARPA, as it was known, was a prestigious organization. Although relatively unknown by the American public, its programs had been responsible for many significant technological breakthroughs; the best known being the development of the foundation for the Internet. Originally named the Advanced Research Projects Agency, or ARPA, the agency was established in 1958 by President Eisenhower in response to Russia's Sputnik space program. Its mission then and now was to ensure that the technology of the US military was more advanced than that of the country's potential enemies. DARPA conducted its research using its own staff as well as private sector companies and universities. Its budget of approximately $3 billion had produced many notable successes, including significant advances related to graphical user interfaces and robotics.

Quickly recovering from his surprise at the arrival of Thomas McAllen, Bill welcomed the three DARPA representatives into his office. After they were seated comfortably at the small conference table and four chairs that were his one concession to CEO-like office furnishings, Bill asked his guests for their coffee orders, which consisted of one black cup of coffee, one Coke, and a glass of water for the unaffiliated George Wilson. He also asked Jane to invite Sean to join them, both because he felt outnumbered, and to provide any advice that might be needed should legal issues arise. He hoped that Jane would have the presence of mind to let Sean know the stature of their visitors before ushering him into the meeting so that he would arrive prepared to join the conversation.

McAllen opened the discussion with a statement that indicated he had been fully briefed by Kevin Goldberg. "Kevin tells me that you've made quite a breakthrough here at JCN. You are to be congratulated."

Bill nodded, accepting the congratulations, and responded, "Now the challenge is to figure out what to do with it. I used the analogy of nuclear energy with my staff, in that MOM has the power of great good and great evil. I feel that deciding on next steps is above my pay grade."

Thomas McAllen smiled at Jaski's false modesty. He knew Bill well enough to realize that he never avoided difficult decisions, but also knew that he favored collaborative decisions, feeling that they had a better chance of success. "Well, let me help you with your decision. We took advantage of the advanced warning you provided this morning to consult with various other agencies as well as the White House. The consensus is that we should continue research related to MOM. In fact, if anything, it should be accelerated. We're prepared to increase your funding to ensure that this happens." McAllen nodded to George Wilson as he paused before continuing his remarks.

During the pause, Bill and Sean stared at each other in surprise. Of all the directions they had anticipated that the meeting would take, the one they had just heard was the least likely. "I expected your reaction," McAllen continued. "But consider the alternatives. We could kill the project, bury the results, and pretend it never happened. But what are the chances of a leak by an employee that either retains documents or remembers enough to recreate the project for someone else, most likely at great personal profit. The other possibility is that we kill the project and one of the bad guys, possibly Communist China, independently develops a similar capability on their own. If this happens, we're at a disadvantage unless the United States has comparable computing power. To continue with your nuclear energy analogy, other countries were well on their way toward developing similar capabilities when the United States devel-

oped the first atom bomb. If we had not pursued its development, the Germans, Russians, and others would eventually have
been in a position to blackmail us." Bill and Sean began slowly
nodding in unison as the wisdom of Thomas McAllen's evaluation began to sink in.

"But the additional funding for the project comes with some
strings. First of all, we're going to have to increase the security
on the project. This includes higher security clearance levels
for all employees before they can work on the project. It may
also require moving MOM to a new facility that can provide the
physical protection against unauthorized intruders that is essential for its new security level. It will also require round-the-clock
guards. As an alternative, it may be possible to provide you with
laboratory and office space at an existing government facility.
That will minimize the cost of establishing your own elaborate
physical security. Do you have any preferences?"

Bill said he would have to think about it, discuss it with
his senior staff, and the affected employees. There were many
things to be considered, including employee commuting distances and the ability of senior JCN managers to oversee any
work being performed at a remote location. The decision would
also be based on the amount of space and laboratory facilities
available at the government facility. Obviously, the decision
was a complicated one, although, unfortunately, it was one that
would have to be made quickly.

McAllen stood to leave. "I've got to get back to the ranch,
but Kevin here is fully authorized to guide the program through
its next steps. Mr. Wilson will help you with any political
issues that might arise." McAllen's reference to Wilson, with
no affiliation offered, was the first time that his presence had
been acknowledged. George looked the part of an upper-level
government employee. With his crisp white shirt and dark suit,
he was in competition with Sean Casey for best dressed in the
room. He obviously worked at a higher level than Kevin, who as
a program manager dressed casually in a sport shirt and slacks.

McAllen continued. "The next steps include needed contract
modifications, along with changes to the security classification

of the program. Let me repeat, all members of the staff who are working on MOM must be cleared at the highest levels. This program is equivalent to the Manhattan project that developed the atom bomb and will be handled in the same way. I cleared my schedule to meet with you this afternoon, to impress upon you the potential significance of this project as well as the need for utmost security. I have complete confidence that you will handle it with the utmost care and discretion."

Following McAllen's brief visit, Bill Jaski suggested that they all take a break to attend to their inevitable personal needs and return cell-phone calls, as is frequently the case with long meetings. During the break, he took the opportunity to summon Jack Vermeer and Joan Toner, the two who were most able to address security and contract issues that were likely to arise. He had wanted to include his chief scientist, Marylou, in the meeting, but realizing that she was extremely busy, he decided to leave her alone, thinking he could always brief her later. Because the meeting had expanded beyond the capacity of his office, the group reconvened in the boardroom.

***

Once everyone was seated and introductions had been completed, George Wilson surprised the attendees by assuming control of the meeting. He indicated in no uncertain terms that security was the government's primary concern. He asked Jack Vermeer to confirm that all materials associated with MOM had been isolated and placed in appropriate security safes. He also asked that JCN hire armed guards from a private security firm, to be personally approved by him, for round-the-clock monitoring of access to the secure facilities containing the project materials. As Wilson was speaking, Bill began to appreciate the significance of this project and continued to wonder about George's relationship with the DARPA.

"We are concerned with two types of security: personnel security clearances and limiting access to the project materials. In other words, physical security. Although we fast-tracked the plans that I'm going to describe, we're confident that they will be effective and believe they're critical to the future protection of your technology. Quite frankly, these plans are not negotiable. They are based on directives from the highest levels of the government."

George's opening statement confirmed Bill's growing suspicion that he was a representative from the White House, the Department of Homeland Security, or the Department of Defense.

Wilson continued. "Beginning with the issue of security clearance, it has been determined that personnel working on the MOM program must have SCI clearances. In case you are not familiar with these clearances, SCI stands for Sensitive Compartmented Information. These clearances are assigned after an extensive background investigation, which is more rigorous than that required for a Top Secret clearance, with an additional special adjudication process used to evaluate the results of the investigation. Individuals with SCI clearances are assigned to compartments separated from each other. In other words, individuals in one compartment do not have access to information in another compartment. The government can, at its discretion, impose stricter criteria on individuals with SCI clearances."

"What clearances do the individuals currently working on MOM have?"

Jack Vermeer's one-word answer: "Secret."

George responded, "That's too bad, since even top-secret clearances require several months for their award. SCI clearances may take even longer. I'll have to see whether I can expedite the process."

He then added, almost as an afterthought, "And one more thing. Only US citizens will be cleared for this work."

This last statement was met with a stunned silence by the JCN representatives at the meeting, since several of the key professionals working on the MOM program had green cards, not the least of whom was Jahmir Al Saadi. Bill Jaski pulled out his cellphone and called Jane. "Ask Marylou to get in here as quickly as possible."

When she arrived at the boardroom, Marylou was introduced to George and Kevin. She already knew Kevin very well from her past dealings with the DARPA program. Once again, no effort was made to provide Wilson's position, both because none of the JCN personnel knew, and because neither Kevin nor George were forthcoming.

Bill briefly summarized the discussion that had occurred so far, ending with a more detailed description of the security clearance requirements that had been described by Wilson. Marylou's reacted to these requirements with a scowl, to which George repeated his earlier statement that these requirements were not negotiable.

She replied, "But Jahmir Al Saadi is an Iraqi citizen who is here on a green card. He is key to this project and is responsible for many of its innovations. Banning him from working on the project would delay its progress, at best, and could result in its failure. I think your restrictions are a potentially costly mistake."

George was unmoved. "As I said, these requirements are not negotiable."

Marylou muttered something that sounded like "bureaucrats" under her breath and lapsed into silence.

Ignoring Marylou's comment, George then handed Kevin a stack of security clearance applications contained in a box marked Top Secret-SCI. "Please see that these are completed as quickly as possible by your eligible employees," he said, emphasizing the word eligible.

The remainder of the meeting was spent discussing alternative government facilities with adequate provisions for physical security in the Washington, DC area, of which many were feasible. If a government facility were to be used, Bill preferred one in Maryland, since the majority of the JCN employees were Maryland residents, and a commute to downtown DC or northern Virginia would mean spending hours in rush hour traffic. George had arrived with a list of candidates, each of which was evaluated by the group. Eventually it was decided that the National Security Agency (NSA) would provide the best venue for MOM because it had available space (although somewhat limited), and its location, in Laurel, Maryland, halfway between Baltimore and Washington, would be the least inconvenient for the JCN employees. Bill told Kevin and George that he would compare this alternative with the possibility of modifications to their existing facility that would meet their new security requirements.

Kevin had been quiet during most of the meeting because, as Bill suspected, he was outranked by everyone present. Now back on more familiar ground, he turned to Joan Toner, the JCN director of contracts. "We would like to know whether or not it might be possible to accelerate the pace of the ongoing work. For example, would it be possible to have an operational prototype within twelve months instead of the sixteen months required by the existing contract? We would also like a list of the applications that might be feasible with the initial prototype and the schedule for their development."

To Bill's delight, he added, "Cost is not the primary consideration here. But be aware of the fact that some very important people will be watching. So please, please, please, do not promise schedules and functionality that you cannot deliver. I would rather have you tell me that something is not possible than disappoint us later."

Marylou could no longer restrain herself. "I hope you are all having a wonderful time discussing a reduced schedule and expanded functionality while forcing us to remove Al-Saadi, our most important resource, from the project. Do you think I'm a miracle worker?"

George responded before anyone else could say anything. "I am completely sympathetic to your problem, Marylou. And believe me, if there were any alternatives, I would aggressively pursue them. But this has not been my decision. It is a joint decision made at the highest levels of several organizations. Don't shoot the messenger."

Bill was anxious to solve the problem as well as pacify the ruffled feathers of his customer's representatives. "Marylou, let's discuss this later. We are not without alternatives here. We could add additional staff members to the project or transfer some of our existing staff. Don't forget that Al-Saadi is not the only talented individual that works for JCN. In fact, it might be possible to move another talented staff member to MOM and replace him or her with Al-Saadi on the project from which they were transferred."

Marylou was obviously not mollified. "We'll discuss this later."

As the meeting broke up, Bill accompanied his visitors to the entrance lobby of JCN, where he glanced at the visitors' log. He noted that Wilson had identified his affiliation as USG, which was an organizational acronym unknown to Jaski.

***

Jaski and Marylou reconvened in his office shortly after the departure of their DARPA visitors. Bill had been apprehensive about this follow-up meeting since he knew that Marylou was upset. When she entered his office carrying her ever-present cup of coffee, he motioned for her to take a seat on the couch while he remained in relative safety behind his desk. He swiveled his desk chair to face her.

She did not wait for him to speak, but immediately began what appeared to be a prepared appeal. "Bill—you know as well as I do that we cannot continue to make progress on MOM at our current pace without James. He's a brilliant computer engineer, and has been responsible for the majority of advances that we've made. In addition, there are elements of both the hardware and software that I suspect only he understands. We've carefully documented all our developments, but documentation only takes you so far. In addition, there is no replacement for his creativity."

"I'm aware of that, but our hands are tied. That guy George, whoever he is, repeated the non-negotiable aspects of the security clearance requirements, at least three times. I'm not sure who George is except that his last name is Wilson and, according to the sign-in sheet, he represents an unnamed agency he identified as USG. I suspect he's relatively high up in the government structure, and he was rather specific in his description of the requirement as having been approved by multiple agencies. You must admit that it would be almost impossible to get the bureaucracy to change their position on this in a timely manner, if at all."

Marylou surprised Bill by laughing. "You don't know who USG is?" she said. "That's the standard affiliation used by government personnel who do not want to reveal their organization. It stands for US Government. I hope you didn't spend too much time Googling it." She laughed again.

Bill was embarrassed, but not prepared to be diverted from his message. "That further confirms my feeling that we are in no position to resist the requirements outlined by George. If he is in the intelligence business, and backed by multiple agencies as well, there would be no way for us to resist his and their demands."

"OK, Bill. Assuming for the moment that I agree with you, what are we going to do? Surely you are not going to agree to accelerate our development schedule? If you do, I quit! I'm not sure how we could accelerate the schedule, even if James were still with us. Without him it would be impossible. Doubling the number of software engineers does not cut the schedule in half, just like two women can't have a baby in four and half months."

She added, "In fact, adding unfamiliar people to a project invariably slows the project down. So what are you going to do?"

Bill knew she was right. "Would it be possible to complete a system with limited capabilities in a shorter time frame than the overall system? If so, we could offer a schedule that appears accelerated in that it develops an operational product with limited capabilities in a shorter time. We could possibly give Kevin a list of options with different capabilities and ask him to prioritize the list. Perhaps these mini systems could be developed faster."

It was Marylou's turn to do some thinking. "That might work," she said after a pause. "Why don't you let me discuss it with James's partner Rick and see if it's possible?"

"We need to be quick about this. Why don't you proceed as you say and get me a list by tomorrow at this time? I'll then set up another meeting with Kevin, you, and Rick to discuss the concept. I believe he'll like it. But we have to move fast since Joan is working with their contracts people on a modification to our contract while we speak."

Then Bill added, almost as an afterthought, "Which reminds me, we've got to make a decision on the use of a facility with enhanced security—theirs or ours. Any thoughts on this?"

Marylou responded, "I've been so wrapped up in this Al-Saadi issue that I haven't thought about anything else. One of my concerns is finding another project for him that he'll find equally challenging. I'd hate to see him leave JCN, although it's a distinct possibility. IT people are mobile and will readily change jobs if they feel that they're not appreciated.

"But as far as the issue of office locations, my vote would be to either renovate and expand these offices, or rent some space elsewhere in this office park. I know there's some space available. Things are in enough turmoil as it is without having to ask people to change their commutes and to ask me to manage a staff that is geographically dispersed." She concluded with a plea. "At least take my problems into consideration to the extent that we remain physically consolidated."

Bill was moved by her arguments and nodded.

The meeting ended cordially. Their relationship had survived many disagreements in the past and would undoubtedly survive others in the future.

Marylou left Bill's office with the additional assignment of working out the phased development of MOM applications, while Bill was now saddled with the planning for an expansion and modification of the JCN facilities. But most critical, Marylou now had to face the unpleasant task of letting Jahmir Al-Saadi know that he was being removed from the project.

CHAPTER 11

THE UGLY MESSAGE

Marylou knew that she couldn't postpone a conversation with Jahmir much longer. It would be terrible if he received the bad news from someone other than her. Yet she wanted to be fully prepared. She quickly scanned the list of JCN projects she had printed out in preparation for the meeting with Jahmir, looking for projects compatible with his background and interests. She had to find a suitable match before calling him, knowing that unless he was intrigued by the project he would leave JCN for greener pastures elsewhere. As it was, she suspected his level of disappointment at being removed from MOM could be so high that he would leave out of bitterness toward the government system that had treated him so poorly. She identified two projects that might work.

Reluctantly she dialed Jahmir's cellphone. It rang for a long time before it was answered with an unenthusiastic "Hello."

Using her most cheerful voice, Marylou replied, "James, is that you?"

"I've been expecting to hear from you, Marylou," Jahmir replied. "I hope you are calling to tell me that we're restarting work on MOM. We're falling behind schedule and badly need to get started."

"I'm calling you about MOM, but not about restarting the project. As you may already know, we just finished a meeting with our bosses at DARPA, and they had both good news and bad news, which we need to discuss. Are you in the office right now? If so, could you please come by my office so we can talk?"

A few minutes later she heard Jahmir coming down the hall, and braced herself for the ensuing discussion.

Philip J. Tarnoff

Jahmir entered her office, slumped into the chair next to Marylou's desk, and without preamble said, "What's the bad news?"

Ignoring his question, Marylou said, "The good news is that DARPA wants to accelerate the project. They want to increase our funding so we can begin to develop expanded functionality and do it more quickly. The bad news is that they've imposed some very strict security requirements on us that will be difficult to meet. Some of these requirements are concerned with the physical security of our facilities, and others are concerned with the security clearances of our personnel. The latter requirement directly affects you. It bans foreign nationals from working on the project."

James started to reply and then lapsed into stunned silence as the impact of her statement sank in. He sat back in the chair and stared at Marylou. "Does this mean that I can no longer be associated with MOM?"

"I'm afraid so. I argued on your behalf and told everyone that you were the key to making any progress on the project. But they answered that the orders for this level of security came from the highest levels of government, and included the concurrence of multiple government agencies. I was told in no uncertain terms that there was no way that this requirement could or would be relaxed."

Ashen faced, James replied, "That's terrible. My entire life is wrapped around MOM. I have many ideas for future developments that would take the system to new levels of capability. What are we going to do?"

Marylou responded, "Have you thought about applying for US citizenship? I know it's a long process, but in the meantime we can productively employ you on some of our other projects. I've identified several that need people with your skills."

Jahmir had looked into the possibility of citizenship in the past and was familiar with the process. "A successful application for citizenship will take between six months and a year. Add to that the time required to obtain the necessary security clearances, and I'll be waiting for between one and two years

122

before I can rejoin the project. Two years of development is a lifetime in my world. By the time I am once again part of the team, they will have progressed too far for me to catch up."

"You know that's not true," answered Marylou. "This is a bad situation, but please don't make it seem worse than it is. In fact, the delay could be closer to one year, and you are bright enough to easily catch up with the team's progress."

Jahmir was in no mood to look at the bright side of things. He said, "Furthermore, the remaining team members will be publishing papers and generally taking credit for all of the developments associated with MOM. I will never achieve the recognition associated with this significant breakthrough, which is likely to revolutionize the computer industry."

"Jahmir, you are forgetting that there is a prohibition against publishing or speaking about this project outside JCN. Your teammates will not be in a position to take credit for anything."

"Well let me think about this situation, Marylou. It would help if you could tell me about the other projects to which I might be assigned."

The remainder of the meeting was spent discussing Jahmir's potential role in alternative JCN projects. None of the projects that were offered seemed to spark his interest. As a result, he was a depressed individual when he left the meeting. Marylou Sachler had the unhappy feeling that he had not been pacified.

***

When Jahmir left Marylou's office, he had an urgent desire to go someplace outside of the JCN offices so he could clear his mind and think about his future. He felt the walls closing in around him as he returned to the office that he shared with Rick. He was relieved that Rick wasn't there as he sat down at his desk and reflected on his new unhappy situation. How could they do this to him? Didn't they realize that MOM was his? He had provided most of the creativity behind their advances, and now they were going to take it away from him. How was this possible? Did this represent an anti-Arab bias? He had hoped that his achievements would propel him into the pantheon of individuals who had revolutionized information technology, such as Alan Turing and John Von Neumann, pioneers of the industry. Now his hopes had been dashed and he was likely to be headed for a career submerged in anonymity. His dreams had been shattered.

He mentally sorted through his various alternatives, which included Marylou's suggestion that he hang in there and apply for US citizenship, with the hope that he would ultimately be able to rejoin the MOM project. He also considered leaving JCN and looking for a position elsewhere that would allow him to pursue his career in other available directions. He thought about the conversation at Rick's apartment the previous evening, where the possibility of forming a new business had been discussed.

One by one he discarded each of these alternatives. The hang in there alternative seemed to be the easiest path to take, but he doubted he could tread water for a year or two while Rick and the other members of the MOM team celebrated their various successes. Leaving JCN for another job was another possibility, although he felt that he was likely to encounter the same problems wherever classified work was being performed. He discarded the possibility of forming a new business with Rick because he wasn't sure how he would even get started. Furthermore, at this point, the idea of working with Rick didn't appeal to him since he harbored some unjustified resentment toward Rick who in his happy-go-lucky manner had survived the situation unscathed just because he was the stereotypical all-American boy.

Jahmir had enough self-awareness to know that he was bitter, confused, and needed advice. He thought of his father. But the old man was a dry cleaner and had no understanding of Jahmir's work. Similarly, it would be of no value to discuss this with his sister Sara, with whom he was very close, but she was a fashion designer and thought that the sole purpose of computers was to gossip with her friends using social media. Jahmir also felt that a trip to New York to visit his family would unnecessarily delay a decision that he felt needed to be made quickly. Normally he would have discussed his decision with Rick, but he didn't feel that Rick could give him honest advice since he had survived the security purge.

This left Kelly Jaffari, the girl with whom he had been living and to whom he was now engaged. He was reluctant to discuss his problems with her because he was afraid she would be upset and might want to postpone their planned wedding. Kelly's one great fault was her insecurity, brought about from her childhood in Syria, where no one could be certain of their future well-being. But Jahmir had little choice. Kelly was soon going to be his wife, and he owed it to her to discuss the future direction of his career. Kelly was also a JCN employee of Middle Eastern extraction and would understand his situation better than anyone else, other than Rick.

Jahmir spent a long afternoon reflecting on his options and reviewing the information Marylou had provided regarding the new projects to which he could be assigned. He also spent some of this time trying to decide how he would break the news to Kelly.

***

Kelly was an outgoing and energetic young lady. Like Jahmir, she had immigrated to the United States with her family, settling in the suburbs of Baltimore, Maryland. Unlike Jahmir, her father had been a wealthy banker in Syria before the instability created by the Arab Spring of 2014 had forced them to leave. The family watched with horror as the Syrian economy and society collapsed. They followed the news closely, watching for information about their friends and relatives remaining in Syria. Email and telephone contacts were possible, but it was intermittent at best. Although some of the Jaffari relatives had come to the United States, many had resettled in other countries of the Middle East. The Jaffaris were a wealthy family, and their arrival was welcomed wherever they went. Kelly's father had been careful to invest his money in the banks of many countries throughout the world, as had many of their relatives, with the result that he was now living a comfortable life in the United States.

When she arrived at the JCN reception area to meet Jahmir for their daily ride home together, she was surprised to find him pacing impatiently. Usually she had to wait as he completed some aspect of his project in which he had become engrossed.

"What's wrong, James?"

Jahmir skipped his carefully rehearsed speech and immediately launched into an explanation of the events of the day. He concluded, "So I've had a rather bad day. I've lost my baby. Now I know how women feel who have had a miscarriage. In this case, however, it's a miscarriage of justice. As I look at it, my career is over. I almost wonder if this isn't a subtle form of discrimination against Muslims."

Kelly's mind was racing. How would this affect the personality of her sensitive and brilliant fiancé? What would it do to their future relationship? Would this affect their wedding plans? What about the suspicion of discrimination? She wisely avoided mentioning any impact that all of this would have on her life, and in fact kept her reply neutral. "Let's not discuss this standing in the JCN lobby. Why don't we go home, have a glass of wine, and continue our discussion there?"

The trip home was quiet, with each of them immersed in their own thoughts. They entered their small apartment, threw their coats over the back of the sofa near the entrance, and poured two glasses of wine. Although both Kelly and Jahmir were practicing Muslims, they both drank alcohol in moderation.

As soon as they were comfortably seated in the apartment's living area, Kelly began. "So what do you plan to do?"

Jahmir replied, "I've spent all afternoon considering alternatives. None of them are very attractive. It may be that for the time being my best option would be to remain with JCN and work on another project. Marylou suggested that I apply for US citizenship with the goal of rejoining the MOM project in the future, but I think that would take forever, since I would also have to apply for the high-level security clearance."

Kelly replied thoughtfully, "Applying for citizenship might not be a bad idea."

"But applying for US citizenship would destroy my father."

"On the other hand, US citizenship would make it easier to travel internationally, and you could keep your Iraqi citizenship at the same time."

"Why would I want to do that?"

"You never know. Someday a foreign government might want to hire you as a computer consultant. A US citizenship might simplify foreign travel."

To Jahmir's surprise, Kelly then abruptly changed the subject. "James, have you considered the discussion we had at Rick's last night about possibly starting your own company?"

"I thought about it briefly, but it isn't practical. First, I doubt that Rick would want to join me since he's happily involved with MOM and JCN. Second, I'm not sure I want him to join me since he may be part of the anti-Muslim effort that is responsible for my current situation. Third, I have no practical business experience, and fourth, and probably most important, is that I would have no means of financial support and no customers. So it really isn't a reasonable alternative."

Kelly looked thoughtful, and then said, "I wasn't thinking that you would partner with Rick. In fact, for many reasons, you might do better on your own. Let me talk to my father about financial support and business advice. What would you say if we could work some of that out?"

For the first time since the morning, Jahmir felt a small ray of hope. But he also felt some trepidation at being alone, without any sources of advice regarding the many issues associated with the birth of a new company. He knew that starting a new company was a long shot and a difficult challenge. He needed to decide quickly in order to give Marylou an answer regarding his continuing employment with JCN. He didn't think he'd be able to postpone his answer for more than a week.

"So do you want me to talk to my father? I'll do it tonight if you give me the go-ahead."

"It can't hurt. But I can just imagine the challenge of talking to bankers about the concepts behind MOM and convincing them that it is a worthwhile investment."

"That might not be necessary. I've been telling Dad about your work in the most general terms, without violating any of the security restrictions. He has a vague idea of its potential."

"There's also another problem," said Jahmir. "We don't have any of the equipment or software that is currently locked down at JCN. I can't imagine sneaking in there and stealing this material."

Kelly replied, "That isn't quite true." James stared at her, waiting for an explanation.

"I've been backing up all our work, both yours and mine, on my personal PC in case JCN's much-vaunted computer systems go down. Remember the incident last year when we lost a month's work because of their computer problems? I wasn't prepared to take a chance of that happening again."

James was concerned. "Let me remind you that you that you are breaking federal laws and violating JCN policy. We could all be in a heap of trouble if anyone finds out."

"But no one will find out. Will they?" Kelly asked.

"But the challenge doesn't end there," replied Jahmir. "If your father is half the banker I think he is, I would expect him to ask me another question that I've been asking myself. Who would be my customer? Right now, even JCN only has a single customer, and that's DARPA."

"Don't worry about that," answered Kelly. "Without trying very hard, I can think of a dozen companies that would gladly pay for the capabilities that MOM offers. And we really should stop calling it MOM. We've got to differentiate between the JCN product and the product offered by your new company."

"One thing at a time. Before worrying about names, let's worry about the company."

"I'll call Dad now." Kelly seemed to have all the answers.

***

It was a beautiful Maryland spring day, and Kelly thoroughly enjoyed the one-hour drive from Silver Spring to the rolling countryside north of Baltimore. She opened the sunroof of her car as she left the interstate for the winding two-lane roads of Maryland's hunt country. As she turned into the gravel drive of her parents' two-story white colonial, Kelly admired the manicured lawn and landscaping. Her parents certainly had the good life here in Maryland. Recognizing the deteriorating situation in Syria, her father had sold all of their material possessions, including real estate and some extremely valuable antiques, and his foresight along with his considerable savings had ensured the good life in the United States. The white colonial sat on a four-acre tract in an upscale community. Although they had no interest in horses or any equine sports, the Jaffaris enjoyed watching fox hunts that took place in the hills beyond their property.

Kelly was always filled with a sense of peace as she approached the Jaffari residence. She was close with her parents and her younger sister, and was glad that they had found such a comfortable existence in Timonium and the Loch Raven Reservoir, near Baltimore.

As she exited her Kia SUV, Kelly was not surprised to see her father, Sami, standing at the open front door. He was always glad to see her, and was frequently shouting greetings to her before she left the car. "Kelly," he shouted, using the Arabic pronunciation that emphasized the last syllable of her name.

"Hi Baba," she answered, using the combination of Arabic and English that had been their conversational custom. She retrieved her attaché case out of the car, walked quickly up the brick front walk, and gave her father an affectionate hug.

"I see you're here on business," he said, eying the case as the two of them walked into the spacious front foyer of the house.

"Yes. As I told you on the phone, Jahmir has encountered a difficult situation at work that I wanted to discuss with you. Although he wanted to come with me, I thought it best if we discussed it alone."

Philip J. Tarnoff

"I agree," replied her father. "We have things to discuss that are best done in private."

"But business can wait. Come say hello to your mother and join me with a cup of good Syrian coffee. We still have more than an hour before lunch."

The formalities of coffee and some general gossip are never refused and are an essential preliminary for any Syrian business meeting. Kelly enjoyed these formalities, and readily accepted her father's invitation to join him and her mother, Lilliane, in the large, well-equipped kitchen, which overlooked the grounds to the rear of the house. Sami and Lilliane were a handsome, outgoing pair who were very popular with their neighbors. When he wasn't managing his many investments, Sami spent his time with his two great loves: gardening and beekeeping. The former had attracted him because the Maryland climate was more hospitable to plant life than that of Syria. Maryland's long, humid summer months permitted him to work with plants and vegetables that had been unknown to him in his former life. He also planted several fruit trees, including apples and peaches, and was delighted with their yield. The fruit trees particularly appealed to him because, along with his flowers and shrubs, they were a significant source of pollen for his bees, which in turn provided the honey used with many of the Syrian cakes and treats that Lilliane was fond of preparing.

Lilliane the artist had taken up watercolor painting along with her piano playing. She was an accomplished pianist, and the Jaffaris were convinced that Kelly's ability as a computer programmer was derived from Lilliane's musical talent. The two are closely connected, a fact that was discovered by IBM in the early days of the software industry before colleges offered computer science degrees.

Sami began the conversation when they were comfortably seated around the kitchen table with steaming demitasse cups of Arab coffee in front of them. "So Kelly, what's new in Silver Spring these days?"

"I'm afraid the news is not good—at least from Jahmir's perspective. As I've told you in the past, his project deals with a

130

new computer named MOM. JCN has decided that the project is critical to national security. They feel that its capabilities are so significant that they've given it the highest security classification. Only American citizens are allowed to work on the project. Jahmir never got his citizenship, and so he's off the project, which has been his baby for the past three years. As you can imagine, he's thoroughly bummed out about it."

"What is he going to do?"

"He doesn't know. He's considering all sorts of alternatives. One thing he's considering is getting his citizenship so that he can obtain the security clearance needed to return to work on the project. Another alternative he's considering is to start a new company that will reproduce the capabilities of MOM. Each of these alternatives has advantages and disadvantages. Right now, he's just depressed. I told him I'd discuss it with you."

Sami listened intently as Kelly spoke. "As I've told you in the past, I'll be more than happy to help. Let's have lunch and then go for a walk in the garden."

Lunch was a pleasant family affair, with discussion of relatives, the latest political situation in Syria, and most important—the health of the bees. Sami's bees had been unaffected by the colony collapse disorder (CCD) that had infected many hives throughout the United States, and he'd been able to collect several gallons of honey each season. The past winter had been cold and snowy, with the result that he was concerned about losing one of the weaker hives that had been short of honey stores. He had tried to save the hive by feeding it saturated sugar water, but his efforts seemed to have been in vain.

While Lilliane was clearing the lunch dishes, Sami said to Kelly, "Let's go for a walk."

They left the house enjoying a sunny Maryland spring day and followed one of the gravel paths Sami used to tend to his azaleas. As they walked he said to Kelly, "I'm never comfortable talking in the house. I don't want to involve your mother in my dealings. In Syria there was so much violence that all she craves is a peaceful retirement. The other reason to leave the house is that I worry about my conversations being monitored by American security forces. We can't give them any reason to suspect our loyalty to the United States. Kelly, be very careful about what you say, who you say it to, and where you say it. Now tell me about Jahmir and his project."

Kelly explained, "Without going into technical details, Jahmir and his ex-friend Rick were responsible for the development of a computer that is many times more powerful than any other computer currently in existence. The US government is concerned that a device with so much power can compromise all of the electronic systems in the country because it can potentially bypass all of the security protection they contain. Jahmir has been removed from the project because their highest security classifications require that all cleared personnel be US citizens."

Sami's cryptic reply: "Very interesting. What can I do to help Jahmir continue his work in a productive manner?"

Kelly had her answer ready. "Baba, I think it is in everyone's best interest for Jahmir to form his own company, independent from JCN. He is so bitter about his treatment by JCN that he would be miserable if he stayed. He is convinced that he is being discriminated against, which may not be true, but it influences his feelings. With his own company he can pursue areas of interest to his customers and his investors." This latter was not lost on Sami.

After a brief pause, Kelly continued. "So assuming you are in agreement so far, I think Jahmir needs some things that you might be able to provide: money, customers, and advice."

In spite of his interest in the subject, Sami could not help laughing. "That's all anyone starting a company needs. Fortunately for Jahmir, I may be able to provide all three. But depending on his needs, I may have to go outside the family. What are his needs and how does he feel about the Muslim conflicts occurring in the Middle East?"

Although she had not discussed the subject with Jahmir, Kelly had enough knowledge of business to be able to provide a credible answer. "Well, we've made some preliminary estimates," she said, lying, "and they are something like this. He'll need enough cash to survive for at least a year. That would include salary for himself, equipment, and rent for office and lab space. Assuming each of these is around one hundred thousand dollars, he would need three hundred thousand to keep him going for the first year."

Kelly then switched to the subject of customers. "I wish that it was as easy to define his possible customers as it is to estimate the money he needs. Assuming he can re-create the computer system known as MOM, potential customers are anyone who needs incredible computer processing power. This could mean organizations, such as weather forecasters and medical researchers, and possibly foreign powers." She said the words *foreign powers* with her voice rising, making it sound more like a question than part of the rest of the sentence.

Sami was fascinated. "Do you suppose it could help with oil exploration?" he asked innocently.

"I suppose. I could see how you could use it to help map underground rock formations."

Returning to the subject of funds, Sami said, "I think your estimate of the needed funding is quite low. First of all, I imagine he'll need additional help. One, possibly two additional staff, one of whom could be you. Second, I doubt that he'll be self-supporting in less than three years. If I use your basic financial estimates, he would need somewhere between one and two million dollars. I could afford to provide this amount of money, but would rather not risk that much money. I think it would be prudent for me to find some additional investors to share the risk."

Kelly nodded as her Baba spoke. His knowledge of business finances far exceeded her limited knowledge, and she was, after all, asking him for a high-risk investment.

Sami continued. "Then there is the matter of customers. As you know, my Syrian friends are interested in oil exploration. Maybe Jahmir could write a proposal that describes how MOM could be used to help the exploration problem. That would be the good side of MOM. Perhaps his proposal could also describe the bad side of MOM, so we could understand her full potential for both good and evil. I think this type of information could be quite useful when I speak with other investors."

Kelly wondered how Jahmir would develop the expertise to write a proposal about oil exploration and evil applications quickly enough for her father. "How soon would you need this information?" she asked.

"It depends how quickly Jahmir would like to get started with his new business. I can begin talking to investors before he gets me the proposal, but I should have a polished document from him within the month."

A month sounded like an eternity to Kelly, but she quickly agreed, realizing it would be a busy month for both of them.

The remainder of Kelly's visit was filled with small talk about relatives, including her brother, who had turned out to be the classical prodigal son, wandering around the United States playing with rock bands. They also discussed the general situation in the Middle East and agreed that they were undecided about its future. She stayed for another hour before returning to Jahmir in their Silver Spring apartment.

***

Immediately following Kelly's departure, Sami told his wife that he had some pressing work to do, and that he shouldn't be bothered for a little while. Lilliane, who had been taught obedience from birth, nodded without question and continued her preparations for dinner.

Sami did not trouble himself with the details of communicating with his business associates in the Middle East and elsewhere. He only knew that most Arab immigrants to the United States were watched carefully by the various American security agencies. As a result, any communications containing confidential information had to be handled with the utmost care. Arrangements had been made for him to give any confidential messages to the maid who cleaned their house every Thursday. When the messages couldn't wait until Thursday, the Jaffaris were to arrange a dinner party with the need to have the house cleaned immediately prior to the guests' arrival. Having spoken with Kelly on a Wednesday, Sami decided to maintain the regular schedule. Too many changes were likely to raise suspicion about a sudden jump in activities. Sami neither knew nor cared how messages were delivered. He only knew that it was a tedious and dangerous process, and that frequent delays and interruptions in service were experienced.

His objective was to compose a letter to his contacts in Syria that would persuade them of the magnitude of the opportunity represented by Jahmir and his new computer. Without their support, it was unlikely that he would be able to provide the funding and business contacts needed for Jahmir's success. He thought for a while, and then began his letter, hoping that a response would be received without undue delay. Unknown to Sami was the fact that Syria was only a transfer point for the letters. Their actual destination was Jakarta, Indonesia.

Now all that Sami, Kelly, and Jahmir could do was to wait for a reply from Sami's friends in the Middle East and elsewhere.

CHAPTER 12
THE WAITING GAME

Jahmir wasn't home when Kelly arrived at the apartment. She was disappointed, since she was looking forward to sharing her tentatively good news with him. She paced for a few minutes before deciding that it couldn't wait. Her cellphone call was answered after two rings by Jahmir, who sounded depressed.

"I was hoping you'd be home. Where are you?"

"I got tired of hanging around the apartment and decided to go into work. I guess I can't break old habits. I ended up having a long conversation with Marylou, who apparently has spent a lot of time trying to find another project for me. I didn't come away with the feeling that she had succeeded."

"Well I had a good meeting with my father. I'll share the results when you get home. How long will you be?"

"I was just getting ready to leave when you called. Should be home in less than a half hour."

"Fine. I'll see you soon. Love you."

Jahmir was good to his word, and walked in the door twenty minutes later. After a brief kiss, he threw his light jacket over the back of the couch, poured himself a Coke, and sat down.

"So tell me about the meeting with your father."

"It was great. He understands the potential of your project, which we are no longer calling MOM, and realizes that you need a lot of money and customers in order to strike out on your own."

"Did he ask for any technical details about the computer?"

Kelly just laughed. "My father is smart enough to know what he doesn't know. He took my word for its potential. However, he did ask for a short proposal describing both the potential good uses and evil uses of which MOM is capable. He was particularly interested in its benefits for oil exploration. I think you could put together a proposal using general descriptions of its capabilities in a few hours."

"Did you discuss money? If so, how much did you ask for?"

"In the car on the trip to their place in Timonium I did a rough mental calculation. I decided that we'd need a hundred thousand for your salary, which I know is a pay cut, but we're dealing with round numbers here, a hundred thousand for office and lab space, and a hundred thousand for equipment. So I told him we'd need three hundred thousand for the first year. He told me that my numbers were way too low and that we'd need at least one million for the first year, and we should plan to need funding for at least three years. I didn't argue."

Jahmir was bowled over. "Three million is a lot of money. I wonder what he expects in return."

Kelly had a ready answer. "I'm sure he expects a financial return on his investment. Perhaps someday you'd sell the company for a lot more money than three million. That's what bankers do. They invest money in growth opportunities with the hope that every dollar they invest returns many additional dollars."

Jahmir did not react, but asked, "What about customers? Did he ask who would be likely to pay for my services?"

"That's why he asked you for a proposal describing MOM's potential applications. He would use that to entice his contacts, some of whom could become customers," Kelly replied. "He thought there was a market for the new computer in Europe or the Middle East. Beyond that he was cryptic. He also thought you needed a new name for your computer. At the risk of appearing to take charge, he thought you should call it Qalb."

Jahmir was puzzled. "But Qalb means heart in Arabic. How does that relate to my computer?"

Kelly laughed. "If you were more familiar with the Koran you would know that Qalb also means intelligence. It intermixes the two terms. For example, when Allah says that *they have hearts wherewith they understand not*, the concept of heart is being interchanged with intelligence. In our, or should I say your religion, it is a common merging of the two concepts. My father was very clever to choose Qalb as the name for your computer."

"With all due respect to your father, his inclination is toward the Old World. If we're going to do well here in the West, we need to adapt. How about a name like Eastern Star? That should be less threatening to prospective Western customers."

Kelly sensed that they were at an impasse. In order to avoid an argument, she answered, "Right now we're arguing over hypotheticals. Let's wait until we have a company and some customers. Why don't we use the initials of our first names as the name of the company? How about JK Computing?"

"At last something we can agree on. JK Computing it is. It's odd that every place we work has a name made up of initials beginning with the letter J. Perhaps that's a good omen. Now that we have a name, all we need to do is turn it into a company. Is your father's attorney available to help us with the bureaucratic details?"

***

The following week passed slowly despite the fact that Jahmir had the dual responsibilities of pretending to be interested in JCN's projects while he was writing a proposal and giving birth to their new baby—JK Computing. The birthing included a series of mundane tasks, such as incorporation, establishing tax ID numbers, and finding office space, tasks which consumed Jahmir's spare time and patience. Kelly undertook the responsibility of enrolling in a health insurance plan and identifying inexpensive sources of used office furniture. They had decided it would be impractical to work out of their apartment because of its lack of space. By the end of the week they were well on their way to becoming a real company, although one without customers.

The proposal prepared by Jahmir described the manner in which MOM, aka QALB, aka Eastern Star, could be used for both good and evil. It was an easy task involving a brief introduction that compared the new processor's similarity to the human brain, followed by the descriptions of good and evil. The good applications featured oil exploration and weather forecasting. The evil applications described the manner in which a powerful computer could gain access to protected computer systems by rapidly bypassing passwords and firewall protection.

Throughout the week, Jahmir worried about their possibilities of success and whether all his work would produce any results.

Exactly seven days following Kelly's visit to her Baba, he called to tell her that he had been successful in his efforts to locate financing for their new company. He had uncovered at least one interested individual who was willing to invest, subject to a review of Jahmir's proposal. But Sami said that it came with strings, and that it would be extremely important to meet with Kelly and Jahmir before proceeding any further. He reminded them that the need for the proposal was now urgent. Kelly immediately agreed to deliver the proposal without even consulting Jahmir.

The next day found Kelly and Jahmir heading for Timonium to visit the Jaffaris. It was agreed that Kelly would drive her car because she knew the way and because her Kia had less mileage than Jahmir's beat-up Toyota Camry, which was approaching the end of its useful life. Although it was a beautiful day for a drive through the rural horse country north of Baltimore, it was all lost on Jahmir, who was worried about the upcoming meeting.

"What do you suppose Sami wants?" he asked Kelly.

"I'm sure he just wants to be comfortable with the investment he's about to make in your enterprise. After all, three million is a lot of money. You can't blame him for trying to understand how you intend to use it."

Mollified, Jahmir lapsed into silence for the rest of the drive.

Once again, Sami greeted them warmly as they drove up the curved driveway. He gave Kelly a big hug and formally shook Jahmir's hand.

"Come in. Come in. Lilliane has been expecting you. She's spent the morning preparing lunch."

Jahmir fervently wished that they would skip lunch. He was so nervous about the meeting that he had no appetite and was anxious to get down to business. However, he understood that Syrian hospitality demanded guests be made comfortable before any discussions could commence.

Lunch passed painlessly with heaping plates of lamb kebab and sides of brown rice and salad followed by baklava for dessert. Lilliane had felt it her duty to know her future son-in-law and had carefully studied Jahmir's habits, including his dietary preferences. Thus it was no surprise that lunch featured his favorite foods. Conversation was innocuous, mostly focusing on Kelly's activities and touching on world events, with particular attention being paid to the plight of the Syrian refugees.

At last the meal ended, with Jahmir and Sami retiring to the library, while Kelly helped her mother clear the table and wash the dishes. Although this was the traditional manner in which Syrians conducted business, Kelly would not normally have allowed herself to be excluded, except that this time she knew the agenda and felt that the meeting would go more smoothly if she weren't there. Furthermore, she welcomed the opportunity to spend some time with her mother discussing subjects of common interest, such as clothing and the possibility of a future wedding.

Sami began the conversation by asking Jahmir if he'd like something to drink. Jahmir shook his head, with his demeanor making it clear that he wished Sami would get to the point.

"Jahmir, I know you're impatient to find out about the funding I have located, but I will not give you the details until we are in agreement on certain points."

"What points?" responded Jahmir, barely able to contain himself.

"What are your feelings regarding the various conflicts in the Mideast?"

Jahmir paused to collect his thoughts before answering. "I haven't given it much thought. I may be an Arab Muslim, but

I'm also a scientist. I guess now that I think about it, my treatment at JCN is probably the result of this unfortunate combination of characteristics."

"There is probably some truth to what you say, but you haven't answered my question. You must have feelings on this important subject."

Jahmir hesitated. Finally, he answered. "The situation is so complicated that it defies forming a single opinion. The only way to answer your question is country by country. So why don't I start with the two countries that we both know best. As an Iraqi, I deeply resent the American policies toward my country, which have essentially destroyed the land that my family knew. We have despaired of ever returning. You must feel the same about Syria, where the situation is even worse. Here again, most of the problems being experienced can be traced back to the United States, which encouraged the overthrow of the existing government and then failed to support the rebels. Then ISIS emerged to take advantage of the chaos."

"That's not a bad summary" Sami said. "You mentioned ISIS. How do you feel about them?"

"I used to feel that they were a barbarian horde," Jahmir said. "But the more I read about their goals and activities, the more I begin to understand them. I've also done some reading about the behavior of the British Empire during the past several centuries and have discovered that their methods were at least as brutal as those of ISIS. This has put the ISIS culture into perspective for me."

"But understanding and approving are two different things. Do you approve of the organization?"

Jahmir was puzzled. "Where are we going with this? Why do you care how I feel about ISIS?"

"I'm not about to ask you to deal with ISIS, but they are partners with one of your biggest potential customers. I can't introduce you to them unless you are in full support of their objectives. And let me emphasize that if you have any doubts, you must tell me. While doubts will kill the deal, as you say in the United States, I will still respect you and support your relationship with Kelly. There are probably other customers for you in this world, but none as well financed as the one we are discussing."

Jahmir found the palms of his hands sweating. He felt as if he was on dangerous ground. He realized that Sami was asking him for an absolute commitment to the ISIS cause. While he felt that he might possibly be able to make the commitment, he recognized the finality of the decision and hesitated to give Sami the commitment he was looking for. So he asked, "How soon do you need an answer?"

"The sooner the better, but I don't need an answer today. Do you want to schedule another meeting here in a few days to discuss your decision?"

"That would be great," Jahmir said.

Sami then suggested an approach that had been on his mind. "I will ask you to look at the websites on the list I will give you. They will help you make up your mind."

Jahmir had read the reports of the proselytizing of American youth by ISIS and was not anxious to become the victim of their propaganda. "I've read articles about the effectiveness of the ISIS websites, which are designed to attract disaffected American teenagers. I'm not an American teenager, although I will admit that I am somewhat disaffected by my treatment at JCN."

"Exactly!" Sami said enthusiastically. "If you analyze the material that I suggest you read, you will see that they make three important points." Using his fingers to emphasize the three points, Sami then recited them to Jahmir.

Raising the first finger of his right hand, Sami tapped it with his left hand. "First, except for Kelly, all your friends are no longer with you. Your social life existed with your coworkers at JCN. If you leave JCN, you leave your social life. Everyone needs a group of like-minded people for their support. A group with which ideas can be exchanged, and a group which ideally thinks about things in the same way you do."

Raising his second finger, Sami again tapped it with his left hand. "Second, you are not the only Muslim to be persecuted for his religion. Muslims throughout the world are experiencing similar persecution. For example, there are some in the United States who are convinced that there are secret Muslim training camps from which we will all emerge to take over the world. ISIS and its partners are ensuring that the persecution stops and that Muslims are treated with the respect they deserve. When ISIS achieves its goals, the persecution will be replaced with respect."

Raising his third finger, Sami continued. "Third, as a Sunni Muslim, you have an obligation to support them in their quest to establish a worldwide caliphate that will ensure we are united in the single purpose of worshipping Allah. I am not aware of the strength of your religious beliefs, but a worldwide caliphate will ensure prosperity for all Muslims, both on earth and in heaven."

Jahmir was overwhelmed by the strength of Sami's convictions as well as their persuasive nature. For a minute he was tempted to accept Sami's offer at the conclusion of his monolog. But he reined in his emotions. "You bring up some excellent points. While I am certainly inclined to agree with them, I would still like a few days to think it over. I promise I will look at the websites during that period."

Sami smiled. "You have promised all that I can ask. Let's get together in three days to continue our discussion. If all is well, perhaps we can finalize our arrangements at that time. Oh, and one more thing, I think I have found a talented computer engineer to help you at your company."

The two men shook hands cordially. After some polite words, Jahmir and Kelly departed for Silver Spring.

In the car on the way home, Kelly asked, "Well how did it go?"

"Did you know that our customer would be an associate of ISIS?" Jahmir replied, answering her question with a question.

"I didn't know who he had in mind. But I do know that he has some ties with organizations that the FBI might consider undesirable."

"More than undesirable, they're terrorist organizations. I wonder if the FBI has your father under surveillance. If they do, and they discover my relationship with him, my chances for a security clearance are dead."

"You're not thinking clearly," Kelly answered. "The United States doesn't seem all that interested in the technology you developed for them. My father's associates are very interested and are willing to pay you significant amounts of money. In addition, their long-term objectives are religious. All they want to do is to establish a caliphate to organize and promote the Muslim religion. They do not intend to use your device for military purposes, such as destroying Syria and many other countries of the Middle East."

"You raise good points. Let me look at the websites recommended by your father, and then we can continue the discussions with him in three days."

Kelly nodded, concluding the discussion. "Just don't take more than three days to make up your mind. The longer we wait, the more complicated your departure from JCN becomes.

***

The three days passed rapidly. Jahmir's time was spent in feigned interest with his work at JCN, continuing the planning for JK Computing, and reflecting on his goals in life generally. He dutifully reviewed the websites that Sami had recommended and found them to be eloquent presentations of the case for ISIS. In fact, the websites helped him accept ISIS recruitment as he thought about the injustices of the American system and his desires for a peaceful existence in which he could pursue his first love, the development of new computer architectures. After reflecting on the online information and his incomplete knowledge of Islam, he decided that the true path to world peace would be the existence of a strong caliphate that could counter the unnatural strength of Western civilization.

***

And so once again, Jahmir and Kelly were riding to Timonium in the Kia. After receiving the same warm greeting and ample luncheon, the men retired to Sami's study. Sami was anxious to learn of Jahmir's decision. Without offering the obligatory cup of coffee, he asked, "Have you made up your mind?"

This time Jahmir responded without hesitation. "Yes, I have, and I would like to work with your organization."

As much as he had hoped for Jahmir's response, Sami felt obliged to challenge his sincerity. "Now you realize that this decision makes you a potential enemy of the United States. The Americans will try to ferret you out, and if they succeed, you could end up in jail. You must be certain of your decision before we proceed."

Jahmir had thought of these possibilities. "I would still like to go ahead. But I hope that you can provide me with the assistance that I might need to escape detection."

Sami's response was unexpected. "I have been considering this problem for some time. After all, I desire your safety almost as much as you do, since my daughter is involved. I have come to the conclusion that the safest path would be for you to conduct your research outside of the United States, in a safe country. Knowing that this is a possibility would mean that both of you would have to leave your native country and your family for an extended period of time. Does this change your decision?"

"I guess it depends on the country," Jahmir said after a pause. "I would rather not subject Kelly to the living conditions of a third-world country, and I would need some basic resources to complete my work. It would not be productive for me to live and work in a country constantly beset by warring factions."

Sami acted insulted. "Do you really think I would want my daughter to return to the conditions I left in Syria? Of course I took these things into consideration."

"I'm sorry. I didn't mean to imply that you would not worry about Kelly. But I felt that it was important to say these things."

"Apology accepted. Now let me tell you what I would suggest. How about using Kuwait as your base of operations? Kuwait City is a sophisticated urban environment. It's a stable society, with an advanced IT infrastructure. I have been there. You would like it. As a side benefit, the city has an active nightlife." Then Sami added, as if it was an afterthought, "In addition, the airport in Kuwait has good connections to cities throughout the world."

Jahmir thought about Sami's suggestion for several minutes before replying. "Let me discuss this with Kelly. Do you know if she's ever been to Kuwait?"

With that, the meeting temporarily broke up while Jahmir went to speak with Kelly, who had never been to Kuwait but was anxious to give it a try. After a brief conference, their meeting reconvened, this time the women were included.

"Well, what do you two think?" Sami asked.

This time Kelly answered. "I think Kuwait would be a wonderful place to live. I've heard generally good things about it. Baba, do you have contacts there that could help us get settled?"

"Don't worry. I'll do everything in my power to help you."

And with that the agreement was sealed.

That evening Kelly asked Jahmir to drive them home from Timonium. While they were driving on the relatively rural roads near the Jaffari home, Jahmir reflected on their conversation about the possible interest of the FBI in their plans. As he drove he noticed a set of headlights that seemed to be following them. *I must be paranoid as a result of my conversation with Sami*, thought Jahmir. But, just to be certain, he told Kelly of his concern and then turned into a randomly selected side street leading into a community of upscale homes. When he turned, the headlights behind him turned also. He wound through the suburban development making random turns, each of which were followed by the headlights behind them. Now they were both worried and somewhat scared.

Jahmir suddenly turned and accelerated up a side street so that the car following them missed the turn and had to back up. With that, Jahmir made an immediate left turn up a second nearby side street, pulled into the driveway of a residence, and turned off their lights. They slid down in their seats and watched the following vehicle drive past. They both breathed a sigh of relief.

Kelly's cellphone rang a few minutes after they had lost their pursuers. She answered to find herself talking to her Baba.

"Why did you flee from my guards?" he asked.

"What do you mean? Were those your men that were following us?"

"Yes, they were. I've been trying to protect you."

"I appreciate your help, but it would have been helpful if you had told me," was her sarcastic reply. "You scared us half to death."

"I'm sorry. I was only trying to help. They will station themselves outside your apartment for the remainder of your stay in Silver Spring."

***

Within the short space of a month, Kelly and Jahmir were able to resign their positions at JCN, dispose of their meager possessions, and prepare for the move to Kuwait. The most complex aspect of their trip was the need to assume new identities that would prevent US authorities from tracing their movements. Both Kelly and Jamir had taken Sami's warning to heart that the FBI would frown on their use of American technology to support the cause of an enemy. The one thing they were both certain of was that the technology in their possession would be considered a threat to US security if it were placed in the hands of their Middle Eastern partners. As a result, they both assumed new names and, with Sami's assistance, obtained counterfeit passports, driver's licenses, birth certificates, and airline tickets that gave no hint of their real identities. Jahmir became James, or Jim Andrews, and Kelly became Mrs. Karen Andrews, James' wife. Everyone laughed at the pseudo marriage that had been created between Jim and Karen, except for Lilliane, who felt that her plans for an elaborate wedding for her daughter were being hijacked. She was particularly upset by the wedding bands and engagement ring that Sami had obtained for the two of them to wear. Unfortunately, she was not able to come up with a better arrangement, and so Jim and Karen became a married couple. It was agreed that once they left the United States, these would become the names by which everyone referred to them.

Philip J. Tarnoff

Sami also felt it would be important for them to develop rudimentary disguises. As he pointed out, all airports are blanketed by security cameras that record the comings and goings of airline passengers. It would be easy for the FBI to check the videos produced by these cameras in order to identify the departure of wanted individuals. The false identification papers would not offer complete protection. So Jahmir, aka Jim, grew a mustache and beard and purchased a set of horn-rimmed glasses. He also let his hair grow so that it fell over his shirt collar. Kelly, aka Karen, began wearing a hajib, much to the approval of her mother. This, combined with a pair of contact lenses that changed her eye color and a new hair style that changed her shoulder-length hair to a page boy hairstyle with bangs, provided the needed change to her looks. They both agreed to change their style of dress from its current preppy look to that of a well-dressed businessman and his wife for the upcoming trip.

Finally there was the question of JK Computing, the new company they had established as an alternative to JCN. It was agreed that JK Computing would continue to exist in rental office space located in Columbia, Maryland. A convenient location in that the driving times from Silver Spring and Timonium to Columbia were about equal. The office would be furnished with the used furnishings located by Kelly. It would have a mail slot for mail deliveries, a telephone and answering machine, and an inexpensive copier. The office would be checked twice a week by one of the Jaffaris, the maid, or their security team, who would pick up the mail and remove messages from the answering machine. In the event that an important message arrived that exceeded the ability of the Jaffaris to respond, it would be sent in encrypted form through multiple servers to James and Karen in Kuwait City.

Sami had thoughtfully booked an Emirates airline first class ticket for the two of them on a fourteen-hour flight with a brief stop at Dubai's new $4.5 billion modern terminal. Karen wished she had a longer layover for some shopping, but recognized the urgency of their arrival in Kuwait. Sami had also arranged for temporary accommodations at the Sheraton Kuwait, which had

148

two favorable attributes: it was located near the city's business centers and featured a sumptuous evening buffet. Because of the Sheraton's amenities, they had to resist the temptation of extending their stay to enjoy its luxuries.

With an abundance of caution, Sami made all of the arrangements necessary for Kelly and Jahmir's change of identities and travel through the same security company that had provided the guards. The president of this company was an old friend of his from Syria and had ways of performing the needed tasks without detection by US law enforcement agencies.

Jim and Karen were able to locate a townhouse large enough to serve as both living and office space. Living at the office would eliminate the need to spend time commuting and reduce their exposure to anyone that might be looking for them. It also eliminated the need to purchase a car and deal with the associated hazards of driving in the chaotic Kuwaiti traffic. Their new apartment was located on a quiet street lined with palm trees. None of the houses had garages, with the result that residents who owned cars were forced to park on the street. All of the townhouses were identical white two- and three-story buildings with a tile roofs. Jim and Karen were relieved to learn that their neighbors generally kept to themselves and exhibited little interest in the new tenants. In short, with the arrangements they had made, Karen and Jim became all but invisible residents of Kuwait City.

When they were settled in their new quarters, Karen took charge of furnishing their living quarters, lab, and office space. Jim assumed the responsibility for purchasing computer equipment, shopping at multiple office supply and computer stores to avoid revealing the extent of their technology purchases. He spent many evenings modifying the equipment they had purchased to duplicate the configuration and capabilities of MOM within their new system, now known as Qalb. As he worked, he wondered about his previous associates at JCN. He was curious to know whether the latest version of MOM was advancing in the manner that had been discussed when he was still part of the project.

Within a short time after they were settled, Karen received an encrypted email from her father asking how they were doing and proposing the addition of another expert to the Qalb team. He emphasized that his partners were most interested in seeing a rapid return on their investment, and wondered whether additions to their staff would speed up their progress. Jim replied, indicating that another person would be a big help if that person was adequately qualified to provide the needed assistance and equally committed to their cause. True to Sami's personality, the next message indicated that the needed assistance would be arriving the following week and provided the time and flight number of his arrival. Jim was curious that the flight on which the new member was arriving originated in Cairo. Sami had also indicated that the name of their new assistant was Hasan Jouda. His message was accompanied by a resume containing Hasan's background. He was Palestinian and had received his bachelor of science degree from Alexandria University, in Egypt. Jim was excited to learn that Hasan's specialty was computer hardware engineering, which complemented Jim's software expertise. If Hasan was as good as Sami claimed, they would make an effective team.

***

Two days later, Jim rented a car using his false ID and made the ten-mile drive to Farwaniyah, the location of the modern Kuwait International Airport. He immediately spotted Hasan entering the terminal, identifying him as the only computer nerd among the deplaning passengers. Hasan was dressed as he had been in Jakarta, wearing the Dockers slacks and sport shirt that made him look as if he were a new college graduate.

Because of their common interests, the two bonded immediately, and Jim was elated to welcome Hasan to their apartment and JK Computing. During the drive, they quickly abandoned any security concerns they might have had. Jim summarized his experience with JCN and described his work on MOM, which he referred to as Qalb during their conversation. He summarized

Qalb's capabilities as well as he could without a blackboard or pencil and paper. On his part, Hasan told of his life in Gaza and his work for Hamas. He described the guidance system he had developed for the Suquur missile along with his plans for future developments. The two computer scientists had thoroughly bonded by the time Jim pulled up in front of their apartment.

Jim marveled at Sami's ability to provide him with a technical assistant who precisely met his needs. As Sami had hoped, Hasan proved an invaluable asset that permitted Jim to rapidly recreate the laboratory facilities he had at JCN. Qalb was operational within a month from Hasan's arrival. With oil exploration long forgotten, the three computer scientists then began the development of applications capable of breaking the security codes and cyphers of the world's most sophisticated organizations. Jim had predicted that the development would be completed in less than a year, and it appeared that they would be able to meet that schedule.

Jim was becoming convinced that with Hasan's assistance, he could change the world.

BOOK 3
THE EMPIRE'S AWAKENING

The result (of Roman conquests) was a strange duality in Roman culture under the empire. On one side, for three centuries legions marched, roads were built, and new provinces were conquered and plundered. Triumphs were celebrated, emperors were deified and great temples were consecrated in their memory. Great monuments like the Colosseum and the Circus Maximus rose on the Roman skyline as the empire's citizens enjoyed an unparalleled prosperity and splendor. Yet Rome's finest minds and spirits found it all empty and meaningless, even a sign of approaching doom.

From Arthur Herman's, *The Cave and the Light: Plato Versus Aristotle, and the Struggle for the Soul of Western Civilization*, p.134.

CHAPTER 13

A STAR IS BORN

He was born on Christmas day in the small town of Wimberely, Texas. His proud and religious parents, Glenn and Marylou Jeffers, immediately named their new baby and first child Christopher, carrier of Christ, in recognition of the propitious date of his birth.

Wimberely is the quintessential Texas small town. Located in the beautiful Texas hill country between San Antonio and Austin, the small town of fewer than 5,000 people is best known for the artisans who operate various arts and crafts shops in town. It is also known for the frequent flooding it experiences from Cyprus Creek, which flows through the town.

Glenn and Marylou were active members of the First Baptist Church, which they regularly attended and enthusiastically supported. The church was housed in a modern facility on a small campus located ten minutes from downtown Wimberely. Marylou was a soprano in the church choir, and Glenn taught Sunday school and actively evangelized the First Baptist religion, encouraging his friends and neighbors to join him in worship.

So Glenn and Marylou were the pillars of their community. Glenn was an attorney and, like many of his counterparts in similar Texas communities, his practice included a mix of divorce cases, property claims, and service delivery disputes. With his persuasive personality, he prided himself in his ability to negotiate agreements between litigants with apparently insolvable disputes.

Marylou was the principal of the Wimberely High School Texans. In that role she enforced a strict code of behavior that was surprisingly appreciated by both the students and their parents. Her take-no-prisoners approach to administering her school was an important policy in a town with limited opportunities for extracurricular activities, other than those available in the varied program of outside activities offered by the high school.

As a member of a successful family with educated and intelligent parents, and a close association with an evangelical church, it was not surprising that Christopher was a popular leader in his class. He was a well-rounded student with excellent grades who was also a star on the Texans track-and-field team. He was class president during his senior year and graduated as his school's valedictorian. The combination of outstanding grades and impressive extracurricular activities ensured that he would be courted by many of the country's most prestigious universities.

After a long debate at the family dinner table, it was decided that he would forgo offers received from Harvard, Yale, and other Ivy League universities and attend Texas A&M University in College Station, Texas. There were many reasons for this decision, not the least of which were the full scholarship being offered and the fact that the chosen university was located in the State of Texas. The Jeffers were philosophically and politically a right-wing conservative family, and Chris felt that he would be more comfortable as a Texas student rather than having a frustrating association with a bunch of liberal Easterners.

At A&M, Chris thoroughly enjoyed classes associated with his political science major and, unlike many of his fellow students, relished many of the required courses. He was particularly interested in studies that included discussions of the US Constitution as well as those that covered the evolution of various forms of government, including the Greek, Roman, and Western civilization thinking on the subject. It interested him that many of these civilizations had experienced various combinations of hereditary-based and democratic governments. One of Chris's observations during these studies was that none of these governments appeared to have lasting power. At some point change was typically imposed on the government, either by internal decay or external invaders.

But the most satisfying experience for Chris at A&M was the evening he met Melissa on a blind date. Melissa, who was one year behind Chris, was also enrolled as a political science major. The two immediately discovered many common interests as well as compatible conservative political philosophies. After Melissa's graduation from A&M, they were married in a large wedding in Melissa's home town of Irving, Texas, a suburb northwest of Dallas. They then led a hand-to-mouth existence in College Station, where Melissa worked in the A&M library while Chris pursued his law degree at the A&M School of Law, passing the bar exam at a youthful twenty-five years of age.

***

Following graduation, Chris's career began as an assistant district attorney in the governor's office in Austin, the Texas capital. Although he was well-qualified for the work, his father was able to guarantee his selection for the position as a result of his relationship with the state legislator that represented the Wimberely district. Chris and Melissa were delighted with the job, since Austin was within a fifty-minute drive of the elder Jeffers' home. As a result, they enjoyed many Sunday evening dinners in Wimberely.

The General Counsel's Office of Texas provided legal advice to the governor and his staff in connection with a broad range of issues associated with governing the second largest state in the United States. During his first year in the office, Chris was given a number of mundane assignments associated with relatively minor initiatives, such as child care legislation and employee benefits. In spite of the low priority of these assignments, his reports were quickly identified as being thoroughly studied and well written. The quality of his work led to assignments of more significant legal matters faced by the state, which were of direct political concern to the governor. His duties led to a parallel assignment as the governor's speech writer and subsequently a high-level position on the governor's campaign team.

Philip J. Tarnoff

Within a short few years, Chris had acquired experience with state-level politics, as well as knowledge of the important elements of the election process. It was a short step from the governor's office to his own campaign for public office on the national stage. The obvious choice for a thirty-five-year-old aspiring politician would have been to compete for election to the US House of Representatives. The Jeffers family was well known in the Austin congressional election district, a consideration that would have simplified his run for an office with a geographically constrained constituency. But Chris was anxious to assume a role in Washington where he could make a significant difference. Along with his friends within the state capital and the congregation of the Wimberely First Baptist Church, he had developed a dislike of the liberal policies that seemed to dominate Washington, DC politics.

While the influence of a member of the House of Representatives might be considerable, the impact of a US Senator can be even greater. The retirement announcement of one of Texas's two senators led Chris to believe that he might actually bypass a career in the House of Representatives and campaign for a seat in the upper chamber of Congress, the US Senate. So against the advice of his parents and the governor, Chris proceeded with his campaign for a seat in the Senate. Melissa was an enthusiastic supporter, encouraging his decision, and actively participating in his campaign. With her blond good looks and bubbly personality, she quickly won over the ruling clique of the Republican Party, whose support was essential to a successful election campaign.

After a grueling campaign, much of which required meeting with potential financial supporters as well as fending off the criticisms of competitors, Chris achieved his dream of a seat in the US Senate. It was a close race, but Texans found his consistently conservative positions on national defense, immigration, marriage, and government regulation to be closely aligned with their own views. He readily overcame the disadvantages of his youth and inexperience with his charisma, winning ways, and attractive wife.

***

158

The US Senate was a learning experience for Chris. One of the challenges faced by all new entrants to that exclusive club was being selected for assignment to one of the more desirable of the Senate's twenty standing committees. Chris's class included fifteen new freshmen senators. All of them had targeted the Armed Services and the Budget Committees as the ones to which they would like an appointment. While Chris was among those whose attempts to join the desirable committees were unsuccessful, he was able to acquire an appointment to the Commerce, Science, and Transportation Committee. This committee was involved with a broad range of issues that impacted many areas of the nation's business and economy. Among its responsibilities were the regulation of the nation's communications infrastructure, oversight of NASA, and funding of the transportation system.

Although he was initially disappointed, Chris quickly realized that this committee, more than most of the others, was one in which he could have an impact on the general welfare of the nation. He was not an expert in technology. In fact, he found working with his cellphone to be challenging, and tended to use a few apps that had proven useful and easy to use. In spite of this deficiency, which he shared with many of his fellow committee members, Chris found many of the legislative issues to be both interesting and significant.

He rapidly became involved with issues associated with the information technology industry, which included cyber security, Internet, fair play within the entertainment and music industries, and regulation of the communications industry. With his conservative background, he tended to favor reduced regulation for each of these areas.

While he felt a sense of accomplishment, after twelve years in the Senate, Chris was growing restless. As he characterized it, his reelection to a second six-year term in the Senate had been a walk in the park. During the second election, his opponent was a Democratic Party hack who had volunteered to serve as a sacrificial offering in opposing Chris. No one was surprised at his landslide victory. Yet in spite of his gradual rise to a position of prominence within the Senate leadership and the assurance of a lifetime of service representing the State of Texas, Chris was looking for other fields to conquer.

The opportunity for change came three years into his second term in the Senate. Chris made a life-altering decision, which he announced to Melissa as they were getting ready for bed one evening. Her reaction was predictable. "Are you out of your mind? Campaign for president?" Melissa exclaimed with incredulity. "Do you have any idea what it would take to run for President of the United States?"

"I've been giving it a lot of thought and feel that I could be successful," Chris said. "I've been talking to some wealthy supporters who seem interested in backing me. I've been in the Senate for nine years, and, frankly, the job has lost some of its luster. I'm sick to death of haggling over the smallest details in pending legislation while losing sight of its purpose. I'm sick of the interparty politics. And frankly, if you'll excuse my French, I'm tired of dealing with assholes."

Melissa sat quietly, letting Chris's announcement sink in. She chose the safest response. "You know you'll have my support for anything you decide."

"I was hoping you would say that. You've always been beside me," He replied, giving Melissa a hug and kiss as they fell into bed.

Their lovemaking that evening marked the beginning of a phase in Chris's life that no one could have predicted.

Beginning with the conversation in his bedroom, Chris relentlessly pursued the dream of the presidency, a pursuit that ultimately ended in his election as President of the United States at the relatively youthful age of forty-seven. But Chris never tired of telling his doubters that he was not alone in the ranks of forty-year-old presidents. Many of his predecessors had been younger, including none other than Ulysses Grant, Teddy Roosevelt, and John Kennedy.

Foreign policy had been the central issue of the campaign. During the years that the incumbent president had been in office, the multiple wars of the Middle East had raged unabated.

The United States had continued to play the game of Whack-a-Mole, a sport in which toy moles pop out of holes at random, and the player has to hit them with a wooden mallet before they return to their hole. Similarly, the US military was tasked with identifying the next lunatic dictator, or the next extremist group, or the next terrorist attack that would occur without warning, and whack it militarily before it morphed into a more dangerous form. Leaders in the form of imams, local army generals, and self-appointed leaders appeared seemingly out of nowhere to challenge local authorities as well as Western powers. Throughout the long nightmare, the civilian populations of the Middle Eastern countries suffered greatly. Many US presidents had unsuccessfully attempted to deal with the problem, which had been euphemistically called instability.

Ever since the attacks on the World Trade Center on September 11, 2001, it was clear that the United States was a target of the Middle Eastern terrorists. While other countries had suffered significantly more during the years following those attacks, it was becoming increasingly obvious that foreign terror organizations had once again set their sights on the United States. This perception, which was based on reality rather than paranoia, had become one of the top concerns of the US public and its leaders. The challenge for politicians seeking national office was to create the illusion that they had the solution to these problems. In most cases, the solution was one in which US military might would be projected to the offending region for the purpose of obliterating the problem organization and its supporters. Although this solution was bought by the public, it was impractical. Obliterating an organization that is fully integrated with the local populace also requires obliterating the populace, including men, women, and children. Sadly, the reality of the situation did not match the oratory.

Chris recognized this insolvable problem as he debated his democratic opponent. He, like his opponent, was forced to make patriotic statements regarding the nature of the response he would order to terrorist attacks, knowing full well from his experience in the Senate that the president's authority for such attacks was both legislatively and fiscally limited. At these times, which often occurred during debates, he wondered why he or anyone else would want to be president.

***

The euphoria of the campaign and ensuing inaugural balls faded quickly as President Christopher Jeffers became immersed in the duties of Chief Executive Officer and Commander in Chief of the United States of America. He had inherited a country that was looked upon as the bastion of freedom for the free world, but which was suffering from crippling debt and beset by seemingly eternal enemies in the Middle East, Africa, and Asia. He sensed that, if anything, the country was plagued by increasing levels of strife, with violence focused against those with different ethnic backgrounds, a deteriorating educational system, and a loss of confidence in the federal government to solve the problems of the US society.

His day began as usual by speed-reading the President's Daily Intelligence Brief, also known as the PDB, which had been prepared by George Wilson, his Director of National Intelligence, known by the bureaucracy as the DNI. But today was unusual in that he customarily read the report over a cup of coffee sipped in the Oval Office. This morning, the PDB had been hand delivered by the DNI. This meeting in the White House occurred less than one month following the Bis Saif meeting in Jakarta.

They were in the green room adjacent to the Oval Office, sitting on the straight-backed chairs that had been pulled up to one of the tables in the room. The president's casual morning dress consisting of a pair of Lands' End slacks, a striped dress shirt open at the button-down collar, and loafers, contrasted sharply with George Wilson's ever-present Brooks Brothers dark suit and white shirt. The president was sipping a steaming cup of coffee, which Wilson had declined.

"How are you doing this morning?" Christopher asked, ignoring the tension in the room.

"I'm great, sir," Wilson said in a forced, casual tone.

"Well George, if everything's so good, why are you here at seven in the morning?"

"Mr. President, there is an item in the PDB that needs your immediate attention," explained the DNI. "You will notice that the second item refers to a recent contact from the Brits, in which they explain that they have found the location of the Boko Haram headquarters in Nigeria. They are requesting an immediate drone strike to destroy the headquarters building and its occupants. They feel it would deal a crippling blow to the organization."

"This certainly is sudden. Did we have any indication that they had found their HQ? I also have some other questions, such as the presence of noncombatants in the area. How certain are they that it's the headquarters, and how can they be sure that the general staff will be there when the lights go out?"

"I expected your questions, and that's the reason I've skipped my beauty sleep this morning. I felt it would be best to meet with you in person to enable a quick decision. I've been personally monitoring the situation."

George continued. "Mr. President, we were contacted by the Director of MI-6, who had requested both satellite photography and drone surveillance of the facility—which we think is located in a Nigerian city called Maiduguri. Maiduguri is a rabbit warren of a city with a population of around one million, mostly Muslims, but also Christians and several native religions. We've been tracking the comings and goings of various military groups within the city and are ninety-nine percent certain that we've pinpointed the headquarters. It has been cleverly disguised as an abandoned warehouse in the center of town. We're certain that we've identified the famed Boko Haram leader General Modukuri entering and leaving the building. MI-6 agrees with our analysis."

George continued. "In answer to your questions, Boko Haram has deviated from the normal procedures of these groups. Rather than locating the headquarters in the middle of a heavy civilian population, they've set up business in a warehouse district, which, fortunately, would minimize the chances of civilian casualties if we were to bomb them. We are speculating that they've done this for security reasons, since it is relatively easy for them to establish a security zone around the building without anyone realizing they have done so. The downside of setting up shop in the middle of a dense civilian population is that it is difficult to maintain a security perimeter without anyone getting suspicious." The president nodded in understanding as George spoke.

"Sir, I believe your second question dealt with the presence of the general staff when and if the facility is bombed. Obviously it's impossible to guarantee their presence, but here again we've been blessed. The members of the general staff follow a relatively repeatable pattern, which includes what appears to be a staff meeting every Monday morning. Today is Friday, so the Brits are asking us to schedule an attack for this coming Monday. They are anxious to avoid the possibility of missing the general due to an unexpected change in his routine."

Chris nodded thoughtfully. This was the first time during his term of president that he had been asked for an executive order that directly involved murder. But his campaign for office had been based on getting tough with the Muslim jihadists, and here was an opportunity to deliver. An opportunity that had been dropped in his lap by the British. He could make significant points with the American public by demonstrating his resolve. With very little hesitation, he made up his mind to proceed. But he didn't want the man sitting across from him to think that his actions were motivated by politics. So after a moment's pause, he asked, "George, what would you do if you were in my shoes?"

George replied without hesitation. "Mr. President, I'd kill the bastards. Think of the atrocities they've committed throughout Nigeria. Killing, stealing, kidnapping, and raping throughout the unprotected countryside. If anything, the quick death we offer them is better than they deserve."

The answer was not a surprise, and it coincided with Chris's decision. "Do it. You have my blessing. Be sure to let me know how it turns out. George, ask my press secretary to prepare a news release to be used following the successful attack."

Without further ceremony the meeting ended. George Wilson stood, shook the president's hand, thanked him, and left the room.

***

The drone attack was a success. General Modukuri and many of his staff were killed, and the building housing their headquarters destroyed. The attack was observed with varying reactions by individuals scattered throughout the world.

In Great Britain, at MI-6, Stan Comstock and his staff breathed a sigh of relief. They had staked their credibility with the prime minister on the information Cecil Breathwaite, aka John Smith, had provided. His credibility climbed to greater heights with MI-6 as a result of the successful attack.

In Jakarta, the trio of John Smith, Adam al-Zhihri, and Abu Ahmed al-Kuwaiti watched the event with interest on Al Jazeera, the Middle Eastern news network. They wondered whether the remaining leaders of Boko Haram would connect the dots and realize that the attack was the result of their refusal to join Bis Saif. Adam wondered whether Udo had survived the attack, and whether they should try to contact him. After a brief discussion with the others, he decided to wait to see whether Udo and his fellow soldiers would figure it out for themselves.

In Nigeria, Udo was way ahead of the trio in Jakarta. He suspected Bis Saif as soon as the bombs began to fall. If only General Modukuri had recognized their power. Udo felt that he had tried to warn the general by describing the extensive Bis Saif facilities in Jakarta. But all the general seemed to care about was raping and pillaging. He had no interest in the overall goal of a united Sunni Muslim caliphate, nor for that matter did he seem to care about a better life for Nigerians. Udo decided to bide his time before he decided on his long-term status with Boko Haram.

In Iraq, Ali and his commander, Mohammed, immediately understood what had happened. Ali brought up the subject during their evening mess. "Mohammed. did you hear about the bombing of the Boko Haram headquarters in Nigeria?"

"Yes, those American dogs did it," Mohammed said. "I don't know how they discovered the location of the headquarters, but I'll bet that your friends in Jakarta were responsible. I had heard that the Nigerians refused to join their cause. I'll bet that the bombing was intended as a lesson to their other partners."

Ali had the same thought. "They are dangerous partners. We'll have to be careful how we deal with them. I wonder what General Hussain thinks of it."

In Palestine, General Murtaja and his staff were oblivious to the message that had been sent. With Hasan Jouda in Kuwait helping with the computer project, they had forgotten the details of his trip to Jakarta. All they remembered was that it had provided a drone fleet that they could use against Israel.

In Kuwait, Hasan immediately made the connection, which he explained to his new partners Jahmir and Kelly. They were not happy to learn that their new investors were, in fact, dangerous killers. But they concluded that it was too late to change directions. They would just have to be careful dealing with Bis Saif.

CHAPTER 14

NO REST FOR THE WEARY

It was six months following the bombing of the Boko Haram headquarters in Maiduguri and nearly ten months following the meeting in Jakarta. The crowd was on its feet as the Washington Warriors had the ball on the Dallas Cowboys fifteen yard line. The Warriors' new name had replaced that of the Redskins in the interest of political correctness, and their fans were still adjusting to the jarring change. The Warriors had been in the lead for the first three quarters of the game. In typical fashion, they had relinquished their advantage midway through the fourth quarter and were now playing catch-up, trying to overcome the three-point lead currently held by the Dallas Cowboys, the Warriors perennial rivals. Although they didn't like it, Washington fans were accustomed to this situation, although they were hoping against hope that they would beat the hated Cowboys. In almost ritual fashion, the Warriors would begin the game aggressively and then become overconfident and blow their lead. Their wins often featured a last-minute scoring drive needed to overcome the advantage they had lost during the game's second half. Would they make it to the end zone, or would this be another disappointing game? Warriors' fans were a resilient bunch. No matter how often they were disappointed, they remained loyal to their beloved home team, which they stubbornly continued to call the Washington Redskins.

Christopher Jeffers, the President of the United States, was also on his feet in the stadium owner's box. He was a minority in the box, since, as a Dallas native, he had been a Cowboys fan almost from the day he was born. President Jeffers and Melissa had arrived at the stadium unnoticed by the press, passing quickly through the underground VIP stadium entrance available to those guests using the owner's club suite. Once in the suite, he joined the Warriors' owner and a short list of invited guests, all of whom were on their feet cheering. Melissa and Christopher were the only Cowboys fans in the suite, but were unbothered by their minority status.

The Warriors' scoring drive appeared to stall with an incomplete pass and a three-yard run. The Washington crowd was then reenergized by a quarterback sneak, which brought the ball to the three yard line and another first down. Dallas called a time out, giving the guests in the owner's suite an opportunity to refill their plates with the gourmet food laid out on the buffet along the rear wall.

As he watched the players huddle on the field, Chris couldn't help reflecting on the similarity between American football games and the spectacles that ancient Rome produced in their colosseums. He felt as if he were the emperor of Rome sitting in the imperial box in the Colosseum, having traveled through the underground tunnel to arrive at his prestigious seat. The United States, like Rome, seemed to be staging football games as a diversion for the general public, keeping their collective mindset away from concerns, such as unemployment, unseen foreign enemies, and a generally deteriorating quality of life.

When pro football wasn't available, many other diversions were, including baseball, basketball, soccer, golf, and ice hockey. Fans could root for their favorite professional and college teams. Sports had become such a diversion in the United States that annual revenue from all sports, including tickets, concessions, and sales of memorabilia, exceeded $600 billion annually. TV viewership for major sporting events such as the Super Bowl and the World Series far exceeded the numbers for news programming or the president's annual State of the Union address. By any standard, the American public was captivated by ongoing sports spectacles at a level that far exceeded the attention they paid to the policies and actions of their government.

As the president was about to return his attention to the game, his cellphone rang. The call from Jan Adams, his administrative assistant, caused him to curse under his breath and momentarily wish that he was not President of the United States. He knew that Jan would not be calling unless it was important. She knew that football was near and dear to his heart and had been warned not to interrupt him for anything except the direst circumstances. Turning to his hosts, he asked, "This call is probably important, but should be taken in private. Is there some place other than the men's room where I can have some privacy?"

With a nod from the owner, the security detail ushered him into the owner's office, which was considered the inner sanctum of the suite.

"This better be important," he said to the indefatigable Jan. Jan was a retired member of the US Marines, and it would take more than a grumpy president to scare her.

"I think you'll agree that it is," Jan said. "I'll put George Wilson on the line."

Wilson's message caused Chris to forget the football game. "Looks like ISIS has increased their capabilities. One of our Air Force F-16s was just shot down by a SAM over Iraq. A second one was damaged, but the pilot was able to return to the base."

"SAMs! I didn't know that ISIS had them. This is beginning to sound like Viet Nam. Did anyone at the Pentagon expect this?"

Wilson's response was not encouraging. "Actually, the attack caught us by surprise. Until now, we've ruled the skies. I suppose we should have expected this, but there was no indication that ISIS had access to these weapons."

"I'd better come home. I'll meet you in the Oval Office in a half hour."

When Chris walked out of the owner's office, Melissa could tell something was wrong, but she knew better than to ask, particularly in public. She rose from her seat and indicated that it was time for the presidential couple to take their leave. Thanking them for their hospitality, she joined Chris and his Secret Service detail to return to their waiting limousine, which took them to the White House through the streets of Washington at a speed that most commuters would envy.

"Well, who won?" asked Chris, regaining his composure.

"I was so concerned about your telephone conversation that I almost forgot to pay attention to the game. Fortunately, I was able to refocus in time to watch the good guys win."

***

The ride back to the White House was a quiet one. Melissa broke the silence asking, "ISIS again?"

Chris replied with a nod. "We'd better not talk about it until we get home."

The limousine followed the police escort with its sirens and flashing lights to the underground entrance of the White House. When they arrived, Chris immediately proceeded to the Oval Office where he was met by the DNI. Once again, their dress was a study in contrast, with the president in casual clothes and George in a business suit.

'Well, let's have the bad news," the President said without introduction.

"It appears to have been a Chinese made missile, although we're not sure. Our experts are still analyzing the electronic data."

"Did either pilot survive?"

"The one plane made it back to the base and the pilot is fine, although somewhat shaken. The pilot bailed out of the plane that was shot down. We've got a search-and-rescue mission underway in hopes of finding him before ISIS does. As you know, captured aviators don't fare well in their hands."

"Let me know as soon as you hear. If there's a fatality, I'd like to personally call the family."

"Will do, sir."

Jeffers then turned to the practical aspect of the tragedy. "Were the planes equipped with countermeasures?"

Wilson replied. "We believe so, but the SAM appeared to have been a Sky Dragon 50, which uses the latest Chinese SAM technology. We don't know much about it, but if I'm right, we're about to take a crash course in that system. All we know is that it was featured in a recent Africa Aerospace and Defense Conference. All of the top arms suppliers were there. Thank heavens we were well represented by our people posing as purchasers from third world countries. So we were able to gather a lot of information."

"We seem to be well informed about foreign military systems, but not very well informed about their customers," George added cynically.

Christopher was unhappy with the tone of the conversation. He felt that they had experienced too many surprises since he became president and was becoming concerned about his country's ability to make the progress against the various terror groups that he had promised to eliminate during his campaign for office. But more important, he was unhappy with the future prospects for a country that was besieged by enemies everywhere. Far from being the defenders of the free world, he felt that they were on the run, concerned only with protecting their own flanks.

With these thoughts in mind, he turned to George Wilson and ordered emphatically, "I want you to redouble your efforts to improve the intelligence picture in the Middle East. I will go to Congress and ask for increased funding, both for your efforts as well as that of the CIA and NSA. We cannot, I repeat, cannot be continuously caught by surprise. If there are too many more surprises, it may be necessary to make some significant changes around here."

Realizing he had just chewed out the individual whose advice he valued the most, the president relaxed his tone and asked, "Keep me informed as this situation progresses. And be sure to let me know about the pilot of the downed F-16. I'll do my part to get you some funding. All I ask is that you put the appropriate agencies on notice that I will not tolerate any more surprises."

With that, George made a hasty exit from the Oval Office.

***

The weeks following the downing of the F-16 were eventful. President Jeffers realized that there were many weaknesses to be addressed if he was to fulfill his promise of defending the country and defeating ISIS and the other jihadists. He assigned his DNI the responsibility for coordinating the country's intelligence agencies and upgrading their monitoring and evaluation capabilities as well as improving the coordination among agencies. He told Wilson to order the CIA and the Naval Research Laboratory to accelerate its technical evaluation of the SAM system, including its capabilities, possible countermeasures, and, most important, an analysis of the manner in which the system was purchased, sold, delivered, and paid for. He intended to make it clear to the Chinese, if in fact they proved to be the source of the equipment, that future sales of this nature would be met with retribution.

Jeffers cancelled his monthly cabinet meeting in order to meet with the individuals most responsible for addressing these issues. He decided that the Washington, DC bureaucracy would only appreciate the gravity of the situation if he became personally involved. He reflected on his decision as he sat at the head of the long table in the Cabinet Room in the White House West Wing. Seated at the table were the leaders of many of the US intelligence and military communities. Of the seventeen agencies that comprised the US intelligence community, only those that were directly related to the issues at hand were invited. These included six agencies: The Office of the Director of National Intelligence (DNI), the Central Intelligence Agency (CIA), the National Security Agency (NSA), the Department of Homeland Security (DHS), the Department of Defense (DOD), and the Federal Bureau of Investigation (FBI). The participants were clustered with the president at the far end of the table. By request of the White House, none of the attendees were accompanied by aides. This group, which was to meet frequently in the future, became known as the President's War Cabinet.

Jeffers opened the meeting. "Ladies and gentlemen, I appreciate your response to my request for this meeting. I believe this will prove to be one of the more important meetings of my administration." He took a sip of water before continuing.

"We are faced with a serious situation. It appears that no matter what we do, and how much money we spend, things continue to deteriorate. I also believe this group of smart, experienced leaders of the intelligence community can jointly develop a plan to turn this situation around. Money is obviously not an issue. The collective budgets of your agencies exceed that of any country of the free world by several orders of magnitude.

"I believe that we have the following problems." With that, Jeffers raised his fingers and listed the results of his analysis.

"First, we don't understand them. Looking around this room full of white middle-aged Christians and Jews, there's not a single individual in this room that can internalize their thought process and who really understands their long-term goals.

"Second, I think our intelligence processes are out of balance. We rely too much on automation. It's as if our system was designed by a bunch of nerds who enjoy working with computers rather than with people. We rely on surveillance of the communications systems, satellites, drones, and TV monitors. None of these devices allow us to get into the heads of the people we are trying to understand and track. I recognize that there are agents throughout the world who risk their lives every day to fill this gap. But I'm not certain that the spending on human intelligence, HUMINT, relative to that which is spent on technology makes sense. In other words, we've got to increase the funding of HUMINT.

"Third, I don't believe we know who *they* are. We keep playing Whack-a-Mole with these various groups. As soon as we beat one down, another pops up. Does anyone understand the relationships among these groups? Does anyone know whether they are aligned with each other? Where do they come from? Are they purely nationalistic, or are they international?

"Fourth, getting back to their long-term goals, what are they? Do all groups have the same goal? Are their various attacks within their own countries following some sort of strategic plan or are they just random spur-of-the-moment ideas? If they're planned, who is planning them?

"And finally, I just don't get it that we aren't better informed. I also don't get it that these groups are so popular within their own regions. I don't get it that with all our money and technology we can't answer these questions. I hope that you can all provide explanations that will make me feel better and also possibly serve as the basis for developing a decent plan. If this group can't answer these questions and make some corrections to its current trajectory, I'll find some people who can. And let me make it clear that I'm not looking for canned answers. I'm looking for creativity, thinking outside the box, and greatly improved performance." Although he hadn't intended it, his final remarks were made with his voice rising.

The president sat down and the room went silent.

After a long pause, George Wilson spoke up. "Mr. President, these are all excellent points, and I'm certain that given enough time they can be answered. I've got a suggestion. Why don't we address each of these issues right now, as a group, for the purpose of assessing both our collective knowledge and the gaps in this knowledge? When we have worked through the list, we can use the gaps as the basis for developing our plan."

Jeffers turned to Jan and asked her to summarize the first of his four points. She said, "What are their long-term goals?" The response was unanimous. The group consensus was that the goals depended on the organization. Their consensus was based on two examples: Palestinians just wanted to get rid of Israel and establish a homeland, while ISIS was trying to establish a global caliphate. There was no discussion of the reasons that followers were attracted to the extremist causes at an estimated rate of 100 per day.

It was then Jan's turn again. "Intelligence processes are out of balance," she summarized. This issue stimulated a long discussion that had been repeated on many previous occasions. NSA, with its telecommunications monitoring program, was very experienced at justifying its program ever since Edward Snowden had walked away with their files. Although everyone in the room was familiar with their justification of the program, Admiral DeForce, the NSA administrator, couldn't be prevented from reciting their long list of successes. It was clear that Jeffers had hit a sensitive subject with his second point. As a result of the NSA defense of its program, all others present felt obligated to make similar presentations. With the exception of Matthew O'Brien, the CIA director, who agreed with the president's point of lack of balance. Most of the speeches reflected the parochial concerns of the individual giving the speech.

Sensing that his suggested approach was not producing the desired results, George Wilson interrupted in an attempt to redirect the conversation. "Let's move on," he said. "I'm sure everyone is doing the best that they can under the constraints of national policy and funding. But there must be something we can do to preempt situations such as this."

Realizing that George was trying to move them off a divisive topic, Jan moved on to the next question without prompting from Jeffers. Rather than repeating the question verbatim, she paraphrased it. "Do we really understand the overall organization of the jihadists, including their relationships with each other?"

Following a brief silence, Matthew O'Brien spoke up. "Mr. President, that is an excellent question and one that we've been trying to unravel for more than ten years. Ever since the Arab Spring at the end of 2010, these groups have been proliferating like rabbits. In the beginning, there was only Al Qaeda as well as the Taliban in Afghanistan. But now there are more groups with unpronounceable names than anyone in this room can list. We estimate that there are more than fifty groups around the world, some of which are affiliated with Al Qaeda and others that aren't. The problem is that the groups appear and disappear. Their relationships with each other change with time. It's the nature of their cultures that they are constantly bargaining to get the best deal for themselves. The terrorist community is something like an Arab rug market. So you're correct when you describe our situation as being something like the game of Whack-a-Mole. Without agents inserted at high levels in all of these organizations, it's impossible to know what is going on. If you would like, I can send you a list of the organizations we're trying to track, but you could get the same information from Wikipedia." And then, prophetically, O'Brien added, "What scares us is the possibility that somehow these factions will become organized against the West. Can you imagine the situation if we were trying to overcome a worldwide terror network?"

Then O'Brien said, "I can also try to answer your question regarding their motivation, internationally. We believe that ISIS terrorist activities outside the Middle East are intended to turn the non-Muslims against the Muslims. Their purpose is to convince the Muslim population that the world is against them, and that they should join the jihad. And it's working. Every act of anti-Muslim bigotry attracts more of them to the jihad. All of our scared politicians with their anti-Muslim campaigning are assisting the ISIS recruiting effort. I tell you, I'm getting very worried."

A statement like that, coming from the director of the CIA, sent tremors through the room.

The president, who had remained silent during these discussions, spoke up. "This is scary stuff. What are we going to do about it? We're the greatest country in the world, and we're running around the globe chasing a bunch of religious fanatics. It's as if we were trying to herd cats."

Several of the Christians in the room had a common thought that they kept to themselves. *Religious fanatics have been responsible for some of the greatest changes experienced by our civilization.*

With the nodding approval of all present, Jan indicated that they had already addressed the president's final point—the overall long-term goal of the extremists. It was clear to all present that the meeting had accomplished little. Everyone in the room shared the common commitment to the defeat of the forces of evil. The problem was that no one knew how to do it.

Jeffers felt as if he were a football coach trying to instill some life into his team. With one final effort to spur them to greater accomplishments, he ended the meeting. "We've all got to resolve to address these issues. We will talk to Congress about additional funding for the CIA in order to improve our HUMINT. I believe a special appropriation is in order. DOD has confirmed that our plane was shot down by a Chinese-made SAM system. We are trying to follow the money trail to understand who financed the purchase and who sold it. If the Chinese are involved, we'll try to solve the problems through diplomatic channels. In the meantime, I want your agencies to redouble their efforts to get inside the heads of the jihadists. I'm determined to resolve this issue by the end of my first term in office, even though there are less than three years left. The American people are depending on us. In the meantime, feel free to contact me if you have any additional thoughts or information. I will always be available to you at a moment's notice."

As the meeting broke up, Jan came up to him and whispered, "There's an urgent call for you from the Prime Minister of Israel. Do you want to take it in the Oval Office?"

***

"Good morning, Moshe, what can I do for you?"

The voice at the other end of the line belonged to Moshe Tamer, the Prime Minister of Israel. Although he and Chris had developed a friendship borne of a common understanding of Israel's security needs, Moshe was obviously not in a mood for idle formalities. "I have an urgent matter to discuss with you. I'm not certain whether your defense department has told you yet, but we were just attacked by the Palestinians on two fronts. One was a guided missile attack launched by a new addition to their arsenal, which our Mossad security service says they have named the Suquur. This missile hit the terminal building of Ben Gurion Airport near Tel Aviv and killed more than fifty tourists and staff. It has shut down the airport, which is our main link with the outside world. The second was an attack by remote control drones aimed at Beersheba that killed more than a dozen civilians. The Palestinians take full credit for the attacks and tell us that more are coming unless we meet their demands at the bargaining table."

Chris replied in a calm voice that belied his inner turmoil. "Horrible! What can we do to help?"

"I'm calling you for two reasons. First, to let you know that we will not accede to blackmail. We have mobilized our military and will be attacking Gaza within the next forty-eight hours. The Palestinians will regret their decision. They have awakened the sleeping lion. I am asking your country's support for our effort, both at the United Nations and with the world community. It is also possible that we will be requesting military assistance to help us absorb the cost of what is now becoming known as the Next War."

Without hesitation, Jeffers responded, "You have our support. Let us know what you need."

"Second, we need to determine how the Palestinians obtained this technology. I don't think they possess the skills needed to construct the missile, and I also don't think that they manufacture their own drones. Where did it come from, and how do we ensure that they don't acquire any additional armaments? Our greatest advantage over our enemies is the technological capabilities of our country. If similar capabilities are being provided to them, we will be in great trouble. The Mossad is working on this, but we need every scrap of intelligence you can provide."

Again, without hesitation, Jeffers replied, "You've got my assurances of cooperative intelligence. Let us speak again tomorrow, and I will let you know what we can provide. If you could tell us of your military needs when we speak again, I will ensure that you are supported."

The prime minister ended the call by thanking the president and telling him that he would call the next day at the same time to see what had been decided.

***

As soon as he hung up the phone, President Jeffers buzzed Jan and asked her to try to catch Matthew O'Brien, General Altman, and George Wilson before they left the White House. Fortunately, they had been standing near the exit discussing the meeting before returning to their cars.

As they reentered the Oval Office, they immediately sensed that something was wrong. "Well we have another surprise. I just received a call from Israel," the president said without preamble. "They have been attacked by sophisticated guided missiles and drones."

Turning to O'Brien, he added, "I want you to find out where they purchased this stuff. I'd like to know whether there's any connection between this event and the SAM attacks over Syria. It's ironic and maybe not coincidental that the two attacks were so close together. I'm wondering what else is in store for us. I'm also wondering whether the next attack will be a terrorist attack against civilians. George, will you alert DHS and the FBI that there may be more attacks in store? Have them place their agencies on highest alert. And will all of you keep me informed about any new information you develop?

"And one other thing," the president added, reflectively addressing O'Brien. "Matt, I think your evaluation of the purpose of the terrorist attacks on the West is correct. Our fellow politicians of both parties are using fear of the Muslims for their political advantage. Their actions are playing directly into ISIS's hands. I'd like to figure out how to bring this Muslim-baiting to an end. There are one point six billion Muslims in the world. If they are unified by the hatred being bred in the West, and turn against the West, it could be the end of our civilization, all because of a bunch of self-centered politicians. I need your help in the form of any ideas you can come up with." He then added reflectively, "I'm president of the greatest power in the world, and I'm helpless to defend our allies, our pilots, or our citizens. What's going on here? Are we still the greatest power in the world?"

The trio stood silently. All they could do was to promise that they would get right on it.

After the three men left, the president asked Jan to join him. The two of them immediately turned their attention to the many items that needed to be addressed. These included press releases, notifications to key congressional staff, and meetings with the majority and minority leaders of the House and Senate. The latter were particularly important since he needed their support for the supplemental funding required by the CIA and DOD to increase their HUMINT. Additional funding would also be required by the FBI and Department of Homeland Security to increase their surveillance of possible troublemakers at home.

Then the president raised a subject with Jan that had been on his mind. Jan Adams had been with him for many years. She first appeared in Washington as a Senate aide when he was the junior senator from Texas. Jeffers developed a deep respect for her intelligence and ability and, as time passed, he relied on her more and more. When he was elected president, it was only natural that he would take her with him to the White House as his administrative assistant.

"Jan, I was unsettled by our meeting with the leaders of the US Intelligence Community. What was your reaction?"

"Mr. President, I thought the meeting was a total failure. No one said anything original, and many spent the time justifying their own existence. I was hoping that the meeting could have turned into a brainstorming session, but that never happened."

"I agree. I think they're out of ideas. I also think that they're already doing everything they can think of, and I honestly believe they've got their staffs pushed to the limit. But one new thought occurred to me during the meeting. I want to get your reaction. Looking around the room full of middle-aged white men, I was wondering how this group could possibly pretend to understand the mind-sets of the Muslim extremists. Do you think it would be useful to meet with a group of Muslims who could give us some insights into the thinking of our enemies?"

Jan thought for a minute before replying. "It could cause problems politically since a meeting of that type might be interpreted as meeting with the enemy. There's also a chance that those who you'd invite to the meeting have as many questions as you do. But if you're willing to take the risk of bad publicity and an unproductive meeting, what can you lose by meeting with them except a few hours of your time?"

"I think I'll go ahead with the meeting," Jeffers replied. "I know you're busy, but I'd like to keep this a secret for as long as possible. In your copious spare time, could you prepare a list of possible participants in such a meeting? I'd like to get something started within the next two weeks and schedule a meeting by the middle of next month."

"Sure. I'd be happy to get you the list."

"Thanks, Jan. And now back to the business of running the country."

Unfortunately, the meeting would never take place.

CHAPTER 15

IN THE DARK OF THE NIGHT

A different meeting from the one that Jeffers had planned began one evening in early December. This meeting, which convened in the Oval Office, included the congressional leadership of both parties. The president enjoyed meeting in the office because of its view of the Rose Garden and other landscaping on the south side of the White House. Tonight it was particularly comfortable with the presence of the newly decorated Christmas tree and a fire in the fireplace. But the comfortable surroundings were lost on the meeting participants, whose minds were focused on the return to their home districts rather than spending extra time in Washington.

The meeting had been organized by Jan at Jeffers' request. Although it had been scheduled for a date that followed the congressional Christmas recess, Jan had prevailed upon the majority and minority leaders of both the House and Senate to delay their departures from Washington for their home states for a few days, saying that the president felt that the meeting was essential to the nation's security. Jan could be very persuasive when she had to.

The five men meeting that evening included the president, Wayne Zyder, a Republican who was the House Minority Leader, Brad Nelson, a Democrat who was the House Majority Leader, Robert McIntyre, the Republican Senate Majority Leader, and Paul Greenberg, the Senate Minority Leader. The split in party leadership, with the Republicans leading in the Senate and the Democrats leading in the House of Representatives, often created problems. The president and the four leaders had agreed to work together early in Jeffers' term, recognizing that frequent meetings were the key to avoiding an impotent Congress. They became known as the Leadership Group, due to the frequency of their meetings.

As if by prior agreement, all five had worn dark suits with white shirts and ties reflecting the holiday season. Because of the meeting's late hour, all five had draped their coats over the backs of their chairs. The two Republicans had also rolled up their sleeves because of the warmth that the fireplace had created in the office. All five also had steaming mugs of coffee in front of them, adorned with the presidential seal along with yellow legal pads that had been thoughtfully provided by Jan.

"Mr. President, what is so important that it can't wait until after the holidays?" asked Brad Nelson, clearly in a dark mood.

Jeffers had been expecting this from Brad, who was an effective politician but could be difficult to deal with. Brad was the stereotypical prickly New Englander, a person who said what he thought with no holds barred. "Believe me, I don't want my holidays interrupted any more than you do. Melissa and I had planned to return to Texas today so that we could spend Christmas and New Years with our families. But I think you'll agree we should set our personal desires aside, considering the deteriorating situation in the Middle East."

"But Mr. President, there have been a few new events, but I think they are just a natural evolution of the situation there. I don't see any reason to panic," ventured Robert McIntyre.

"Bob, I can't believe you're saying that," replied the president. "We've both supported the Republican platform of getting tough on ISIS and their friends with the goal of solving the Middle East problem. Not only are we failing to meet that goal, but things are getting worse. In the last two weeks we've lost an F-16 to a SAM system, which was deployed by ISIS for the first time, and the Israelis have been bombarded with new high-tech guided missiles and drones. I think that the nearly concurrent timing of these two developments is not a coincidence. I also think that both the Palestinians and ISIS have found a new source of technical assistance. The question is, what next?"

183

No one said anything, so the president continued. "There are a number of things that are scary about this. First, we didn't have a clue that these developments were taking place. This points to a major weakness in our intelligence in spite of the billions of dollars we've been pouring into it. Second, until now, the Palestinians and ISIS had scarcely paid any attention to each other. In fact, the Palestinians have been so focused on burying Israel that they have not cooperated with anyone unless they could advance this goal. Yet here we have possible evidence of cooperation. Third, I've convened the upper echelon of my security council, which we now call the President's War Cabinet, in an effort to identify new actions we could take to defeat the various Sunni Muslim terrorist groups, or at least weaken them. No one could come up with any ideas other than to do more of what we're currently doing. Yet we've got to do something. We're in the middle of an ideological battle, and our side is intellectually bankrupt. Bob, I will deny ever saying this, but yes, I'm getting close to panic."

Brad Nelson stood up and began to pace. He ran his fingers through his wavy gray mane, looking for all the world like a reincarnation of Everett Dirksen, a Republican who had been the Senate minority leader for more than a decade. "Now you're making me feel uneasy. But what do you want us to do? Come up with ideas that your own staff couldn't produce?"

"No, I'm not coming to you for ideas, although I'll accept good ideas from any source, including you," responded Jeffers with a smile. "What I need from all of you is support for a supplemental budget proposal that I am about to submit that will provide increased funding for the intelligence agencies—primarily the CIA, as well as additional military aid for Israel. Our lack of knowledge about technology developments and collaboration is truly frightening. We've got to solve the problem or we'll be continuing to fight a war against an enemy we don't understand. It's as if we're a prize fighter trying to box with an opponent while wearing a blindfold." Then, not quite as an afterthought, he added, "I would also like to discuss my existing war powers with you and determine if and when they should be expanded."

Paul Greenberg, a strong supporter of Israel, in part because of his Jewish heritage, asked, "How much do you want?"

As he opened his mouth to answer, the president was startled when the lights in the White House flickered briefly followed by the hum of the building's emergency generators. Reflexively, the five men in the Oval Office meeting that included the most powerful man on the planet looked out the windows and were surprised that the glow of the Washington, DC horizon had disappeared. It was as if the city had disappeared, the result of a citywide power failure.

Their meeting was interrupted as six Secret Service officers rushed in and politely but forcefully herded the top leadership of the United States out of the Oval Office through the White House hallways to the Situation Room, located in the basement. The Situation Room provided a focal point for incoming information as well as the secure communication capabilities required for coordination with emergency and military services. It also provides a safe haven for its occupants in the event of enemy attack. It is permanently staffed by approximately thirty military personnel who provide the maintenance and operations needed for collection and dissemination of information and other communications.

"My God, what's happening?" said Paul Greenberg, who had no military service and had never experienced a life-threatening situation. "All I did was ask how much you wanted. You didn't have to respond in such a spectacular fashion," he added with an attempt at humor.

One of the Secret Service agents answered, addressing Jeffers "Mr. President, we don't know much, but we think that the entire city as well as the surrounding suburbs are blacked out. It's too early to determine the cause, but hopefully power can be restored soon. You can imagine the chaos. There are hundreds stuck in elevators, traffic is a mess without working traffic lights, the Metro and VRE Express aren't operating, and high-rise buildings are being evacuated. I sure hope that PEPCO and VEPCO figure out the problem soon. Why do these things always happen after dark?"

***

Philip J. Tarnoff

As the Leadership Group and their supporting staff puzzled over the power failure, the news media described a continuously deteriorating situation. A lieutenant colonel from the Situation Room watch team approached the conference table around which the four legislators and the president were seated and saluted. President Jeffers nodded and asked, "What's on your mind, Colonel?"

"Mr. President, in addition to the regional power failure, there was a terrorist attack at Union Station. The station was crowded, as you'd expect on a Friday evening before Christmas, and blacked out due to the power failure. People were already panicking, the trains had stopped running, and the station was running on emergency lighting. It seems as if somewhere between four and five terrorists entered the station with automatic weapons and grenades. The situation is very confused, but there are lots of deaths and injuries. You can imagine the mayhem. To make matters worse, it looks as if all the terrorists escaped in the dark because of the absence of police, who were attending emergencies elsewhere. The police couldn't get to the station because traffic is so snarled due to the power failure. And even worse, it wasn't possible for ambulances and other medical assistance to get there quickly either. There are some doctors and nurses in the station, who were traveling, and they're trying to treat the wounded. Lord knows there's nothing else for them to do; they can't travel with the train service knocked out. The mayhem at the station is incredible."

It was all that Jeffers could do to control his emotions. His first thought was that the concurrent timing of the attack and the power failure could not have been a coincidence. Like the timing of the ISIS and Palestinian incidents, it was as if there were a puppeteer behind all of this calling the shots. "Thank you, Colonel. That will be all. I'll call you if I need anything."

Jeffers knew that he should do something or say something that gave the impression he was in control and would solve the problem. But at that moment he was out of ideas. Once again the massive intelligence and law enforcement community that he commanded had let him down. Something was going on and he was powerless to strike back.

Suddenly the video display at the end of the conference table facing the president came to life. There were no images or audio displayed. Instead, lines of text appeared and slowly scrolled through the display. "Get me five copies of that as soon as possible," he ordered. Then he added, "Get all members of the National Security Council here as soon as possible."

The message was brief and the Situation Room staff efficient. Within minutes, the five men were studying the message. Additional copies were printed for the perusal of the members of the NSC as they arrived.

You are witnessing small sample of our capabilities. We are able to turn off the power to the Washington, DC region, the entire East Coast of the United States, or your entire country. We will turn off your power for as long as it takes for you to beg for mercy. You may have enough supplies to last for an emergency of a week or even a month, but could your people last for a year?

At the same time, you have witnessed our ability to attack your people without repercussions. You do not know us, but we know you. We know that you have not found the terrorists who attacked Union Station. We know that you have no idea where they are. We also know that they live to attack another day to inflict countless horrors on your people.

Why are we doing this? You may not realize that you are at war against us, but we do. We are at war with you, and it is a war we intend to win. We have won the first battle, and perhaps the only battle of the war. We will not make the mistake of stopping short of our goals. We intend to establish a worldwide caliphate. We intend to rule all the territories of the Levant. We intend to eliminate Israel. We are going to accomplish this with your assistance.

If you do not begin removing your troops, planes, and ships from all of the Levant within one week, one fourth of your nation will become dark. If you do not end your support of Israel within two weeks, one half of your nation will go dark. If all of your troops, planes, and ships are not removed from the Levant within one month, your entire country will become dark. While this is happening, there will be a cascade of terror attacks. Your population will be at our mercy. We will unleash the forces of Jahannam on them.

There will be no negotiation and no opportunity to discuss this either in person or by text. Your actions will be your response.

Bis Saif

***

Members of the War Cabinet began arriving as the president and the four congressmen finished reading the message from Bis Saif. Their trip to the White House had been harrowing. Those that could traveled from their offices to the White House helipad by helicopter to avoid the snarled traffic. Those that did not have the luxury of airborne transportation arrived hours later.

George Wilson was the first to arrive since he had been at his office in the White House East Wing when the power failure occurred. General Altman arrived soon after, having taken a helicopter from the Pentagon to the White House. The two of them walked into the Situation Room together as the others were reading the Bis Saif message.

His immediate reaction matched those of the others: "Who the hell is Bis Saif?"

George called one of his contacts at the CIA, realizing that Matthew O'Brien was in transit by helicopter and could probably get the answer quickly once he arrived. But George was not willing to wait and hoped that his contact could provide advice in a timely manner. After a long conversation, George put his cellphone back in his pocket, turned to the president, and said; "They'll get back to me."

Reading between the lines, Jeffers replied, "That tells me they don't have a clue who they are. I hope they have some better knowledge of the way we can survive a nationwide power failure, but I'm not hopeful. How long will it take for Janice to get here?"

The colonel took the lead in answering the president's question. He knew the president was referring to Janice DeBeers, the Director of the Department of Homeland Security (DHS). "We're in contact with all members of the War Cabinet. Ms. DeBeers should be here within thirty minutes. She may end up walking when they get close since DHS doesn't have a helicopter, and she's stuck in traffic about a mile from here."

General Altman then asked the question on everyone's mind, but who were afraid to ask. "Can someone tell me what Jahannam means?"

The colonel was expecting this and had quietly Googled the definition while the participants were arriving. Without divulging his source, he said, "Jahannam is the Muslim word for hell."

And with that simple exchange, one piece of the puzzle, albeit a small piece, fell into place. The Bis Saif terrorists were Muslims.

Little by little the members of the War Cabinet straggled in. Those with helicopters arrived soon after General Altman's arrival. Matthew O'Brien arrived during the discussion of Jahannam. O'Brien's stature belied his power as director of the CIA and hid his considerable intellect. He was short and stooped and wore permanently wrinkled clothes. Jan used to joke with Melissa, who she called the boss's wife, that he used a dry cleaner that specialized in pre-wrinkled clothes. He was also a Harvard-trained computer expert with a PhD in cybersecurity.

O'Brien listened to the exchange with interest. "In all honesty, the CIA has no knowledge of Bis Saif. We know it's an Arabic word for *by the sword*. But that's the extent of our knowledge. We've asked NSA to comb the phone records for use of the word, but so far no luck."

Almost on cue, Admiral DeForce, the director of the National Security Agency, arrived. It was the NSA's responsibility to monitor all electronic communications originating or terminating in the United States. They were well known for the mountains of information accumulated and stored for situations such as this.

Having heard O'Brien's comments as he walked into the Situation Room, the admiral concurred. "We received the CIA's request an hour ago and have made a request to the Internet providers to search their databases for the words *Bis Saif*. Ever since the Edward Snowden catastrophe, which required us to leave the records with the communications companies, our processes have been slowed down. While the courts and the general public may feel that their privacy is secured by keeping their records away from the government, our ability to search these records has degraded. It will be days, at best, before we can respond to the CIA's request. Yet I believe we remain the best hope of finding Bis Saif since we don't know where in the world they're even located."

O'Brien nodded, agreeing. "We've already notified all of our station agents throughout the world to press their sources for any scrap of information they can produce about Bis Saif. We've made it a high priority, more important than anything else on their plates."

As the discussion of Bis Saif wound down, Janice DeBeers walked into the room. Normally a statuesque, well-dressed woman, she had just walked more than a mile and limped in carrying her high heeled shoes in one hand. She was highly qualified for her position in that both her educational background and work experience was related to the management of large complex organizations. Jeffers was relieved that she had arrived. In his mind, response to the present blackout and possible future blackouts had assumed priority over that of finding Bis Saif.

"Janice, we've got a big problem," he said, motioning to the ultimatum still displayed on the monitor at the end of the room. "I'll give you a moment to read it before grilling you."

The room lapsed into silence while Janice stood in front of the big screen and read. It only took a few minutes for her to finish. "Wow! Have we got a problem. Before we talk, let me make a few calls to get the FEMA staff moving. We've got to activate our plans to deal with extended power failures. Although knowing my staff, they're already working on this." FEMA, which was the acronym for the Federal Emergency Management Agency, was a major activity within DHS. The agency was responsible for coordinating response to major catastrophes, such as earthquakes and hurricanes, as well as man-made catastrophes, such as power failures and terrorist attacks.

With that, she took her cellphone out of her purse and speed dialed the director of FEMA. She spoke into the phone for an extended period of time, while everyone in the room watched her speak. When she finally wrapped up the conversation, she turned to the group with her report. "Well, the power failure is extensive. It covers the entire service areas of PEPCO and VEPCO. PEPCO serves the District of Columbia as well as most of Montgomery and Prince Georges counties in Maryland. Virginia is not as clean cut since VEPCO serves parts of many counties, including Arlington, Fairfax, Fauquier, Loudon, Stafford, and Prince William. Quite a list. As a rough estimate, we're guessing the power failure is affecting more than five million individuals. Local fire departments and police are dealing with people trapped in elevators and other electrically operated spaces. Police are also directing traffic at all major intersections, except those in Washington, DC. If I could editorialize, the city always seems unprepared to deal with unusual situations. Water supplies are OK since the water utilities have emergency generators at most of their pumping stations. In fact, some transportation agencies also have emergency generators operating their traffic signals at important intersections. So we're doing OK for now."

The president smiled weakly, and then asked the question that had been on everyone's mind. "Assuming this power failure lasts for a while, how long can we sustain our population before we have to start considering mass evacuations or other dramatic measures? I'm assuming that resumption of rail service is out of the question since it would be unlikely that they'd have any backup power. True?"

The Director of DHS answered without hesitation. "True. We can forget about Amtrak or Metro for the time being. But freight service and bus transportation are OK since they rely on diesel engines." She then continued. "Our plans are adequate for a power outage of two weeks to a month. We can sustain the population by trucking in food, gasoline, medicine, and other supplies. We have portable generators that can be installed at a scattering of gas stations so that people can get gas for their cars. We can truck in diesel fuel for backup generators at hospitals, nursing homes, and other critical facilities, such as the White House," she concluded with a smile. "All this will work well for a regional blackout such as the one we're experiencing. But a widespread blackout such as the one they describe in their message would be a big problem, since we wouldn't be able to import supplies as easily from more distant areas. We'd also need significantly more supplies. I doubt we have the resources to feed a million people, for example. I sure hope that PEPCO and VEPCO can get the power on quickly. I also hope they figure out what happened and take steps to make sure it doesn't happen again." Without realizing it, everyone in the room was nodding in agreement with her comments.

The president felt that it was important to refocus the discussion. "It appears that DHS and their emergency management people have things under control for the time being. Now we need to decide how to deal with the threat itself."

Up to this point, the four congressional leaders had remained silent, observing the evolving preparations to deal with the existing situation. Breaking their silence, Wayne Zyder spoke up. "I interpret these actions and the threatening message as a declaration of war. With my colleagues' agreement, I intend to request an immediate emergency meeting of Congress to address this issue. We need to provide President Jeffers with all the authority he needs to take immediate and forceful steps necessary to combat this Bis Saif organization along with its allies. So far, we've been far too easy on them with our controlled response to their threats. It's time to take on these barbarians as ruthlessly as they have attacked us. We've got to put the country on a war footing in order to wipe them out." His three colleagues nodded in agreement, and without waiting for the president's concurrence, immediately began making calls to their staffs, who would recall Congress to address the needed actions.

Jeffers responded enthusiastically. "Wayne, I agree with your recommendation. And I agree that this message is tantamount to a declaration of war. I would hope that Congress would review the provisions of the War Powers Act in order to provide me with the expanded authority to take any actions needed to protect the country. I cannot keep asking for permission to do this and that as the situation unfolds. I need expanded and unlimited authority to take any actions needed to protect the country. But keep in mind the fact that we do not know anything about Bis Saif. It is really difficult to go to war against an invisible enemy. I am hoping that O'Brien and DeForce can solve this little problem, and solve it quickly."

The remainder of the evening was spent on two subjects: the response to the threatening message and the actions needed to deal with both the current emergency, as well as possible future emergencies that could be even more severe.

There was unanimous concurrence that there would be no capitulation to the terms of the Bis Saif message. The group also recognized that the search for the terrorist organization with its frightening technology could be a long one. And finally, it was agreed that the United States would create the illusion of a major troop withdrawal through the chaotic use of transport and cargo aircraft flying in and out of airfields in Iraq, Turkey, and Syria. Similarly, ship movements would be increased in random patterns that could not be interpreted as either a withdrawal or repositioning. General Altman agreed to initiate these actions. By doing this, the assembled group felt that they could buy a week of time from the Bis Saif message. Secondly, they would privately assure Israel of the United States' continuing support, while at the end of the first week publicly stating that the country was withdrawing its financial support. This could buy a second week of badly needed time.

Janice DeBeers took the lead for the next part of the discussion. "I figure that in spite of your best efforts, there is a good chance of a major blackout combined with terrorist attacks that will affect one fourth of the country. This is a horrifying possibility since it means that nearly eighty million people will be without the basic necessities—possibly for as long as a month, or possibly longer. We will immediately begin stockpiling the food, fuel, and medical supplies needed to support this population for an assumed two-month period. We will also create stockpiles of temporary shelters for some percentage of the refugees who are likely to leave the affected areas. And finally, we will have to identify the transportation facilities needed to get this material to the people who need it. I hope you all realize this is a herculean task that will involve the expenditures of vast sums of money. While these assignments do not have a one-hundred-percent chance of success, the future of our nation is at stake. We've got to give it our best shot."

President Jeffers succinctly summed up the results of the discussion. "Then we've all got our marching orders. Altman is to create the image of a troop withdrawal. DeBeers is to prepare for a major blackout. O'Brien and DeForce are to track down Bis Saif. Our friends from Congress are to call a special session. I will take responsibility for communicating this situation to the public. And George, I would like you to be responsible for coordinating this entire effort and keeping me informed of any and all new developments. This will be particularly difficult, since it is impossible to keep the Bis Saif demands under wrap, but at the same time we don't want everyone to panic. These are all tall orders with doubtful outcomes. But the nation is depending on us. You are all welcome to remain here and use the facilities of the Situation Room as well as other White House facilities. Our staff will do everything in its power to ensure that you have all the things that you need to perform your duties. I hear that congestion has died down, so if you want to go to your offices or return home, this is now possible. After all, it is after midnight. Best wishes for success."

With very little additional discussion, the country's top officials dispersed to perform their assigned tasks.

CHAPTER 16
THE SEARCH FOR DAYLIGHT

At 5:00 a.m. on the day following the receipt of the Bis Saif demands, the press secretary and his staff were hard at work crafting a speech for the president to deliver nationally. It was one of the most difficult speeches they had ever prepared, having received their instructions that the speech should be honest and straightforward, while at the same time leaving the impression that things were under control. It wouldn't do to throw the country into a panic. The speech was to be delivered from the Oval Office at 6:00 p.m. that evening—dinnertime, to ensure the largest possible audience. There were to be no questions from the press. A single camera and microphone would be used with feeds being provided to all interested news networks. There were no uninterested networks.

Promptly at 6:00 p.m., President Jeffers entered the Oval Office wearing his signature dark suit, white shirt, and red tie. He calmly sat at his desk, looked at the camera, and, at a signal from the director, began the most important speech of his life.

"Good evening, my fellow Americans. As most of you know by now, we have experienced a power interruption in the Washington, DC area accompanied by a major terrorist attack at Union Station. These events were accompanied by the receipt of a threatening message from an organization that has named itself Bis Saif. The full text of the message has been provided to members of the press and is available on the White House website. I am certain that it will be printed in tomorrow's edition of most of the nation's newspapers. In short, the message threatens repetition of similar incidents if we do not comply with their demands, which include troop withdrawals and cessation of our support for Israel. We find these demands to be nothing short of blackmail. We are the most powerful nation on the face of this planet. We pride ourselves in our ability to help maintain the peace, support the weak against the enemies of darkness, and provide our citizens with opportunities to lead comfortable and prosperous lives. We find the demands being made by this shadow organization of terrorists to be both preposterous and abhorrent. They are contrary to everything we stand for, and, as I have said, they are nothing short of blackmail.

"The Bis Saif blackmail letter contains specific threats about widespread power failures and terrorist attacks. The government along with the electric utilities are both repairing the existing system and taking steps to ensure that the power failure in the Washington, DC area will not be repeated. For security reasons I cannot be more specific regarding these steps. In addition, the government, as well as the power companies, are increasing their cyber security defenses to minimize the possibility of additional terrorist attacks. In addition, law enforcement agencies at every level of government are intensifying their efforts to find the perpetrators of the Union Station attacks and to protect the public against future attacks. As we speak, individuals on terrorist watch lists are being arrested and interrogated. Appropriate local law enforcement agencies and the FBI are being supplemented by members of our armed forces to provide the personnel needed for a comprehensive security sweep.

"To provide one additional level of protection, FEMA, the Federal Emergency Management Agency, has initiated a major program to provide the supplies needed in the event of a major power failure. We are stockpiling the food, medicine, fuel, and other items needed to help affected areas deal with an extended loss of power. This combination of activities will provide American citizens with the assurance that their lives will not be disrupted by the actions of a group of barbarians with selfish and self-centered goals.

"I pledge to keep you informed as we advance against these maniacs. America is a great power, and we will not become hostages to a rogue state whose aim is to take over the world."

With those concluding remarks, the cameras were turned off as the president crossed himself, sank back in his chair, and said to himself, "Whew! I only hope that most of that is true."

***

The president's speech dominated the media for the rest of the day and well into the following day. The consensus was that the speech was short on details. Questions abounded: Was the United States considering agreeing to the Bis Saif demands? Who is Bis Saif? What about Israel? Did our allies receive similar messages? The only response to these questions was speculation by the media's hired experts. The administration and congressional leaders remained silent, refusing to fuel speculation. Little by little the more experienced reporters began to realize that their government did not have answers to these questions. Their silence was covering up ignorance. They were observing a work in progress. This conclusion was reinforced by the refusal of high-level government officials to participate in any interviews.

When the Bis Saif message had been analyzed, discussed, and dissected until there was no more to extract, the media then turned its attention to the power failure and the Union Station massacre. This dual horror, in juxtaposition with the threats of the Bis Saif message, was leading to an increasing public restlessness that was verging on panic.

The morning talk shows of the major networks, including NBC's *Today Show*, ABC's *Good Morning America*, CBS's *The Early Show*, and the FOX show known as *Fox and Friends*, all had scheduled interviews with politicians in the know. By prior agreement, the four leaders of Congress who spent the evening in the White House Situation Room had each signed up with one of the four major networks. They had agreed with each other and the president that their interviews should be used to pave the way for quick and decisive congressional action that would give Jeffers the tools he needed to combat this new threat. No one was concerned about security leaks during their interviews

197

since there was nothing to leak. The CIA, NSA, FBI, and their friends in the foreign intelligence community had come up dry after twenty-four hours of searching for Bis Saif.

Rather than focusing on the Bis Saif message, the power failure, and the Union Station attacks, the four legislators agreed that they would focus on the legislation that was to be rushed through Congress.

Robert McIntyre's interview with Matt Lauer of the *Today Show* was typical.

Matt's demeanor was grave as he reviewed the past twenty-four hours with McIntyre, whose position as Senate Majority Leader scrolled across the screen.

"Senator McIntyre, were you in the White House Situation Room as the events of the night before last unfolded?"

"Yes, Matt, I was present, and I can tell you that the mood was the same as it probably was in every American living room throughout the country."

"And what was the president's reaction when he saw the message from this mysterious organization that calls itself Bis Saif?"

"I believe it was a mixture of anger and frustration. Anger because of the hubris associated with the demands being made by a ragtag bunch of hoodlums. Frustration both because it caught us by surprise and also because, at the time, we didn't have any knowledge of this organization."

Lauer immediately picked up on the phrase "at the time" and asked, "So you're saying that our intelligence services are hot on the trail of Bis Saif?"

McIntyre recognized that the question was a trap. "Matt, I'm not saying that we either have or do not have information regarding Bis Saif. With my concurrence, we've decided to keep our progress a secret in order to retain the element of surprise in our response to their ridiculous demands." McIntyre was experienced with interviews of this nature. So he forced Lauer to change the subject by saying, "But my specialty does not lie in the intelligence field. As I'm certain you know, legislative foreign policy is my specialty."

Matt instinctively understood McIntyre's change in direction and went along with it. "I can appreciate your position on this entire complex situation. No one can be an expert on everything. We'll let the experts address the security and recovery issues. This entire incident is so serious and complex that it has filled our discretionary programming for the next two weeks."

"I can appreciate that, Matt."

"So tell me what's going to happen legislatively."

McIntyre sat back on the couch he was sharing with Lauer and prepared to deliver a speech that he had carefully prepared the night before and memorized.

"Matt, as you just said, this is an extremely complex situation. So let me provide you with a little background. I apologize to you and your viewers if some of this appears very basic, but it's important to understand the basis on which we intend to proceed. However, before giving you my Civics 101 lecture, let me say that there are four of us in the lead on this issue, including the majority and minority leadership of both the House and the Senate. This is not a partisan issue. We're in lockstep on it. We feel that our mission is to provide the president with every available tool in the nation's military and intelligence arsenal to protect the United States of America."

He then began his lecture. "The basis for everything we do in Congress is the US Constitution. This is our Bible, so to speak. When we try to address a complicated situation, we often turn to the Constitution first to ensure that we are proceeding in a way that is consistent with the vision of our Founding Fathers."

Matt Lauer began shifting in his seat as he realized that his audience was going to be subjected to a rather dry monolog courtesy of Bob McIntyre, who continued unabated, ignoring Lauer's discomfort.

"Matt, as you know, the US Constitution divides the determination of activities associated with war between the Congress and the president. Congress has the power to declare war, raise and support the armed forces, control the war funding, and has the power, and I'm quoting from Article One, Section Eight here, '...to make all laws which shall be necessary and proper for carrying into execution other powers vested by the Constitution ....' The president is the commander-in-chief of the military. This role gives the president the power and responsibility for repelling attacks against the United States and in general leading and directing the armed forces." McIntyre concluded his discussion of the Constitution, saying, "This seems very clear, Congress declares war and the president executes it, but it isn't; many presidents have sent our military into battle without declaring war. This was true in Laos, Cambodia, Yugoslavia, Haiti, Iraq, and many other instances. Both parties have been guilty of this."

Trying to hurry McIntyre along, Lauer spoke up at this point. "Well, I understand there are some gray areas here, but in this instance, it seems obvious to me that the Bis Saif message is their declaration of war against the United States, and all Congress has to do is to declare war on them, and we're off and running."

"Matt, I agree that the declaration of war is a relatively easy step. It is the other associated powers that we can provide or withhold from the president that must be addressed. These so-called powers are provided in legislation that has become known as the War Powers Act. And let me tell you, there have been a bunch of them. But rather than boring you some more with the entire history of War Powers Resolutions, I'd like to summarize the terms of the act that was passed during World War II, which are probably the most extensive powers ever authorized. This act gave the president enormous authority, which included the ability to reorganize government agencies and corporations for the war, censor mail and other forms of communication with foreign countries, and condemnation of land for military purposes. It also repealed the confidentiality of census data so the FBI could round up Japanese Americans and changed contracting procedures for war-related production. These extraordinary powers given to the president, in addition to those already granted by the Constitution, represented a range of authority that would have made the emperors of ancient Rome jealous."

McIntyre paused to take a breath, allowing Lauer to jump in. "Are you telling me that consideration is being given to provide President Jeffers a similar level of authority?"

"Similar but not identical. First of all, let's define the word *consideration*. We intend to introduce legislation that will have similar objectives and organization to that of the first War Powers Resolution. Obviously the contents will be modified. But this Resolution will be debated in both houses of Congress and revised by a joint committee. So our considerations could be significantly modified by the time a final bill reaches the president's desk. Second, to your point of similar level of authority, I should emphasize that many of the circumstances here are considerably different than they were during the Second World War. In that case, we were fighting a relatively well-defined enemy that operated in a well-defined territory. In this case, we aren't even certain who our enemy is, and the conflict is global. This is more of a world war than WWII, although I hesitate to label it WWIII."

Lauer persisted. "I recognize the differences, but the War Powers Resolution we're discussing here had certain key elements that you've already summarized, including reorganizing the government and corporations, censoring the mail, modifying contracting processes, setting up internment camps for the Japanese, and condemnation of land. Would these key elements be in the draft bill that you're preparing for Congress?"

McIntyre refused to be pinned down on these points. "Matt, I can't tell you yet what will be proposed since it is a work in progress. I can tell you that many of these elements are likely to be included." And then in an attempt at humor, he added, "Of course, we do not have plans to set up internment camps for Japanese Americans."

McIntyre soon regretted his attempted humor when Matt latched onto that issue. "But are there plans for internment camps for Muslims?"

"Certainly not. One of the mistakes that we've made consistently over the years is to put all Muslims in the same basket. Just as many Japanese were loyal Americans during the Second

World War, and the same is true of Muslims. Although Muslim-bashing has become a popular form of campaign rhetoric, it is not the American way. There have been many instances in history during which Christians have committed the same atrocities as those being committed by ISIS and Bis Saif today. In fact, some Christian sects have recently terrorized their Muslim neighbors. Having said that, I believe that we should give the president the discretionary ability to proactively incarcerate or ban entry into the United States of groups which in his judgment pose a threat to our citizens. Defining that authority as well as its limits will be the responsibility of Congress."

Recognizing that he had pursued this topic to its conclusion, Matt Lauer ended the interview. "We have been speaking with Robert McIntyre, the Senate Majority Leader. Bob, thank you very much for providing us with an update on the legislative directions we can expect from Congress. We look forward to speaking with you again as this situation evolves."

In a jarring juxtaposition of subjects possible only on television, he then added, "And now stay tuned for advice on preparing your Christmas dinner for the upcoming holiday season."

***

It had been two days since the Bis Saif attack. Power had not yet been restored to the Washington region. DC police, with the assistance of the FBI, were still searching for the terrorists that had killed seventy-eight and wounded 312 travelers at Union Station. They had gathered few clues as to their whereabouts.

George Wilson had accepted the Jeffers' offer to camp out at the White House, which had the disadvantage that he was away from his family, trapped in the dark in Bethesda. But it had the advantage that he could spend an extra hour in bed before having to report for the daily intelligence briefing. He needed the extra sleep since the past two days had been the most harrowing period of his entire life.

Now it was 6:00 a.m., and he was seated with the president in the Oval Office gazing out the French doors at the view of the White House gardens, a view which was normally beautiful at this time of year, having been decorated with Christmas lights that illuminated the unusual December snowfall. But the sun had not yet risen above the horizon, and the lights were dark due to the power failure, turning the usual fairy-tale scene into a depressing vista. George could not help but think of his family freezing in their darkened residence in Bethesda.

The daily intelligence briefing with the president did not go well. George had little news to report other than FEMA's efforts to deal with the power failure. Since it had occurred in a relatively limited geographic region, there were adequate resources on hand to ensure that the public safety, health, and well-being could be maintained. Emergency generators had been shipped from throughout the country to ensure that many gas stations continued to operate, water supplies were maintained, hospitals were fully electrified, and deliveries of basic goods, including food and medicine, could continue. The ability of the government and the non-governmental organizations (NGOs) to deal with these types of emergencies had been proven during numerous similar events in the past, including most recently Hurricane Sandy in the New York/New Jersey area.

Jeffers was consoled by the report, but still very worried. "Have the utilities made any progress in identifying and repairing the cause of the blackout?"

Wilson paused a minute, trying to decide how much background to give the president. Much of the explanation for the blackout was highly technical and the president was not a technophile. In fact, George didn't understand much of the stuff himself. "Mr. President, in order to understand the problem, we have to know a little about the power distribution system. As I understand it, the system works like this: The electric power that we use in our homes and businesses begins at a generation facility that contains a large electric generator. Energy is required to spin the generator, which may be turned by water flowing through a hydroelectric dam, steam power produced by burning coal or nuclear energy, a diesel engine, a gas turbine, or wind. The electricity leaves the generator and enters a transmission substation that uses huge transformers that increase it to a very high voltage of between 155,000 and 765,000 volts. This extremely high voltage is used because it can be transmitted efficiently over great distances by the transmission lines that can be seen on towers throughout the United States. Are you with me so far, Mr. President?"

"I think so, although I'm not certain about the function of the transformers."

"Transformers are electrical devices that change the voltage level of an incoming source of electricity into a different voltage at their outputs. They are used to either increase or decrease the incoming voltage level. Those in the business call these step-up and step-down transformers. In this case, the relatively low voltage of the electricity produced by the generator is greatly increased to hundreds of thousands of volts by huge, expensive step-up transformers. As an interesting sidelight, transformers will only work with alternating current, which is one of the reasons our power distribution system is based exclusively on the use of AC. Another significant fact is that the transformers used to step up the voltage to the high levels needed by the transmission lines are in short supply. These large power transformers, known as LPTs, are very expensive, costing between $3 million and $10 million each. Since they are tailored to the company's specifications, they cannot be mass produced and about seventy-five percent of them are purchased from other countries. Needless to say, there is no inventory of LPTs. So if either a physical attack or a cyber attack were to incapacitate multiple transformers, the large regions served by the transmission lines would go dark. It would take months and millions of dollars to procure replacement transformers."

Seeing that he now had Jeffers' complete attention, the director of national intelligence continued. "When the transmission lines reach their destination, they are terminated at a power substation, which contains step-down transformers that reduce the voltage to a level of less than ten thousand volts. The power substations also distribute this power to multiple sets of ten-thousand-volt lines. These lines carry the power to individual neighborhoods, where additional transformers step down the voltage to the two hundred and forty volt level that is connected to residences and businesses. So it appears to be a very simple system—generator to transmission line to local distribution lines. A transformer at a power substation is involved with every step of the process."

George concluded his lesson with a prophetic statement. "It's such a simple process. What could go wrong?"

Jeffers concurred. "I agree. There doesn't seem to be anything in the process that could explain the blackout that's hit us."

The DNI continued. "In the interest of understandability, I left off the complexity of the process. Power companies are challenged by the need to balance the supply of electricity against the demand. Too much power on the transmission lines and they overheat and in some cases actually sag. Too little power and the voltage levels at the customers' premises drops, which reduces the efficiency of their devices and in some cases damages their equipment. The solution to this problem is that the power companies use computers to keep their electrical loads balanced. Different parts of the country need more or less power at different times of day. For example, on a hot summer day, the East Coast may need power at midday, while it is still early and relatively cool in the morning on the West Coast. The companies buy and sell electricity in the same manner that stocks are traded, with purchasing companies attempting to meet high demand and selling companies making money from their excess electricity. Computer-controlled equipment is used to buy and sell power as well as to monitor the condition of the lines to ensure that all transmission lines and local distribution lines are operating correctly. This same equipment is used to quickly identify outages, to which field repair crews can be dispatched."

He added with a slight attempt at humor. "If you want to act knowledgeable, the two types of equipment that perform these functions are known as Surveillance, Control, and Data Acquisition, or SCADA, systems, and Energy Management

Systems, or EMS. Although there is some overlap among their functions, the SCADA systems generally perform the monitoring functions while the EMS systems control the distribution of all this power among multiple transmission lines. Since they are computer controlled, these are the systems that are potential targets for hackers. I'll bet that when you speak with the industry officials, they will immediately begin talking about the SCADA and EMS systems. And speaking of industry officials, there are really three primary players with whom we need to coordinate: PEPCO for Maryland and the District, VEPCO for Virginia, and, most important, PJM, the company that manages the long-distance transmission lines that serve both of these companies. That concludes my lecture for today," George said, sitting back in his chair and taking a sip of coffee, which had become cold during his speech.

The president reacted to the lecture. "Phew! I can only imagine how many transformers, miles of transmission lines, SCADA and EMS systems could be targets for potential hackers. There's no way we can protect all these systems and rely on the many companies that operate them."

In their give and take environment, the DNI relaxed and took the liberty of addressing the president by his first name. "Chris, you're right. I can provide you with a mind numbing list of numbers. But perhaps the most significant is the fact that there are about three thousand and three hundred electric utilities in the United States involved with some portion of the generation and transmission of power. Some are well-funded giants, and others are struggling small companies. In one way or other, they all represent access points to the grid. Once you get to the grid, you can get to the SCADA and EMS systems and do some serious damage by placing excess electricity on the high-voltage lines, or shutting them down completely. Not all of the LPTs are well protected, which makes them susceptible to physical attacks. There are many vulnerabilities in the system. Bis Saif demonstrated its sophistication by shutting down a well-defined geographic region on a schedule that they had defined. I think we're in big trouble."

"Speaking of Bis Saif, how are our intelligence agencies doing with the identification of their people and their location?"

Although he was anxious to deliver some good news to his president, George came up dry. "I'm afraid that they're nowhere. NSA has been combing through the telephone records for mention of the Bis Saif name and has come up dry. We've also contacted all of our usual sources throughout the world. So far nothing."

"Give me some good news," Jeffers said, sensing the need for some bit of information he could use to encourage the public. "Have we found the terrorists that shot up Union Station? How are we coming with supplies for the general public?"

George answered, looking down at the Oval Office carpet. "No progress on finding the terrorists. The only good news is that relief supplies and generators are flowing into the region. FEMA and local agencies have gained a lot of experience with major disasters as a result of various hurricanes, tornados, and earthquakes. They've responded relatively quickly and even the ever-critical press has been positive. Not to pile additional worries on you, but we need to be concerned about the fact that we've obtained these supplies from other parts of the country. If there is a more widespread power failure within the next few weeks, we would not be able to respond as effectively."

The president thought for a moment before speaking. When he did, it was a thoughtful response. "This Bis Saif organization must be incredibly smart and well organized to pull off a stunt like this. They've demonstrated as high a level of competence as Al Qaeda did during their 9-11 attacks on the Pentagon and World Trade Center. But they're even more competent at hiding themselves. We can't attack them since we don't know where and who they are."

Jeffers continued. "I could call the directors of our intelligence agencies and yell at them, but I doubt it would do any good. I'm sure they've applied as much pressure within their own agencies as possible. There's no need to impress the urgency of this situation on them. I could also go on TV to reassure the public that we're making progress, but that would be a little bold, even for me, since it wouldn't be true and would soon be uncovered by our friends in the press."

The room was silent as the two men sipped their coffee and contemplated the depressing scene outside the windows. Finally Jeffers sighed and rose from his chair, put on his suit jacket and walked toward the door of the office, saying, "I guess we'd both better get to work. I've got to attend to the legislative issues, and you'd better begin coordinating the intelligence agencies. Maybe a joint effort among the warring agencies will turn up something that has been overlooked. I sure wish these guys would play nicely together."

***

The president hadn't yet left the office when his telephone buzzed. "Mr. President, it's Jan. I've got a call on hold from the CEO of PJM. He insists on speaking with you. Says it's urgent."

"Jan, what are you doing at your desk at 6:00 a.m.? Did you go home last night?"

"Mr. President, I slept on the couch last night. With the power out, travel in DC has become impossible. I'm not much to look at this morning."

"You always look just fine to me," responded the president.

"I've always said that as a politician, you're the best. Now do you want to take that call?"

"Why not? Put him on. Do you know his name?"

Always prepared, Jan responded, "David Powers," and connected him with the president.

Thinking that Powers was an appropriate name for someone in the lead of a major electrical utility, the president picked up the phone. "Good morning, David. What can I do for you this morning?"

Somewhat taken aback that the president knew his name, Powers paused briefly before responding. "Mr. President, thank you for taking my call. I'm sure your schedule is extremely busy, and I wouldn't have interrupted you unless it was on a matter of utmost importance." Barely stopping for breath, Powers continued. "I've got good news and bad news. The good news is that we think we've determined the cause of the power failure. The bad news is that it is the result of an extremely sophisticated hacking attack that caused our EMS to redirect the power in such a manner that it overloaded our high-voltage power lines, causing several of them to fail." Then realizing he had used technical terms with which the president may not be familiar, he began to explain. "I'm sorry, I should explain our terminology. EMS is a reference to our Energy Management System, which is fully computerized."

The president smiled to himself and silently thanked George Wilson for his technical briefing. "No need to apologize. I already have a passing familiarity with your distribution system, and understand that the EMS computers try to keep the load on your power lines balanced."

With relief, David Powers continued. "Our problem is that we don't have the personnel with the ability to diagnose the source of the hacking attack, nor do we completely understand how they were able to take control of our EMS equipment. I'm calling to request, no, to plead, for federal assistance with the identification of the source of the attack as well as some guidance as to what we can do to defend against future attacks. This is an urgent matter. The attacks caused a lot of damage, some of which will take months to repair. We've requested assistance from other power companies around the country to provide both temporary and permanent repairs to the network."

The president responded without hesitation. "I will guarantee you that we will provide assistance using the best resources available. It may be that these resources are available from private industry, but we have some influence among those folks as well. I'll have George Wilson, our director of national intelligence, contact either you or whoever you designate within the next few hours. The information you're seeking is the same as the information we need, so let's work together for everyone's benefit. Promise you'll call me directly if you're not getting what you need."

Powers sounded greatly relieved. "Thank you very much, Mr. President. I regret that this crisis occurred in the first place, but we've got to figure out how they did it before we can make sure it doesn't happen again."

"Before we end this conversation, I have two questions for you," responded the president. "First, are you already working with PEPCO and VEPCO, or do they need similar assistance?"

"Yes, we have a joint team. I'll inform them of our conversation, and we'll provide you with a single point of contact to ensure that things are handled as efficiently as possible," Powers said. "What was your second question?"

"What is your best estimate of the recovery time for the system? I know you're not certain, but I need something that I can use to hold off the press."

"I can't give you a single number since power will be restored area by area. My best guess is that some areas will have power within a week. These will be the sections that are on the fringes of the blacked-out area. But the central part of the region, including Washington, DC, will be much later. Somewhere between one and three months. I wouldn't pretend to tell you what to do, but it may not be good to be too optimistic. All hell will break loose if you say one month and it takes us three."

Without telling him what he was going to do, the president thanked Powers and ended the conversation, passing the call back to Jan so that she could get the contact information.

He called George Wilson, told him of the conversation and gave him his marching orders for supporting PJM, including instructions to find the best cyber-security experts in the country immediately, with NSA's assistance.

CHAPTER 17

HOPE SPRINGS ETERNAL

It was 7:00 a.m.in Rafah, and the dusty streets were barren of the Christmas decorations that adorned other cities throughout the world. The Gaza Strip had undergone an ethnic cleansing encouraged by the Arab Brotherhood in nearby Egypt. This morning, the rush hour traffic included a battered Toyota Camry, whose condition made its color indistinguishable, although it was likely to have originally been the blue found on Toyotas throughout the world. The driver and passenger of the vehicle were dressed in traditional local clothes, wearing khaki pants and shirts and the hardhats of construction workers. An inspection of their vehicle would have revealed that it carried construction tools and vests.

The Toyota slowed as it entered the central city. Parking was at a premium in this area, and to the casual observer, the pair in the vehicle were on their way to a nearby construction site and were looking for parking. As they cruised past a partially destroyed apartment building, they stopped and removed wooden barricades that had been placed near the curb to reserve their parking place. The two occupants took out a large dented metal thermos of coffee, which they poured into Styrofoam cups while they settled back to wait.

Their wait ended with the arrival of a smoking city bus that turned the corner and stopped to discharge a single passenger. The two coffee drinkers hastily poured their coffee into the street and exited their car, carrying a small bundle, which was nothing more than a simple canvas bag. As the passenger who had been discharged from the bus passed the car, the bag was slipped over his head, tied tightly, and the struggling man was bundled into the trunk of the vehicle. The entire process was concluded in less than a minute.

It was a short drive from downtown Rafah to the nearby countryside, which was fortunate due to the banging coming from the trunk. As soon as they left the city limits, the car turned onto a dusty dirt road that ended at an abandoned shack that looked as if it had been deserted for years. After pulling behind the shack, the two got out of the car, opened the trunk, and dragged their struggling captive into the shack.

When the bag had been removed, Abdul Nasser shook his head to clear his vision and his mind. There were only four pieces of furniture in the shack: three chairs and a table. A dirty sink in the corner looked as if it hadn't been used in years. The single window had a broken pane of glass covered with an oily cloth. The two kidnappers stood over him with hoods over their heads and their pistols pointed at his head. *Not a good place to die*, thought Nasser.

The taller of the two spoke first in accented Arabic. "We have some questions. If you answer them completely and honestly we will not harm you, and we will let you go after you've answered all our questions. Do you understand?"

Nasser mutely nodded, being too scared to trust his shaky voice.

With the preambles completed, the two kidnappers grabbed him under his arms and dragged him to the heavy wooden chair that made up twenty-five percent of the shack's furnishings. They tied his hands behind the chair, lashed his ankles to its legs, and for good measure tightly tied a belt around his waist and to the back of the chair. He was completely immobilized.

The shorter of his two captors dragged one of the other chairs over in front of Nasser with its back facing him. The man then sat backward on the chair facing Nasser with his arms folded over the back. "Tell me what you do," he asked in a soft voice. In his mind, Nasser named him the inquisitor.

"I'm an engineer with the Hamas," was Nasser's response.

"What are you working on?"

"I repair equipment that is broken," Nasser lied.

"What type of equipment?"

"Items like navigation equipment. You know, things that use GPS. They're used so people don't get lost." Nasser lied again, but with enough of a thread of truth that he felt that he was neither lying nor providing any useful information.

"Who uses the equipment?"

"The army. It helps their troops pass through the desert without getting lost." This was a total lie.

"What are the model numbers of the equipment?"

This time, Nasser was stopped cold. He did not know whether the army used GPS equipment at all, and he certainly did not know any model numbers. Who were these men, and why were they asking these questions? His arms were aching in the hot, smelly shack, and he was afraid. He remained silent.

"I thought I told you that you would be released unharmed if you cooperated?" said his inquisitor.

The tallest of the pair walked over to him and hit him in the face with a closed fist. Nasser felt certain that the punch had knocked out one of his teeth. He felt the blood collecting in his mouth and began coughing. "Don't kill him yet," said the inquisitor.

"Now let's go back over the information you have provided us. You said that you are an engineer, and that you work for Hamas. We believe that to be true." Nasser nodded.

"You also told us that you repair broken equipment. We don't believe that this is entirely true. Is it?"

Nasser protested. "I understand that I will be safe as long as I tell the truth. That's why I am not lying to you."

The tall man walked around behind Nasser, grabbed the index finger of his bound left hand, and slowly began bending it backward. Nasser screamed and blurted out, "Well it's almost true. I build new equipment, and when it breaks I repair it." He felt the pressure on his finger easing.

The inquisitor then moved on to Nasser's next answer. "You said you work on navigation equipment but you couldn't provide us with a model number or name. Obviously your answer was a complete lie. Unless you tell the truth, your damaged finger will be nothing."

Nasser hesitated before answering, thinking, *Who are these people? What will they do with the information I give them? How long would I be able to hold out anyway? Should I just give in?*

The inquisitor pressed harder. "I am going to ask my friend to coax you to tell the truth unless you answer me truthfully within the next five seconds."

The big man moved behind Nasser's chair and this time grabbed the index finger of his right hand. As he began bending the finger, Nasser screamed. But he held on until the finger snapped—a horrible sound accompanied by horrible pain.

The man then took the next finger in his hand. Nasser couldn't stand the pain any further and sobbed out "Okay, okay. I'll answer your questions. Just make him stop."

The inquisitor nodded to the big man, who stepped back from the chair.

"Okay, Nasser. Now suppose you tell us about your work."

"Well, I'll tell you what I know if you promise to let me go."

"We'll let you go if we believe you're telling the truth. Don't forget, we know some of what you are going to tell us, so it will be easy to figure out if you're giving us accurate information."

"You wanted to know what I worked on," answered Nasser with a sob. "I was a member of a team that developed the guidance system for the Suquur."

The inquisitor interrupted. "What is the Suquur?"

Summoning his last ounce of courage, Nasser responded. "If you knew Arabic, you'd know that Suquur means hawk. It's the name of our new missile, which is developed to kill Jews."

With that, the tall man punched Nasser in the face again. Loosening another tooth.

"That's a good start," the inquisitor calmly interjected, ignoring Nasser's new source of pain. "Now let's move on to other subjects. What do you know about Bis Saif?"

Nasser turned pale, unintentionally displaying a knowledge of the subject. He responded, lisping through his broken and bleeding teeth. "I know very little. I only know their name."

The inquisitor shook his head and answered sadly. "I'm afraid I'm going to have to ask my friend to encourage you to be more forthcoming."

Nasser didn't answer, and the tall man moved behind the chair to which he was tied. He took another finger in his hands and began to bend it.

"No! No! Not that again. I'm telling you the truth. I know very little. But if I tell you what I do know, they'll kill me."

"We'll kill you too if you don't tell us what you know. Except your death at our hands will be much more painful."

Nasser hesitated a long time and did not respond until receiving a little more encouragement from the tall man in the form of increased pressure on his fingers. "I only know that they are an extremely well-financed organization. They provided us with the drones we are using to strike at your cities."

"How do you communicate with them?"

"I don't know. Another of our group is responsible for this communication."

"Who is the other member of your group?"

"His name is Hasan Jouda. He was a member of our laboratory, but he is not here anymore. He left six months ago," answered Nasser, now speaking freely since he was at the end of his knowledge of the subject and anxious to preserve what was left of his body.

"What was his role at the lab?"

"He was the engineer that developed the Suquur guidance software."

"How does he know Bis Saif?"

"I'm not sure, since his activities with them were top secret. But I believe he traveled to their headquarters to arrange their support of our movement."

"Where is he now?"

"Believe me, I don't have any idea. He disappeared mysteriously without leaving me any information about his location. Believe me, I would like to find him also since I've got some questions about his design."

"Is Hasan a computer specialist?"

"Yes, and he's a very good one," responded Nasser proudly.

"I didn't think any of you Hamas goons were smart enough for technical work."

"Well you're wrong," snapped Nasser. "He graduated with honors from Alexandria University in Egypt. I guess we're not so stupid after all, are we?"

The inquisitor and the tall man nodded to each other. They believed that they had wrung Hassan dry, and further interrogation would produce little payoff. The tall man opened a small satchel out of sight of Nasser, extracted a hypodermic needle, and inserted it into his arm. Nasser winced briefly and then passed out. As soon as they were certain that he was unconscious, the two men untied him, took off their hoods, cleaned up any evidence of their presence, removed Nasser's shoes and drove off in their Toyota, taking his shoes with them.

As they left, the inquisitor said to his partner, "Shouldn't we talk to Hasan's parents and get more information about him? Maybe a physical description."

"No need to take additional risks of getting captured," he said. "We can easily hack into the files of Alexandria University. They'll have photos, addresses, and physical descriptions. Also useful—they'll have a list of some personal contacts, work experience, and courses that he's taken."

The two then lapsed into silence as they drove toward the northern border of the Gaza Strip.

When Nasser woke up several hours later, they were long gone. He then began the long trek back to Rafah. On wobbly legs and with bare feet, it was a long, painful hike that took most of the day, a day which gave him time to work out a story that would explain his injuries without revealing his conversation with the inquisitor and the torturer.

***

Things were becoming tense at the White House. Four days had passed since the blackout and the terrorist attack at Union Station with little progress to show for the intense worldwide search being conducted for Bis Saif and the domestic search for the terrorists. Power was being restored sporadically in the suburbs, but downtown Washington, DC was still blacked out except for occasional lights powered by generators. Traffic was not as congested as might have been expected since most downtown workers remained within the relative comforts of their homes rather than commuting to cold, darkened office buildings.

President Christopher Jeffers and Senate Majority Leader Robert McIntyre were deep in discussion at a small table in the corner of the Oval Office, working on the list of special war powers about to be considered by Congress. "Bob, we've got to get a list that will give me the ability to control the country and fight these Bis Saif characters, but one that has a chance of being passed. And we've got to prepare that list right now, so you can write a bill to be debated by Congress tomorrow. We're running out of time."

"Chris, I know that you think the war powers list is important, and I agree. But equally important is a declaration of war by Congress. If we don't have that, there's no need for war powers legislation. After all, we're not at war."

"That's why I'm going to introduce the declaration of war bill," added McIntyre "There's little doubt that it will pass, but I feel that my introduction of the bill will ensure it receives the urgency it deserves. But I would also appreciate it if you would have George Wilson on standby in case we need some expert witness testimony. You never know when someone will come up with a killer question that will derail the bill. I want to be fully prepared."

"He's yours. Now let's turn our attention to the war powers."

No sooner had the president said that then the intercom on his desk buzzed. It was Jan and she sounded excited. "Mr. President, I'm sorry to disturb you, but you have an urgent call from Moshe Tamer." There was no need for her to add that he was the Prime Minister of Israeli, since Moshe and Chris had developed a close working relationship due to the escalating attacks from Hamas.

The majority leader rose to leave the Oval Office, but the president motioned for him to remain as he picked up the phone. "It's good to hear from you, Moshe. How is everything?"

"Chris, this is no time for formalities. I have very important news for you, and I need your help to follow up."

Clearly intrigued, Jeffers asked, "I hope it's good news. We could use some of that around here."

Moshe continued without responding directly to Chris. "We have a lead on Bis Saif. We have identified a Palestinian who has been in contact with them. That is the good news. The bad news is that we do not know where he is. And that is one of the reasons I am contacting you. We need the American intelligence resources to help in a worldwide search for him."

"I am impressed and delighted with your success. I'm assuming this is the work of your Mossad. Of course we'll help. Please send your information to George Wilson as soon as possible. He'll make certain that the search for this Palestinian begins immediately. Jan Adams will give you his contact information. How was Mossad able to identify the source?"

"Of course, I'll make certain that your George Wilson receives the information. I cannot give you all the details, but the source was bragging to his friends about the good fortune of Hamas to have attracted the support of Bis Saif. Needless to say, we were alerted to the existence of this dangerous organization from contacts made by your CIA." Then Moshe added, following a brief pause. "But Chris, I need to tell you more. While we were investigating the Bis Saif lead, we discovered the laboratory where the Hamas guided missiles are being produced. They call their missile the Suquur. I want you to know that their facility is being bombed while we speak. We would appreciate any assistance you can provide in deflecting negative world opinion that is likely to be created by this action."

"I understand," replied Jeffers curtly. "You do what you have to do to defend yourselves."

Moshe Tamer continued as if he hadn't heard Jeffers' reply. "Those missiles could have wiped us out. As their payload capabilities increase they could destroy our country. I can't let that happen. I also hope that you are not unduly influenced by the threat from Bis Saif. We are very concerned about their demand that you discontinue your support of my country. We feel as if we are under attack from all directions. The Arabs are beginning to get organized and my people are very scared."

Hearing the tension in Tamer's voice, Jeffers softened his response somewhat. "I understand your concerns. You are used to living under the threat of annihilation. These types of threats are new to us in the United States. We'll have to work together to solve this problem. And there is certainly no need for you to fear that we'll agree to any of Bis Saif's demands, much less that we would withdraw our support of Israel."

Tamer exhaled and answered with evident relief. "Thank you, Mr. President. I was hoping we could count on you."

***

While Tamer and Jeffers were talking, two Israeli Air Force F-15E Strike Eagle fighters, known in Israel as the F15I Ra'am, took off from the IAF base on the extreme tip of southern Israel near Eilat. The base was collocated at Ovda airport, a dual-use facility that served both military and civilian flights. Civilian flights were delayed for their departure. When the F-15s reached cruising altitude, they turned northwest for a brief trip of less than 200 miles to Rafah on the Mediterranean coast. Before crossing the border into Palestine, they rapidly descended to a low altitude of below 150 feet and accelerated to maximum speed to avoid interception. Arriving at Rafah, their navigation systems guided them to their target, a partially destroyed apartment building. They made multiple passes over the building, dropping their bunker-buster bombs until the building was completely destroyed, including its basement and subbasements. They made a tight turn over Rafah and returned unchallenged to their Ovda airport base.

The destruction of the building was complete. It included the death of Abdul Nasser and Ossama, his superior. Shadi, the website developer who was replaced by Hasan Jouda, had the misfortune of visiting the facility at the time and also died. But most important, the attack terminated the short-lived Suquur program that had been the pride of Hamas.

Hamas protested loudly that their airspace had been violated and numerous civilians killed in the raid. They complained that the destroyed building had housed numerous refugees from previous Israeli raids, who were now either dead or homeless. Their protests at the UN led to a vote in the General Assembly to censor Israel for their brutal actions. The Israeli government with United States support voted against the bill, indicating that the raid had been an attack on a Hamas missile production facility. The evidence produced by the Israelis did little to influence the vote of condemnation.

***

Turning to McIntyre, who had only heard the president's end of the call, Jeffers quickly summarized the telephone conversation. McIntyre's reaction matched that of the president. "Well that is certainly hopeful news. But we've got a way to go and not much time."

"I agree," responded Jeffers. "We've got to be careful not to be distracted by the uproar that Hamas has created over the bombing of their missile facility. But I must say that we would do the same thing if there was an enemy threatening to rain missiles on our civilian population. We've got to support them in the press and at the UN. Now let's get down to business. I'd like to get out in front of the new war powers bill with specific proposals."

McIntyre nodded and added, "Let's get to work. Why don't we begin with the list of war powers included in previous bills and determine which should remain and which should be deleted. Then we can add additional items as we see fit."

With this preamble, the two rolled up their sleeves and developed the following list.

First: The ability to reorganize the agencies of the Executive Branch without the prior approval of Congress, providing such changes enhance the nation's ability to conduct the war. However, any changes to the budget caused by the reorganization require the approval of Congress.

Second: The ability to censor all communications, including mail, telephone, digital communications of any form, and video communications being transmitted outside of the United States.

Third: Condemnation of land or facilities for military purposes, providing there is no alternative readily available.

Fourth: Streamlining procedures to permit the Department of Defense and the intelligence agencies to contract with private sector organizations bypassing the time-consuming competitive selection process. To ease concerns, this item suggested that Congress retain the ability to review and cancel such contracts after the fact if abuses were demonstrated.

Fifth: The ability to assassinate terrorists or their leadership, including leaders of rogue nations, without requiring the approval of Congress or the need to report on the existence of these acts.

Sixth: The ability to expand the war beyond any geographic or political areas defined by the declaration of war without the prior approval of Congress.

The majority leader sat back in his chair and exclaimed. "Whew! That's quite a list. Do you think it has a chance to get past Congress?"

"It is likely to pass, but undoubtedly with changes. It's in your hands now. I assume that your first step will be to get together with the Leadership Group. They should be a big help." With a laugh he added, "Now let's have a drink."

***

While Jeffers poured modest glasses of bourbon on the rocks for the two of them, McIntyre briefly left the Oval Office in order to ask Jan to round up the other three members of the Leadership Group. Following his drink and small talk with the president, McIntyre climbed into his limousine and motored to his office in the Russell Senate Office Building, where he met with the rest of the group.

Surprisingly, the meeting of the Leadership Group and subsequent debates in Congress moved quickly and without rancor. Within forty-eight hours from the meeting in the Oval Office, war was declared on Bis Saif, and, for good measure, ISIS and al-Qaeda. The New War Powers Bill was passed, including a list that was substantially unchanged from the one that the president and the majority leader had developed, except that the ability to censor communications was deleted.

As a result, Jeffers now found himself with undisputed power to wage war with only minimal oversight from the legislative branch, which, according to the Constitution, was to provide advice and consent related to many of these items.

***

The president and Bob McIntyre, his war powers ally, had reconvened in the Oval Office for a second time. Jeffers opened the conversation. "Bob, thanks for your valuable leadership. I think this is an important step in preparing for the oncoming catastrophe."

"But Chris, you now have more power than any president has had since Roosevelt. What if it isn't enough?"

"I've thought about that. But there are some other powers that might be useful, but I'd be reluctant to push our luck unless there's a dire need for them."

"Like what?"

"Well, I'll tell you about my list, but I guarantee that you wouldn't get it through Congress as readily as the current list. Additional powers might include:

First: The ability to overturn judicial rulings that hamper our ability to wage war.

Second: The ability to initiate searches of suspects without requiring compelling evidence typically needed for search warrants.

Third: The ability to move funds between departments without congressional approval as needed for the conduct of the war.

Fourth: The ability to define classes of citizens by race, religion, or occupation, who are to be detained both for their protection and ours.

Fifth: The power to temporarily extend the terms of office of selected federal officials whose presence in the government is essential to continuing the war."

Sixth: The ability to arrest, detain, and question both citizens and aliens without compelling evidence, for a period of not more than ninety days.

McIntyre didn't respond right away. It was clear that he was turning over the president's list in his mind and was not in complete agreement with some of the more extreme items on the list. After a pause he began his carefully framed response. "Whew! That's quite a list. I'm not sure that all of this would be very popular with Congress. I'd be particularly concerned about overturning judicial decisions and detaining classes of citizens. As you know, I'm a student of the US Constitution, and your list reminds me of a document that George Mason wrote objecting to the draft of the Constitution before it was ratified by the states. I thought the quote was so significant that I've memorized it. I believe it went something like this: "This government will set out a modest aristocracy; it is at present impossible to foresee whether it will, in its operation, produce a monarchy, or a corrupt tyrannical aristocracy; it will most probably vibrate some years between the two, and then terminate in one or the other." The bottom line is that the current War Powers Act is the beginning of the vibration foreseen by Mason. The additional powers you are proposing certainly seem as if we are headed toward a monarchy. Although, in your case, I am confident it would be a benevolent monarchy." He quickly added with a smile at the end of his statement.

Jeffers was not offended by McIntyre's brief speech. He just smiled. "I'm afraid this does sound like a monarchy. But somehow we've got to get this situation under control. Between you and me, a massive national power failure could lead to a nationwide panic, with millions dying from starvation, or just fighting over a dwindling food supply. Things would not go well without a firm hand on the controls."

McIntyre replied, "I thought our Israeli friends had made some progress?"

"Yes, their lead is a big breakthrough. But that's all it is. We've got two days before they deliver on their next round of threats, and we still don't understand their organization or the location of any of their facilities. I'm starting to panic myself, although so far I've succeeded in maintaining a calm exterior."

"I'll see what I can do about getting this through Congress, although I hate to go to the well a second time so soon after the first bill was passed. Let me discuss this with the other members of the Leadership Group. In the meantime, maybe we should have another drink."

CHAPTER 18

TIME IS RUNNING OUT

Five days had passed since the power failure of the Washington, DC region and the terrorist attack, and the citizens of the region had seen little progress. Power had been restored in limited areas at the fringe of the region, mostly through the efforts of the power companies to serve these areas with energy diverted from other undamaged utilities. Many residents were suffering from the lack of power in the early winter chill typical of the Middle Atlantic Seaboard. Their misery was further compounded by the need to wait on long lines to pump fuel for their cars at the few gas stations equipped with FEMA furnished generators. In an effort to reduce the pressure on the gas stations, the three jurisdictions of Maryland, Virginia, and the District of Columbia had imposed rules on traveling that had been unseen since the Arab oil crisis in 1973, during which vehicles with odd-numbered license plates could be driven on odd numbered days of the month, while vehicles with even-numbered license plates could only be driven on even numbered days of the month, and only ten gallons of gas could be pumped by each customer.

Supplies of groceries and other basic necessities were also in limited supply. Only stores equipped with generators were open, and many of their shelves were bare due to the difficulties associated with getting deliveries. Here again, long lines waiting for entry to the stores, reminiscent of the lines at Moscow's departments stores, were the rule.

Local fire departments were kept busy responding to calls that resulted from the use of candles and kerosene lamps by a public unfamiliar with the basic safety rules associated with these devices. Emergency evacuation centers were opened at local schools and other public buildings to house those displaced by fire, or whose health required a more comfortable and safer environment.

The misery was generally being tolerated by the public, who understood the difficulties faced by the officials charged with their protection. But the unhappiness of many bubbled over when it was announced that the final game of the Warriors football season was going to be indefinitely postponed. The cancellation decision was made because the stadium was without power. This was a critical game that determined the Warriors playoff chances. The cancellation seemed to break the back of the public's patience with the power failures. It spawned spontaneous demonstrations, both at the stadium parking lot and in Lafayette Square across from the front entrance of the White House.

As he often did, the president was observing the demonstrations on a monitor in his living quarters, accompanied by Melissa, the First Lady. When he first met her at Texas A&M, Chris had quickly realized that his wife-to-be was a bright individual, and he had grown to value her opinion on a variety of subjects, not the least of which was her uncanny ability to evaluate members of his staff. The video they watched was furnished courtesy of a closed-circuit television setup installed by the Secret Service.

Both Christopher and Melissa preferred to use the sitting room in the northeast corner of the second floor White House residence quarters. The room was comfortably furnished and offered a beautiful view of the White House grounds through its floor-to-ceiling windows. The Jeffers sat together on a loveseat positioned on the wall facing the windows.

As they watched, a crowd began to gather in Lafayette Park across Pennsylvania Avenue from the White House main entrance. The protestors had gathered in the shadow of President Andrew Jackson mounted on a prancing warhorse. Protest signs began to appear seemingly out of nowhere as the protestors organized themselves. The square was ringed by members of the Metropolitan DC Police and Secret Service to ensure that the protest remained peaceful. A police mobile command post along with buses to transport arrested individuals were parked out of sight of the cameras.

Many of the signs featured clumsy acronyms created to provide supposedly memorable messages to the TV broadcast audience. Melissa read the signs as they appeared. "Chris, look at that one. Stop Lethal Arab Muslims or SLAM." She editorialized, "It didn't take long for racial hatred to appear. SLAM seems to be taking aim at both Muslims and Arabs. No matter how much you remind people of our Constitution, the bigotry takes center stage."

"Mel, I know it's frustrating. But just keep reminding yourself that they represent a relatively small percentage of the population," Jeffers said.

"If you didn't like SLAM, perhaps you'll like this next one. Citizens United for Football, or CUF. Glad to hear that the public has their priorities straight. This group places football above all our current difficulties. They're upset because their precious football game was cancelled. I wonder whether Americans haven't had it too soft for too long when football becomes most important."

Melissa's statements reminded Christopher of his reaction to the crowd at the Warriors vs. Dallas football game he had recently attended. "I agree. Our sports seem to have become the opiate of the masses. We have it so good in this country compared with most of the rest of the world. I think that the only purpose people can find is to root for their favorite team." Then he added half in jest, "I just hope that they don't discover that unseating their government can become an alternative form of entertainment."

Melissa shivered. "Don't even think like that. It isn't funny."

A new sign appeared while they were talking. It was Chris's turn to read this one. "Citizens United Against Taxes or CUT." This sign contained additional detail. Chris continued to read. "No Power, No Security, No Food = No Taxes." Well this is the first semi-political sign we've seen. It is an interesting proposition. We're not providing citizens with basic necessities, so why should they pay taxes."

"Chris, you can't be serious?"

"Well it's an interesting idea. Suspending taxes on the affected areas for a few weeks won't bankrupt the country, and it may help to reduce the discontent." Then Christopher added, "At least no one's talking about impeachment. We've got to destroy Bis Saif before things get worse. I think this demonstration is just the beginning."

And having said that, he rose and kissed Melissa on the forehead. "It's time to get back to work."

***

A motley crew assembled at the Lowe House of Delegates Office Building in Annapolis to assess progress, exchange information, and decide on next steps. The meeting had been convened by George Wilson and was in Annapolis both for its accessibility and the availability of power. The power failures experienced in the Washington, DC region had not hit Annapolis or the Maryland Eastern Shore, presumably because they were outside of the region served by the damaged portions of the power grid.

The Lowe Building served the legislative branch of the State of Maryland. Its marbled floors and older style wooden desks mirrored an older, more peaceful era of government. The governor of Maryland had offered the building as a meeting site to minimize the discomfort and inconvenience of those that otherwise would be meeting in the Capital. The Lowe Building also featured hot water and shower facilities that could be used by those attendees currently suffering from the lack of power at their own homes. As a result, many arrived with small suitcases and a change of clothes. The dark suits and crisp white shirts were absent, having been replaced by casual clothes, and in some cases denim jeans. The one exception was Janice DeBeers, the director of Homeland Security, who as always was dressed to perfection in a dark blue suit and white blouse. George wondered whether she slept in that outfit.

Wilson had selected the attendees based on their direct relevance to the Bis Saif problem. The press was excluded, and the meeting was limited to those individuals holding senior positions with the involved organizations. In addition to the ad hoc group known as the President's War Cabinet, there were two private-sector participants—a representative from PJM, and one from Google. PJM had been invited to the meeting because of its role in restoring power to the Washington, DC region. The Google representative was a well-known cyber specialist whose wisdom was essential to preventing future attacks on the electrical grid. The ever-present Jan Adams was in attendance in order to record the proceedings and handle the needs of the attendees. The unstated reason for her participation was to provide an independent assessment of the discussion to the president, who would not be attending the meeting.

George opened the meeting. "I want to thank you all for taking time out of your extremely busy schedules to meet with us. I know you're all under a lot of pressure to produce results, and the last thing you need is another meeting. Recognizing that, we'll try to keep this meeting short. Two hours max. But the president and I felt that it was important to spend some time in person discussing our agencies' activities with the hope that coordination among us will expedite our efforts. Any questions or comments?"

George briefly paused before continuing. "Jan, I'd appreciate it if you would pass out the agendas. As you can see, we've organized the meeting into broad areas of concern, including first and foremost locating and destroying Bis Saif. Second, we'll move into infrastructure protection, and finally recovery, both from the current crisis and the next crisis. So let's begin with the first item—Bis Saif. Matt and Arnie, could you give us a status report?" he said, indicating Matthew O'Brien and Admiral Arnold DeForce, the directors of the CIA and NSA respectively.

Philip J. Tarnoff

O'Brien was the first to respond. "As most of you know, our Israeli friends were able to identify a Palestinian who has been in direct contact with Bis Saif. His name is Hasan Jouda, and he had been employed by Hamas in connection with the development of their Suquur surface-to-surface missile, which had the potential to create a great deal of destruction in Israel. We believe that the Israeli air force has leveled the Suquur R&D facility in a strike that probably killed most of their key staff. Hasan Jouda left the country several weeks and possibly months prior to that. With the help of our friends at the NSA, and many overseas allies, we are currently searching for him. I have no doubt that he will ultimately be captured—hopefully alive so we can learn more about Bis Saif as well as his computer-related activities. Before entertaining any questions, I'd like to give Admiral DeForce a chance to speak. Then we can do the collaborative thing," O'Brien concluded sarcastically.

Wilson thought, *Thanks for nothing, Matt. There wasn't a single new fact in your brief talk, and in fact there weren't many facts at all. Hopefully, we'll be able to squeeze something out of him. Doesn't he have any concept of how important this is?*

"Thanks Matt," began Admiral DeForce. "As you know, the challenge of finding the communications of a single individual is equivalent to finding a needle in a haystack. We monitor billions of communications every day. But we have a few advantages here in that we know the name and email addresses of the individual for whom we're searching. We also know his parents' names and email addresses as well those of his friends. We've found a few messages which are being analyzed, but so far nothing useful. And now," he said, turning to the rest of the participants, "any questions?"

James Proctor, the director of the FBI, had been sitting quietly. But it was clear that he had some questions for the director of his sister agency. "Matt, you didn't specifically mention the manner in which your overseas search is being conducted. Are you looking at airport security footage, credit card usage, etcetera? I would imagine he departed from Cairo, and if we could trace his route it would sure be helpful."

O'Brien struggled to maintain his self-control. "Of course we're doing those things, Jim. After all, we're not novices at this game. But the world is a big place, and while we've identified his presence in Cairo, he disappears after that. I intentionally kept the details out of my presentation on the theory that the fewer people who know the details, the better we'll be."

Wilson, sensing the competitive nature of the discussion, sought to calm things down. "Thanks to all of you for your presentations. Are there any other questions? Is there anything the White House can do to help? Are you getting the cooperation from our allies that you need?"

O'Brien responded in a calmer voice. "Yes George, our allies are really pitching in. We're checking security camera footage from around the globe." And in an attempt to mollify Proctor, he added, "It would be very helpful if the FBI could help us with your facial recognition processing facilities. We're swamped with all the footage we're receiving."

"Of course. I'll tell our lab that your tapes are the highest priority."

"Thanks."

So nothing new, thought George Wilson. *I really wonder how this is all going to end.* Then, with effort, he said out loud to the group. "We'll move on to the next subject—infrastructure protection. I'm using this fancy term as a reference to keeping hackers out of our power grid. I'd like to ask our expert from Google to lead off this discussion," he said, referring to Bill Solenski, a tall, lanky individual who was obviously a techie not used to participating in meetings of this nature. He was dressed in jeans and a plaid flannel shirt and wore sandals on his bare feet.

Bill unwound from his chair and walked to the front of the room as if he were addressing a classroom. It was clear that he had prepared a formal presentation, which he recited in a monotone. "Thank you, Mr. Wilson. I appreciate the opportunity to be here. I have studied the issues associated with the protection of the nation's electrical grid and concluded that it is pathetically easy for an experienced hacker to do some serious damage."

Philip J. Tarnoff

Solenski's opening statement caused obvious consternation to the PJM representative and others in the room.

Ignoring their reaction, Solenski continued. "Think of the security features of the power grid as a giant hot air balloon. The challenge is to keep the air from escaping, or in other words, the challenge is to keep an unfriendly party from breathing the escaping air. The surface of the balloon is made up of nearly three thousand pieces of fabric. These are the three thousand independent companies that have access to the grid. These three thousand companies must all provide perfect security for the balloon. In other words, there cannot be any points on the surface of the balloon from which air can escape. Once it begins escaping, the entire balloon is deflated. This is the challenge of the security of the electric grid. Some of the larger suppliers, such as PJM, PEPCO, and VEPCO, use higher quality fabric to keep the air from escaping. But no matter how good their fabric is, the overall security of the balloon can still be affected by the weakest fabric. This is the problem we're facing."

Seeing he had the attention of everyone in the room, Bill proceeded with his lecture. "I have analyzed the security of the grid and found that at best it is uneven. Some companies, including those in this room, have excellent security. But some of the smaller companies, either because of insufficient resources or a focus on profitability, have not done as well. We define security in terms of vulnerabilities, which include quality of password protection, frequency of password changes, employee protection of password information, presence of firewalls, and monitoring of security breaches. We've evaluated these vulnerabilities for a small sample of the overall system and found them to be present in the majority of companies. By far, the greatest vulnerability is the employees of these companies. For example, a control center operator in a Midwestern power company had his password written on the bottom of his desk blotter. To make matters worse, the password he used was the word *password*. When we discussed the issue with him, his reaction was: 'Why should I worry about it? We're a million miles from anyone. Why would anyone want to hack our system?' In many compa-

232

nies this would be grounds for reprimand or even dismissal. But when we told his manager about the problem, they were equally unimpressed. So you see, we have a problem."

As Bill paused, David Powers, PJM's CEO, interrupted. "Give me the name of the company, and I'll see that it's taken care of."

Bill responded, "As much as I'd like to see that happen, we are operating under strict rules of confidentiality that prevent me from giving you that information. But let me put this all into perspective. First, it might surprise all of you to realize that the hackers got through the PJM system and not those of the small Midwestern company I used in my example. Second, and perhaps most significantly, the manner in which they breached PJM's security defenses tells me that they found the needed passwords through a random search process. Given the nature of PJM's passwords, this process would have required centuries of computer time if a conventional computer was used. The computer that cracked PJM's passwords was one helluva super computer, more powerful than any I've ever seen."

"Have you discussed your findings with the DOD, FBI, NSA, or CIA?" asked George.

"Yes I have. My contact at DOD seems to remember a project funded by the Defense Advanced Projects Agency, or DARPA, in your hieroglyphics, that was developing a super computer."

Wilson was stunned. All of a sudden he remembered his visit to JCN and the demonstration of MOM. He must have gasped out loud since everyone in the room turned in his direction. The room went silent. Then James Proctor spoke up. "This might turn out to be the FBI's responsibility. George, why don't you fill us all in?"

It was George Wilson's turn to tell a story. "About two years ago, Thomas McAllen and his program manager invited me to join them on a visit to a company named JCN. As I recall, they were located somewhere in the Washington suburbs—possibly Silver Spring, Maryland. We were astounded to learn that they had developed the prototype of a computer that was more than

1,000 times faster than the fastest computer in existence. It was modeled after the calculation processes of the human brain." Everyone in the Lowes Building was so focused on Wilson's narrative that you could have heard a pin drop in the room.

George continued uninterrupted. "We were awed by the demonstration as well as the potential of the new device. In follow-up conversations with the CEO of JCN, it became obvious that an invention of this nature was similar to the discovery of nuclear energy, in that it could be used for tremendous good or tremendous harm. The one thing that was evident to all of us, including several in this room, was that individuals working on this project should have the highest security clearance. Since the project manager and brains behind the project (no pun intended) was Iraqi, he would not be eligible for such a clearance. My assumptions may be premature, but as I recall, he left JCN over this matter and seems to have disappeared somewhere. This could either be the break we're looking for in our search for Bis Saif, or a dead-end. I agree with Proctor that this is the FBI's business. Jim, I'm not going to tell you how to run your shop, but I would suggest that you get in touch with Thomas McAllen, the Director of DARPA, immediately. Jan can help you with phone contacts so that you can get things started before leaving this meeting. I would also remind you, as if you need reminding, that the New War Powers Bill recently passed by Congress gives the president the right to authorize a search warrant without the existence of compelling evidence."

There was a sense of excitement in the room, as if they might be on the verge of their big break. But George was anxious to continue the meeting. It was a rare occasion to get all of the concerned parties in one room, and he wanted to take advantage of their presence. He began by excusing Proctor, whose schedule had suddenly become crowded. He then turned to the remaining participants and asked if they had anything to report regarding enhanced cyber security and recovery from the power blackout. They all seemed to have lost their appetite to discuss these matters, with the result that their reports were brief and follow-up questions were perfunctory. George then turned to Janice DeBeers asking for the status of the DHS recovery efforts. She responded with a brief progress report, anxious not to interrupt the group's renewed efforts to identify those responsible for the power failure. Realizing momentum had been lost, Wilson adjourned the meeting, reminded everyone of the availability of showers, and returned to the White House.

CHAPTER 19
THE SEARCH BEGINS

Day six was clear, sunny, and unusually warm. The two FBI agents arrived at JCN's offices at 7:00 a.m. They were met at the door by a yawning Bill Jaski, the company's president. Jaski opened the conversation. "What brings you gentlemen to Silver Spring at this ungodly hour? Don't you know that computer programmers start late and work late? But I understand this is a serious matter. I don't suppose you'd be willing to show me some identification?"

The two agents introduced themselves and showed Jaski their credentials. When he was satisfied, he led them to a small conference room adjacent to the lobby. One of them opened the conversation. "Mr. Jaski, we're here on a most serious matter. Normally we don't provide the background of our investigations during an interview, but given the severity of this situation, we want you to be fully informed. Undoubtedly you're familiar with the power failure and terrorist attacks in the DC area. Our investigations have led us to believe that the power failure was due to the fact that the electrical distribution network had been hacked by the mysterious organization that identifies itself as Bis Saif. Our experts believe that this could only have been done by an extremely powerful computer. You may remember that representatives of the government visited your facility approximately two years ago. You demonstrated a new computer you had named MOM, which seems to have the capability needed to hack into the distribution system. We would like to check all your employees to determine whether any of them could have ties to Bis Saif or any other terrorist organization. In addition, we may want to interview all employees. So let's get started."

Bill was nodding as he listened to the agent's explanation. "I wish you had alerted me to the purpose of your visit. You would need our personnel records as well as the documentation of the security clearances that have been granted. My staff hasn't arrived yet."

"Could you please call them at home and ask them to get here as soon as possible?" was the polite response. "You can understand the urgency here since the message with the threat to repeat the attack on a more widespread basis gave us seven days. We've managed to use up six of these days identifying your organization as a possible source of the trouble."

Anticipating the agent's request, Jaski already had his cellphone out and was calling Jack Vermeer, his security officer, and Marylou Sachler, his chief engineer. Jack could provide information related to security clearances, and Marylou would have access to the personnel files as well as knowledge of possible ways in which MOM might have been compromised. Both Jack and Marylou complained about the need to rush into the office an hour before they had planned, but both immediately responded to Jaski's urgent request for their help.

While they waited for the two to arrive, the FBI agents asked Jaski about the history of MOM. He patiently responded to their probing question, explaining the development of the computer, its theory of operation, and capabilities. When he reached the point of the meeting with DARPA and George Wilson, he suddenly paused and hit the table with his fist. "Of course! I should have thought of this from the beginning. Jahmir Al-Saadi was one of the two principal developers of MOM. His girlfriend, Kelly Jaffari, worked with him on the project. When George Wilson insisted that all employees working on MOM have top-level security clearances, it became clear that Jahmir would not qualify since he was not a US citizen. He became very upset after all his requests to make an exception for him were refused. Shortly after, both Jahmir and Kelly disappeared."

The agents were rapidly taking notes as Jaski spoke. "Where are they now?"

Jaski continued. "That's where things get interesting. At first Jahmir told us that he was going to work for a competitor. Then he told his ex-coworkers that he was going to start his own company and compete with us. I believe the company he formed was called JK Computing, using their first initials. Then all of a sudden he completely disappeared, although they do seem to have acquired some office space in Columbia, Maryland."

"Does he have a residence?"

"I believe so. He and Kelly lived together in an apartment not far from here. I'm not sure whether they still own or rent the place, or whether they've moved out. Their closest friend at JCN, Rick Springer, might know. He still works here."

"Could you ask him to come in also?" Jaski was immediately on his cellphone again, speaking to another complaining late riser.

While they were waiting for Jack, Marylou, and Rick to arrive, the two agents were busy on their phones, forwarding the information about Jahmir and Kelly to Lee Sanders, the agent coordinating the search. Within twenty-four hours, every detail of the two would be known, including residences, relatives, photographs, outside interests, professional backgrounds, and clothing styles. The more the FBI investigated Jahmir and Kelly, the more convinced they became of their culpability.

***

Both the CIA and the FBI were energized by their new leads. The CIA was engaged in rounding up all airport recordings throughout the Mideast in their search for Hasan Jouda. They had spotted him on a video recording made at the boarding gate of Cairo Airport. The FBI began a similar search of the video recordings of the airports serving Washington, DC, including Baltimore-Washington International, Reagan National Airport, Dulles International Airport, and even Philadelphia's airport. Unfortunately, they had no immediate success.

The recording of Hasan showed him boarding a KLM flight to Amsterdam's Schiphol International Airport under the assumed name of Mohammed Ali. This facetious choice of the name of a famous American boxer enabled the CIA agents in Cairo to rapidly identify him among the passengers of the KLM flight. Unfortunately, they lost him at Schiphol, where presumably he had changed names for the next flight to his possible destination. Thus the CIA, like the FBI, became bogged down with the laborious task of running hours of video recordings through their facial recognition software in an attempt to identify Hasan Jouda, aka Mohammed Ali. While they were confident of their ability to locate him, they were uncertain whether it would be possible to complete this task before the Bis Saif deadlines. The terrorists would have been pleased to learn that a significant percentage of the CIA operatives and analysts had been removed from their existing assignments to support the search for Hasan.

At the same time, the FBI had been busy tracing Jahmir and Kelly's activities in the United States. A search of their apartment yielded very little, since, as the disgruntled building superintendent told the agents, he had re-rented their apartment after having had it thoroughly cleaned and repainted. He told the agents that they had left nothing behind except for a few empty pizza boxes and beer cans. They also came up empty at JK Computing offices in Columbia, which consisted of a central work area and a supply closet. It was obvious that this space had only been occupied for a brief time, and that no serious work had been conducted. The only information gleaned from the search of the JK offices were fingerprints of the two suspects.

The FBI's investigation offered the promise of bearing fruit as the investigation moved to the home of Kelly's parents. They arrived in Timonium unannounced bearing search warrants and arrest warrants that had been issued under the newly enacted War Powers Act. As interpreted by the FBI, this act gave them virtually unlimited access to the house and the grounds. It also granted them the authority to detain Sami and Lilliane Jaffari. Although the detention was limited to ninety days, the agents saw no benefit in informing the Jaffaris of this fact.

As the two Jaffaris were hustled out of the house in hand-cuffs, Sami protested loudly, stating that he was an American citizen and should not be subjected to these fascist tactics. He also requested an immediate call to his attorney, a request that fell on the deaf ears of the arresting agents. The two found themselves in the back seat of a black FBI SUV that immediately headed for a little-known facility at Ft. Meade, the headquarters of the National Security Agency. Placed in separate holding cells at Ft. Meade, the two were left to contemplate their fate.

On its way to Ft. Meade, the black SUV passed an equally black motor home headed in the opposite direction. One of the occupants of the motor home was Lee Sanders, one of the Special Agents in Charge, or SACs, as they are known, of the Washington, DC District. Lee had abandoned his traditional business dress for a windbreaker emblazoned with the FBI lettering on the back. A tall and imposing individual, during his twenty years at the FBI, Lee had made his reputation from his success with a number of terrorist- and drug-related cases. He was an obvious choice to lead the search for Bis Saif. After a full week of investigation, he had been frustrated by the lack of evidence produced from any of the bureau's traditional sources. He was initially elated when the big break produced by George Wilson was received. But a search of Kelly and Jahmir's home and business office resulted in further frustration through the lack of evidence it produced. He had never been involved in a case like this, where every lead ended in a dead-end.

By the time the motor home pulled into the Jaffaris' drive-way, Lee had developed a comprehensive plan for an efficient and rapid search of the property. He had requested and received a team of fifteen individuals experienced with these types of searches. They included many FBI personnel with specialized skills, including x-ray techs, fingerprint analysts, computer scientists, a photographer, a locksmith, as well as drug, explosive, and firearm experts. They were to be assisted in their search by two handlers with their dogs, one for drugs and the other for explosives. Now the challenge was to ensure that their work was thorough, efficient, and quick.

As he assembled the team in the motor home's cramped quarters, Lee began his briefing. "You all know we're here to establish a connection between the Jaffaris and any terrorist group, including in particular al-Qaeda and Bis Saif. We're also trying to determine whether they've had any interactions with Kelly Jaffari and Jahmir Al Saadi, and if so, what they were. We'd be very interested to learn where those two have gone."

Lee then moved on to describe the procedures that would be used for the search. "The search of the premises has got to be conducted as efficiently as possible. We've got to ensure that everyone is gainfully employed without running into each other or compromising any evidence. So here's what we're going to do. First, the search will proceed from attic to basement—or in other words, it will be a search from top to bottom." When no one laughed at Lee's attempt at humor, he continued. "We will begin with the non-intrusive elements of the search in this order. First, the photographers will make a complete record of every inch of the premises before anything is moved or touched. When the photography is completed, the dogs will move in to determine whether any drugs or explosives are present. Then the x-ray technicians will scan all padded furniture, mattresses, etcetera to determine whether anything is hidden inside. When this phase of the search has been completed, the more intrusive physical search will begin. This will begin with fingerprinting, which will be followed by the removal of anything that is not nailed down for analysis at the lab in the motor home. You know what that includes. Finally, the physical search begins for hidden compartments, safes, and other niches in which valuables can be stashed, including the trite but still used fake books. I would suggest that your physical search be preceded by the process of measuring the dimensions of all rooms to be used in drafting a floorplan that can be used to identify any hollow walls. The measurement can take place while the x-ray technicians are working. I would suggest that once the non-intrusive search of the attic is completed, the searchers will move to the upstairs floor, while the intrusive searchers are working in the attic, and so forth. Any questions?"

There was no need for questions, since most of those present had participated in similar searches in the past. When no one responded, Lee wrapped up the meeting. "Then let's get started. Let me know immediately if you find anything that might be of interest."

The team quickly and efficiently broke into groups and entered the Jaffari residence through the front entrance. The non-intrusive group finished their work in the attic in about fifteen minutes and moved to the second floor. Lee could tell that the work of the intrusive group was underway when garbage bags full of potential evidence began to arrive. He sorted the material into electronics and physical evidence. Some would be analyzed using the facilities of the motor home, and others would be sent to the FBI laboratories at the Marine Corps base in Quantico, Virginia. He was particularly interested in the two personal computers that were removed, a laptop and a tower, as well as an Apple iPad. The computers remained in the motor home to be analyzed by the technicians that had arrived with Lee.

As he waited in the motor home, Sanders monitored the discussions among the searchers for early updates on their results as well as any indications of a need for assistance. He heard one say, "Here's a wall safe. Where's the locksmith?" The locksmith was immediately dispatched to the master bedroom, where the safe had been discovered.

The reports from the technicians as well as the searchers were discouraging. Lee couldn't believe that these suspects of high interest who appeared to be a middle-aged Syrian banker and his wife could possess the sophistication to avoid leaving any useful clues. The wall safe contained a modest amount of cash that could be readily attributed to a rainy-day fund for emergencies. The computers yielded some interesting email pertaining to the Jaffaris' personal lives, but nothing terrorist related. The searchers turned up some bills from a security firm for furnishing two bodyguards for a period of time. Lee noted that the guard service had been hired a week before the disappearance of Kelly and Jahmir from JCN and continued for only two months. He wondered whether there was any relationship.

As the searchers began to run out of material, the evidence arriving at the motor home diminished. Lee was discouraged by their lack of success. They had checked the fingerprints in the house, finding Sami's, Lilliane's, Kelly's, Jahmir's, and three additional sets, which turned out to belong to the maid and the two bodyguards. They had collected DNA samples from unwashed dishes and toilet articles. They had x-rayed the furniture and the walls. When the room measurements revealed a space within the walls that could not be explained, they removed the wall. They ran a fiber optic camera through all the heating ducts. They checked the binding of every book in the library. They sent the bank account numbers to the specialists at the Quantico lab. None of this produced any useful information.

Lee left the motor home and began to wander around the premises. Admiring the landscaping, he wandered through Sami's rose garden. He mused that this garden must be beautiful in the summer. These roses needed a lot of attention, particularly during the humid summers of Maryland. He mused, *Sami must have a lot of time on his hands. Maybe we should take a look at his financial profile.*

Since the radio chatter in his earpiece was dying down, Lee continued wandering around the well-kept grounds. He saw a curved concrete bench under a dogwood tree adjacent to the rose garden and sat down on it in the cold December air. A gentle slope led down to a pond a short distance from the rose garden. Absent mindedly, Lee enjoyed the view of the pond, noticing a weeping willow tree with its long, drooping branches swaying gracefully in the breeze. He noticed three objects looking like stacks of white boxes near the willow tree. Whatever they were, they probably deserved a closer look, and he stood up and wandered down the slope toward the boxes. As he neared the boxes he heard a buzzing noise that got louder as he got closer. He realized with a start they were beehives. Beating a hasty retreat up the hill, Lee thanked his good fortune that he had discovered the hives before the bees discovered him.

As he walked back to the motor home, Lee thought, *We've searched every inch of the house and attached garage. Unless*

243

the evidence is buried in the garden, it just may be hidden in the hives. A ridiculous idea, but can't lose anything by looking. It was just a hunch, but many FBI cases had been solved by an agent's hunch.

Returning to the motor home, he placed a call to headquarters. "This may sound ridiculous, but we need a beekeeper at the Jaffaris' house," he told the incredulous dispatch operator. "And we need him ASAP."

"That's a tall order, but I'll do what I can. I'll call you when I have an ETA," came the reply.

As Lee waited for the beekeeper to arrive, he reviewed the evidence

Four hours later after an interminable wait, Lee heard a car approaching. The red Chevy Impala pulled into the driveway and parked behind the motor home. The driver emerging from the car couldn't have looked less like a beekeeper. He was wearing a pair of Oakley sunglasses, chinos, a sport shirt with the top two buttons opened, and a light sports jacket. He strode confidently up to Lee and introduced himself. "Hi, I'm Charles Ardley, beekeeper from the University of Maryland. I understand you're in a hurry. Sorry it took so long to get here, but I was in the middle of teaching my apiary course. What can I do for you?"

Lee liked Ardley immediately. "I've got a problem. We suspect the occupants of this house are up to no good. We've searched their house for evidence, but couldn't find anything. The only place we haven't searched are the beehives. I need you to look through the hives to see whether they contain anything but honey."

"I've brought an extra outfit if you'd like to join me."

Lee was torn. He was ashamed to admit that he was afraid of the bees, since FBI agents are supposed to be fearless. He also felt that he should witness the search of the hives in case any evidence was discovered. His presence would ensure that the chain of custody would remain unbroken. Screwing up his courage, Lee replied as casually as he could. "Sure. I'd be happy to join you, providing your suits offer adequate protection."

Charles's response provided some degree of comfort. "Trust me, Agent Sanders. This will be a walk in the park. I've opened hundreds of hives, sometimes without even wearing a bee-keeper's outfit. If you're stung at all, it will be less painful than a flu shot. But first let me ask you a few questions. First, let me know if you're allergic to insect stings. Second, tell me if you're wearing an after shave lotion or a strong cologne of any sort."

"None of the above," Lee responded seriously.

"In order to save time, I've just brought the beekeepers jackets, gloves, a hat and veil. No need for special pants, but I also have a set of rubber bands that you should use to seal the bottoms of your slacks. You don't want a bee flying up your pants, after all."

The two of them got dressed in their beekeeper outfits while the idle members of the search crew watched and provided moral support. "If the bees decide to chase you, run in the other direction!" yelled the lab technician, laughing.

Charles then removed a bucket containing a smoker stuffed with straw and a hive tool from his car. The latter was a metal instrument with a curved end that was useful for removing the top of the hive as well as the frames. The resinous propolis, which is a mixture of sap produced by the bees, occasionally made these objects difficult to separate.

As they walked down the gentle slope toward the hives, Charles began to explain their structure. He did this partly to keep Lee from worrying about the upcoming visit to the hives, and partly in case he needed Lee's assistance in their search.

"The white boxes you see stacked in front of you are called hive bodies. On the top of the stack, which is called the hive, is a cover. Underneath the cover is an inner cover that provides some degree of ventilation. Underneath the hive is a bottom board that serves as the entrance. But of great interest to us is the internal structure of the hive. Each of the hive bodies contains ten frames inserted vertically into the hive body. The frames are nothing more than a rectangular framework some-thing like a picture frame. The frame is used to support sheets of plastic or embossed beeswax called foundation on which the bees construct their beeswax cells. If this isn't completely clear to you, it will become evident as soon as we begin taking the hives apart."

"You mean we're going to disassemble the hives?" asked Lee incredulously.

"Yes. It disturbs the bees somewhat, but as soon as we reassemble the hive, they return to their business," replied Charles as they neared the hives. "It's no big deal. We'll distract them with smoke from the smoker. There will be a lot of bees flying around, but as long as you don't swat at them or annoy them, they'll leave you alone. One or two might land on you or fly around your head. Just ignore them."

Easier said than done, thought Lee, who was trying his best to remain calm.

As he spoke, Charles set the smoker on the ground, took out a lighter, and ignited the straw it contained. The straw didn't burn, but just smoldered, giving off healthy wisps of smoke. Charles squeezed the bellows on the smoker to increase the amount of smoke being expelled.

Charles continued to talk as they neared the hives. "I've been thinking since you explained the problem. If someone were to hide something in a beehive, it could be in several places. It could be inserted as a false frame, it could be a false hive body, or it could be hidden under the bottom board. A thorough search will require taking apart the entire hive and looking at every one of the frames. My hope is that we will discover anything hidden in the hive quickly, since I'm certain that Mr. Jaffari would want to be able to access the information easily without having to disassemble the entire hive."

Lee concurred with enthusiasm. "That's my hope as well. I'm not looking forward to spending a lot of time here."

Charles squeezed the bellows on the smoker again, causing a puff of smoke to exit the spout, which he aimed at the hive. The buzzing in the hive immediately increased, much to Lee's consternation. "Don't worry," Charles laughed, "completely normal."

He then proceeded to remove the cover and inner cover from the first hive. Lee soon forgot his fear of the bees and became fascinated with the activity in the hive. Charles removed the frames from the top box one by one, examining each one carefully. The frames in the top box were sparsely populated, with the bees beginning to build new cells.

Charles then removed the top box, laid it on the ground, and examined the next box, which was much busier, crowded with bees busy with the process of creating cells, laying brood, and creating honey. He repeated this process until the four boxes of the stack had all been separated. Lee was unhappy with the quantity of homeless bees that were filling the air, and wished that Charles would complete his examination of the hive. They were both disappointed when the disassembled hive failed to produce anything that could be interpreted as evidence. Charles quickly reassembled the first hive and the two watched as the bees returned to their interrupted activities.

They had more success with the second hive. As Charles removed the outer cover and prepared to remove the inner cover, the two of them saw a manila envelope in a plastic baggie taped to the bottom of the cover. As Charles reached for the envelope, Lee stopped him, saying, "Let me remove it. It's evidence, and it should be handled with the utmost care. If it wouldn't harm the bees, I would take the entire cover with me."

"I've got another cover in the car," replied Charles as he replaced the cover on the second hive. "I'll get it for you, and then you can have the cover, envelope and all."

Lee breathed a sigh of relief. His instincts had been vindicated.

***

The significance of the discovery in the beehives was so great that Lee bypassed the chain of command and phoned the director's office. As he expected, the call was answered by his assistant. "Director Proctor's office, may I help you?"

Philip J. Tarnoff

"Anna, this is Lee Sanders, one of the SACs from the DC district. I need to speak with the director ASAP."

He was pleased with her response. "Hi Lee. I was told that if you called, I was to put you through immediately."

In less than a minute, he heard "Jim Proctor here. Lee, what have you got for me? Time is short."

"Director Proctor, I've got a lead that needs top-priority examination. We searched the Jaffari residence, and you won't believe this, but we found an envelope containing what looks like encryption keys. And that's all we've found. I need the NSA to search their digital message haystack to see if they can find the needle that was sent using these codes. It's a tall order, but I can give them a range of dates during which the messages would have been sent, and I can also give them the likely point of origination of the messages."

"Anything else?"

Unfortunately, no. As you know, we've arrested the Jaffaris, and they are being interrogated now. But a search of their residence as well as those of Kelly and Jahmir has turned up nothing. I'm afraid they're long gone. I've also got our techs reviewing all available videos from the four airports in the DC region to see whether they boarded an international flight. So far, nothing has turned up. They're either very clever or very lucky. Right now, these codes seem to be our best bet."

"Stand by. You'll receive a call from NSA within the next ten minutes," the director said as he disconnected.

While he waited for the call from NSA, Lee removed his beekeeper outfit and replaced it with the more familiar FBI jacket. No one could accuse the intelligence community of being inefficient. Lee's cellphone rang as the timer on his digital watch showed ten minutes.

The voice on the other end was obviously that of someone with a military background. "Admiral DeForce, NSA, I understand you may have something for us," came the curt response to Lee's greeting.

After telling the admiral that the call was with respect to the Bis Saif case, Lee quickly described the material he had removed from the bee hives. The admiral responded without hesitation. "There will be a chopper at your location within thirty minutes. We would appreciate it if you would be so good as to accompany the evidence to our offices." The latter sounded more like an order than a request, but Lee had already decided he wouldn't let the evidence out of his sight.

The helicopter arrived in less than thirty minutes, but Lee was ready. Having instructed his team to pack up the evidence from the house and transport it to the FBI labs at Quantico, and thanked Charles Ardley for his assistance, Lee stood at the edge of the clearing that would serve as a helipad. The thirty-mile trip from Timonium to NSA's headquarters at Ft. Meade was accomplished in fifteen minutes. Before he knew it, Lee was seated in a conference room with the top managers of NSA's Office of Cryptology.

Everyone knew who he was when he walked into the conference room carrying the cover of a beehive with the envelope taped to the bottom and wearing his FBI jacket. The Director of NSA was also obvious, wearing his Navy uniform with its admiral's insignia. In spite of the obvious fact that he was the one in charge, the admiral stood when Lee entered the conference room and introduced himself. "Welcome. I'm Arnold DeForce, Director of the NSA. Please call me Arnie."

Not knowing what else to say, Lee responded in like manner. "I'm Lee Sanders with the FBI. special agent in charge of the Bis Saif investigation."

Either by oversight or intentionally, Admiral DeForce failed to introduce Lee to the others in the room. He knew that NSA was a very secretive organization, so it would not be unusual to maintain some degree of anonymity for the staff. Instead, DeForce guided the conversation to the question of the codes. "Lee, why don't you tell us what you have and let us take it from there?"

Lee immediately began his briefing, including the reason for their interest in the Jaffaris, the FBI's search of their home, and the last-minute discovery of the codes within the beehives. He also provided the group with the likely dates at which Kelly and Jahmir fled the country, which in turn provided the NSA with a range of dates to begin their search for coded communications from the Jaffaris. When he completed his briefing, he reminded the group of the urgency of the investigation and its significance to the future of the United States. The questions flew at him from the assembled group, which was obviously experienced at this sort of thing.

"Do you think the messages were sent from the Jaffaris' computer?"

"Do you have the email address of their computers?"

"Could the messages have been sent from another computer? If so, do you know which computer it might have been?"

"Could the messages have been embedded in another medium, such as a photograph?"

"Is the computer from which the messages might have been sent in your possession? If so, could we borrow it?"

Lee had to profess ignorance to most of these questions. He gave them the name and phone number of the specialist at Quantico who was performing a postmortem on the computer, hoping that the NSA and FBI would play nice together. He concluded by saying, "I hope that the messages were sent from their own computers. If not, I'm not sure how they might have been transmitted. We're currently canvassing the area for coffee shops or other computer cafes that might have been used. I wish we could tell you more. We're hoping that you might be a source of new leads." Then Lee added hopefully, "How long do you think this will take?"

The admiral answered for the group. "I know you're in a hurry. We're all in a hurry. I just wish I could answer your question. It could take anywhere from five minutes to five months, depending on whether we get lucky. The more information you can provide my team, the more efficient the search. All I can tell you is that we've got all hands working on this. I've pulled everyone off of every other project."

He then concluded the meeting by saying, "Lee, thanks for a very complete and clear briefing. Now if you will accompany my secretary into the next room, we'll make a copy of the codes so that you can keep the original in your possession." Smiling, he added, "I think you'll also need a ride home."

Turning to the group he said, "Let's get to work, folks."

BOOK 4

GENERATIONAL DECAY

*The decay of the city (Rome) had gradually impaired the value
of the public works. The circus and theaters might still excite,
but they seldom gratified the desires of the people: the temples
which had escaped the zeal of the Christians were no longer
inhabited, either by gods or men; the diminished crowds of the
Romans were lost in the immense space of their baths and porti-
cos; and the stately libraries and halls of justice became useless
to an indolent generation whose repose was seldom disturbed
either by study or business.*

Gibbon, Edward. *The Decline and Fall of the Roman Empire.*
Amazon Kindle File. Chapter XXXVI.

CHAPTER 20
PLAYING CATCH-UP

It was a grim group that met in the White House Cabinet Room with less than twenty-four hours to go until Bis Saif carried out its next threatened blackout. As before, the President's War Council was present, the group, which included senior level representatives from all agencies, responsible for dealing with the crisis. This time, however, the meeting was chaired by the President of the United States rather than the director of national intelligence.

Usually an upbeat individual, President Jeffers began the meeting with a depressing, for him, opening statement. "Ladies and gentlemen, we are facing a difficult situation. Congress has set a precedent. It has declared war on a shadow group, Bis Saif. The declaration implicitly activates the New War Powers Act, a piece of legislation that gives me virtually unlimited powers to combat them and their affiliates. The only problem is that we don't know who they are or where they are. The second equally serious problem is that the citizens of this great country are beginning to panic, and I have nothing with which to reassure them. So I ask you all to provide me with something, anything, that I can use both to console myself and the general public.

"Before turning the floor over to George Wilson, I'd like to welcome General Elliott Drake, Chairman of the Joint Chiefs of Staff. General Drake is here to listen and to ensure that needed troops are available when needed. General, is there anything you'd like to say?"

Sitting rigidly erect and at attention in his chair, if such a thing was possible, the general was the stereotypical marine. The rows of ribbons on his uniform hinted at a distinguished

253

career. As everyone expected, his reply was a verbal salute to the president. "No, sir. As you said, I'm here to listen and learn. I'm honored to be part of this hard-working group."

Jeffers then stepped aside and let George Wilson, the DNI, lead the discussion. "OK then. Let's first discuss what we know about Bis Saif. Hopefully we're making some progress. Director Proctor, would you please fill us in on the FBI's progress?"

"Well I've got some encouraging news, which I will summarize. George, as you know, we've followed up on the lead you provided regarding JCN and their super-duper computer. We found that two of their principal developers of the computer had left the company shortly after your visit. Their names are Kelly Jaffari and Jamir Al-Saadi. It turns out that both are immigrants from the Middle East. Kelly's background was particularly interesting, since she is the daughter of Syrian expatriates who are quite wealthy. Her parents' names are Sami and Lilliane Jaffari. They are now under arrest and incarcerated in a holding cell at Ft. Meade under the authority of the New War Powers Act. Also under the authority of the act, we've literally taken their house apart, and to make a long story short, we discovered a set of encryption keys. In all places, they were hidden in a beehive on the Jaffari property. We've given the codes to NSA, where they are being used to decode messages sent from the Jaffaris or their security company during the time period that they disappeared. One final note is that we're interrogating the Jaffaris, who are not being very talkative, and we're analyzing all other material removed from their premises. Now I'd like to turn the floor over to Admiral DeForce." And with that, James Proctor concluded his report.

The director of NSA picked up the story where Proctor had ended. "First, let me commend the FBI and their SAC, Lee Sanders, in particular, for their creativity in conducting the search. Can you imagine thinking about searching a beehive for evidence? Sanders brought the evidence to us yesterday, and I have turned the agency on its head in order to track down messages sent using the codes he discovered. Every single staff member within the cryptography group has been assigned to discovering the encrypted messages. As a result, we're days behind in our normal surveillance of digital traffic. But the good news is that I received a report while on my way to this meeting that we have uncovered the messages in question. It appears that Sami Jaffari sent three coded messages: The first was to an unnamed party with presumable ties to Bis Saif, asking for funds to pay for the development of an incredibly powerful computer. The second was a message to Bis Saif thanking them for their support and suggesting that the development take place in a third location—neither the United States nor at their location, which was unnamed. The third message indicated that Sami had Kuwait City as the location for the development of the new computer. Unfortunately, we were not able to identify the replies to these messages, but this information is more than enough for us to move forward."

As soon as the admiral had concluded his report, Matthew O'Brien, the director of the CIA, spoke up. "This is very good news, and it confirms my information regarding Kuwait City as the likely location for the super computer. Have you passed it on to my agency?"

Admiral DeForce was ready. "It was passed on to your people before I entered this room."

O'Brien then took over the briefing. "It appears that a third person is working on this computer. His name is Hasan Jouda, and he's a member of the Hamas in Palestine. With the assistance of the Israeli Mossad, we discovered that he recently left Palestine and boarded a plane for Kuwait that originated in Cairo. He's using an assumed name and passport, but we were able to spot him using video tapes from the security cameras. We've ID'd him both in Cairo and Kuwait. Now we've got to search for Kelly and Jahmir. It's important to find them in case they've altered their appearance and changed their names."

Turning to President Jeffers, O'Brien asked, "Mr. President, I believe we could use your assistance. Would you be willing to call the emir and ask for his assistance in searching Kuwait City for the suspects?"

His response was immediate. "Of course, I'll call him right now. I'd like to commend all of you for a first-class investigation. I've also been impressed with the degree of cooperation and focus you've all brought to this problem. I just wish we could speed up the process. And now, why don't you all take a break while I call His Excellency. I'd like to be present for the rest of the discussion."

***

The president returned in fifteen minutes, which gave those in the room an opportunity to update their subordinates with the information they had just received.

Jeffers shared the results of his conversation with the emir as he was resuming his seat at the head of the table. "Well he's on board. The emir told me he would immediately activate the national police in a city-wide search for our fugitives. It goes without saying that he thought it would be helpful if we had recent photos of Kelly and Jahmir. Jim, could you see that he gets them?"

Changing the subject, Jeffers added, "Now let's turn our attention to the massacre at Union Station. It may appear less important than finding Bis Saif, but it is an increasing source of panic for the American public. In fact, they seem to be more upset at the prospect of another mass murder than they are of the power failure. Frankly, I'm not sure which scares me the most. So let's turn our attention to the subject of the Union Station massacre. Any progress?"

Once again it was Proctor's turn to respond. "We've made considerable progress. Although the gunmen wore ski masks, one of them took off his mask as he was getting into their SUV. Although the photo was not perfect, we were able to identify him as one of the Syrian refugees that we had on our watch list. We've issued a nationwide alert for him. We've also found the SUV, which was stolen, and are currently dusting for fingerprints. We've found one latent that matches another individual in our database. Another refugee. If our past experience is any indication, we should have arrests within the next few days. These guys are not very sophisticated, and in addition, they're not US citizens, which should make them stand out. Our friends in the Syrian refugee community are anxious to help, since they don't want to be painted by the same brush. The Muslim community is in turmoil."

"This is exactly what I've been worrying about. The terrorists were Muslim refugees. We've already got a witch hunt on our hands for individuals with these backgrounds. I'm afraid that we're going to be faced with another anti-Muslim movement, led by the crazies in the general public. Congress is already muttering about internment camps. We've got to get this problem under control. I'm going to meet with our Leadership Group this afternoon," Jeffers said, referring to the House and Senate leaders with whom he had coordinated the passage of the New War Powers Act.

"Now let's get to the elephant in the room. The problems of dealing with the current power failure, and a new, more massive failure. Janice, what's the progress at DHS?" Jeffers added, turning to the DHS director.

Once again dressed in her typically stylish business suit and white blouse, Janice DeBeers began her response with praise for her staff. "First, let me say that the DHS crew is working sixteen-hour days, seven days a week, to deal with the existing problem and to prepare for the future. If our experience in the DC region is any example, I'm afraid that the next power failure could also last for several months. We were shocked to learn that the utilities don't have spare high-voltage transformers and other equipment to repair damage of the sort that we've experienced in DC. We're shipping massive supplies of food and fuel into the DC region to help folks weather the current storm. Think of it. Approximately eight million people are affected by this power failure. I don't want to bury you in statistics, but the average American consumes about one ton of food each year, which equates to more than a hundred and sixty pounds per month. So we need to provide six hundred and forty thousand tons of food for the region each month. Since an eighteen-wheeler can carry around forty tons, this equals to sixteen thousand full truck loads per month. You might ask why this is a problem since this is the rate of deliveries normally shipped to the region. The problem is that much of this is perishable, so there's a problem of refrigeration without power, and there's also the problem of finding fuel for sixteen thousand trucks each month. Also, don't forget that traffic is a mess, so normal deliveries to supermarkets, assuming they're open and able to keep the food from spoiling, is difficult at best. A very messy problem."

Before continuing, DeBeers paused to let the complexity of the situation sink in. "So we've come up with what I think is a very creative solution. We've established twenty distribution centers around the region where the public can shop for the essentials they need. Each of the distribution centers is powered by a large diesel generator that provides lighting and refrigeration. We've contracted with the major supermarkets to staff the center, including pricing and checkout facilities. We've also had to install a new computer system to deal with the retail transactions so that the government is not footing the entire bill. The distribution centers are existing centers, such as the ones in Jessup, Maryland, or large warehouses wherever we can find them, or venues such as the DC Convention Center. These venues are not being used anyway due to the power failure, so they're more than happy to accommodate us.

"Here's how it works. Let's say a truckload of tomatoes is being shipped from Florida. They typically arrive at DC from Florida by truck traveling north on I-95. The trucker will be stopped at the rest stop north of Fredericksburg by the Virginia State Police. He will be given a scheduled departure time and a route to follow. The routes are truck-only routes. At certain times of day, trucks will be convoyed along these exclusive routes directly to the distribution center. The convoys will be unloaded, and diesel fuel will be available, if needed. As soon as the truck is unloaded and fueled, it is directed to immediately leave the area using the same truck route in the opposite direction. Within the distribution center food can either be purchased directly by consumers or vans will be used to deliver the food to individual neighborhoods for folks that cannot get to the distribution centers. We've set up a phone bank for people to place their grocery orders. When they've placed their orders, they must pay by credit card or check. This system has been in place for two days now, and except for a few snags, it seems to be working relatively smoothly. We get complaints from people who cannot get the merchandise they are used to, or cannot get a particular brand. But I've got little sympathy for our spoiled American public, who are used to infinite variety at nearby supermarkets."

Jeffers reflected the reactions of the assembled, who were clearly impressed. "Wow! I can't believe you put all of that together in five days. How did you accomplish it?"

"We assembled the management of all the local supermarkets, and this was the scheme that was jointly developed with our staff. This was one of the best public-private partnerships I have ever seen. I think it will enable us to get through the next month or so with only minimal problems. But don't let this small success lull us into complacency. First of all, I can't begin to describe all the local problems that have occurred. Without power there have been many medical emergencies as well as small catastrophes with people trapped in elevators and people unable to get to work because they don't have transportation. We've scoured the area for generators, and have purchased them from major retailers such as Lowes and Home Depot, as well as smaller hardware stores and rental stores. I don't think there's a generator of any size left for sale in the region. In spite of our efforts, only five percent of gas stations and ten percent of pharmacies have power. Everything is being rationed except water. We're OK with water since all pumps are on backup power. Needless to say, people are not very happy, and they're blaming their problems on Muslims, immigrants, Middle Easterners, the federal government, or anyone else they can find."

George Wilson spoke up for the first time. "I've been afraid of this. The problems you describe will pale by comparison with a more widespread power failure. How will we handle that?"

"Our problem with the Bis Saif threats is that they are not geographically specific. We don't know what part of the country will be affected, nor do we know the duration of its impact. We obviously can't pre-position food and drugs for the entire country. The impact of such a power failure would be devastating. Think of it as if it were twenty times the impact of Hurricane Katrina, which hit New Orleans in 2005. Katrina affected only one quarter of a state. A power failure would affect entire states, and possibly multiple states, depending on which grid they hit. We're trying to warehouse as much nonperishable food supplies as possible at depots throughout the country, with the help of our friends at DOD," She said, nodding to the Secretary of Defense. "But I'm afraid that our efforts will barely make a dent in the need that could occur with a massive regional power failure of the type they're threatening. Gentlemen, I think we're in big trouble here!"

"That sure was a depressing conclusion to an upbeat presentation," Jeffers said. "But I think your conclusion is accurate. You aren't suggesting we capitulate to their demands, are you?"

DeBeers responded vehemently. "Heavens no! We're supposed to be the greatest power on earth. I don't think the prospect of some inconvenience for our citizens should cause us to cave in."

"Since we're on the subject, how do the rest of you feel?"

It was unanimous. They all thought the United States should stand firm. No capitulation.

"I agree with your feelings and intend to pass our decision on to the Leadership Group when I meet with them this afternoon. By the way, if anyone in this room let's their nickname out, I will deny it to my dying day and reprimand the culprit."

Jeffers then added, "Janice, what can we do to help in addition to adding supplemental funding to your budget?"

"At some point, but not yet, I'm sure we'll need National Guard troops activated in the areas hit by the next power failure. I also think we'll need some transport facilities, such as trucks and aircraft. We've already been in touch with DOD and received first-class cooperation. Other than that, we've sorta got things under control. I believe that everyone recognizes the severity of the situation and they're all helping to the greatest extent possible. So we've sorta got things under control," she repeated with a wan smile.

"Well that about wraps everything up. We'll meet back here in another week. Keep on pushing for results, and pray to God we survive the year."

***

There was a fire in the Oval Office fireplace as the president and the Leadership Group met. Sitting in the comfortably furnished room, the five most powerful men in the country couldn't help but reflect on the plight of those living in the DC region without power, which meant no heat, no hot water, no light, except candles and kerosene lamps, food and drug shortages, and many scarcities.

The president opened the meeting. "We've got to get this under control. I just met with key members of my cabinet and they're all making progress, but no breakthroughs. I've got a Navy Seal team on standby to take out the computer facilities being run by Bis Saif, but right now we don't know where in the world to send them, although we have some suspicions."

"Chris, you wouldn't be willing to share the location with us, would you?" asked Wayne Zyder, a Republican and the House Minority Leader.

"We'd like to treat that as highly classified information," responded Jeffers. "If I told you and word leaked out, whether or not you were the source, you would always be under a cloud. Worse yet, if there were leaks, it would alert Bis Saif to move their facilities."

"I understand," replied Zyder.

Returning to the purpose of the meeting, Jeffers began. "First, I want to thank you all for your assistance in passing the New War Powers Act. Although you may not be aware of it, we've already put it to good use. Although we've started out on a good note, I'm not optimistic that you'll be able to hold everything together in Congress as we experience more power failures and the senators and representatives begin receiving pressure from their constituents to solve the problem."

"You got that right," Brad Nelson, the House Majority Leader and Zyder's counterpart on the other side of the aisle, said. "You wouldn't believe the crazy talk that is taking place, on the floor of Congress, no less."

"Like what?"

Brad Nelson was a big man who had obviously spent his younger days outdoors working on his Wyoming ranch. He was highly regarded in Congress as a straight shooter. His colleagues knew that a promise made was a promise kept, and that he told things exactly as he saw them. With a booming voice and a good sense of humor, he was universally liked. But now he was clearly upset. He stood up and paced around the Oval Office as he spoke. "I know we've got our share of crazies in Wyoming, but I didn't realize they were also bred in other parts of the country. Would you believe that one of my counterparts, Donald Squlo, the junior Republican representative from California, actually suggested that we drop an atomic bomb on Syria? This is an exact quote: 'Why don't we nuke the bastards?' My response was that one reason not to do that is we don't know where the bastards are. How do you know they're in Syria? Second, the individuals we're trying to find are probably point zero zero one percent of the Syrian population, even assuming they're Syrian. Would you kill everyone else?"

"What was his answer?" asked Paul Greenberg, the Democratic Senate Minority Leader.

"His answer floored me. He said that it would be worth it as long as the American people were not inconvenienced."

"That's scary."

But Nelson wasn't finished. "I just related the nuke story to give you an idea of the extremists we've got in our government. But they don't worry me nearly as much as the anti-Muslim coalition. Many of these politicians were elected on an anti-Muslim political agenda. And they seem to be ganging up on the other members of the House. Fortunately, they don't seem to have reached a consensus around their solution to the problem.

Proposed solutions include deportation, immigration restrictions, and internment camps. I've also heard rumors of planned book burnings, confiscation of religions artifacts, and closing all mosques. In addition, there are rumors of underground groups being formed by the public to carry out vigilante raids on Muslims and their mosques. I don't think I need to convince you gentlemen of the degree of hysteria that is evolving in this country. What if the Muslims decide to fight back? I'm sure that ISIS and Bis Saif would be more than willing to provide their support. We'll have a civil war on our hands."

"Sounds like a return to Hitler and the Jewish problem. Isn't this part of the Bis Saif plan? So far, their plan is working, and we're helpless to do anything about it," observed Greenberg, who was Jewish and wearing a black yarmulke, which somehow seemed to conflict with his Ivy League dress of a V-necked cable-knit sweater, chinos, and loafers.

"I agree," concurred Jeffers, who had been quiet up until that point in the conversation. "But what can we do about it? The things you are hearing in Congress, you could also hear on the streets of any town in rural America. The Union Station attack was probably more damaging to the Muslim cause than the power failure, which may be the reason it was carried out. The more that Bis Saif is able to polarize our population—Muslims against Jews and Christians—the more effective they'll be. Somehow, we've got to bring this to an end."

Bob McIntyre, Senate Majority Leader, spoke up. "Not only do we have to figure out the solution, but we need to do it in less than twenty-four hours." Then, not realizing this had already been discussed with the President's War Cabinet, he added speculatively, "Chris, we're members of the same political party. What would be the impact on our party if we caved in to the Bis Saif demands?"

"We discussed that at our War Cabinet meeting, and the group was unanimously opposed to giving into the Bis Saif demands. I'm in agreement with their feelings."

"What if we pretend to concede to their terms, without actually giving in?" responded McIntyre, unwilling to give up on the idea.

"George Wilson has discussed that with DOD, and they all agree it might buy some time. But it would not amount to a lot of time. A day or two, maybe even a week. But you might remember that one of their demands was to give up support for Israel. They can test this demand easily by attacking Israel and watching our response. If we do nothing, they will know we were truthful, but they might also win the war while we're sitting on the sidelines."

At that point, McIntyre conceded the point. "I guess I'm all out of ideas."

Jeffers continued. "I'm not certain there's much we can do at this point, except pray. My feeling is that we'll have to endure one more power failure before we can shut them down. It's true that we're making progress. I want to address the nation tonight on all aspects of the problem, including power failures, terrorism, and Bis Saif. I think my effectiveness would be enhanced if the four of you were with me on the podium. I'll give the address from the press briefing room rather than the Oval Office so that you can join me. If you want, I will also give you a chance to speak."

All four nodded in agreement to join the president when he spoke. Bob McIntyre responded directly. "Chris, I think you should do the speaking. Too many words water down the message, and all we'd be able to do is to repeat what you'd have already said. So I'll be happy to join you and look wise, but the words should be yours."

Again the others nodded in agreement.

"One more thing I'd like to discuss with you," added Jeffers. "I'd like to make a hate crime involving murder against any race or religion a capital offense, punishable by death. Do you think we could get that through Congress? I'll tell you why this is so important. The FBI thinks that the terrorists that shot up Union Station were Syrian, Muslim refugees. Also, I think it is likely that the next power failure, which is due tomorrow, will be accompanied by another terrorist attack. These are ingredients for a nationwide panic and purge of perceived enemies. If the Muslims decide to defend themselves, we could be on the verge of a civil war."

Again Bob McIntyre spoke for the group. "I think it would be tough fight, but I'd like to give it a shot."

And again, the three others nodded their agreement.

"Why can't everyone work together as well as we do?" answered Chris warmly. "It's truly a pleasure working with you, gentlemen."

Jeffers then shook hands with each member of the congressional leadership as they returned to their unenviable tasks.

***

Six days without electricity was beginning to strain the resources and energy of the Crain family. David, the family's breadwinner, was employed by the US Department of Transportation, where he was responsible for analyzing the cause of traffic deaths. When his agency had announced that their work-at-home policy was in effect, there wasn't much that David could do, since without power his PC was no better than a rock. As a result, he commuted to his office building in Southeast Washington three days a week using METRO, which was providing reduced service to conserve the emergency power that was keeping the system running. At work, he had access to a workstation in one of the areas of the building that was powered by an emergency generator. For the remaining two days of the week he used his annual leave, which fortunately he had in abundance. David felt sorry for other families working for less benevolent employers than the US government, who were living on their savings.

When David was not at work he was kept busy finding fuel for the car, cutting firewood illegally in Rock Creek Park, located a few blocks from his home, and helping Joanna entertain their two terminally bored kids, Steve, age eight, and Megan, eleven.

Perhaps one of his most important duties was grocery shopping. The food distribution center nearest their Silver Spring residence had been established at the Strathmore Performing Arts Center in Bethesda, approximately thirty minutes from

265

their home. Traffic congestion was less than usual, as motorists tried to conserve their fuel supplies by restricting their travel to essential trips. Although the selection was very limited, the distribution center had all of the essentials: milk, bread, eggs, chicken, some beef, paper towels, and the ubiquitous toilet paper. The center also carried a limited selection of canned soups, canned fruit, and canned vegetables. It didn't carry any fresh or frozen fruit or vegetables. Nor did it have any cheese or yogurt. He was impressed with the system they had established with the assistance of Safeway and Giant, the region's two largest grocery chains. He called in his order before leaving home. When he arrived at Strathmore, the order was already waiting, packed in bags and cartons. All he had to do was pay for it and carry it to the car.

No one in the family required critical medicine, such as insulin or heart medication, which relieved him from the time-consuming need for trips to a local pharmacy with long lines and limited supplies.

One of the most difficult tasks David faced was to locate firewood to heat their house. He quickly realized that his tall, lanky, out-of-shape frame was not intended for cutting firewood. It was even less well suited for carrying firewood from the receding tree line to his car. Fortunately, the weather was relatively mild, with low temperatures of forty degrees in the evenings. But this was an uncomfortable temperature for an American family used to living at a climate-controlled seventy-two degrees year round. As a result, they had a fire continuously burning in their inefficient living room fireplace. Rock Creek Park was rapidly being stripped of its trees as nearby residents poached its wood, while the park police looked the other way out of sympathy for the shivering locals.

But it was the psychological impact on the kids that was most upsetting. The absence of electricity meant no television and no electronic entertainment. They found board games to be a poor replacement for the quick-moving animation of e-games. Their lives had devolved to that of the family of the early twentieth century, and they didn't like it. Joanna and David, when they could, tried valiantly to amuse them. They resorted to a primitive form of home schooling during the day, but even this was difficult without the online instruction that had become the backbone of home schooling. They read books and even spent time reading the Bible. On nice days, David took them to a nearby park, where they played soccer. Yet, in spite of these efforts, Steve and Megan spent much of the time during that first week complaining. They missed school, they missed their friends, they missed their iPhone, they missed Netflix, and they missed TV. Furthermore, they found the monotonous food boring, and they were cold. One evening David couldn't take it any longer. He slammed down the book he was trying to read and shouted, "The two of you are spoiled silly. Kids have been doing without all these things for hundreds of years. Believe me, you'll survive the deprivation for a few more weeks."

Megan whined in response, "Weeks? I thought we'd be without power for just a few days. How long will this last? I don't think I can stand it."

"I think we're looking at least one or two months, so you'd better get used to it."

"What if I can't get used to it? Dad, why can't you do something?"

"I'm not a magician, and you aren't the only person suffering. In fact, many others are suffering more than you are. Look at this time as something you'll be able to tell your children about."

"I don't want children. And if I have any, I don't intend to tell them about this."

David felt his blood pressure rising. He was working hard to sustain the family, and all they could do was complain. To avoid the threatening argument, he turned to Joanna. "Why don't you call your sister in Dayton? Maybe the three of you could stay with her until power is restored. In the meantime, I'll hold down the fort here and try to keep my job."

Joanna, the love of his life, was a tall, willowy blond. Although she complained about her looks and was convinced she was overweight, he thought she was beautiful. He would

Philip J. Tarnoff

miss her if she agreed to visit her sister in Ohio. "I could do that, but are you sure you'd be okay on your own? I'd sure miss you."

After a phone call, rapid packing, and a long wait on a gas line to fill up the car, Joanna loaded the kids into the car and headed west to Ohio. David's decision to send them packing was reinforced by the complaints from Steve and Megan about having to spend a month with their Ohio cousins, whom they claimed to hate. He spent some time reveling in the silence after they drove out of sight.

That evening, only the sixth day of the power failure, even though it had felt like a year, David decided to walk into downtown Silver Spring to a local bar for a drink and some conversation. As he leaned on the bar and nursed his warm beer by candlelight, the guy next to him struck up a conversation. "This really sucks, doesn't it?"

"Things could be better. Do you live around here?"

"I live in the townhouses on the west side of Georgia Avenue. My name is Gus. How about you?"

"I'm David," he replied as the two shook hands. I live a few blocks east of here. Just sent my family out of town. Couldn't stand the whining. Darn kids are so spoiled they thought their life was ending because there was no TV and no games."

"The damned Arabs have done it to us again. I don't know why we don't blow them off the face of the earth. I belong to an organization that will force the government to use some force to solve this problem once and for all."

David was on his third beer and still simmering over his frustration with the kids. "In theory, that sounds good. We'd all be so much better off if there were no crazy people in this world. I often think of the amount of money we spend on defense in this country, and how well-off we'd all be if we didn't have to spend so much. But I'm not sure I'd be in favor of wiping out the entire Arab world. Think of the women and children. I'm not a religious person, but a slaughter of the type you're describing would be horrible."

His new friend was not discouraged. He handed David a business card. "Well, David, we meet every Thursday night at this address. Meeting starts at eight. We're going to compare the current situation with that of the Romans when they were being invaded by the barbarians. The ending of the Roman Empire was not a happy one. Hopefully the United States will be more successful. After all, we've got nukes. Why not come by next week? I'm sure you won't have anything better to do."

"Sounds good. I'll see you then."

With that, the two finished their beers, paid the tab, and went their separate ways.

CHAPTER 21
THE END OF THE WAITING

5:00 a.m. A week had passed since the Bis Saif threats had been received. After a restless night of tossing and turning, Chris woke up and gave up trying to go back to sleep. Melissa, in bed at his side, quietly said; "Worrying won't solve the problem."

"I know, but I still can't sleep. Might as well get up and get ready for the next catastrophe."

6:00 a.m. Chris and Melissa were in the sitting room adjacent to their bedroom. The sitting room was part of a master suite that included a dressing room for Melissa as well as a large walk-in closet that led to their elegant bathroom. Melissa and Chris frequently used the sitting room in the mornings to prepare themselves for the upcoming day. Today was no exception, as they sat quietly and enjoyed the cup of coffee that had just been served by the White House valet.

The silence between them was palpable, broken only by the sound of the ticking clock on the fireplace mantle. Although they each held a mug of coffee, neither had taken a sip. The White House was silent. Even though many members of the staff often reported for duty at six, it was as if everyone was holding their collective breath.

Finally, Chris couldn't take it anymore. He broke the silence with an insipid phrase, but at least it was a sound. "If anyone had told me that the presidency would be like this, I'd have turned down the damned job. Never could figure out why it was in so much demand anyway."

Melissa, dressed in a yellow blouse and black slacks and looking as if she had just left the beauty parlor, sensed that

Chris's calm exterior belied his inner turmoil. She took a sip of her now lukewarm coffee before replying in her soft Texas drawl. "Now Chris honey, you've done everything possible. You're surrounded by competent people who are nearly killing themselves trying to solve this problem. Driving yourself crazy over this isn't going to help."

"I know you're right, but I'd like to call everyone right now to see how they're doing. It's a stupid idea since I know they'll call me as soon as they know something. There must be something that I've overlooked. Something more that could be done. I'm sure if that's the case, the press will uncover it."

"Honey, you're right. If and when anything happens, you'll be the first to know. Why don't we get dressed and have breakfast, and then you should go about your normal business instead of sitting here on pins and needles."

7:00 a.m. Chris, taking Melissa's suggestion, left for the family dining room, where they quickly ate their traditional light breakfast of juice, coffee, and toast. Chris, who normally had a hard-boiled egg with his breakfast, declined, saying he didn't have much appetite this morning. They were both grateful to have electricity, provided by the large diesel generators that had been installed for the White House ten years earlier, even though others in the region did not have the luxury of a shower followed by a hot breakfast. Chris had skipped his morning workout on the treadmill in the White House gym since he wanted to be fully available if anything should happen.

8:00 a.m. The time was creeping by. Chris began the day by meeting with leaders of the Washington region to discuss ways in which the effects of the power failure could be relieved. His crowded schedule began with a meeting with the director of the Metropolitan Washington Council of Governments, who described the issues associated with emergency management and transportation. Chris hadn't contemplated the issues that were described, which included communications difficulties due to lack of backup generators. As a result, many police and firemen were not able to communicate with their dispatchers during emergencies. While the base stations were operational,

271

power was required by the repeaters scattered throughout the area. The absence of repeaters meant the absence of communications in many areas of the region. He wondered how this could have been overlooked when the system was designed. But this was just one problem of a long list of other issues that the director brought with him. He promised to see what he could do as the meeting concluded and left the room conscious of the ticking clock on the mantle.

9:30 a.m. As he passed Jan Adams' desk, he told her about the generator problem and asked her to call Janice DeBeers office to see if there was anything they could do to help with the generators. "Please have someone call the director and let him know the disposition of the problem."

Jan responded with a worried frown. "You're not doing real well today, are you?"

"I'll be a lot better when the day ends, however it ends. If you need me, I'll be with Paul working on my pronouncements for this afternoon's press conference. Wish I had something intelligent to say." Paul Lynd was Jeffers's press secretary. He relied on him to orchestrate his press conferences so that they ended on as positive a note as possible.

"On second thought, I think I'll call Jim and Matt first to see how the FBI and the CIA are doing. We could sure use some sort of a breakthrough to counteract the depressing prospects for the future. Could you get Jim on the line first?"

Chris then retired to his office to speak with James Proctor. "Jim, just wanted an update before preparing for the press conference this afternoon. Any news?"

"Yes, Mr. President. We've made a little progress, but I didn't think it was significant enough to bother you." What Proctor really meant was that he wanted to be certain that the information they had was not leaked. In his opinion, the senior levels of the government were nothing more than a security sieve. Whatever went in came out somewhere.

"Jim, nothing is insignificant here. I want continuing updates no matter how minute," Chris answered, barely able to hide his annoyance.

"Well the answer is that we've got the location of one of the four gunmen. We want to be sure to get him alive so that he can be questioned. His residence is being watched and every move is monitored. He'll be arrested and questioned at the appropriate time. If we take him alive, I'm confident we'll get the information we need. The only question is how long it will take. It's unlikely that we'll have enough information to prevent another attack tonight, if such an attack is being planned."

"That's good news. I just wish we could speed up the process. But I'm not going to tell you how to conduct your business. Any word on other possible attacks elsewhere in the country?"

"We've turned up the heat on our informants nationwide. A few interesting leads but nothing solid. The most promising lead seems to be in California, where a lot of communications chatter is occurring. Our Los Angeles office is conducting raids on several known cells. I'm waiting to hear from them now."

Chris ended the conversation with a subtle reminder. "Thanks, Jim. Very helpful. Please be sure to keep me up to date."

Turning to his intercom, Chris said, "Jan, I'm ready to speak with Matt O'Brien."

A few minutes later, his intercom buzzed. "Matt, how are things at the CIA?"

O'Brien's response annoyed Chris in the same way that Proctor's had. "Well I've got some good news and some bad news. The good news is that we've identified the aliases adopted by Jaffari and Al-Saadi. They're now called Karen and Jim Andrews. Light disguises, such as Karen has changed her hair style, dyed her hair and wears colored contact lenses. Jim has grown a beard. We've discovered that they traveled to Kuwait, where they spent a few days at the Sheraton Kuwait. After that they disappeared. It seems that they were driven to their new residence in a taxi that was stolen and appears to have been driven by an ISIS sympathizer. We've got the Kuwaiti police, Interpol, and our own people searching for them in Kuwait. We'll eventually find them, but I'm not sure how long it will take."

10:30 a.m. The rest of the morning was spent with his press secretary. "Paul, we need to practice for this afternoon's press briefing. Unfortunately, I don't have much to tell the vultures, but I'd at least like to feed them some tidbits and also be prepared with meaningless pronouncements. So why don't we go through the normal role playing. Shouldn't be too difficult for you to act like a reporter and pretend to be grilling me. As usual, I would appreciate your honesty in evaluating my responses."

"Okay, you asked for it," Paul answered before beginning the practice.

"Mr. President, have we made any progress in finding the Union Station terrorists?"

"Paul, I'll be happy to report that we've made considerable progress. Although I can't reveal the classified details, we've identified some key individuals and are currently tracking them down."

"I'd like to ask a follow-up question. Have you identified all of the terrorists?"

"Since we are not certain of the number of terrorists involved, that's a difficult question to answer. All I can tell you is that we've made significant progress."

"Another follow-up please. When will you begin making arrests?"

"Soon. I'm afraid that's as specific as I can be."

"Moving on to another subject. Have our intelligence agencies located Bis Saif?"

"Here again, we're making progress and hope to be able to provide good news soon."

And so it went for the next hour. The hypothetical reporter and the president practicing for the press conference. At the conclusion of the session, they took a break to answer some phone calls and make use of the restroom facilities adjacent to the press room. As they reconvened, the president asked, "Well, what do you think?"

"I think you've done as well as you can. Obviously you can't be too specific without playing our cards in public. It would be good if you would include a statement to that effect in your opening remarks. It might help minimize the frustration associated with vague answers."

"Speaking of opening remarks, do you think you could have something for me to use within the next two hours?"

"Have I ever let you down?"

"No, you haven't. But I really need you now. When you prepare those remarks, you might add the fact that we are well aware of the seven-day deadline given to us by Bis Saif, and that we don't intend to knuckle under to their demands. Furthermore, we're prepared as we can be for their next cyber attack. You might also include the successes we've had in dealing with the DC region's power failure. I'm sure that DHS can give you statistics of the number of generators provided, the tons of food shipped into the region and distributed, etcetera."

"I'd better get on it. You'll need something by two, since the press conference is at three."

"I just hope we don't have another attack before the conference. I'd be naked on the podium if an attack of unexpected dimensions occurs while I'm speaking."

In an attempt to ease the tension in the room, Paul responded, "That would be a vision. I'd guarantee it would make the front page of every newspaper in the country."

"See you at two," replied the president humorlessly as his cellphone rang with Jan Adams reminding him of his luncheon appointment with the Israeli ambassador.

12:00 noon. "Good day, Mr. President."

"Good day to you, Mr. Ambassador," Jeffers replied, momentarily forgetting the ambassador's name and wishing he had remembered to ask Jan. "And how is Prime Minister Tamer doing today."

"Quite well, thank you, although he would be doing better if we had the Bis Saif problem under control and could get some additional assistance combatting the drone problem."

"Why don't we discuss these matters over lunch?" said the president, ushering the ambassador into the Oval Office dining room, an informal dining room a few steps from the Oval Office. "Have a seat, and please order something to drink from the steward while I step out for a minute to speak with my administrative assistant."

Jeffers returned in less than a minute, having established the fact that the ambassador's name was Paul Akerman. He wondered how someone with a distinctly American name could become ambassador from a Middle Eastern country.

Lunch proceeded amiably while the president labored mightily to keep from glancing nervously at the advancing hands of the clock, wondering when and where the next attack would occur. Conversation covered the entire range of Israeli security issues, including their latest problem with the drones and missiles being launched by Hamas. Fortunately, Jeffers realized he had the complete support of Congress and was able assure Ambassador Akerman that the United States would provide all of the assistance within its power to combat the attacks. At the conclusion of the lunch, Akerman asked the question preying on the mind of every Israeli citizen. "Mr. President, can I assure my government that the United States will not agree to the terms of the Bis Saif threat and abandon my country?"

Chris had been prepared for the question and answered unequivocally. "I am prepared to personally guarantee our continuing support of Israel. In saying this, I am also speaking for the US Congress and the US public. We will stand one hundred percent behind you."

The ambassador's relief was palpable. "Thank you, Mr. President. I will quote you to our government and to our public as well. The United States has always been a good friend, and your continuing friendship is greatly appreciated."

Akerman then brought up the second most important subject on the minds of the Israeli government. "These attacks, as well as increased security, are proving to be a significant financial burden. Would the US Government consider increasing the level of foreign aid it provides? We understand that this is a one-time supplement to the funds we receive annually, but we are facing difficult times."

Although he appreciated the difficulties being faced by the Israelis, Jeffers had financial concerns of his own and was not feeling particularly generous. He realized that they would ultimately provide additional financial support, but was not prepared to make any promises over lunch. His answer was carefully phrased. "Paul, I can imagine that you are being faced with serious financial problems. You must recognize that we have some financial concerns of our own. I'm not prepared to make a commitment at this time, but we're certainly willing to consider it. How much additional funding would your country require?"

Akerman, the diplomat, answered carefully. "We've made some very preliminary estimates and concluded that our shortfall, to use your terminology, could be in the range of one to two billion dollars. I realize this is a large sum of money, and we are working very hard to reduce that sum to the minimum amount."

Jeffers tried hard not to show any reaction to an amount he considered to be exorbitant. "Paul, that's a lot of money. It represents a thirty-percent increase of the military funding we currently provide to you. As you can imagine, we don't have those amounts of money just lying around ready to be mailed to our friends. I will have to reexamine our budget to see whether that much money could be provided, even if Congress is in agreement. So I won't be able to give you an answer today. In the meantime, I'd advise that you continue to examine your budget to determine whether you could make use of less than one billion dollars. So I'll have to answer you at a future time."

And with that, the luncheon concluded.

1:30 p.m. As he returned to the Oval Office, Chris glanced nervously at his watch, thinking, *Well, we've gotten through the morning without any problems. I hope the rest of the day goes as smoothly.*

As he sat down at his desk, he saw a draft of the opening remarks that had been prepared by Paul Lynd. Paul was an experienced hand at this business. His resume showed a stint with CNN as a news commentator, four years covering the White House for the Washington Post, and one year as the president's press secretary. As expected, his work was nearly perfect. Penciling in a few minor changes, Chris gave the speech to Jan for loading into the teleprompter for use at the upcoming news conference. Always an appreciative boss, he then called Paul to thank him for a good job.

2:30 p.m. It was time for a quick wardrobe check and some minor makeup before the press conference began. Chris also used the thirty minutes to check over the notes he had made containing various statistics that might be needed in response to reporters' questions. He then proceeded to the anteroom outside of the press briefing room where he waited for the announcement signaling his entrance. While he waited, he glanced nervously at his watch and prayed fervently that a Bis Saif attack would not occur during the press conference.

3:00 p.m. The briefing began as planned. As Jeffers entered the room, everyone rose respectfully. The gathered reporters listened closely as he presented his opening remarks. Some were taking notes in the traditional manner, while others were recording his talk. When he had finished, the usual bedlam broke out with reporters trying to out-shout each other so they could ask their questions, partly out of a genuine desire for more information, and partly so that they would be shown on camera asking the question. The questions generally followed the pattern that had been anticipated by Paul, who orchestrated the discussion from his position at the side of the podium.

As the news conference progressed, the questions became more antagonistic. These reporters were experienced at their jobs and were unhappy at the vague answers being provided by the president. When a reporter from *The New York Times* was recognized by Paul, it was clear that his frustration had reached its limit. "Mr. President, you warned us in your opening remarks that you would have to be vague for national security reasons. I accept your explanation to a point. But you have avoided specific answers to questions that can't possibly be related to national security. For example, you won't even provide us with the number of attackers at Union Station. Surely Bis Saif knows how many terrorists were there. If you revealed the number, whose security would have been breached? I've got to conclude that we don't know how many terrorists were there or you would have told us. From that, I've got to conclude that we have made no progress in the investigation."

His statements were followed with a murmur of approval from the gathered reporters. Chris thought for a minute before answering. "This situation is more complicated than you describe. I am unwilling to release any of the details of the investigation since it would provide a number of clues to the enemy regarding the status of our investigation as well as the degree to which we are preparing to arrest the participants in the attack. In spite of your understandable desire to know more, I can only repeat that national security prevents me from going into more detail. Be assured that we are making definite progress. Like you, I wish that things would move more quickly, but the entire weight of the FBI, CIA, DHS, and DOD is behind this investigation. We *will* succeed."

Paul Lynd, the experienced press secretary, used Chris's statements as the closing remarks for the conference. He was anxious to avoid letting the conference get out of hand, so he stood and said, "Thank you, Mr. President."

4:00 p.m. Chris glanced at his watch again as he walked to the Oval Office. *The day is two-thirds over,* he thought. *Eight more hours to go before midnight.*

He spent the remaining time until dinner addressing the numerous issues that face every president. He met with Jan to discuss tomorrow's schedule. He reviewed the current draft of the State of the Union Address that was being prepared for his upcoming meeting with Congress. He spent some time with his chief of staff discussing the new Social Security legislation currently being debated by the House of Representatives. In short, he was being presidential.

6:00 p.m. Nothing left on the agenda for the day. Chris decided to return to the White House living quarters and spend some quiet time with his family. As he poured himself his usual end-of-day Bombay Sapphire martini, straight up with two olives, Melissa joined him with a glass of red wine. "How did things go today?" she asked, massaging his tight back muscles.

"About as well as could be expected. Paul Lynd did a good job of ending the press conference just as things began to get ugly. And more important, we've gotten through most of the day without any Bis Saif attacks. Couldn't ask for more than that."

They discussed the events of the day quietly. Melissa told him of her visit with the Girl Scout Troop of the Year, and described some of the cute discussions she had with the girls. They also discussed an upcoming gathering to be held following the State of the Union Address. With their drinks finished, they retired to the family dining room for a simple dinner of good ole Texas barbecue with sides of slaw and baked beans.

8:00 p.m. The tranquility abruptly ended with an emergency phone call from Janice DeBeers.

***

"Mr. President, we've been attacked again!" she said, trying to keep her voice under control.

"Get a hold of yourself, Janice. We need your leadership during this crisis."

"This time was worse than the other time. They hit the California Independent System Operator grid that serves around eighty percent of California and parts of Nevada as well." She then elaborated on her statement. "When I said hit, I mean they disabled the high voltage grid. A number of high voltage transformers were destroyed along with some of the transmission lines. It will take months to repair the damage."

It was Chris's turn to fight to keep his voice even. "How on earth are we going to keep the state electrified until the grid is repaired?"

"Now you understand my hysteria. We can't even come close to finding the generators needed to keep the lights on in California. We're stretched thin in DC and have requisitioned generators from all over the country. They're currently in short supply everywhere."

"It would probably take too long to manufacture additional generators," said Chris thoughtfully. "What are the chances of importing additional equipment from our friends in Canada, Europe, South America, or Asia?"

"We're looking into that. It appears that Canada and Mexico are the only major users of sixty hertz power. Most of the rest of the world, except for some third-world countries or small islands, use fifty hertz. We can't use fifty hertz generators for backup as they could burn out electrical equipment. We're trying to purchase generators from those two countries, although they're being somewhat protective since they're worrying about their own potential power failures. But even if we successfully negotiate a purchase, it is likely to only scratch the surface of our need. I figure we've got about three days before Californians begin to panic."

"What about relocating some of the Californians temporarily to hotels, motels, military bases, and other facilities until power is restored?"

"We're working on all of that and hope to have some answers by tomorrow. I assume you'll want another of your all-hands meetings tomorrow to figure out how to respond?"

"I'm going to call the meeting as soon as I hang up the phone. I'll let you get back to work since you're probably going to have a busy night. Plan on a meeting at eleven tomorrow morning."

As Chris hung up the phone, he mentally developed an action list, beginning with the meeting he had just discussed with Janice. He assumed that all members of the all-hands group, as Janice had called them, were already familiar with the situation.

***

Once again, the president was presiding in the Cabinet Room with the assistance of George Wilson, his DNI. Attendance was the same as it had been yesterday, including General Elliot Drake, Joint Chiefs; Matthew O'Brien, CIA; Janice DeBeers, DHS Director; Admiral DeForce, NSA; James Proctor, FBI; and Bill Solenski, Google. Everyone in the room looked as if

281

they had not slept in twenty-four hours. Even Janice DeBeers had abandoned her stylish pants suit for a pair of jeans and a sweatshirt with her alma mater, U Penn, emblazoned on the front. Except for Drake, who was in uniform, the others were also dressed in jeans or casual slacks.

Jeffers opened the meeting as he had the day before. "It occurs to me that we really should have a full-blown cabinet meeting since every aspect of life in California will be affected, from education to health to business. But there isn't time to call a meeting, and you are all on the front line of this Bis Saif problem, which we've *got* to solve. General Drake, I'd appreciate it if you would take responsibility for keeping the Secretary of Defense up to date. He really should be here except that he's out of the country."

"Yes sir," was Drake's military response.

Chris continued. "There isn't time to bring everyone up to speed. At some point I'll also have to deal with Congress, which I'm sure is full of opinions. Why don't we begin with status updates? If nothing has changed, say so. We don't have time for speech making. After all, we were together less than twenty-four hours ago. George, why don't you take over the meeting?"

Without standing up, George Wilson nodded to Janice DeBeers and said, "Why don't you begin?"

"As you know, Mr. President, the power failure affected eighty percent of California and some of Nevada. We estimate that providing backup power for the next three months to ten percent of the gas stations, individuals on emergency medical equipment, and other critical services will result in a need for approximately ten thousand emergency generators of various sizes. Since we've drained the supply of available generators for the Washington, DC area, we're really stuck. The DHS staff is working on a plan to move citizens of northern California north into Oregon, and citizens of southern California either into Mexico or Arizona. Nevada can't be used since they're dealing with their own power failure. So we can evacuate the northern and southern parts of the state and will concentrate our available generator supplies on central California, in other words, the LA area. If we get lucky, we can dig up the three thousand or so generators we might need."

Janice paused for breath and then continued. "That leaves us with two problems, which we are currently addressing. First, is the problem of providing food to the remaining population, and the second is finding money to pay for all this. We could handle the food in the same way as we're handling the food for the DC region, except on a much bigger scale. The second is paying for three months of housing for approximately two-thirds of the population of California. Mr. President, I'm hoping you can find funding for this. California has a population of nearly forty million people. If two-thirds of this population needs room and board, at a rate of twenty dollars per person per day, this works out to forty-eight billion dollars for a period of ninety days. This is nearly equal to the DHS sixty billion dollar billion budget. If we tried to pay for this mass migration it would bankrupt our agency." And with that depressing news, the DHS director resumed her seat.

Rather than discussing the problems of California's lack of power, Chris decided to continue with the meeting. "Hopefully we can find creative ways of reducing that cost. I admit that twenty dollars per day per person is not much of a per diem, but forty-eight billion diverted from fighting ISIS and Bis Saif would put quite a dent in our budget. Let's address that issue later. I don't want to bore everyone with budget discussions."

George Wilson then resumed control of the meeting. "Jim, I wonder whether the FBI has anything to report."

"I've got some good news," James Proctor said. "We've arrested one of the terrorists from the Union Station attack, and he seems anxious to talk. He drove the getaway car, and is the younger brother of one of the other terrorists. He's given us several names and a few locations. It appears that the terrorists are all connected with ISIS. We haven't been able to establish their relationship with Bis Saif. Additional arrests will be made soon."

In an attempt at humor, George Wilson said, "I won't ask why the younger brother was anxious to talk. But that is definitely good news." No one laughed, but the tension in the room eased slightly. Proceeding from his failed attempt at humor, George called on the next speaker, Matthew O'Brien. "Tell us how things are going at the CIA. Hopefully you've been able to make some progress."

O'Brien began speaking as soon as his name was mentioned. "First, I would like Jim's confirmation that the FBI has not been able to obtain any additional information from the Jaffaris. It's my understanding that they've given us everything they know and that their prosecution as aiding and abetting a terror group will shortly be underway." He paused and continued after Proctor nodded his head in agreement.

"As far as tracking down Kelly and Jahmir, aka Karen and Jim, we have made some progress, but are currently at a dead-end. I would also remind you that they're now working with a third individual, a Hamas Palestinian whose name is Hasan Jouda. With the assistance of our Kuwaiti friends, we've found their apartment in Kuwait City. It's a three-bedroom flat in a residential area. We've seen the three of them leaving the airport two months before the threats were received. The problem is that we don't know where they went. They appear to have flown on a multi-leg trip using a different name for each leg. The first leg of their trip was to Amsterdam on KLM. We found video footage of their arrival in Amsterdam, but can't find footage of their departure. It's possible, even likely, that they changed their disguises in Amsterdam. Hasan took a different flight from Karen and Jim. We are working with Interpol to obtain video footage from all the cameras at Schiphol, the Dutch airport. Our analysts are currently reviewing the tapes. I've got every analyst at Langley working on this. We've *got* to track these three, since that's the only way we can find the headquarters of Bis Saif."

Chris looked downcast. "That doesn't sound good. Somehow we've got to find them within the next week. It's the only way we can avoid further catastrophes." Turning to Elliot Drake, he said, "General, when we locate them, we'll have to take them out. Do you have a Special Forces team standing by?"

"Yes, sir, we've actually got several teams standing by at various sites around the world. We've also got transports loaded with their equipment sitting on their respective runways. Just tell us where and when, and I personally guarantee we'll solve the problem."

"General, while you've got the floor, I'd like to return to the subject of the power failures. I think we cut the FBI report short. They've told me that a number of anti-Muslim groups are mobilizing to take their frustrations out on those people. We are likely to need military assistance in combating these groups. It's also likely that we'll need the assistance of your military police to supplement local police in guarding public venues and the general populous so that we don't have a recurrence of the Union Station incident. Do any of you remember the riots in 1968 when Martin Luther King was assassinated? At that time, National Guard troops in full battle gear patrolled the streets of many American cities. We may have a similar situation. Have you had any discussions with the FBI and local agencies on this subject?"

"Mr. President we are actively engaged in these discussions. In addition to the problems you mentioned, there is also the issue of guarding the residences and businesses of individuals who have been evacuated to other states for three months. The California, Maryland, Virginia, and DC National Guards have all been activated by their governors for police, transportation, and medical support. All of the installations in these states are also on alert with instructions to provide any and all assistance as it is requested."

"Thank you, General. Finally, I'd like a report from our Google representative, who is exploring ways to provide improved cyber security to the power distribution facilities."

It was Bill Solenski's turn to speak. "Mr. President, we're continuing to work with the affected companies as well as those of other distribution companies. Fortunately, there are only four or five companies that serve the large geographic areas Bis Saif is trying to cripple. In all cases, security has been upgraded, and three of the companies have been disconnected from the

Philip J. Tarnoff

Internet to prevent remote access by Bis Saif. This is leading to incredibly inefficient power sharing among utilities, but it is the only certain way of protecting their facilities. We have reverted to mid-twentieth-century technology as a result of the disconnection. The Bis Saif computer is so powerful that it is impossible to provide one-hundred-percent assurance of protection. We've also initiated a training program for all employees of the distribution companies to impress on them the importance of protecting all passwords. The disconnection might at least provide the temporary protection we need to avoid future catastrophes."

Jeffers sensed that the participants in the meeting were anxious to return to their urgent tasks and concluded the meeting. "So it sounds as if everything that could be done is being done. The one loose end is finding Bis Saif and destroying them. We've got one week to solve that particular problem. In the meantime, I'd like to thank all of you for attending two long meetings within twenty-four hours. Once again, I would remind you to keep me up to date if anything changes."

CHAPTER 22

HELP FROM ABROAD

During the 1970s, Nigeria began planning for a new capital city. Located in the middle of the country, the site for Abuja was selected as a neutral location that did not favor any one of the religious or ethnic groups within the country. Since its official designation as the country's capital in 1991, Abuja has been one of the fastest-growing cities in the world, with a regional population of eight million and an annual growth rate that exceeds thirty percent. Located approximately 600 miles from the equator, Abuja experiences a tropical climate with year-round temperatures in the eighties and nineties and comparable humidity.

But the weather and growth of Abuja were of little interest to Udo as he made his way through the crowded streets toward the American embassy. He was nervous about the letter he carried, which if discovered in the pocket of his tan cargo pants would guarantee his execution by either Boko Haram or the Nigerian Army. Udo had planned the process carefully, and if everything went well, today might be his last day in Nigeria.

His disillusionment with the warring factions of Nigeria had begun when he witnessed the incompetence of the army in his home town of Baga, which led to his defection to Boko Haram. After serving with Boko Haram for nearly a year, he realized that they also suffered from a high level of incompetence, which was further compounded by their brutality. His unhappiness had peaked when, following his visit to Jakarta, General Modukuri had refused to become part of the Bis Saif movement. The subsequent bombing of the Boko Haram headquarters in Maiduguri and the death of General Modukuri had been the last straw.

He was convinced that Bis Saif had been behind the bombing, which had been carried out as revenge for the general's refusal to unite with their organization. As he observed the never-ending conflict between the army and Boko Haram, he had concluded that life in Nigeria was a dead-end existence. He was aware of the American's dilemma over the Bis Saif threats, and felt that his knowledge of their operation was a ticket out of Nigeria.

Now that he had written his letter to the American ambassador and was ready to execute his plan, he was nervous. His hands shook as he extracted the letter from his pocket and approached one of the numerous street urchins who eked out a living begging and running errands for local politicians. He grabbed a surprised boy, who appeared to be around fourteen years old, by the collar of his tattered shirt. "Would you like to earn some easy money?"

"Sure, man. What do I have to do? Kill someone?" he said.

"No, it's easier than that. All you have to do is give this envelope to one of the guards outside the American embassy two streets away, and then run. Don't let them catch you or question you. I'll give you one hundred Naira now and one hundred Naira when you return if you do what I've told you," Udo said, offering the boy a sum equivalent to one US dollar.

"We have a deal," answered the streetwise boy.

Udo handed him the envelope and the money and watched the boy dash down the street in the direction of the embassy. He positioned himself outside the view of the cameras surrounding the embassy's fence and watched the boy as he ran up to the marine guard, hand him the envelope, and dash back down the street and around the corner to where Udo waited with another 100 Naira note.

The boy took the money and disappeared down the street with as much money as he could have expected from a day of begging on the street.

Udo's note, handwritten in poorly printed English, had been direct and to the point:

"I wish to desert from Boko Haram today. I know many things about Bis Saif. I will tell you everything I

*know if you take me to America. I will not tell you until
I arrive in America. If you agree, meet me at Abuja Airport in cafeteria near entrance at 7:00 tonight. I wearing
tan pants and shirt says Yale University. My name Joe.
Contact should look like Nigerian and not American."*

Udo could scarcely imagine the stir his note created at the
embassy. As soon as it had been opened by the CIA station
chief, it was taken to the ambassador, scanned, and sent to CIA
headquarters in Langley, Virginia. Plans were immediately
made for Udo's extraction.

***

It was 7:00 p.m. at the airport, and Udo was seated at a
table for two to the right of the entrance to the cafeteria. He
was wearing the Yale tee shirt that had been given to him as a
parting gift in Jakarta as he reflected on the irony of the gift and
the purpose of this meeting. He glanced nervously around the
cafeteria, looking for signs of Nigerian army soldiers, police, or
his ex-comrades from Boko Haram. All he saw in the crowded
cafeteria were travelers—businessmen with carry-ons, families
with tired and bored children, and elderly women who appeared
to be traveling to see their grandchildren. He thought, *All I have
to do is stand up and leave, and life can return to normal. What
am I doing here?*

While he was immersed in his fears, he failed to notice that
two armed security guards had entered the cafeteria with an
obviously irate woman, who pointed at him and yelled, "There
he is. That's the one who stole my purse. Arrest that thief."

Udo couldn't believe she was pointing at him and looked
around to see whether there had been some mistake. The two
guards walked over to him and asked him to stand up and come
with them. His heart sank with the realization that this could
mean his exit from Nigeria was being blocked by a stupid mis-
understanding. Udo obeyed. As he stood up, each of the guards
grabbed one of his arms and hustled him out of the cafeteria,
while the other customers stared in curious silence. As the

guards marched him down the concourse, with the accusing woman in tow still muttering about the theft, they turned suddenly at an unmarked door and shoved him into a bare room with a table and four chairs. One of the guards turned, locked the door that they had just entered, sat down, and offered Udo his hand. "Are you Joe?" he asked.

Udo's reply reflected his shock and the fact that in the excitement he had forgotten the alias he had selected. "I guess so. I mean—yes, I am Joe. Who are you?"

"It's better if you do not know our names. We're from the American embassy, and we received your note. What is it that you want to tell us?"

Udo recovered quickly. "As I said in my note, I will not discuss anything with you unless I'm in America."

"We understand, but we cannot help you unless you can give us some idea of what you know. What is the name of the terrorist organization you want to discuss?"

"Bis Saif," he said.

"Do you know what country they are in?"

"Yes, but I'm not going to tell you here."

"Do you know what city they are in?"

"Yes, but I'm not going to tell you here."

"Did you meet their leaders?"

"Yes, but I'm not going to tell you here."

"This is our last question. We will only get you to America if you answer it. How did you come to meet them?"

Udo realized that he was going to have to give these fake security guards some information if they were going to meet his demands. "I was a Boko Haram soldier. My general got a request from Bis Saif to send a representative. He chose me."

"What was your general's name?"

Although this was another question after the last, Udo answered without hesitation. "General Modukuri. He was killed by the Americans in a bombing attack within a few weeks after I returned from my meeting."

Udo's two replies appeared to satisfy the three from the embassy. They looked at each other and nodded. "I'm sure you realize that your information is of great interest to the American government. We are going to great expense to get you to America as quickly as possible. After that, you will be questioned at great length by our people. Please answer everything as completely and truthfully as possible. You may already know that there is a reward being offered to people who can help us locate Bis Saif. If you are able to provide us with the information we need, you could be a very rich man."

"I'm not doing this for money, although I would accept money gratefully," Udo replied. He had no idea that a reward was being offered.

"Have you ever flown in an airplane?"

Udo hadn't contemplated this possibility and gulped before answering. "Yes, I flew for my visit with Bis Saif."

With that the three rose and left the office by a second door that Udo hadn't noticed. They walked down a long corridor which led to another door, through which they exited to the airport tarmac. A two-person Jeep with a flag on top was waiting with the engine idling. The guard who had done all the talking clapped Udo on the shoulder and said, "Have a good trip." And with that, the Americans were gone, while Udo and the taciturn driver sped along the airport taxiway to a hanger on the edge of the runways. Inside the hanger was a white, unmarked Gulfstream G650 executive jet with a cruising range of 6,000 miles and a top speed of 600 mph. The cabin was beautifully appointed, with reclining leather seats, deep-pile carpeting, and fluorescent overhead lighting. The driver indicated that Udo should climb the stairs leading to the jet's cabin. As he entered the plane's cabin, he was awed by its luxurious appointments and the presence of two armed US Army soldiers, one of whom said, "We were told not to speak with you unless it concerned the details of this flight. So let us know if there's anything you need—food, drink, clothing, etcetera, and we'll see what we can do. You are dressed for the tropical climate of Abuja. But we're flying to Andrews Air Force Base, which is near Washington, DC. It is winter in Washington, so you'll need much warmer clothes. We've brought some clothing for you. Hope it fits."

Too overwhelmed to speak, Udo just nodded at the soldier before asking, "How long is our trip?"

"About twenty hours. We'll stop very briefly in Spain to refuel, and then cross the Atlantic to America."

As the conversation was taking place, the cabin door was closed and the plane was being pushed backward out of the hanger by one of the airport tugs. As soon as it cleared the hanger, the engines started and the pilot began his rotation for the airport departure taxiway. Udo didn't realize that this was an extremely high-priority flight, and its takeoff had received precedence over other traffic at Abuja Airport. The CIA had moved heaven and earth to ensure his safe and rapid travel from Nigeria to his ultimate destination, somewhere near Washington, DC.

***

Udo had eaten well and was in a deep sleep, dreaming about his native Baga, when one of the soldiers roughly shook him to wake him up. He awoke disoriented by the strange surroundings of the Gulfstream's cabin, and it took him several minutes to realize where he was. "Sorry. I guess I fell asleep for a few minutes."

The soldier laughed. "I'd say you were asleep for five hours. You missed most of the long, boring flight across the Atlantic Ocean. We'll be landing near Washington, DC in a little while. But first, we want to convince you that we've kept our part of the bargain and brought you to America. Before the pilot lands, we will fly around Washington, DC so you can see the capital and the monuments. Then we will land at Andrews Air Force Base, which is near the city. So look out the window and watch the scenery."

Udo did as he was told and stared with great interest out of the large, oval cabin windows, watching the US coastline unfold beneath the plane. It was 10:00 a.m. in Washington, DC, and Udo watched as the plane passed over Chesapeake Bay and then turned southwest to the city. The soldier pointed out various landmarks as they flew over Mt. Vernon, the birthplace of the first president, the Pentagon, Jefferson Memorial, and Kennedy Center for the Performing Arts. Udo could also see the Capitol, the White House, and the Washington Monument. Flights taking off and landing at Reagan National Airport had been suspended because Udo's sightseeing tour crossed their flight paths. The CIA was taking no chances that he would back out of his offer to share his knowledge of Bis Saif, and they felt that these extraordinary arrangements were worth temporarily inconveniencing other air travelers.

When the tour had been completed and Udo was significantly impressed, the Gulfstream reversed its course and headed for Andrews. After landing, they taxied to a hanger on the edge of the airfield, where the plane was attached to a tug and towed into a nearby hanger. After the hanger doors had been closed, one of the soldiers opened the cabin door and motioned to Udo that he should proceed down the retractable stairs. At the foot of the stairs he was met by four men dressed informally in sports shirts, slacks, and casual jackets. They escorted him to a sparsely furnished office adjacent to the hangar.

"Welcome to the United States of America," said the one who was obviously their leader. "My name is Al. We are representatives of the US government. We will take you to a nicer place after we've had time to speak, but right now, it is urgent for us to learn what you can tell us without delay. After that, you will have time to relax and learn about your new country. And if the information you provide us is useful, you will be eligible for a very great reward. Joe, it's good to meet you." He concluded by extending his hand.

Udo was momentarily taken aback. He had again forgotten that he had used the name Joe as an alias. He shook Al's hand and laughed. "That's not really my name. I didn't want to use my real name while we were still in Nigeria. My name is Udo."

Al smiled. "That's a good beginning to our discussion. We figured your real name was not Joe, but have not had time to figure out who you are. Why don't you tell us about yourself?"

Udo took a deep breath and began his story. "My name is Udo. I was raised in the small village of Baga, in the Borno

Province. My family had been fishermen on Lake Chad, which is near Baga, but the lake is drying up, and my father could no longer find enough fish for the family. So we began raising vegetables and hunting to support ourselves. One day Major Maduka, from the Nigerian Army, came and said we were about to be attacked by Boko Haram. He promised to tell us when Boko Haram was coming and that the Nigerian Army would provide us with rifles to defend ourselves. But the army's help never came, and we were attacked by a great force of Boko Haram soldiers. I was one of the few who escaped by hiding in the jungle. My entire family was killed, after the women were raped and our village was burned." He paused to wipe a tear away.

Al was anxious for Udo to continue, but felt that it would be important to give him time to collect himself. "Udo, would you like something to drink? We have coffee, tea, water, Coca Cola."

"No, thank you. I would like to finish my story. After that I will have something to drink."

Al realized that the boy in front of him was tough and that he had been through a lot. So he lapsed into silence.

"I was enraged," continued Udo. "I felt that Boko Haram was brutal, but the Nigerian Army was worse. Not only did they allow my town to be destroyed, but they had lied to us and did not provide any support. Also I have heard that the Nigerian Army had conducted as many atrocities as Boko Haram. Although it might not seem right, I made the decision to join Boko Haram so that I could fight the Nigerian Army, which seemed to me to be the worst of the two groups. I had to belong to one of them in order to survive.

"I did not enjoy being with Boko Haram. They are also brutal, and I saw them kill many of my fellow Nigerians. In spite of my feelings, I fought in many battles and gained their respect. One day, the leader of our fighting group came to me and said that General Modukuri wanted to speak to me. I did not know what he wanted, and was surprised when he told me he had a secret mission for me. He told me that I was chosen since my English was good."

Al held his breath, realizing that the information they needed was about to be revealed.

"The general told me that a group named Bis Saif had contacted them, and that they wanted to make an offer to us. They had told the general that he should send a representative who he trusted to speak with them. That they could not discuss these matters any other way."

"So you were the one who was chosen to represent Boko Haram?" asked Al, urging Udo on.

"Yes, General Modukuri told me that Bis Saif would provide me with transportation, and that I was to follow their instructions. One week later, airplane tickets were given to me by someone I did not know. I flew on three airplanes, using three different tickets and three different names. Bis Saif provided me with a passport that matched each of the names. When I arrived at my destination, I was met by their representative. I was taken to a van without windows and told to get in the back. We drove a long way, but I could tell I was in a big city. When the van stopped, I was blindfolded and taken out of the van into a house. Then we went down some stairs. When my blindfold was removed, we were in a tunnel under the ground. We then walked a long time in the tunnel until we got to their offices."

The four men interviewing Udo had a thousand questions at this point. But the one overriding concern was the location of the Bis Saif headquarters. Restraining his impatience, Al asked, "Udo, you never told us the city in which the final airport was located. Did you know where your last flight landed?"

"Yes, it was Jakarta," responded Udo, in one sentence answering the question that US intelligence agencies had been asking for the past two weeks.

With that, one of the four men in the room stood up. "I've got to take a leak. Would you excuse me for a minute?"

Everyone nodded. Udo was the only one in the room who did not realize that the trip to the men's room was a cover being made by George Wilson, the US Director of National Intelligence. As soon as he left the interrogation room, George made a phone call to Jan Adams, who was waiting for the call. "It's

295

Jakarta," he said. "You know who to call. It also goes without saying that the president should call the President of Indonesia and ask for his assistance in tracking down these assassins."

Jan's crisp answer: "Consider it done."

As Wilson returned to the room, Udo was saying, "When I returned to Nigeria, I presented the proposed arrangement in the most positive terms. But General Modukuri was not impressed. In spite of the large amount of assistance they offered us, he decided to refuse their offer, saying, 'I will not give up my freedom to an outside power.' I was very troubled that I had risked my life and returned with a good offer and it was refused."

"Go on," encouraged Al.

"Well, two weeks after the general had refused the Bis Saif offer, a strange thing happened. Our headquarters in Maiduguri were bombed by American warplanes. The general was killed in the bombing attack. This could have been a coincidence, but I think it was a message from Bis Saif to anyone else who was thinking about refusing their offers. To me, this was another sign of the incompetence of our leaders. I often wondered how Bis Saif got the Americans to work for them."

Al glanced briefly at one of the other men in the room with his eyebrows raised.

The meeting continued for another hour until Udo was yawning and visibly exhausted. He was questioned about every detail of his trip, including the airlines he used, his seat on the plane, and the names on his passports. But most of the time was spent quizzing him about the details of the Bis Saif headquarters. He described the rooms, the equipment he saw, the food they served, the size of their staff, and the means of entry and exit. They were particularly interested in his impression of the goals of the organization and the capabilities of the men that he met.

At the end of the hour, Al stood up and said, "You must be exhausted from your long trip. Why don't we take you to your new home in America, where you can get a hot meal and some rest? You're fortunate that we could find a place for you outside the area that has been affected by the power failure. As you know, most of the Washington, DC region has no electricity."

Udo just nodded, realizing that he had given these men control over his entire life. He was in America without any knowledge of the place. He had no money and no identification papers. He just hoped he had done the right thing.

***

The two agents who had not been introduced then escorted Udo to the waiting car. George Wilson and Al Kaplan were left behind. Al immediately downloaded the recording of the interview to his staff at CIA headquarters, Lee Sanders at the FBI, and General Drake of the Joint Chiefs at the Pentagon. The three organizations immediately began squeezing every ounce of intelligence information out of Udo's story.

As soon as Kaplan had finished with the mechanics of the download, he turned to Wilson and said, "Whew. That's quite a story. I can understand why Udo's emotions are in turmoil. I'm surprised he decided to flee to the United States since he knew that we were the ones who bombed the Boko Haram headquarters."

"I'm more interested in the two significant items that emerged from his story. First is their location in Jakarta, and second is the supposedly coincidental bombing. Do you know how we got that location?"

"No, but I'm going to find out ASAP." As he was replying, Kaplan was again picking up the phone for a brief conversation with someone at the CIA. "They'll call me back as soon as we know something."

"Maybe Drake can find out quicker," suggested Wilson

"I doubt it. We were the ones who figured out which building to bomb. I want to know how we knew the HQ was in Maiduguri." With that, Kaplan made himself a cup of coffee from the Keurig coffee pot on a table in the corner of the room.

Although Kaplan was a career CIA employee, he did not look the part. He was overweight, and his clothes were perpetually rumpled. His suit appeared to have been obtained from a Goodwill store. His tie hung loosely, and his shirt was unbuttoned at the neck. But looks can be deceiving, and Al was generally considered to be one of the best analysts employed by the CIA. He had been given unlimited access to personnel and funding in the urgent quest to find Bis Saif.

Wilson and Kaplan did not have long to wait. In less than ten minutes, Kaplan's cellphone rang. Although George could only hear one end of the conversation, it was enough.

"You're kidding! Our info came from MI-6? Don't the Brits vet their sources?"

A pause and then, "Contact them immediately. Find out how they got their information and what they know about their source."

Another pause. "Don't let them alert their source that we're onto him. We need to track him back to their HQ."

***

It was 3:00 a.m. in Chelsea when the phone rang. "Bloody hell," swore Stan Comstock as he rolled over in bed and felt for the phone on his nightstand in the dark. He growled into the phone, "Hallo, who is this?"

He knew the voice on the other end of the call immediately. It was Al Kaplan, his contact at the CIA. "We need your help as soon as possible. I know it's the middle of the night over there, but this can't wait."

Comstock was instantly awake. "What's the problem?"

"There's no problem, but you might have some information that we badly need. Who was it that told you about the Boko Haram headquarters being in Maiduguri? What do you know about your source?"

Stan was always willing to cooperate with the CIA, as their relationship was a good one. But revealing names of their agents went far beyond cooperation. "You know I can't reveal that information. Why do you want to know?"

"You know about our little difficulty with Bis Saif. You know that almost half of the United States is without electricity, and they're responsible. Until recently, we did not know where they were located, which would make it difficult to take out their computer. But we recently received information that they may be located in Jakarta, Indonesia. But where in Jakarta? That's the question. It's like looking for a needle in a haystack."

"What does that have to do with our agent?"

"We also discovered that Bis Saif hosted representatives from various Sunni terrorist groups. One of the groups was Boko Haram. They asked these groups to affiliate with them. Boko Haram turned them down. Within a week after their refusal, you magically came up with the location of the Boko Haram headquarters. Our source thinks it was an act of retribution that you asked us to level the HQ. We've got four days to find Bis Saif before we experience another widespread power failure. We're determined to solve the problem. We think that your agent might have connections with Bis Saif. That's why we need you to double-check his background, and if it is at all suspicious, we'd like to ask you to call him in so we can follow him back to his nest full of vermin."

Comstock needed no further convincing. "I'll call you in less than two hours."

He was at his desk at 4:00 a.m. after getting dressed and an unusually quick early hour drive to the headquarters. Pulling Cecil Breathwaite's personnel file, he began reading. As he scanned the file he was left with the uncomfortable feeling that it only described Breathwaite's immediate family: mother, father, and sister. No effort had been made to examine the backgrounds of his other relatives or the parents of the mother and father. He remembered the investigation, which had been considered urgent because of the value of the information that Breathwaite appeared to offer. Comstock now had a problem. He couldn't complete the investigation without alerting Breathwaite to the fact that he was under suspicion. He finally concluded that the only solution would be to come clean with the Americans.

Stan made the call. It was answered at the first ring. "Hello?"

"Comstock here. I'm afraid we all have a problem. I looked at the file, and it appears that the investigation of his background wasn't as complete as it should have been. We can't pursue the investigation without alerting him of our suspicions. So my suggestion is that we immediately begin tracking him to see where his trail leads."

"You haven't given me his name yet."

Comstock took a deep breath. "You realize I am about to violate a security regulation which could lead to my prosecution. I would appreciate it if you would treat this conversation with the greatest secrecy."

"You have my word."

"His name is Cecil Breathwaite. We can only contact him through a security drop in London. I suspect his sister watches the drop. By a twist of fate, he's due to arrive at our offices this afternoon."

"Now here's another coincidence," replied Kaplan. "He must be visiting you in order to receive an update on our progress to date in tracking his organization. The timing of his visit confirms our suspicions that he's our man. What's his excuse for the visit?"

"He claims his sister is very sick and he's here to visit her. I'd really like to check that out, but I'm afraid of spooking him."

Kaplan agreed. "I would be very careful with him. I don't think you should be checking on anything. When he stops by to visit, I would tell him that we haven't made any progress in finding Bis Saif, and that we're starting to panic."

"That's exactly what we'll do. Now I've got to say ta-ta. I've got a lot to do before Breathwaite, or whatever his name is, arrives."

"Good luck, and let us know if there's anything we can do to help. Breathwaite doesn't know any of our operatives, so it might be good to call on our local office to see if they can help you track him without raising any alarms. I'll send them a message that you might be calling right away. But please don't lose him."

Comstock replied with a growl. "Don't worry, this one will not be lost."

CHAPTER 23

PROGRESS

The Indonesian government was facing a dilemma. Just as Christianity was the majority US religion, the Muslim religion was the majority in Indonesia. As a democratically elected leader, the President of Indonesia could not risk angering his political base. He was also concerned that actions perceived as being taken against Muslims could spark terrorist attacks similar to those that occurred since the turn of the century. During a fifteen-year period, nearly 300 people had died in nine major terrorist attacks in Indonesia.

Yet the government was afraid to impose strict anti-terrorist laws because they were afraid that it would anger the large conservative Muslim population. For example, they couldn't arrest Indonesians who had fought with ISIS and then returned home unless they had already purchased explosives or other weapons. The radical population was rapidly increasing as those who had been imprisoned mixed with other inmates who were recruiting new jihadists. So it seemed that Indonesia, the home of the largest Muslim population in the world, was rapidly becoming a powder keg. Certainly, Jakarta was a good choice for the Bis Saif headquarters.

Thus, President Sutanto of Indonesia was not a happy man when he answered the call from President Jeffers. Jeffers was asking for his assistance in tracing the location of Bis Saif. He was also asking for Sutanto's agreement that the Indonesian security and police forces would not interfere with the operations of the US Special Forces personnel who were about to be embedded in Jakarta.

President Sutanto's reply proved him to be the wily politician he was. "President Jeffers, I greatly sympathize with your difficulties. And as an ally of the United States, we will do everything in our power to assist you. But as you know, our resources are limited, and everyone in our population would not agree to our support of you Americans. I think it would be best if we helped you by doing things that your people cannot do. This could include speaking to local informants known only to our police and our intelligence group, the Badan Intelijen Negara, or the BIN, as we call them. We might also help you track people of interest since your CIA and Special Forces do not look very Indonesian. Finally, I can offer to ignore the presence of any Americans that are attempting to capture the Bis Saif leaders. If your people are caught in their illegal activities, I will offer to help them avoid prosecution through some sort of prisoner exchange. But if this happens, I will be very horrified and will ask for a formal apology from your government."

"I think that's fair. We can certainly work with that arrangement," replied Jeffers.

Sutanto continued as if Jeffers had not spoken. "Of course, Mr. President, you may be aware of the fact that our BIN has been requesting some listening devices from your CIA for some time now. We have never received a reply to our request. In our new spirit of cooperation, do you think it would be possible to consider our request?"

"I will look into it immediately, and thank you, President Sutanto, for your assistance."

And with that, the phone call was concluded, with both parties having recorded the discussion.

Jeffers buzzed Jan as soon as the call was completed and asked her to look into the issue of the listening devices. "Whatever they were," he added, "unless there is some compelling issue of national interest associated with their release, they are to be dispatched to Indonesia immediately."

Jeffers then sent high-priority, classified emails to both General Drake and Matthew O'Brien to inform them of the conversation with President Sutanto. Al Kaplan and the colonel in charge of the Navy Seal team knew of the arrangement within minutes after the emails had been received.

***

As a result of the telephone call between the two presidents, the wheels of the United States, UK, and Indonesian governments were turning at a high speed. In the US, two units of an Army Special Forces team were boarding planes with their equipment, bound for Jakarta. Photos of Udo, Hasan Jouda, and Karen and Jim Andrews, aka Kelly Jaffari and Jahmir Al-Saadi, were distributed to agencies throughout the world, including Interpol, Mossad, Indonesian security, and MI-6. Their value would be in identifying transit points that any of these individuals might have passed through on their way to the Bis Saif headquarters in Jakarta. Hundreds if not thousands of pairs of eyes would be scanning security videos at airport screening facilities looking for them. In Jakarta, the review of video would include curbside transportation services in the hope of identifying any of these individuals entering a van for transportation to the Bis Saif facilities. The CIA and their counterparts recognized that although they had found the city in which Bis Saif operated, they did not know their location. Jakarta is an enormous city, with a population of nearly ten million within an area of 250 square miles. Searching for the headquarters would be like looking for the proverbial needle in a haystack. They needed more information.

In the UK, security forces had been mobilized to track the movements of Cecil Breathwaite.

This was a complex undertaking since Breathwaite had worked for MI-6 for many years and knew their personnel and their tactics. He operated with extreme caution, which explained his longevity as a double agent. But Stan Comstock was also experienced, and had enlisted the assistance of a number of experienced trackers from outside MI-6, including the personnel from the CIA's London office in following Breathwaite as he visited MI-6 for a relatively brief one-hour meeting, followed

303

Philip J. Tarnoff

by a lengthier visit with his sister. During the time with his sister he could be seen at the window of her second-floor flat, constantly checking the street for loiterers that might be tailing him. He remained with her overnight and left early the next morning to catch a flight to Istanbul, Turkey on Turkish airlines using an assumed name. In Istanbul, he changed to Singapore airlines and used a different assumed name and passport for the second leg of his trip, which took him directly to Jakarta. Much to the frustration of the trackers, Breathwaite flew first class while they were consigned to the cramped coach seats in the rear.

As Breathwaite exited the plane in Jakarta, another set of trackers was assigned to follow him on this, the most critical leg of his trip. These men were BIN operatives. The BIN had received increased funding since 2002, when a terrorist bombing on the Indonesian island of Bali had killed more than 200 people. As a result, they were well equipped and trained for the assignment of tailing Cecil Breathwaite.

As Breathwaite left the international arrivals terminal with its red tiled roof and waited on line at the taxi stand, pulling his carry-on bag behind, the newsstand vendor spoke surreptitiously into his radio. "He's waiting on line for a cab. I'll give you the cab number as soon as he gets in."

A long pause and then. "OK. He's getting into a Blue Bird cab, number 3875."

As the blue cab pulled away from the curb, two BIN Toyota Corollas also moved into the traffic lanes for the airport exit. Travel time from the airport to the center city was unpredictable, taking between one and four hours, depending on the time of day and day of week. Breathwaite, who had become John Smith upon entering Indonesia, was fortunate, in that his arrival time of 8:00 p.m. was well after rush hour had ended. As they drove along the limited access roadway, the trackers exited every five miles to be replaced by BIN agents driving different cars. They leapfrogged each other, fell back, and were replaced. It would have been impossible for Breathwaite to detect their presence.

The cab then took a downtown exit, forcing the agent driving a white RAV4 to close the gap between his vehicle and the

304

cab. They drove for several blocks on city streets before the cab suddenly turned left and stopped. The agent in the RAV4 radioed the event to the second car, a blue Camry, which pulled over to the curb as if it was being parked while the RAV4 continued straight without stopping. The second driver took his time leaving the Camry while he appeared to fumble with packages inside the car. He observed Breathwaite, aka Smith, pay the cab driver and join the pedestrian traffic along the street pulling his carry-on suitcase. The second driver got out of his car and watched Breathwaite enter a house surrounded by a neatly manicured yard shaded by a large palm tree. It was clear that this small tile roofed residence was Breathwaite's destination. The BIN agent returned to his Camry and drove to headquarters.

***

Al Kaplan read the high-priority email from the Indonesian BIN with interest. He had spent the time waiting for the message interviewing Udo in the northern Virginia safe house. It was a unique experience for Udo. He had never met someone with such an intense focus on detail. Kaplan asked question after question, and when he asked something that Udo couldn't answer, he asked him to close his eyes and picture his surroundings, hoping some additional scrap of information might be recalled.

Kaplan's focus had been on identifying the location of the Bis Saif headquarters. He asked Udo to picture his trip from the airport. Did they travel fast or slow? Were they in stop-and-go traffic? How long would he estimate he was in each type of traffic? Did he think that they were traveling in circles to confuse him? How many people were in the van beside him? Were they all men? Did they speak with accents? When the van stopped and he was blindfolded, could he tell what type of building he had entered? Were there any cooking smells? Was the floor smooth or rough? Was the floor made of something polished like marble, or was it more like a wood floor? Were there other people in the place that they took him? If so, how many and what type of people? If he was in a tunnel when they took the blindfold off, how did he get there—by elevator or stairs? If stairs, how many stairs? Were they metal stairs or wooden stairs? On and on went the questions. When Kaplan finished asking the initial series of questions about Udo's entrance to the headquarters, he asked another series of questions about his exit. He then moved to a discussion of the headquarters themselves.

At the completion of this first round of questioning, Kaplan concluded that the headquarters had multiple entrances (and exits, of course). He also concluded that many if not all of the entrances were connected to the headquarters by a labyrinth of tunnels that were likely to have been booby trapped and were undoubtedly equipped with surveillance cameras. He had mapped out a likely zone to which Udo had been taken based on his estimates of travel times.

The information he had received from the Indonesian BIN included a definite location of an entrance to one of the tunnels. It was interesting to Kaplan that this entrance was not within the zone that he had mapped out based on Udo's information. This could mean that either Udo's information was incorrect or he had been taken to a different entrance.

Kaplan rocked back in his chair and stared at the ceiling. The interrogation had been as tiring for the questioner as it was for the one being questioned. As he relaxed, he remembered something that Udo had said when they were discussing the facilities themselves. When describing his quarters, he had said that there was a recurring noise like that of an electric motor. It would be quiet for a period and then start up for a few minutes. It was noisiest in the mornings and evenings, running almost continuously. At the time, Kaplan thought he was describing the noise from a ventilating fan. Then it hit him. The noise Udo heard was an elevator motor. He had been in a high-rise office building!

Kaplan then called the tech expert on his staff. "Jeffrey, what do you know about elevators?"

"Nothing Al. That's a strange question, why do you ask?"

"My Bis Saif source was in a building for a week and heard elevator noise all week. We're trying to find the building. I need to know whether all elevators sound the same, and whether it's possible to play recordings of various elevator motors to my source to see whether he recognizes any of them. It would also be helpful to know how many different elevators are installed in the various high-rise buildings of Jakarta."

"Wow. You never come up with easy questions."

"This is really serious stuff. Can you get me some answers in an hour?"

"I'll try. In the meantime, you've been working for twenty-four hours straight. Why don't you take a nap for that hour you've given me?"

Ignoring Jeffrey's suggestion, Al added, "And one other thing. Ask whether it's possible to estimate the height of a building from the time that the motor was running. It goes without saying that anyone you include in your research shouldn't know why you're asking."

"I'll be back to you within the hour."

True to his word, Kaplan's cellphone rang with the answer to the elevator questions in less than an hour.

The voice on the other end had a few answers, but not enough to provide definitive information. "There are only a few manufacturers of elevators for high-rise buildings. We're not sure yet which of them sells equipment in Indonesia. They include Mitsubishi, Schindler, and Otis. Our guess is that Mitsubishi is the biggest supplier. We're trying to contact them now to see what they might have installed in Jakarta. There are no recordings of elevator motors that might be useful to you. In fact, I doubt that any would be useful to you since the motor is usually located at the top of the building. The noise your informant heard was probably the cables and the movement of the cab. So even if we could find the recordings, it wouldn't be very useful. However, if he has any idea of the length of time of the longest duration noise, we might be able to estimate the height of the building."

"That's a start," replied Kaplan. "I'll ask him about the duration. In the meantime, let me know what Mitsubishi tells you. I'd be particularly interested in any special designs that might be required by any of their customers."

"I'll keep on it."

***

Kaplan had no sooner finished his discussion of the elevators than he received a call from the CIA station chief in Jakarta. "Al, I think we've got a hit at the airport. One of the arriving passengers has a striking resemblance to Hasan Jouda. He did not try to disguise his identity the way the two Americans did. In fact, we've seen him twice in the videos we've been reviewing. The first time was the initial visit that your source made, and the second more recently."

"Did any of the outside cameras record Jouda getting into a van or other vehicle?" Kaplan said, beginning to feel as if things were coming together and hoping that they would come together before the end of the week.

"We only saw him leaving the terminal in the most recent sighting."

"Did you get a license plate number or any distinguishing markings on the van?"

"Yes. The van had a company logo on the outside. SL Teknik was the name. We've contacted our counterparts at BIN, and they're looking at every video they can find on the route from the airport to the center city. We're lucky that the governor of Jakarta asked all building owners to install closed-circuit televisions on their buildings to monitor their surrounds, after a terrorist attack in 2015. And the police are experienced at analyzing the tapes. The president is urging the police and governor to cooperate. It also helps to have the time and date that we're looking for. Unfortunately, this could take a while, but we're pushing as hard as we can. I'm optimistic that we'll succeed. I just don't know when."

"Keep up the good work and please get back to me as soon as you know more." Kaplan wished he hadn't given up smoking. He could sure use a cigarette right now.

***

As soon as he disconnected and laid his cellphone on the desk, he heard a polite knock on his door. It was the analyst who had been assigned the problem of locating the tunnels being used by Bis Saif to access their headquarters in the building. A map of the tunnels would help pin down the location of the building, access points for the Special Forces, and potential escape routes for the occupants. This was not only a critical task, but also the most difficult to accomplish.

"Sir, I've made some progress and feel as if we need to make some decisions," the analyst said nervously. He had only been assigned to Kaplan for a few months, and was in awe of his reputation and intensity.

"Let's hear it."

"Well, sir, it appears that there are a number of technologies available for detection of tunnels. Unfortunately, all of them have advantages and disadvantages. I can prepare a report on the results of my research, if you would like."

"You obviously don't appreciate the urgency of this situation. Skip the report and the exhaustive presentation of alternatives. Just give me the bottom line. Answer two questions. Is it feasible to map the tunnels, and if so, how?" said Kaplan impatiently.

"Sir, this is a complex subject, made more so by the need for speed and secrecy. I'll try to make this as brief as possible. Tunnel detection is of great interest to the Israelis, South Koreans, and US Border Protection. It turns out that there are three or four different techniques for detecting tunnels. The only technique that seems appropriate for the urban environment, with its sewers, water pipes, heating vents, and cabling, would be radar, which is particularly good for detecting concrete tunnels

Philip J. Tarnoff

with rebar and wiring. Radar is relatively effective at a depth of ten meters, but can be used for tunnels as deep as one hundred meters. It can be made portable if we use a van with a removable floor to map the area of interest. I was able to identify several experts on this subject, some of whom are Israelis."

"How soon can you begin the mapping, assuming unlimited funds along with the cooperation of the Israelis and the Indonesian government?"

"We could probably be underway in a week, and the mapping might take as long as a month," responded the unfortunate analyst who was ignorant of the reason for the search.

Kaplan exploded. "Figure out how to be underway in twenty-four hours and complete the mapping in two days. I will give you areas of the city in which to focus your search. Get back to me when you've figured it out. I'll take care of getting the Israeli specialists for you. Ask my secretary to come in on your way out. She'll get you the contact information for the specialists. Come back when you have an action plan. Hopefully within the hour."

The analyst rapidly backed out of Kaplan's office, saying "Yes sir" as he left.

***

It was 10:00 p.m. and although he was exhausted, Kaplan sensed that the tide was turning. All of a sudden, useful information was arriving from multiple directions. As he waited for the return of the analyst with the plans for the tunnel search, the phone rang with a call from Jeffrey, the newly anointed elevator expert. "I didn't get answers to your specific questions, but we've gotten really lucky. We received a return call from Mitsubishi. Maybe they appreciated the urgency of the situation because I called the president of their elevator division at 3:00 a.m. his time. It turns out that they are the biggest supplier of elevators for high-rises in Jakarta. One of their recent installations was in a high-rise in East Jakarta known as the Citibank Tower. Apparently the elevator design included a lot of special

310

requirements. What makes this interesting is that the project was completed on time and within budget, but their project manager, who was also the chief designer, was mysteriously killed in a hit-and-run auto accident in downtown Jakarta one week after the project was completed. That might be considered a coincidence, except that all the plans and operational details of that elevator system have disappeared."

"What were the special requirements?"

"The Mitsubishi guy was a little vague on that point. But he said that the display showing the location of each of the elevator cars was modified so that in some cases if a car was going down, the display would show it going up. Also it was necessary to use a special key card to access some of the basement floors as well as the suites near the roof. The key card wasn't that unusual, but the modifications to the display were unique."

"Great job, Jeff!" said Kaplan enthusiastically. "Let me know if you can squeeze any additional information out of them. But what you have gotten is pure gold. Gotta go now."

Kaplan turned to his computer and began a Google search for the Citibank Tower. As he was printing out its location and address, his administrative assistant, who was also working late, shouted from her desk, "I've got a call from Jakarta. Do you want to talk to them?"

"Right away," answered Kaplan, picking up the phone. "I hope you have some good news for me."

The caller was the CIA station chief at the Jakarta Embassy. "It is definitely good news. Our friends at BIN have been talking to some of their snitches to see whether anyone knew of tunnels being dug within the past two years. They hit pay dirt. Identified the locations of two tunnels, including both their beginnings and ends. They both end in a high-rise called Citibank Tower, and they both begin in different residential districts less than a mile from the tower. I'm emailing you a map of Jakarta with the locations highlighted along with the route of the tunnels."

"Fantastic. Keep up the first-class work, and keep pushing the BIN for more. We're tentatively planning on a raid for the day after tomorrow. The specifics are highly classified. I'll let you know how it works out as soon as the raid is completed," Kaplan said.

He had decided not to tell the station chief that he already knew about the tower, believing that his information was invaluable since it confirmed the information that had been received from Mitsubishi. He had also decided not to tell the analyst locating the tunnels about the information regarding the tunnel routes since he wanted independent, unbiased confirmation of these as well.

The call from Jakarta had just ended when the nervous analyst entered Kaplan's office without knocking. "What've you got?" asked Kaplan without preamble.

"I've put together a plan I think you'll like. I've located nine radar units that can be used for underground mapping. When they heard why we needed them, the Israelis immediately contributed four units with operators, who are now on their way to Jakarta. The Mexican government contributed one unit that they use for detecting drug runners' tunnels, and the US Border Patrol is contributing three units that they've been using along the Mexican border. The four units are on their way to the Davis-Monthan Air Force Base, in Tucson Arizona, where they will be flown nonstop to Jakarta with the benefit of midair refueling."

"Go on," encouraged Kaplan.

"Well sir, I've asked our station chief in Jakarta to find nine used vans. He will be taking them to a friendly garage where the needed modifications will be made to the floorboards to allow the radars to operate. We're also installing digital recorders in the vans so that their exact position along with the radar returns will be continuously recorded. The four Israeli operators along with a border patrol volunteer will be set up in an office in Jakarta with all needed computer equipment to analyze the radar data. So all that we need is a map of the locations to be covered," concluded the analyst, turning to Kaplan with a questioning look.

"Good work, but we've still got a way to go. Your job is probably the most important of all the efforts we've got underway. Fortunately, I've just received the location information that I believe you will need. It is likely that the tunnels you are looking for begin at a building known as the Citibank Tower. I'll give you the address. It should be possible to travel from this building to another address, which I will give you, either directly or through some combination of tunnels. Maybe you should lay out a grid that defines the paths of each of the vans. Your job is to discover *all* tunnels leading to the building and to identify their entrances. It is essential that you discover all the tunnels, and it is critical that the work be completed within two days after the equipment arrives. I want you on-site supervising this entire operation. So pack your bags."

Kaplan didn't know why he was so rough on the nervous analyst, except that, for some reason, the kid's nervousness annoyed him. But he couldn't deny that his work was thorough. He just wished that he was more aggressive about pursuing his assignments.

***

It was now time to bring the other players up to date. Kaplan placed two critical phone calls. The first was to Matthew O'Brien, who was also working late. "Mr. Director, I think we're almost ready to move on Bis Saif."

"That's the best news I've heard all day. What do you know, and what's the schedule?"

"We've located their headquarters, which are well protected and equipped with multiple escape routes through hidden tunnels. I've got some thoughts about the way in which we should approach this, but will leave the details to the Special Forces boys. They've got the experience. The challenge is ensuring that no one escapes. To do this, we need to be sure we've ID'd all of their escape tunnels. We know about three of the tunnels, but there are likely to be more. By tomorrow we'll have nine crews looking for more tunnels using ground-penetrating radar. Hopefully they won't miss anything. I need your OK to let our people move in."

O'Brien answered without hesitation. "You've got the green light from me, but give me less than an hour to get the go-ahead from the White House."

Then Kaplan placed his second call. This time to his counterpart at the Pentagon. The call was short and strictly business. "I've got the information needed to initiate our assault. Only waiting for the needed release, which I'll forward to you as soon as it is received. Sending you an email with all details. Plan to move out in two days."

Then he huddled with his administrative assistant while the two of them put together an information package to be sent to the Special Forces units waiting patiently on the aircraft carrier USS George Washington (CVN 73), currently stationed in the Java Sea, near Jakarta Bay. The carrier was to serve as the point of deployment for the Special Forces troops. Unfortunately, the bay was a relatively long drive from East Jakarta, which was closer to the airport. As a result, the assault would require a helicopter ride from the carrier to the airport, and from there to the vehicles needed to actually carry out the assault. Logistically complicated, but certainly not impossible.

The package included detailed maps of Jakarta and identified the locations of Citibank Tower and the tunnels that had been identified so far. It provided the physical details of the tower, including its specially fabricated elevator. It also included lists of known Bis Saif personnel, including the three computer experts and Cecil Breathwaite. It admitted that the CIA had no idea of the number of other personnel and their armaments. It emphasized the importance of capturing all occupants and either capturing or destroying all computer equipment. The package also included a document that Special Forces personnel rely on. This document provided Kaplan's thoughts about the situation. What was known and what was unknown. The likely schedule and what would be known before the mission was launched. It also clearly defined the mission objectives, including, most importantly, who was to be captured alive and who was expendable. In addition, it listed the equipment that was to be preserved, if possible, and that which could be destroyed. In short, it served as their set of orders in essay form. Kaplan also apologetically made some suggestions about the best approach for carrying out the assault. When the package had been completed, the administrative assistant began assembling its contents as an attachment to a highly classified email that would be transmitted to the Special Forces units using an encrypted satellite link.

While they were working on the Special Forces information package, Kaplan received a call from O'Brien that contained three words. "It's a go."

When their work was done, Kaplan told everyone to go home while he passed out on the couch in his office.

CHAPTER 24
DEFINING SUCCESS

The War Cabinet was meeting again. The representatives from the power industry and Google had not been invited to this particular meeting because of the highly classified nature of the material on the agenda. There was good news and bad news to be discussed. As usual, there was more bad news than good news. The good news related to the identification of the location of Bis Saif. The bad news was that the power restoration was proceeding very slowly, leading to the general unrest of the American public and the appearance of a strong anti-Muslim movement. All the meeting participants were fully engaged in the subjects to be discussed.

As usual, the president opened the meeting. "Good morning, ladies and gentlemen. I hope that we'll be able to do away with these weekly meetings within the next few months. But unfortunately they're still critical. First," he began sympathetically, "how are you and your families making out in the dark? I can imagine it's quite a trial living without electricity."

George Wilson answered for the group. "I suspect that we're all annoyed with the inconvenience, but most of us had the foresight to install backup generators at our homes. If they're powered by natural gas, we're all doing just fine, except for the miserable trip into the District each day. I feel for the people who are not as fortunate as we are."

Jeffers nodded, acknowledging the truth of Wilson's response. He then continued with the meeting. "Moving on, I'd like to begin with a quick summary of our efforts to hunt down Bis Saif. Since the CIA is in the lead with this, I'll ask Matt O'Brien to begin."

316

O'Brien began what sounded as if it were a rehearsed response. "As the president indicated, we've found the Bis Saif lair and hope that we'll be able to eliminate that organization by the end of the week. General Drake, I assume you're aware of this activity and will place the entire focus of the US military on ensuring its success."

General Drake's answer was without hesitation. "Yes Matt. I am fully aware of it, and we've got one half of the Pacific Fleet providing support." The general then hedged his bets ever so slightly. "Of course, the success of the mission depends on the quality of the information we receive. I know the CIA is moving heaven and earth to ensure that it's as complete as it can be. But nothing is one-hundred-percent certain on these missions, is it?"

Jeffers was not in the mood to accept hedging. "This one had better be one-hundred-percent certain, at least as far as ending attacks on our power grid."

Drake was not prepared to argue a hypothetical point. So he answered, "Yes, sir."

Yet they both knew that a complex mission of this nature, even with a cooperative government such as the Indonesians, could often fail to end with totally satisfactory results.

O'Brien then continued. "I'm sure you'd all like to know the details of this activity, but unfortunately they can't be shared without endangering the mission. I do not feel that we should place the lives of our servicemen and women in danger, nor will I put the mission at risk through an early release of its details. Tempting as it may be."

The room remained silent since they all knew that he was correct.

Jeffers then resumed control of the meeting. "So, now let's move onto more difficult subjects. I'd like to begin with the easy part. The recovery of power for California and the Washington, DC region. Janice, please bring us up to date."

"Well, sir, some things are going well, and others aren't. The distribution of food and other supplies seems to be working out fairly well, thanks to the help we've received from the retail industry and the Department of Defense. Although there have admittedly been a number of complaints about the availability of certain goods," she added, in an attempt to lighten everyone's mood. "There was the case of the famous toilet tissue riots when one of the centers ran out of that critical commodity. But we've solved that particular problem.

"On a more serious note, the relocation of the residents of California is not going well. People are afraid to leave their homes because of the potential for looting. They also don't want to move to unfamiliar surroundings. The absence of schooling is a problem, with the result that we've got gangs of kids from junior high to high school roaming the area. People in California are tired of life in the dark, but at least they're not freezing. People in the East have been without power longer, and those that have not left the area are miserable in the winter cold. I sure wish we could get the power turned on, but that is falling behind schedule due the lack of spare parts, particularly the high-voltage transformers, which have to be shipped from Europe. I'm afraid we're going to have uprisings soon if the power companies can't complete their repairs."

She continued. "To begin with the relatively easy problem of the Washington, DC region, the power is scheduled to be turned on within the next month. I'm reluctant to provide any specific dates until I am more certain of the schedule. But the news media is hounding us for more information. Most people in the region seem to have adjusted to life without electricity. We've been able to provide the generators needed for service stations to pump gas, the water supply is functioning, and the distribution of food and other goods is functioning relatively smoothly. We've distributed LP canisters to people with barbecue grills to enable them to prepare hot meals. We've also opened as many emergency shelters in the public schools as we can power. So life is miserable but bearable. Many people have moved out of the area to stay with friends and families in unaffected regions of the country, which has relieved some of the pressure on the essential services we're trying to provide. So I think we're going to make it.

"But there is some bad news associated with the DC situation. First, we've drained the country of its supply of backup generators. Between hospitals, prisons, gas stations, food distribution centers, critical government facilities, and emergency shelters, we've cornered the market on all the generators in the country. To say that we were woefully unprepared for this situation would be an understatement. Think of that in terms of the unmet needs in California, as well as possible future unmet needs if Bis Saif is allowed to execute its next threat." Janet then paused to let the bad news sink in. The group looked appropriately glum, but no one spoke up.

So DeBeers continued with her bad news for the DC region. "In spite of the assistance of the National Guards of Maryland, DC, and Virginia, we've got some problems with looting as well as occasional riots at the distribution centers. But more important, we're seeing the formation of vigilante groups anxious to take their frustration out on the Muslims in the region. The FBI is leading our efforts to keep these grou)s under control. I'll let Jim Proctor address this situation."

Jim Proctor was ready to pick up the report. "Janet is correct. Vigilante groups are springing up all over the country, with Muslims identified as the cause of their problems. I'll discuss the situation in California when we get to that part of her report, but we've already got our hands full in the DC region. One particularly virile group is led by a man known only as Gus. We still don't have his last name. He operates out his home in Silver Spring, Maryland. We're in contact with a guy who seems to know him. I'm not going to give you his name. Our guy met Gus in a bar. He also lives in Silver Spring as a bachelor. He sent his wife and kids to Ohio to live with the wife's sister. Our informant is now undercover with Gus's unnamed vigilante group.

"Their reason for existence is a shared hatred of the Muslims, whom they blame for all of their problems. Not only the power failures, but also difficulties at home and at work. Typical profiles for disenchanted people looking for a way of venting their frustrations. These tend to be the most dangerous individuals. We're hoping that with our informant's help we'll be able to anticipate any threats posed by the group before they do anything stupid. We're also hoping that his work will lead us to other groups around the country, particularly California."

Proctor then went on with barely a pause for breath. "To make a bad situation worse, many of the Muslims see this as a threat to their homes and their families. They're not going to take this lying down. We have information that Muslim gangs made up of teenagers and young adults are beginning to arm themselves, mostly from the stores of looted gun dealers. Some of these gangs have joined ISIS, which is welcoming them with open arms and providing them with the equipment and other assistance needed to support their terrorist activities. We're afraid that there will be a war on the streets of DC between Gus's group and the Muslim gangs before this terrible situation comes to an end. And remember, I'm just talking about DC."

Jeffers had remained silent for the two reports. He interrupted, feeling he needed to provide some sense of leadership to these two senior members of his staff. "What can the rest of us do to help? Do you need more money, more equipment, more manpower?"

DeBeers jumped in, answering for both the DHS and the FBI. "Yes, yes, and yes. But we both know that there are limits to what you can provide."

"I'm thinking that there are two sets of resources that you haven't yet tapped. One is the National Security Agency, and the other is the Department of Defense. NSA should be able to monitor messages originating in Silver Spring that could give you some leads on Gus's identity and some idea of what they are planning. My guess is that these newer groups are not nearly as sophisticated as ISIS or Bis Saif when it comes to encrypting their communications or hiding their locations. Is that true?" he said, turning to Admiral DeForce.

"It's absolutely true, and I'd be happy to divert considerable resources for this purpose."

Jeffers continued. "General Drake, can you provide resources in addition to those of the National Guard, both to prevent looting and to help the FBI monitor the activities of these vigilante groups?"

"DOD can provide considerable policing assistance. Don't forget we served in this role at the end of the Iraq war. We have soldiers trained as MPs who are used at military bases and other installations. We can provide as many as you need."

Although he was trying to remain as upbeat as possible, Jeffers was frustrated by the reluctance of this group to collaborate. "I've got to remind you that this is the United States of America. Not just the FBI, DHS, NSA, or DOD. Taken as a whole, we've got extensive resources. It's up to all of you to cooperate. We've got to apply every resource at our disposal to solve these problems."

"Janet, please continue with your report. I suspect it doesn't get any rosier."

"You're right, Mr. President. The situation in the DC area pales by comparison with California. First of all, remember that their power failure is more recent than the DC power failure. So the population in that region isn't as used to living without electricity. Second, this is a much bigger region, and we've drained our resources for DC. You may remember that our plans for the region included relocation of approximately two-thirds of the California population that had been hit by the blackout. In other words, twenty million people. This is a huge number, and our budget would be wiped out paying for it. Fortunately, Mr. President, you were able to identify funding that might have made this possible. But to date, only two million people have taken advantage of our offer for relocation. Another three million have left the state to live with friends and relatives in other parts of the country. This leaves twenty-six million people living in the dark. This is more than three times the population we're trying to serve in the DC region. As I said earlier, those who haven't relocated are worried about looting and moving to an unfamiliar part of the country. This is good news for our budget, but awful news for the support needed by the state in the way of hospitals, emergency generators, water supply, distribution centers, etcetera. Frankly, we're running out of ideas. Jim, could you please pick up the story from the FBI's perspective?"

It was Proctor's turn to spread more bad news. "The vigilante groups in California are dwarfing those in the DC region. As Janet said, we're dealing with a problem that is many times larger than that of the DC region. To make matters worse, Hispanic groups see this as an opportunity to further their supremacy over another ethnic minority. So they are forming gangs of their own to prosecute Muslims. As on the East Coast, the Muslims are arming themselves and have constructed encampments in the desert that they use as their bases from which to attack the white groups. ISIS is in its glory, providing support to US citizens fighting each other and potentially destroying our way of life. Like Janet, I'm rapidly running out of ideas. We're already receiving some support from DOD, but California law enforcement agencies need all the help we can provide."

General Drake then spoke up. "Mr. President, I fully understand your remarks regarding the need for cooperation among our agencies. I hope you can appreciate the degree of support we're already providing primarily in California. We've already committed one entire brigade of nearly five thousand troops along with untold amounts of equipment to provide this support. But here's the situation. The support provided on the ground is primarily furnished by the Army. Aircraft carriers and fighter planes are of no value with this conflict. The Army is already stretched thin with its various assignments around the world. In order to address the problems here we'll probably need to expand our assistance to include an entire division of three brigades, along with all of its support equipment. If we're going to increase our support beyond this point, we'll need to begin withdrawing troops from the Middle East, Afghanistan, Europe, and South Korea. As soon as we begin do that, Bis Saif has won the conflict. In essence, we're conceding these regions to the various Muslim sects. As DeBeers has said at previous meetings, we're also becoming concerned about funding. I realize that the War Powers Act has given you the authority to shift funds around to support this conflict, but at some point other parts of the government will begin to seriously suffer. I'll add my thoughts to those of others in this room. We're running out of ideas."

Jeffers was momentarily speechless. It was almost as if the entire group was about to give up. He had to reenergize their efforts or the United States as they knew it was lost.

"Ladies and gentlemen, we're not about to give up. The United States is the greatest power on earth, and we're not going to cave in to a bunch of thugs. We're certainly not going to give in just as we're on the verge of wiping them out. During my election campaign, I pledged a more forceful approach to combatting terrorism. So here is what I am proposing to do. First, General Drake, send a full division of troops to California. We've got to get that situation under control. Then, following this meeting, I'm going to have lunch with the leaders of the House and Senate. The purpose of the lunch is to discuss long-term restructuring of the budget in order to pour more money into defense and rebuilding the parts of the country damaged by the power failure. We will do this, even though it might be at the short-term expense of other priorities. This afternoon, I am going to address the nation on the subject of intolerance. You all know I'm a religious man, and the anti-Muslim movement runs counter to my religion. I will not tolerate this situation on my watch. I am completely open to any suggestions any of you might have of additional measures that can be taken. We can either discuss them here, or in private if you would prefer."

He then paused as if waiting for suggestions. "Hearing no suggestions, I'd like to end this meeting. I know you all have a lot to do. Tomorrow is the planned date for the attack on the Bis Saif headquarters. I'd like you all to be in the situation room when the attack takes place in case any quick decisions are needed. Matt, I would appreciate it if you would bring your lead man from the CIA. I believe his name is Alan Kaplan. I hear nothing but good about him. And Jim, if you would bring Lee Sanders, your Special Agent in Charge, tomorrow, I'd also appreciate it. General Drake, I leave it up to you whether you'd like to bring one additional participant who might contribute to the event. But please no additional people. Too many becomes counter-productive. Jan will call you all one hour before the attack is scheduled to begin. We will meet in the situation room where we can watch it unfold in real-time. Again, thank you all for coming."

***

Knowing that a speech to the nation was critical, Jeffers asked Jan to get Paul Lynd, his press secretary, on the phone. "Paul, we've got to schedule a speech to the nation for prime time tonight. I don't care how much the networks complain, I'd like to reach as many people as possible on this one."

He listened for a minute to Paul's reply. "No, I don't want the press to be there. I want to address this issue of discrimination against the Muslim community. And I want to hit it hard. I don't care about the political repercussions. We've got to nip this in the bud. Could you get your staff working on this immediately? I'd like to review it by midafternoon. Just call me when it's ready. I've cleared my afternoon schedule for this one."

As soon as Jeffers hung up, Jan buzzed him to tell him that the four representing the leadership of Congress, which had become known as the Leadership Group, were waiting.

He met the four at the door to the small dining room adjacent to the Oval Office. All were dressed in the same manner, with their obligatory dark suits, white shirts, and solid color blue or red ties. As usual, Paul Greenberg, a religious Jew, was wearing his ever-present yarmulke. When they had filed into the dining room, Jeffers skipped the small talk and began immediately as they sat down. "Gentlemen, I trust you're all surviving the power failure in tolerable shape. But rather than discussing our personal situations, I hope you'll forgive me if I skip the discussion of our various discomforts and get right to the heart of the matter. We've got the beginnings of a real crisis on our hands, and I could use a little help from Congress in dealing with it. But first, let me give you the abridged version of our current situation."

With that, Chris summarized the discussion of the morning's meeting. The four congressmen listened silently without interrupting. When he had concluded, Bob McIntyre, who as the Senate Majority Leader had become the spokesman for the group, spoke up. "Well, Mr. President, I believe a lot of that is good news. There doesn't seem to be a reason to be so glum. Once we get rid of Bis Saif, we can turn our attention to rebuilding the regions that have been affected."

"Bob, you've always been the optimist. I don't think that's necessarily the case. First of all, when we get rid of Bis Saif, don't forget there's ISIS and a dozen other groups of fanatics around the world. Second, this power failure has given all the religious bigots, who have been itching for an excuse to get their hands on the Muslims, with the support of much of the US population. I believe we could be on the verge of a religious civil war. The army has already committed five thousand troops to California alone and is expecting to triple that number. We're rapidly running out of money for all these adventures."

Wayne Zyder, the House Minority Leader, and a member of the president's own party, then spoke up. "So Mr. President, that's the real reason you've asked us here for lunch. You've got fiscal problems. I should have known that there's no such thing as a free lunch."

Chris responded when the weak laughter had died down. "This is going to cost you much more than a free lunch." Then he continued. "I need to know your impression of the mood of Congress. Sometimes I feel that the executive branch is fighting this thing on its own with very little input from Capitol Hill, except for the occasional sniping that has become standard for that great body. We're up to our ears in problems, and we're running out of money to deal with them. The public is unhappy with the situation and becoming less happy by the minute. We'll all be out of a job if this continues, and, worse yet, the nation will be in chaos."

Brad Nelson, the Democratic House Majority Leader and the pessimist of the group, answered for the other three congressmen. "Mr. President, I'm afraid that there are limits to the additional assistance we can give you. The War Powers Act allows you to shift funding to execute this war. A liberal interpretation of the words gives you the ability to do almost anything you want to with the budget. There's not enough unity in Congress to do any more than that."

Wayne Zyder spoke up again. "Brad meant you can do anything you want with the budget except for taking money from entitlement programs and paying interest on the national debt." Again the result was weak laughter from the group, which recognized that two-thirds of the national budget was used to pay for those two budget items.

Jeffers said; "How about raising taxes?"

Everyone in the room turned white, as Jeffers had expected. Wayne responded, "I should amend what I said to mean you can do anything you want except taking money from entitlement programs and raising taxes."

Jeffers said, "I'm serious."

No one said anything. They were all making political calculations about the prospects of success for a tax increase, as well as their prospects for reelection if they supported it. Jeffers could read their minds.

At that point a healthy lunch, consisting of Caesar salad topped with salmon, was served with iced tea and not-so-healthy eclairs for desert. Wayne Zyder, who was from Tennessee and not a big fan of seafood, carefully picked his salmon off the salad and decorously placed it on his butter dish, where it was quickly removed by the attentive wait staff. The lunch was a welcomed break from the discussion that had been underway since it gave all the participants time to consider their positions.

As they began eating their salads, Jeffers returned to the conversation. "I know that tax increases are anathema to our party. In fact, I ran on a platform that opposed any new taxes, as did all of my Republican predecessors. But this is a serious war, unlike any that we've seen before. Even after Bis Saif is eliminated, which I hope will occur soon, we're still faced with all the other gangs. This whole situation is tearing the country apart. I wish I could come up with a quick fix, but the only solutions I see will take a long time and cost a lot of money. In the meantime, our infrastructure is crumbling, and our population is aging. We're running out of options."

Brad Nelson then spoke up. "As house majority leader and a member of the political party that is famously blamed for raising taxes, I can tell you that this one isn't in the cards. Mr. President, it's no secret that my fellow Democrats would love to see you either propose a tax increase and fail, or try to scrape by with our existing budget and see you fail. They're just not inclined to help you out on this one."

Jeffers could feel his blood pressure rising and made a conscious effort to respond with an even voice. "Doesn't anyone in Congress realize the gravity of this situation?"

Zyder spoke up again. "Let me give it to you by the numbers. Speaking solely about the House of Representatives, approximately five percent feel we should give in to Bis Saif's demands. Another fifteen percent feel we should bomb the hell out of anyone who professes to favor the creation of a Muslim caliphate. Another five percent feel we should drop an atomic weapon on the Middle East. The remaining seventy-five percent want to stay the course with some variations. One of the variations is that many would like us to stage a major invasion of the problem countries in the Middle East, although they're having difficulty identifying those countries. A great many on all sides feel we should set up internment camps for all Muslims in the United States. Some of them feel we should confiscate their possessions and use them to pay the extraordinary costs we're encountering due to the power failures. There are so many differing opinions in both parties that it would be impossible to pull the House of Representatives together on any issue associated with this war. I think that with some variations, these statistics and the general atmosphere reflect the feelings of the Senate as well. Don't they, gentlemen?"

Both Bob McIntyre and Paul Greenberg, the majority and minority leaders of the Senate, nodded in agreement.

McIntyre, who Jeffers greatly respected, summed it up. "So there you have it Mr. President. Congress is essentially frozen in place. I hate to say it, but it's up to you to conduct this war. Our fearless representatives on the Hill are incapable of providing any meaningful guidance or assistance. A sad situation, isn't it?"

"Well, all I can do is thank you for your forthright answer to my question. It isn't the answer I wanted, and it is of little help, but it's an answer nonetheless."

Jeffers thought it would be useful to move to a less toxic subject. "So, who do you think is going to win the Super Bowl?" he asked, knowing full well that his favorite Dallas Cowboys were favored to win.

Paul Greenberg, who was from Boston, answered without hesitation. "My money's on the Patriots. Would you like to make a little wager?"

"I'm a big spender. How about twenty dollars with no point spread?"

"You're on."

Zyder then brought the discussion to another unhappy ending. "I hate to throw cold water on your illegal gambling, but will there be a Super Bowl? Remember, it's supposed to be held at the Los Angeles Colosseum, and they don't have any power."

"Oh no! I forgot about that, with all the focus on eliminating Bis Saif. I hope we don't have rioting over that."

And with that, the luncheon ended on a rather sour note.

***

President Christopher Jeffers was about to give the most important and possibly the most powerful speech of his life. He was seated in the Oval Office, with the cameras of the major TV networks trained on him. With the pre-speech publicity, more than one-half of the American public was watching. He was determined to get things under control.

"My fellow Americans," he began. "By that I mean my fellow Christians, Jews, Muslims, Buddhists, Hindus, atheists, agnostics, Native Americans, and followers of dozens of other religions. Yes, we're all Americans. 'All men are created equal. They are endowed by their creator with certain inalienable rights, including life, liberty, and the pursuit of happiness.' This is a quote from the US Declaration of Independence, a document revered by our Founding Fathers as well as most

American citizens, and whose concepts are encapsulated by the First Amendment of the US Constitution, which guarantees unimpeded freedom of religion for all of us.

"I am a believer in the US Constitution, and in my oath of office I swore on a Bible that I would uphold and protect it. I intend to support and defend its principles against religious intolerance of any sort. I do not intend to incarcerate or mistreat in any other way the practitioners of a religion because of some misguided followers who claim to share the same religion. Let me rephrase that in case you didn't understand me the first time. I will not follow a course of bigotry out of irrational fear. Nor will I close our borders to refugees from anywhere in the world seeking asylum in the United States of America.

"The majority of you listening to this speech are Christians, like me. Let me remind you of the commandment unequivocally written in Mark 12:31 of our Holy Bible, which states that you shall love your neighbor as yourself. There can be no mistaking the meaning of this simple directive. You cannot call yourself a Christian unless you follow this commandment, which is derived directly from the Ten Commandments. The Bible does not say that you should only love your neighbor if he isn't a Muslim."

Jeffers was warming up to his subject. "As you might expect, a group that is persecuted will not stand by idly and allow the persecution to continue. The result is that we now have Muslims defending themselves by striking back. They are also ignoring the teachings of their Koran, which says that 'He (God) would have made you a single community, but he wanted to test you regarding what has come to you. So compete with each other in doing good. Every one of you will return to God and he will inform you regarding the things about which you differed.' This comes from the Surat al-Ma'ida, forty-eight." As Chris cited the passage in the Koran, he stumbled over its pronunciation. However, this did little to lessen the impact of his quotation.

"These are just two examples of many that could be cited from the religions that exist within our borders. The common theme is preaching harmony with other religions and peaceful coexistence with other members of the community. None of these religions excuse the existence of terrorists or vigilantes. Being a Christian myself, I will obey the commandments of my religion and take any action necessary to ensure that there is no conflict among the followers of the various religions that make up our population.

"We are all Americans together in this country we call the United States of America. What has made our country great has been our acceptance of immigrants from all over the world. Very few of our inhabitants can claim to be the original occupants of this land. We can only remain great if we continue to work together and honor our varied backgrounds and abilities.

"It is my responsibility and my intent to prevent the actions of a few fearful and intolerant individuals from tearing this country apart. For this reason, I have ordered the army to send a full division of fifteen thousand troops to California to maintain order. In addition to arresting anyone disrupting the peace, they will patrol residential neighborhoods, along with local and state police, to apprehend looters. Anyone accused of looting, rioting, or any other illegal action will be immediately imprisoned without bail in detention camps, also being established and operated by the army. We will eventually get around to hearing your individual cases, but you will be waiting in uncomfortable surroundings for an undetermined time. Trust me when I say that you will regret your actions.

"I urge those residents of California who have chosen to remain in your homes during the power failure to reconsider your decision. We have arranged for more comfortable lodgings in the surrounding states. All you have to do is report to your nearest post office to receive a list of your options and to complete the paperwork needed for your relocation. The government will pay the costs of lodging and provide you with a subsistence allowance to cover the costs of food and any other unusual costs that may be associated with your move. We are experiencing great difficulties providing food, emergency medical care, and other services for those of you who have decided to remain in place. I can promise that you will find the quarters we have arranged will be more comfortable. In most cases, the states to which you relocate have arranged for expanded classroom facilities so that your children can continue to attend school during this unfortunate period. As I said earlier, the US Army, in cooperation with local law enforcement, will provide security for your residences.

"I intend to speak to you often as our current situation unfolds to ensure that you are well informed and not swayed by every malicious rumor that appears on the Internet. Believe me when I say that the government to which you have entrusted us is in good hands. There are untold numbers of public servants working sixty- and seventy-hour weeks to ensure that our recovery from this situation is as rapid and as painless as possible. We will not allow a few misguided souls to derail our society. But we cannot do it without your help.

"The United States is the greatest country in the world. We've got a diverse and talented population, incredible natural resources, and one of the most stable and resilient governments to be found anywhere. In my oath of office, I swore to preserve, protect, and defend our Constitution, which is largely responsible for our success. I took my oath seriously and will do everything in my power to live up to its promises. As citizens of this great country, I'd urge you to do the same. Help me to preserve this great nation and the values that it stands for. Stand up to new and unpleasant situations as your ancestors have in the past. Let's continue bravely forward, overcoming situations that seem unpleasant or threatening. Do what is right. Obey the tenets of your respective religions and respect the rights of others. Let's work together to ensure that the United States of America remains the greatest country on earth."

As President Christopher Jeffers concluded his speech, those watching TV saw the image of the Oval Office dissolve and be replaced by a picture of the American flag waving in the breeze along with a band playing "America the Beautiful."

In the Oval Office, Jeffers slumped into his chair and turned to George Wilson, who had been waiting at the side of the room. "Do you think it did any good? I sure hope someone was listening."

"I think it was a good speech. Let's see how it's spun by the news media."

"Hopefully tomorrow I'll be able to give a more positive speech if we succeed with our attack on Bis Saif. I'm praying that it goes well."

All George could say in reply was, "Amen!"

CHAPTER 25
THE CLIMAX

The tension in the White House Situation Room was so heavy you could cut it with a knife. Everyone who had been invited was present, including representatives from the security agencies and the armed services. Paul Lynd, Jeffers' press secretary, was also in attendance, since as Chris had told him, he didn't want to have to repeat the story when the time came for a news conference with the press. All present had positioned their chairs to view one of the multiple large video screens arrayed around the room. Except for the representatives from the military, dressed in their ubiquitous uniforms, all others present were dressed casually, prepared for a long and hopefully successful afternoon. It was 1:30 a.m. in Jakarta and, conveniently, 1:30 p.m. in Washington.

Al Kaplan had the floor. "While we're waiting for the action to begin, let me provide you with some background. As you know, our target is the Bis Saif headquarters in Jakarta, Indonesia. Obtaining the information I am about to give you was an arduous task, involving multiple agencies from around the world, including the Indonesian secret service, known as the BIN. It goes without saying that this information is highly classified. Fortunately, all of you have top secret clearances.

"The good news is that we have been able to pin down the location of the Bis Saif headquarters. As you'd expect, these facilities have been carefully designed to prevent attacks and to provide multiple escape routes for the occupants. The headquarters is in the subbasement of a twenty- story office building in East Jakarta. The roof of this building is equipped with satellite dishes and radio antennas, presumably for the legitimate tenants of the building, but also for Bis Saif communications. There are several access points to this facility, all of which can also function as escape routes. One way to access their facility is by using the lobby elevator. In order to do this, one must have a special pass card, which is inserted in a slot in the elevator. The use of this card causes the elevator to descend to the Bis Saif headquarters, while falsely displaying that the elevator is ascending.

"The bad news is that a network of tunnels has been constructed leading from the headquarters building and which terminate at various locations in the city. For example, some of these tunnels have exits inside of residential structures outside of the central business district. Mapping the network without being discovered by a member of Bis Saif was quite an undertaking, involving extensive manpower and the use of ground-penetrating radar. I should emphasize that because of the need for speed and secrecy as well as the fact that the radar is not completely reliable, we can only be ninety-five-percent certain of the results. In other words, there's a chance we haven't found all the exits."

At this point, a few in Kaplan's audience appeared ready to interrupt with questions. But he held up his hand, saying, "Let me finish before asking questions. We don't have much time before the assault begins, and I want to be sure to have covered everything.

"Ideally we would have liked to have a large contingent of Marines backing up the Special Forces troops, but unfortunately this isn't possible. The Indonesian government wanted to maintain a position of deniability if the raid is unsuccessful, with the result that we've been forced to sneak our people into the city under cover of darkness. Until they deployed for this raid, they were on an aircraft carrier just offshore. As a result, we have a total of twenty Special Forces troops involved in the raid, who have spent the past week preparing. They will be flown to the airport from the aircraft carrier using four helicopters, which will be protected by two more helicopter gunships. The six choppers will be met at the outskirts of the airport by five armor-plated black Chevrolet Suburban SUVs, of the type we use to transport our president on international visits. The SUVs will proceed to both the high-rise building and the exits of the tunnels.

"The soldiers at the high-rise building will have two assignments. One contingent is to proceed immediately to the roof, where their assignment will be to disable the antennas immediately after the attack begins. A second contingent will be stationed in the lobby of the building to prevent any escape using the elevators or stairs. However, they will not try to enter the headquarters using the stairs, assuming that they're heavily alarmed and may be booby-trapped.

"The remaining soldiers will be assigned to enter the headquarters using the tunnels. Four tunnels have been identified. Four soldiers will enter each of the tunnels. They've all been furnished with maps of the tunnel network, and will be carrying explosives to destroy any barriers they encounter. Their first task on entering the headquarters will be to disable the electrical system, leaving the occupants in the dark and hopefully disoriented.

"Final point is that we're not certain of the number of personnel in the headquarters. We're reasonably certain that the two Jaffaris are there, along with our Palestinian friend. We can assume a staff of at least half a dozen others associated with the leadership and support of Bis Saif will also be there. It is our hope that we will be able to capture all of them. They are likely to be outnumbered and certainly outgunned. We want to maximize the confusion through the use of stun grenades, smoke grenades, and tear gas. That about covers it. Any questions?"

To no one's surprise, General Drake was the first to speak up. It seemed to him that this was a CIA operation, and he was unhappy that he hadn't been consulted. "I see some holes in this plan. Did you consult anyone in the army while it was being developed?"

Kaplan had been expecting this question and was ready. "Yes. Actually, the plan was prepared by the Special Forces units on the scene using the information we provided. We would never advise them how to do their job. But having said that, where do you see holes?"

General Drake was somewhat mollified, but Kaplan's question demanded an answer. "I guess I'm worried about the noise and confusion caused by six choppers landing at the airport."

"I'm worried about that too," replied Kaplan. "But there didn't seem much we could do about it. The trip from the water to the target was too long to undertake by SUV. The airport is much closer. But at this point, this is an academic discussion, since, if they're on schedule, the choppers have already landed and the troops are on their way to the target. Are there any other questions?"

The realization that they were approaching 2:00 p.m. in Washington (2:00 a.m. in Jakarta) and should be watching the screen that had just come to life had dawned on everyone, so there were no additional questions. The group fell silent and held their collective breath.

***

Chris had overseen actions of this nature from the White House Situation Room in the past. He could never get over the feeling that watching displays of military action occurring in real-time on the four video walls was surreal. It was as if he were seeing a large-screen made-in-Hollywood action movie.

Al Kaplan resumed his role as narrator of the attack. "All of the soldiers are equipped with helmet cams so that any or all of them can continuously transmit live video to this room. We are always receiving video from all the cameras, but the operator has been instructed to display the video from only one camera of each team. We will use the tiled format of these video walls to display eight simultaneous videos: five from the tunnels, one from the lobby, one from the roof, and one from the command center. If there is a need to enlarge one of these feeds, we will request the operator to do so."

The video walls came to life as Kaplan ended his explanation. As Kaplan had explained, each of the four walls displayed identical sets of eight tiled videos. The action began slowly and quietly. One member of the building team quietly picked the lock to a rear door of the building. The team watching the elevator crept into the lobby and disabled the guard while the team responsible for the rooftop began its stealthy but rapid climb up twenty flights of stairs to the top of building. Watching the activity, George Wilson thought, *I just saw them effortlessly do two things that I would be incapable of doing: run up twenty flights of stairs and pick a modern lock. I hope they're as good at everything else they do.*

While this was occurring, four other videos showed the Special Forces troops leaving their SUVs with the soldiers surrounding the dwellings that hid the tunnel entrances. The SUVs remained on the scene to provide a relay for the transmissions from the squad, which could not be transmitted directly from the tunnel without the insertion of an antenna in the mouth of the tunnel to receive the video and voice signals being transmitted from the soldiers. An unseen command was given and the squad of four soldiers waiting near the tunnel entrances simultaneously entered both the front and the rear of each dwelling, using flashbang grenades. In each case the residents were in bed and appeared in the video dazed, holding their hands in the air. At least one soldier in each group had learned rudimentary Indonesian. "Where's the tunnel entrance?" was shouted repeatedly. In four of the houses the residents immediately guided them to an entrance, which was often a trapdoor concealed under a throw rug.

At the fifth house, the occupants resisted, repeating that "There's no tunnel here." Although the audience at the White House couldn't understand the conversation, the intent of the conversation was clear. "Either show us the tunnel or we'll tear this place apart. We don't have time to discuss this."

The response was repeated, this time in a high-pitched voice. "There's no tunnel here."

The soldiers used plastic cuffs to handcuff the residents to each other and then began methodically tearing the house apart. Lifting floorboards, throwing carpets in a pile in the corner, tearing out the walls. They had finished destroying the first room when the occupant capitulated. "OK. OK. I'll tell you. It's in the bedroom under the bed."

The four soldiers immediately raced to the bedroom, moved the bed, and then the video showed them climbing down a ladder into the tunnel. The other displays also showed soldiers descending into the tunnel. There was no need to consult maps of the tunnel network since these had been committed to memory before they deployed.

The simultaneous entrance into multiple tunnels, signaled by the sensors at their entrances, could only have signaled an attack. Adam al-Zhihri had been awakened by the Bis Saif night guard and immediately set off the facility-wide alarm. His close friend and associate Abu Ahmed-al Kuwaiti was quickly awake, dressed, and armed, as was Cecil Breathwaite, aka John Smith, and Leroy Williamson, their technical expert. As planned, the four Bis Saif leaders assembled with the rest of the staff in the control room of the headquarters. From this room they could watch the monitors installed in each of the tunnels. They could also remotely trigger the improvised explosive devices, or IEDs, buried in the tunnels. As they were huddled around the monitors in the control room, Adam passed out arms and ammunition to the staff, which normally didn't carry armaments to avoid accidental shootings. Each person received a pistol and an automatic rifle.

The audience in the White House Situation Room was not aware of the preparations taking place at the headquarters. All they knew about was the incredibly slow progress being made by the Special Forces troops as they inched along the tunnels. They had anticipated the possibility of IEDs as well as the release of poison gas in the tunnel and they were prepared with gas masks and magnetometers. But they needed to check every inch of the tunnel floor before they could proceed. Kaplan sensed the impatience of the watchers and made a quick mental calculation. He saw that the soldiers were progressing at a rate of about a foot per second. If one assumed that the tunnel was one-mile long, it was going to require more than 5,000 seconds, or an hour and a half, to traverse its length. "Well everyone, you might as well relax and get a cup of coffee while we watch the soldiers creep patiently through the tunnels. We expected this, since it's important not to get someone blown up."

In spite of Kaplan's invitation, the group in the situation room remained mesmerized by the action that played out in slow motion in front of them. The tension in the room was palpable. Occasionally the squad leader would raise his hand and everyone would come to a halt. Occasionally the delay was caused by the need to disable a video monitor attached to the tunnel wall. But other times the delay was caused by the discovery of an IED, which had to be carefully disabled before proceeding. The Special Forces had come prepared and were using jamming devices to prevent their remote detonation from the Bis Saif control room. And so the ballet of the tunnels continued, with the rapt audience in the situation room following every move. The senior squad leader then radioed the group on the roof to begin destroying the communications gear. He then radioed the group in the lobby to warn them that progress was extremely slow in the tunnels, and they might be expecting a breakout through the stairwell or the elevator.

Suddenly two tunnels converged, and two of the squads arriving at the same time met. Automatically the senior leader took command. He motioned them forward a few feet before encountering a heavy steel door. The door, like the video cameras and IEDs, had been anticipated. The squad leader placed plastic explosives around the edge of the door and motioned everyone back along the passage, unwinding the ignition wire as they retreated. When they had located themselves 100 feet along the corridor, he motioned everyone to get down and huddle together with their backs toward the door, then he ignited the explosives. The blast was tremendous. It disabled one of the helmet cameras while the video on the operational camera momentarily turned white.

The soldiers who had prepared for this recovered immediately, got to their feet, and raced through the door toward the headquarters. One minute later the remaining two squads met in another tunnel and followed the same process. While they ran, they radioed the group in the lobby and told them to be prepared for "rats fleeing the nest."

As they neared the end of the tunnel, the troops donned gas masks and poured copious amounts of tear gas into the headquarters. They met up at the headquarters facility. One soldier was posted at each of the tunnels while the remaining troops conducted a room-by-room search of the facility. They watched from the situation room as various individuals were brought into the conference room with the yellow wall, which had been converted into a holding facility for prisoners. Kaplan identified individuals as they were brought into the room, handcuffed, and placed face down on the floor. "Those two must be the Jaffaris, who must bear most of the responsibility for our power failures." Kelly and Jahmir were unarmed and clearly had not been prepared for the assault. It was as if the Bis Saif leadership had thrown them to the wolves.

"I don't know who the black man is, but I'm certain that he's not their leader," Kaplan said with surprise. He was later to discover that the black man's name was Leroy Williamson, a Bis Saif technical expert on armaments and other useful devices.

The sound of gunfire interrupted the flow of prisoners into the conference room. It also silenced the conversation in the White House Situation Room. The relatively inexperienced Bis Saif fighters were no match for the highly trained Special Forces soldiers, so the fight was brief. It became obvious that the Special Forces personnel had not been able to satisfy the objective of avoiding fatalities when a body was dragged into the conference room and dropped unceremoniously on the floor. This was someone Kaplan could identify. "That's Cecil Breathwaite, our British spy. Too bad we couldn't keep him alive. I'll bet he could have told us some interesting things."

Several others arrived in rapid sequence. These included several who were obviously Indonesians hired to support the headquarters. From their dress they appeared to be cooks, maids, and some soldiers. None of the locals had much desire to fight. This was not their fight. They were just hired hands. And then another individual who Kaplan could identify arrived alive. "There's Hasan Jouda, our Palestinian. I'll bet our Israeli friends would like to get their hands on him."

And then another body arrived. Kaplan couldn't identify him either and remained silent. Upon subsequent questioning, Leroy Williamson, who turned out to be an endless source of useful information, told them that this was Abu Ahmed-Al Kuwaiti, the leader's closest friend and ally. Leroy subsequently told them that the leader's name was Adam al-Zhihri. But this was revealed during subsequent interrogation.

The sounds of fighting died out as the Special Forces troops searched the headquarters for others Bis Saif personnel. Suddenly one of them heard the elevator moving and realized that it had left its parking position on the first floor and was now headed upward. He quickly radioed the squad stationed in the lobby and told them to be prepared for the elevator doors to open. But they never did. The elevator proceeded upward without any floor numbers registering on the display above the doors. It stopped, and silence returned to the building.

The soldiers quickly realized that there had been an escapee. The squad leader assigned two soldiers to guard the prisoners and then assigned each of the remaining troops to one of the building's floors, beginning at the lowest level. He told the troops on the roof to look over the edge of the building's parapets to see if they could discover anyone escaping. It didn't take long to realize that the second floor was connected to a parking garage. Their subject was soon seen exiting the garage at a high speed, driving a BMW 320i. They were out of position, and intercepting the vehicle would have been impossible. Philosophically, the squad leader said, "Well, we got most of them, and I think we've got the computers as well. We'd better settle for a ninety-percent victory."

***

It was standing room only in the press briefing room the next day. The word was out that progress had been made in the hunt for Bis Saif, and all of the media representatives in Washington wanted to get the news first-hand. The normal chatter in the room was louder than usual with the excitement of the news

Philip J. Tarnoff

they were about to hear. Things died down quickly when Paul Lynd, the president's press secretary, entered the room ready to provide the background on the story. Paul intentionally portrayed the image of being in a hurry, forgoing his usual business suit for casual attire, consisting of a plaid open-necked sport shirt, khaki slacks, and loafers.

"Ladies and gentlemen, the president will not be participating today since, as you can imagine, his plate is currently rather full. So I guess you'll have to be satisfied with me." His comment produced some polite laughter, but the overall sentiment in the room was that they wished Paul would get on with it. He continued sensing their impatience.

"As you may have already heard, yesterday two platoons of Special Forces soldiers attacked the Bis Saif headquarters in Jakarta, Indonesia. The raid was a ninety-five-percent successful in that it completely neutralized their operation. The computers that had been used to compromise the US power grid were captured and removed to Washington for further examination. All of the Bis Saif staff except for their leader were either killed or captured. Those that were captured are now in the United States, being subjected to intensive interrogation. With one exception, they are all cooperating with our investigators and providing a wealth of information regarding the Bis Saif operation. All will be prosecuted on US soil, according to our laws. You have all received a handout with the names of those who were captured and their status. The handout also provides the name of Adam al-Zhihri, the leader of Bis Saif, who unfortunately escaped during the attack. We have initiated a worldwide search for him, with the help of our European and Asian friends, and hope to apprehend him soon. Adam's objectives were similar to those of ISIS in that he dreamed of establishing a worldwide caliphate for Sunni Muslims. He hoped that Bis Saif would serve as an organization that would bring the various fragmented Sunni Muslim tribes together in a coordinated program to overthrow the governments of the West."

As Lynd paused for a sip of water, pandemonium broke out among the attending reporters. He held up his hand as an indication that he had not completed his briefing.

"I'll take your questions in a minute, and I'm sure you have many of them. But first I'd like to address the issues of the power disruption. The president recognizes that the two major disruptions, in the Washington, DC region and in California, are causing significant suffering. The government as well as the utilities are doing everything they can to restore the power as quickly as possible. Neutralizing Bis Saif eliminates the possibility of future disruption but does nothing to accelerate the repair of facilities that have already been damaged. The utilities are faced with a difficult task. Some of the major components that were destroyed during the failure are difficult to replace. As a result, it is likely that the DC region will be without power for another month, and California will be without power for another two months, at least. We have moved an entire army division into California to help the local law enforcement agencies maintain the peace. In both Washington and California, we have set up distribution centers for food and other goods in order to supply those who are living in the dark. We have procured every available generator in the United States and Canada to provide power for critical facilities. And finally, we have reserved quarters at government expense for those who are willing to temporarily relocate out of the affected areas. Most of our citizens have adjusted to these emergency conditions and are bearing their discomfort with patience and grace. Many have elected to relocate to the temporary quarters, although we would appreciate it if additional people would consider doing so."

Then, taking a deep breath, Paul added as forcefully as he could. "Members of the press, you can help us weather this storm in two ways. First, by encouraging more people to relocate. As you can imagine, the task of providing goods and services for ten million people in an area without electrical power is a daunting task, which could be made easier if more people would temporarily leave the area. And second, by calming groups that would like to take revenge on those that they perceive are responsible for their discomfort. The president and I feel that it is reprehensible to attack other individuals because of their religious faith. Particularly when most if not all of the people that

Philip J. Tarnoff

worship in this faith bear no responsibility for the problem. It is wrong and frankly unchristian to seek revenge because of the inconvenience or the fear that the power disruption has caused, particularly since the inconvenience is short-lived and the fear is unfounded. So once again, we in the administration are counting on you in the press to provide needed outreach to the American public to do away with the conflicts occurring on both coasts."

And with that, he nodded to the assembled gathering, indicating he was ready for questions, and there were many. Press briefings are not noted for their organization. Reporters shout out their questions and are recognized by the speaker. Typically, the loudest or best-known shouter is recognized first, and this was the case today.

Questions ranged from the mundane to the philosophical. The reporters wanted to know the time of the attack, the names of the Special Forces soldiers, more of the backgrounds of those arrested, the locations at which the prisoners were being held, the manner in which Adam had escaped, the route followed by the Special Forces troops, the manner in which the headquarters had been discovered, the layout of the headquarters, the degree of cooperation received from the Indonesian government, and on and on. Paul answered most of the questions to the best of his ability except for the names of the Special Forces soldiers and the locations of the prisoners. He answered questions regarding the location and layout of the headquarters in very general terms. What the reporters did not know was that one of the reasons that Paul was representing the administration was because of his limited knowledge of the situation. What he didn't know couldn't be answered.

When the reporters had squeezed every drop of information from Paul regarding the attack, their attention turned to the power disruption. Another long list of questions developed regarding the cause of the power failure, the equipment that had to be replaced, the likelihood that the restoration schedule would be met, and the extent of the affected area. Again, Paul answered all questions for which he knew the answer. He had a reputation for being a straight shooter and the reporters knew

344

that he wouldn't fabricate answers to questions that he couldn't answer.

Then the questioning became more probing. This began when the reporter from the *Wall Street Journal* asked the question of the day. "Paul, the actions being taken by the government for the benefit of the public in the regions affected by the power disruption have got to be expensive. What are they costing, and how are they being paid for?"

This was a question that Lynd wanted to answer. In fact, the question had been suggested to the questioner in advance. The administration had been unsuccessful in getting Congress to address the problem, and possibly a public airing would get them moving. If he had brought it up in his prepared statements, the administration would have been accused of lobbying Congress through the press. But if it was asked by a supposedly innocent reporter, they couldn't be accused of taking this action.

"As your question implied, these actions are extremely expensive. The cost of relocations is nearly equal to the DHS annual budget. Obviously this is an expense that cannot be borne by a single agency without a major budget supplement or by shutting all other activities of that agency down. This would mean that the Coast Guard, Border Patrol, Airport Security, FEMA, and many others would all be furloughed for the year. It also means that two hundred and forty thousand employees would find themselves without a job. Obviously, this is not feasible, so a budget supplement is critical. To date, in spite of the president's pleas, Congress has not been willing to consider a budget realignment. For this reason, the president has drawn on the terms of the New War Powers Act, which authorizes him to divert funds intended for other purposes to support our response to Bis Saif. The power disruption is considered by the administration to be part of our response to Bis Saif."

The reporter wasn't satisfied with this answer. "I had assumed that the only way in which such massive funding could be accommodated would be through diversion of funds intended for other purposes. This is the basis for my question. What are the other purposes from which the funds are being diverted?"

Philip J. Tarnoff

Once again, Paul was only too happy to answer. "Well, unfortunately, there is no single activity within the federal government that can readily provide the billions of dollars needed. As a result, the Office of Management and Budget has been analyzing the federal budget to find the needed money. Although I can't provide you with exact amounts, I can provide you with some of the top candidates to serve as funding sources for this effort. I don't think either you or the American people will like the answers, which include highway repair and reconstruction, NASA space programs, big military weapons programs, medical research, foreign aid, education, law enforcement grants, and various construction programs. We will not touch Social Security or health care. We will also leave the operations and maintenance portions of the defense budget untouched. The list is going to gore everyone's ox. No one is going to be happy with the cuts. But the only other alternative is an increase in taxes, and no one is going to like that either." He then ended the meeting by adding sarcastically, "This should please the conservative wing of the Republican Party, since it will result in a much leaner government and a reorientation of services without raising taxes. I know you all have deadlines to meet, so why don't we now call it a day. For your information, the president is planning to address the nation again within the next few days, so stay tuned."

And with that, the reporters raced for the door to file their articles.

BOOK 5
THE BEGINNING OF THE END

The concept of democracy is not new. As early as 100 BCE, the Greek philosophers had accurately evaluated the potential of democracy and its prospects for success. This was applied to the Roman Empire as well as the Western democracies.

On the one hand, Rome had the most perfect constitution in history. In fact, Aristotle's notion of the mixed constitution as distilled by Polybius would pass down from the Romans into the mainstream of Western political thinking, including America's Founding Fathers. On the other, Rome was doomed to failure as Plato turned Aristotle's formula for constitutional success into a warning. A mixed constitution required every group in society pulling its appropriate weight. Allowing any one element, the monarchical (in America's case, the presidency), the democratic (in America's case, the House of Representatives), or the aristocratic (in America's case, the Senate), to gain undue influence over the other parts became a death knell of doom, and the end of any self-governing republic.

Herman, Arthur, *The Cave and the Light*,
Random House, New York, pp 116-117.

CHAPTER 26
MOVING THE CONFLICT

The BMW sped through the empty streets of downtown Jakarta toward Soekarno—Hatta International Airport. Adam knew better than to arrive at the airport on his flight from the country early in the morning on the day of the attack. He had cultivated numerous friendships with fellow Sunni Moslems scattered throughout the city. Some of his support was the result of employment he had provided during the construction of the Bis Saif headquarters, and other support was the result of true belief in the objectives of his organization.

He turned off the airport expressway into a middle-class residential district with palm tree lined streets and houses with neat yards and red tiled roofs. He drove the BMW around to the back of a house and parked it under a palm tree in the backyard, being careful to avoid the toys and sandbox scattered about. Carrying the backpack he had grabbed before escaping the headquarters attack, Adam quietly knocked on the back door of the residence. In a few minutes, a light came on and the door was unlocked by a stocky middle-aged Indonesian in his underwear carrying a pistol.

"It's me," whispered Adam. "I need to activate my escape plan."

"Come on in, man. We can get you fixed up and on your way."

Adam entered the house and was shown to a spare bedroom. He was familiar with this house and was friends with its occupants. Recognizing the possibility of an attack such as the one that had just occurred, Adam had prepared a carefully thought-out plan for a rapid departure from Jakarta, and these folks were a key part of the plan.

"The car is parked behind the house. I'll change the license plates before I leave and let you know where I've left it at the airport. You can keep it."

With that, Adam walked to the spare bedroom of the house, where he lay down for a quick nap before changing his dress and looks. When he left at five that morning, he was the picture of a successful US businessman, complete with a dark suit, white shirt, striped tie, and briefcase. He was clean shaven, wearing dark-rimmed glasses, and had a new passport to match his new name and appearance.

He arrived at the airport in plenty of time for his 6:45 twenty-six-hour overnight flight to Boston. It would be a grueling flight, but one he had done before. For Adam, flying to Boston was like returning home, after having spent four years at Yale in nearby New Haven, Connecticut. Anxious to avoid leaving tracks, upon his arrival he avoided visiting friends from his days in college, tempting though it might be.

The flight arrived in Boston's Logan Airport on time at nine the following evening. Adam had booked a first-class ticket and had a restful flight, featuring gourmet food and seats that reclined into beds. As the plane neared Boston, he retired to the cramped lavatory, where he shaved and brushed his teeth in order to debark looking as if he was going to begin the day in downtown Boston at corporate meetings. Carefully selecting a taxi stand that was out of sight of security cameras, Adam took a cab from the airport to the Parker House hotel, famous for its introduction of the Parker House rolls. He checked into the hotel using a third passport, different from the one he had used in Jakarta, making it impossible for anyone to trace his movements after leaving the airport.

After checking into the hotel, Adam went shopping for clothing and equipment appropriate for those of a company field technician. After returning from his hasty shopping trip, he opened his laptop and began work on unfinished business. *Nothing is more dangerous than a wounded tiger,* thought

Adam. *Those Americans think they're pretty smart, destroying our headquarters. But Bis Saif still exists. It's time to move to the second phase of my plan. I'm more determined than ever to complete our work in the names of Abu and John Smith. They were my friends, and their martyrdom deserves to be honored.* With that, he sent two messages using the encryption software on his laptop.

When Adam left for the airport the next morning, his business suit had been traded for a set of jeans and a Hawaiian-style sport shirt, covered by a nondescript windbreaker. His dark hair had been dyed blond, and he was carrying a tool kit typical of those used by electronics specialists and pulling a roll-aboard suitcase. His next flight was a nonstop American Airlines flight to Los Angeles airport, or LAX, as it is known to frequent travelers. The flight was scheduled to leave at 8:00 a.m. and arrive before noon local time. Flying from east to west had its advantages.

The flight left on time, but was forced to circle LAX when it arrived in Los Angeles. The pilot explained the situation as they circled, saying, "As you know, all of California is without electricity. LAX is running on backup power, which means that only one runway is opened. It also means that only four of the eight terminals are opened, which means that there is also a shortage of available gates. While we have reduced the number of flights to compensate for the lower capacity, there are still significant delays. The good news is that ground traffic at the airport is significantly reduced since the number of passengers has decreased. We should be on the ground in approximately twenty minutes. Thank you for your patience, and we appreciate your business."

Adam's flight eventually landed, as they inevitably do. He retrieved his roll-aboard suitcase from the overhead rack, walked rapidly down the jetway, and proceeded through the terminal to the pickup area outside. The battered green Ford F-150 pickup he was looking for was waiting at the curb. The driver, a wizened farmer wearing a cowboy hat, waved when he saw Adam, recognizing him by the prearranged sign of a Green Bay

Packers decal on his roll-aboard. As soon as Adam was belted in, the pickup left the airport, taking advantage of the absence of the usual swirling congestion on the LA roadways.

The driver introduced himself as Tex, indicating that everyone in the LA area had adopted false names and disguises to prevent being identified as Muslims. "I even shaved my beard. It'll take me a lifetime to regrow it," explained Tex forlornly.

"I've had to shave my beard also," Adam replied in the spirit of consoling Tex.

Adam was anxious to learn about the local situation and plans. So ignoring the issue of Tex's beard, he began, "So what's the plan? Are we going to meet your congregation at a mosque?"

"No, we're going to meet at one of the member's homes. The mosque is being watched closely by army troops. We've managed to smuggle a few weapons into the mosque, but find it much more convenient to operate out of private houses. It would be impossible for the law to search all of our homes in the dark."

"Were my ISIS contacts able to help with the weapons?"

"Yes. We heard from both Ali and General Hussein from Iraq. I understand that Ali has done quite well in ISIS as a result of the SAMs you provided through Bis Saif. He now runs their air-defense system. They seem most anxious to help our efforts here in California."

Adam was buoyed by the news. "I had hoped they would help. ISIS is always eager to pursue any opportunity to disrupt relations between Muslims and Christians, particularly when Sunni Muslims are involved."

"You certainly did your part by destroying the California electric grid. Were you sorry that the Americans attacked your headquarters?"

"Of course I was sorry. But I expected it and had been preparing to move to the second phase of our disruption of their society. We've got the money and cooperation of Sunnis throughout the world. I've always felt that all we need is better organization and more cooperation among our various factions."

Tex reflected on Adam's comments. "So we're at the beginning of your second phase?"

"Yes, you are. It's my hope to stir up conflict between American Muslims and American Christians. The US Christians are a cowardly bunch. They've gotten soft and all they care about is good food, computer games, and their sports entertainment."

"Sadly, you're right. I grew up in this country and always felt that it was a good place to raise a family. During the past twenty years, I've watched the country go downhill. They think their God will save them and that they don't have to do anything but drink beer, watch TV, or play electronic games on their goddamned iPhones."

And so the conversation went as Tex drove from LAX to the neighborhood surrounding the Hadad-Mahmood Mosque, located in a middle-class neighborhood on the fringes of downtown LA. The mosque was designed as a block building with Middle Eastern decorations around the roofline and at ground level. Its role as a mosque was identifiable by the dome on its roof. On this day, its significance was further emphasized by the Humvees in the parking lot and the soldiers with loaded M-16s patrolling its perimeter.

As they drove past the mosque without slowing, Tex advised Adam, "Don't turn your head or show the slightest interest or they'll record my license number and track our movements. Our destination is just a couple of blocks away."

He turned off the arterial into a neighborhood of well-kept houses, many with palm trees and hibiscus bushes in their yards, and turned into one of the larger dwellings on the street. Barely slowing, he drove up the driveway, timing his entry into the garage to coincide with the opening of the automatic garage door so that it just missed the truck's antenna as he entered. The door was then immediately closed.

"Come on in," he said as he motioned for Adam to follow him. "The boys will be glad to meet you."

Adam followed Tex into the sparsely furnished house, where he met a group of five men sitting on rugs around a large room looking like some of the photos that Adam had seen of the al-Qaeda camps occupied by bin Laden in his heyday.

After the mandatory introductions, Adam was pleased to sense that the group was turning to him for instructions. Adam was an intuitive leader, and in this case he felt that his guidance was needed if the Bis Saif goals were to be achieved.

Feeling his way with his newly acquainted allies, Adam began, "How have things been going here?"

Tex, who appeared to be the leader of the group, responded. "Tensions are escalating. As you might expect, everyone around here is blaming the power failure on us. It's not at all unusual for one of our women wearing a hijab to be attacked, either verbally or physically, and told to go back where they came from. We all feel it's time to fight back."

This is exactly what Adam had hoped to hear, so he began his prepared speech. "I completely agree with your feeling that it's time to fight back. I don't think we should be timid. I think we need to let the American Christians know that we've had enough. We need to make a statement."

Seeing that everyone was nodding, Adam laid out a plan for an attack that would make such a statement. The group spent the rest of the afternoon working on the details of the plan. Ideas were offered and either accepted or rejected by the group. It was decidedly a collaborative effort. When they were done, the participants scattered to alert their compatriots of the plans for the evening.

***

At 2:00 a.m. the following morning, a motley group of cars and pickup trucks departed from various houses scattered in the community surrounding the Hadad-Mahmood Mosque. Each of these vehicles carried two to four heavily armed men. As they approached the mosque, each turned off their lights and parked inconspicuously on a side street within a five-minute walk of the mosque's parking lot. It was a moonlit night, and they could see the soldiers leisurely patrolling the parking lot and surrounding grounds. A few were leaning against the fenders of the Humvees, smoking cigarettes and quietly talking. All carried M-16s, and a few were wearing night vision goggles, although there was little need for them in the light of a full moon.

The Muslims quietly deployed behind the shrubbery of the surrounding residential areas. They were also aware of the fact that several of their number had secreted themselves inside the mosque following the evening prayers and were waiting for the signal from Adam to begin the attack.

At precisely 2:30 a.m. a flare was lit and thrown into the parking lot, a signal for the mayhem that was about to follow. As soon as they saw the flare, gunfire erupted from inside the mosque, hitting one of the soldiers, who screamed as he fell. The soldiers, believing they were being attacked by a suicidal group from inside the mosque, took cover behind their Humvees and began pouring a withering fire into the mosque. Their action was a perfect complement to Adam's plans. It both exposed their backs to the group hiding in the bushes outside the mosque, and the deafening noise of their firing masked the fact that they were being attacked from behind. It was obvious that the troops guarding the mosque had little battlefield experience.

What followed was a massacre. All of the troops were killed before they even had a chance of radioing for assistance. When it was plain that the resistance had been eliminated, Adam motioned to the group that they should load their bodies into the Humvees for removal from the mosque's property. The Humvees were quickly driven to an empty lot several blocks away. The group then disbanded, returning to their homes and hiding their weapons in preparation for the inevitable police sweep of the area, looking for evidence. Many of the weapons were simply buried in backyards. Others were placed with relatives located at a distance from the mosque. All returned to bed for the evening, waiting for the arrival of the long arm of the law. Tex drove Adam to a parking garage at the airport, where they spent the night sleeping in the truck to avoid his discovery by law enforcement personnel sweeping the neighborhood in the vicinity of the mosque.

It didn't take long for the police to arrive. As the last attacker was at home and leaping into bed, sirens could be heard in the distance. The police, accompanied by the news media, soon arrived at the scene of the battle only to find a parking lot with spent shell casings, but otherwise deserted. They also found the walls of the mosque pockmarked with bullets fired by the soldiers. They found neither the soldiers nor the Humvees, a situation that was temporarily puzzling to the police, US Army, and news media.

The mystery didn't last long, however. Early the next morning, the Humvees were spotted by a crew on a garbage truck heading out for early morning collection. The area was quickly taped off with yards of yellow tape and examined by a swarm of forensics experts. Little was learned except for the fact that the soldiers had been killed by individuals using a variety of automatic weapons. The mystery was subsequently solved by a text message sent to the *Los Angeles Times*, in which Bis Saif and ISIS took collective credit for the attack.

***

The president was at his desk in the Oval Office with his hands supporting his head as he stared at the numbers that had just been delivered by the Director of the Office of Management and Budget. OMB was responsible for the preparation of the federal budget for the president, and Jeffers had made an emergency request to them for a budget that could support the war with ISIS, help the recovery from the power failure, support the cost of troops stationed in California to defend the local residents, and provide supplemental military aid to Israel. The budget was always a challenge to Jeffers, who was determined to run the country without raising taxes, a Republican mantra, but he was increasingly at a loss as to how this might be accomplished. Now with the loss of the power grid and the problems of Bis Saif, the country's financial problems had taken a turn for the worse. Jeffers was beginning to realize that he had three alternatives: raise taxes, increase the national debt, or cut services.

He was about to call Jan on the intercom when George Wilson burst into the Oval Office with Jan on his heels, saying, "I tried to stop him, but he blew right by me!"

Ignoring Jan, George breathlessly said, "Turn on the TV. Any channel will do."

The president, together with Jan and George, watched the CNN broadcast of the murder of the soldiers in Los Angeles. The newswoman was saying, "It appears they were ambushed by unknown assailants from the surrounding neighborhood. Both ISIS and Bis Saif are taking credit for the attack. All of the soldiers were murdered by their attackers. We will broadcast their names after their next of kin have been notified." Then, recognizing the short attention spans of the typical TV viewer, she moved on to other subjects. "Now, in other news, the National Football League announced today that due to the power failure, there is a possibility that the Super Bowl, scheduled to occur in two weeks, may be cancelled. Unless they can find an acceptable venue in a part of the country that still has power, they will have no choice but to cancel the game. League representatives have indicated that every effort will be made to relocate the game. The cost to the networks, the local hospitality industry, and the NFL would be incalculable if the game is cancelled. And now, after a short break, we'll be back with more information about the mosque attack."

George was the first to break the stunned silence. Turning down the volume on the TV, he said, "Now we're really going to have some trouble. I can't imagine that the anti-Muslim crowd is going to take this lying down."

He had no longer finished expressing the thought than the phone on Jan's desk rang. She rushed out of the Oval Office to answer, and in a few seconds buzzed the president to let him know that General Drake was on the phone. Jeffers opened with his sympathy. "General, I want you to know how distressed we are about the loss of your infantrymen and women."

"Not nearly as distressed as I am. But I'm calling with more bad news. Two more of our F-16s were shot down over Iraq, bringing the total to four aircraft destroyed. Once again, we think that ISIS is to blame, since they appear to have been shot down using surface-to-air missiles. We've made some progress analyzing the first two casualties, and it appears that somehow they've obtained some Chinese-made SAMs. One of the pilots survived and was captured, and the other died. So in addition to the loss of our airmen and equipment, we're faced with yet another public relations nightmare. If it was ISIS, and we'll know soon enough, my guess is that the pilot will be subjected to another gruesome trial. Right now we're in the information gathering phase, but if our guesses are correct, we may be recommending a Seal raid to free both him and the first pilot who was captured."

Chris was dumbfounded. "It never rains but it pours. Keep me informed."

The general continued as if he had not heard the president's response. "Now about the LA massacre. Those troops were ambushed. It was murder plain and simple, and we've got no one to blame but the Muslims. I want to move another division to California. It isn't cheap to move fifteen thousand men with all their equipment. We need money from somewhere other than our existing budget, or we're going to have to reduce our commitments in other places around the world."

Although General Drake didn't explicitly make the statement, Jeffers finished it in his mind: *And if we reduce our commitments, Bis Saif will have won. We may have destroyed their headquarters, but we definitely haven't destroyed them.*

"General Drake, I'll get back to you with answers within twenty-four hours. In the meantime, plan to move another division to California. The current situation is unacceptable."

"Yes, sir," replied the general as he disconnected.

***

When the discussion and speculation came to an end, Jeffers asked Jan to call an immediate meeting with the senior congressional leadership. It required an hour to find the four congress-men who had been his advisors and consultant throughout this crisis. It was early afternoon when they were finally able to meet. The period before the meeting gave President Jeffers an opportunity to continue his study of the budget in the hopes that some magic would occur to solve the country's financial problems. Perhaps a misplaced decimal point or an addition error. But unfortunately, the folks at OMB were efficient and no errors were evident. He knew that the approximate cost of two army divisions in California was approximately $4 billion. Add to that the additional $48 billon cost of relocating the California families displaced by the power failure and the incalculable cost of lost aircraft and pilots in the Middle East, the $1 billion he had promised Israel, the cost of the DC power failures, and he had some big problems. Chris wondered again why he ever wanted to become president. As the famous idiom goes: "Be careful what you wish for, lest it come true."

When the congressmen arrived, he was no closer to solv-ing the budget dilemma than he had been that morning. But he had pulled himself together from his troubling thoughts and was more determined than ever to see this problem through. As a lifelong conservative with a strong Christian ethic, he was determined to do whatever it took to save the United States from itself.

As the four leaders of Congress filed into the Oval Office, it only took one look at Jeffers face to recognize that this was not the time for levity. As usual, Bob McIntyre, the Senate Major-ity Leader, opened the discussion. "Mr. President, I fear we've got some serious problems in this country. I sure hope you have some solutions."

"Bob, I also wish I had some solutions. This is exactly what I've been worrying about. I can't do this by myself. I need some help from the Hill, and I'm depending on the four of you to see that it's provided."

"What sort of help did you have in mind?" questioned Brad Nelson cautiously. As the House Majority Leader, he would bear a significant part of the burden of seeing that needed legislation was passed. His job was not made any easier by the fact that as a Democrat, he and the president were members of different political parties.

"We've got some serious financial problems," explained Jeffers. "The combination of repositioning troops to California to restore peace, and relocating millions of its residents to surrounding states, is putting a serious strain on the budget. We estimate that the combined cost of these two items will be more than $50 billion. On top of that, we've got the cost of replacing downed aircraft, additional foreign aid to Israel, and $5 billion of costs in the Washington, DC region. I expect that the bill will continue to grow as we try to combat unrest in other parts of the country and deliver on our promises for a more aggressive attitude toward ISIS and Bis Saif in the Middle East. We're rapidly approaching a total cost of more than $60 billion for all of this. I realize that the New War Powers Act gives me the latitude to move money from other parts of the budget to pay for all of this, but I've scoured the federal budget for discretionary expenditures that can be reallocated for these expenses, and I've run out of ideas. I'm open to anything that the four of you can suggest."

His request for suggestions was met with silence by the four men.

The exception was Wayne Zyder, a fellow Republican and the House Minority Leader, who exclaimed, "Those Muslim bastards! Maybe the idea of nuking them wasn't such a bad one after all."

Chris's face reddened, which belied his otherwise calm demeanor. "This is the very attitude that I've been trying to combat. Blaming the Muslims for all our problems is not going to keep the country together. What kind of Christian would blame an entire religion for the actions of a few? Don't forget that half of our problems are due to intolerant and irrational Christians."

Zyder remained silent, although it was obvious he was not swayed by the president's response.

"So in the absence of any suggestions from the four of you, I'll acquaint you with the available alternatives, which include the following." Jeffers ticked off the three options on the fingers of his hand as he spoke. "One, we can increase the national debt by another $60 to $100 billion. Two, we can cut services. This would include some pretty significant cuts, which could include our infrastructure renewal, health care, and Social Security. Three, we can raise taxes. None of these are very desirable, and all require the support of Congress. How do you want to proceed?"

Bob McIntyre spoke up again. "Your first alternative is the only one that's feasible. I know you pledged to balance the budget when you ran for office, but no one anticipated this situation. I just can't see Congress agreeing to another tax increase."

Jeffers nodded. "I have trouble bringing myself to further increase the debt. You know that it is currently approaching twenty trillion. That is the number twenty with twelve zeros behind it. That translates to a hundred and sixty thousand of debt per taxpayer. Who in their right mind would willingly accept such a financial burden? Don't you guys ever worry that someday our creditors will lose confidence in our ability to repay the debt and require some of it to be repaid?"

"Mr. President, we've been over all of this before. We've all heard these statistics, and in fact we've used these arguments ourselves. Remember the counterarguments used by liberal economists. The interest we're paying on the debt is only around six percent, which is lower than it has been for the past fifty years. Admittedly this is due to low interest rates, but it is an important consideration. Also, it is very unlikely that our creditors will be calling in their loans to us at any time in the foreseeable future since we have far more assets than debt. Assets which include infrastructure, land, equipment, and other facilities. These assets are quite solvent. Our debt isn't equivalent to a home mortgage that has to be repaid in thirty years. People are quite willing to continue to lend us money. I know I'm using the arguments used by the liberals, but there is some truth to them. In any event, what are our alternatives?"

Everyone in the room appeared to concur with McIntyre's selection of the first alternative.

361

Philip J. Tarnoff

"Since we're approaching the debt ceiling, it's up to the four of you to see that Congress passes a bill raising the ceiling once again. I know that I've itemized sixty billion in unexpected costs, but in the event that the debt ceiling is raised, the increase should be closer to one hundred billion since these initial cost estimates always seem to be low. And the ceiling needs to be done quickly or the country is going to fall apart. I'm not being overly dramatic here. This is a serious situation."

The leadership of the US Congress nodded in agreement. With that, the meeting adjourned following some additional discussion of the manner in which the process would be fast-tracked through Congress.

CHAPTER 27

A RELIGIOUS WAR

Gus sat at the front of the all-purpose room of the First Baptist Church of Santa Monica. Twenty-three members of the church with their friends sat facing him on metal folding chairs that had been set up in advance of the meeting. The men were all dressed in various types of work clothes. Most wore blue jeans and knit golf shirts, some wore coveralls with denim work shirts, and others were dressed in chinos. It was clear that they had all come from work, and in the case of this neighborhood, it was blue-collar work.

As the leader of the group, known as Bear because of his size, made the introductions, Gus noticed a single black man in the group. "Who are you?" he asked rudely, revealing one of his long list of prejudices.

Bear quickly jumped in. "His name is Damian Johnson. His brother was in the army and was killed at the Hadad-Mahmood Mosque. He's one of us."

Gus read Bear's body language correctly and quickly moved to change the subject. He began the meeting with a brief speech that he had prepared during his flight from Dulles Airport. "We have been without power in the Washington, DC area for nearly three months now. We're lucky because the end is in sight. I hear that it might take longer to restore power in California, although for your sake, I hope not. In the Washington area we've started a program intended to drive the Muslims out of our communities. We're doing that through a program of harassment intended to deliver the message that they're not welcome. We're also putting pressure on our representatives in Congress to get rid of them."

He paused for effect. There was a scattering of applause. "You are new to the problem in California. I'm sure that no one is enjoying life without power. Your kids are not going to school, groceries are hard to get, television is not available, and life in the dark is no fun. To make matters worse, there's talk of cancelling the Super Bowl."

A collective gasp was heard at the mention of cancelling the Super Bowl.

Gus continued with a raised voice. "I believe it's time to take matters into our own hands. Obviously the federal government isn't capable of handling the situation. If they had been more capable, an entire platoon of their troops wouldn't have been wiped out by the Muslims. We've got to strike back. That's the only language those rag heads will understand. I'm here to help you do just that."

This time, the applause was more enthusiastic.

When the applause died down, Gus continued. "Here's my proposal. I think we should destroy one of the biggest mosques in the area. I'll let you decide whether you want to do it while worship is underway, or wait until it's empty. Not everyone has the stomach for murder, even though that's what they've done to our people, so I'll leave it up to you. But I'll tell you one thing. Once the deed is done, we will all have to guard our own churches because Muslims are great ones for avenging actions that have been taken against them."

Gus failed to recognize the irony of his statement. The bombing of a mosque was the same type of revenge that he was attributing to the Muslims.

The group collectively decided to bomb an empty mosque. They reasoned that if that did not discourage the Muslims from remaining in the area, they could always resort to more forceful measures in the future. Although a few were in favor of bombing the mosque during services, the majority was squeamish about resorting to murder and worried about the possibility of arrests and prison.

The Hadad-Mahmood Mosque was selected for the bombing, so there could be no question as to whether it was an act of retribution. The scene of the crime against the soldiers was to be leveled. The process for producing explosives was then discussed. It was agreed that the most effective approach would be the one that had been used by Timothy McVeigh and Terry Nichols on the Murrah Federal Building for the Oklahoma City bombing. McVeigh used ammonium nitrate, a form of fertilizer mixed with fuel oil to create the bomb. This was a low-cost approach using readily accessible materials with effective results. The Murrah bomb destroyed or damaged more than 300 buildings within a sixteen-block area, so its effectiveness was beyond dispute.

After giving a pep talk and a warning about secrecy, each member of the group was assigned a task related to the bombing. As with the Murrah bombing, the explosives would be contained in a box truck to be stolen by a group member possessing that particular skill. Others were to obtain the ingredients from hardware stores and garden shops scattered throughout the city, so that no single purchase would be large enough to raise suspicion. And one final group of volunteers would drive the truck toward the mosque's parking lot. All of this was to occur on the following night, giving the participants an evening and a full day to complete their preparations.

***

The next evening was a typical Los Angeles late winter day. The temperature was in the mid-fifties, and there was a full moon. But nature's beauty was lost on the conspirators as they prepared the truck for its final trip. Without prior discussion, everyone had chosen to dress in black to minimize the chances of discovery. Preparations were made in the garage of one of the men who lived near their destination.

When all was ready, the truck with its lights out was driven to within a block of the mosque. The steering wheel was tied to ensure that the truck would travel in a straight line from the point at which it was released toward the mosque. A cinder block was placed on the gas pedal, and the idling engine began racing. The brake was released, the gearshift placed in drive, and the two men leaped out of the cab. The one on the driver's side walked along the truck as it gathered speed, making small adjustments in the steering wheel to ensure that it was headed in the right direction. As it crossed the street adjacent to the mosque, two soldiers looked up in surprise to see a driverless truck heading toward them. They both sprinted out of the way, and then one said speculatively, "I wonder if that's a bomb?"

They both recognized the truth of that statement simultaneously and both yelled "Bomb!" into the night to their fellow soldiers, most of whom instinctively dove for the nearest cover.

No sooner had the soldiers hit the ground then there was a blinding flash and a deafening explosion. Gus had detonated the bomb just as it reached the mosque. Two soldiers at the rear of the mosque, who were without the benefit of the warning, were both knocked off their feet and both sustained serious concussions. Only their helmets and their flak jackets saved them from additional serious injuries or death.

The mosque was in ruins. The entire front wall of the building was demolished and without its support, and the dome toppled forward and landed upside down in the parking lot. The inside of the building was rubble, and everything made of wood was on fire. A fire alarm sounded uselessly in the ensuing quiet.

After viewing the destruction with satisfaction, the men from the First Baptist Church disappeared into the night. Most of them returned immediately to their homes and beds. A few hearty soles, including Gus, assembled at a prearranged bar located several miles from the scene. Except for the two GIs with concussions, no one had received so much as a scratch from the attack.

***

Lee Sanders, the FBI's SAC for the Baltimore region, sat in James Proctor's office prepared to provide an update for the director on the destruction that had occurred in the LA area. Jim and Lee had worked together at the FBI for many years and each respected the other's ability. Lee was looking forward to the discussion, hoping that Proctor might see something in the case that he had missed.

Proctor opened the discussion. "Lee, as you might expect, pressure is increasing from the White House to do something about the LA situation. It seems to me that we're on the verge of all-out war. Now that our troops are being killed, you can imagine the political heat being felt by the president."

"I've been worrying about that ever since the attack on the guard," responded Sanders. "We've been through a lot together, but I don't ever remember times as grim as these."

"You're right. We've got Gus stirring up the Christian crazies, and we suspect that Adam al-Zhihri from Bis Saif is stirring up the Muslim fanatics. A toxic combination, if I've ever seen one. I know your plate is full with your SAC responsibilities, but I need your help resolving this one. So I've made a command decision. I'm temporarily relieving you of your SAC responsibilities and making you the point man on the case of Christians vs. Bis Saif. You'll have to coordinate with Al Kaplan at the CIA, who coordinated the Special Forces attack on their HQ in Jakarta."

The director's phrasing of his assignment had a familiar ring to Sanders. "You mean I'm the point man on the case of Rome vs. the barbarians? What am I supposed to do, prevent Rome from falling to the barbarians? I sure hope that the end result is better for the United States than it was for the Romans."

"What a depressing analogy," answered the director. "I'm with you in the hope that we pull this one off. You've got the full resources of the FBI behind you, and probably the CIA as well. I think you should plan on traveling to LA as soon as possible so that you're closer to the action. But first, let's discuss this latest attack on the mosque."

"This looks like our friend Gus's work," opined Lee. "We've seen similar bombings in the DC area, but none as effective as this one. Thank God no one was killed."

"Why don't you interview your friend David and see what you can find out?" Proctor said.

"I'm pessimistic that he'll be able to shed much light on this, but nothing ventured nothing gained. As soon as I meet with David, I'm off to sunny power-free California." As Sanders left the director's office, he could hear him giving the president the bad news. Things were rapidly spiraling out of control in California, courtesy of individuals like Gus and Adam.

Prior to the director's suggestion, Sanders had contacted David Crain, the guy who had run into Gus in a Silver Spring bar, and who had volunteered to serve as an informant. It was Lee's plan to ensure that David's cooperation remain confidential, with the result that the two of them had gone to great pains to make sure their meetings appeared accidental. This time, Lee had suggested that they meet in a Silver Spring movie theater, sitting toward the rear of the theater and talking while the commercials were playing. No one watched the commercials anyway, so casual conversations in the theater weren't particularly noteworthy.

"So what do you know about Gus's current activities?" whispered Lee.

"He told me that he was going to get out of this cold weather and spend some time in the sun."

"Did he say where he was going?"

"He only said he was going to the West Coast."

"Did he say how he was going?"

"Yes, as a matter of fact, he did. He must have been flying because he said he had to be at Dulles by 7:00 a.m. He was complaining about the early hour."

"That's great. Very useful," Lee said. "You wouldn't happen to have a photo of him, would you?"

"No, I sure don't. How on earth would I get his picture without raising his suspicions?" Dave answered with his voice rising above a whisper.

"Yeah. You're right. Can you describe him? Any unique tattoos or other identifying characteristics?"

"Well, he's a big man. He's got a short beard. Hair is longish, combed back from his forehead. Just covers his collar. Dark hair, dark eyes. Favors jeans and plaid shirts. I'm afraid that's the best I can do."

"I think you've been a big help. Let's watch the movie." Lee's expression and voice were reassuring. David's information had actually been quite helpful.

The two of them sat through a Star Wars rerun they had both seen before, but if one of them had left, their rendezvous would have been noticed. As soon as the movie ended, they parted. David went to the men's room while Lee sprinted out of the theater to convey the information David had provided to agents waiting for his call.

Videos from Dulles Airport were immediately obtained, and agents watched hours of tapes for the time period during which it would be likely that Gus would have caught a plane to California. They were all keeping their fingers crossed that he had elected to take a nonstop flight and were soon rewarded to see a man matching David's description of Gus boarding a Delta flight for Los Angeles. Using facial recognition software, the FBI lab was able to identify him as Gus Waters, a professional protester with no fixed address. He had been arrested numerous times for misdemeanors in connection with his protest activities. The FBI had placed him on their watch list as a result of threatening letters he was suspected of having sent to various elected officials.

As soon as the identification was confirmed, he was placed on the FBI's ten most wanted list, which was sent to all law enforcement agencies, post offices, rail and bus stations, and TV stations in the United States. Within two hours, an agent at National Car Rental contacted the local FBI office to inform them that Gus had rented a white Chevrolet Impala and was headed for points unknown. The FBI notice was updated to reflect this additional information. The alert to the California Highway Patrol was reinforced by a phone call to the patrol to inform them of the importance of apprehending this individual.

Then Lee and his new California staff shifted their attention to apprehending Adam al-Zhihri, the leader of Bis Saif. This task was made easier by groundwork that had been performed by the CIA. Al Kaplan had furnished Lee with pictures of Adam from the Yale college yearbook, which had been photo modified to account for the years that had passed since his graduation. The CIA had also produced multiple versions of his possible appearance with a beard, with just a mustache, with eyeglasses, and with differing hair styles and colors. Approximately a dozen pictures in all. Lee and his California team produced circulars incorporating the CIA's pictures and distributed them along with Gus's photos. As part of his briefing of the FBI's local staff, army forces and local law enforcement agencies, Lee made it clear that their primary mission was to prevent war from breaking out between the Christians and Muslims.

***

With Tex's assistance, Adam was able to reconvene the group from the Hadad-Mahmood Mosque. At Adam's suggestion, they met in the ruins of the newly bombed mosque to ensure that they would be energized to extract the necessary revenge from the Christians.

Adam was a magnetic speaker, and he intended to prepare the group for a long-running conflict with their enemies. He began by reviewing the slights they had endured from other citizens in the LA area. He reminded them that Hispanics and blacks received preferential treatment from the federal government, while Muslims were treated with suspicion. He spoke of insults suffered by their wives and daughters when they were seen wearing a hijab or other head covering. When they were sufficiently aroused, he began telling them of the long-term goals of Bis Saif. He told them about the dreams of a worldwide caliphate that would unite all Muslims into a powerful force that would control the civilized world. When he finished his monolog, the congregation was ready to take on the world.

At the end of his pep talk Adam described the Bis Saif plan. "So now that you're all familiar with the possibilities worldwide, we need to discuss our next steps. Our friends in Iraq have already begun increasing their pressure on Western forces in the Middle East. With the assistance of Bis Saif, they have acquired surface-to-air missile systems that are shooting down the American war planes. We hope to arm them soon with surface-to-surface missiles they can use to sink American naval ships. Now it is up to us to begin increasing the pressure on the Americans here in California. The power failure was a start. Now we've got to increase the pressure. Are you all with me? If not, please leave now. There will be no repercussions from your departure."

Adam paused and looked around the room. Tex answered for the group. "Looks as if we're all on board. You got our adrenaline pumping."

Seeing everyone nodding, Adam laid out his plan. "We'll begin with an attack guaranteed to get the attention of the American government. Without doubt, it will get the attention of the FBI and the army. So we can expect a lot of attention. Make plans to disappear into the general population so that our group becomes invisible. Find a friend or relative who will swear that you were home on the night of the attack. As soon as we return from our target, immediately resume your normal routine. Anyone caught revealing the existence of our group will be dealt with. We are a brotherhood. We live and die together." He concluded with his voice rising. "Allahu Akbar!"

Everyone loudly and emotionally repeated "Allahu Akbar." Adam now had the support he needed to execute the first phase of his plan.

That evening, three cars mysteriously vanished from the valet parking lot at the Green Turtle Restaurant in Santa Monica. Their theft was carefully timed to occur shortly after their owners had arrived to dine at the restaurant, and during a period when the cabinet in which the valets had placed the owners' keys was not being watched. The "borrowed" cars were driven from the valet parking lot at a sedate pace, only accelerating as they continued south to Anaheim, when they were out of sight of the restaurant. The three cars trailed each other as they left Whittier for the I-5 freeway. Taking the Lincoln Avenue exit, they headed directly for Disneyland, the first of the Magic Kingdoms. Each of the cars carried four passengers, all dressed in black and all carrying rapid-fire automatic weapons. They drove through the large Disneyland parking lot, ignored the barricades, jumped the curb, and drove onto the large plaza with the mosaic pattern intended to welcome visitors to the Magic Kingdom. It was a busy day, and there were long lines at the eight entry gates waiting to purchase their tickets and celebrate the season at Disney's fairgrounds.

As they drove onto the plaza, ignoring the orders of the security guards and other members of the Disney staff, each car braked to a halt, disgorging its four rifle-carrying passengers who began pouring automatic fire into the waiting crowds. The lack of resistance from security guards or anyone else encouraged the terrorists, so that they abandoned their plans to restrict their attack to the entry gates. They ran through the now-unattended gates onto the plaza and continued their slaughter inside the manicured grounds of the theme park. It was as if they were mowing a field of wheat. Everywhere they turned with their blazing rifles, people were falling. After what seemed an eternity to the survivors, but was only ten minutes, the twelve terrorists calmly walked back to their vehicles and slowly drove away. They were out of sight by the time sirens were heard in the distance. By then, the terrorists were well on their way back to Wittier.

The massacre was horrific, with a total of 105 dead and 264 injured, many seriously.

The entire operation was completed within forty-five minutes. The three cars were driven to a long-term parking lot at the Los Angeles Airport. Their drivers were picked up by Tex and driven to their homes. By the time the Bis Saif twitter message was received by the news outlets in the LA region, taking credit for the attack, the drivers and their passengers were tucked into their own beds.

The tweet was crafted to inflame the growing conflict between the Christians and Muslims. "Bis Saif and the Muslim community is proud of its strike against Christians. Citizens of America, be prepared for a second crusade. Eventually we will witness your downfall."

***

"We're not going to take this lying down. The namby-pamby government may tolerate the murdering bastards, but the only solution is to teach them a lesson and force them out of the country. We don't want them here, and we need to let them know." As he spoke, Gus gradually got himself worked up until he was nearly screaming at the end.

The group was with him. The end of his speech was accompanied by a cacophony of supporting "Yeahs."

Gus now had his allies eating out of his hand. "I've been thinking long and hard about this, and I've come to the conclusion we've got to do something that will really make a difference. So here's my plan. We've got to start with serious harassment of the ragheads. By harassment, I mean fire-bombing their mosques, homes, and businesses, beating up their people on the street, annoying their women, and anything else that you can think of that will convince them they don't want to live here. We'll be giving you a course in making Molotov cocktails after we're done here. How does that sound?"

Everyone in the room was excited by the prospect of being part of a program of creative violence. So Gus's little speech was met with applause. Encouraged, he unveiled the rest of his plan.

"There are about thirty of us here right now. Eventually the army or the FBI will be able to find us and shut us down. So here's the second part of my plan. I believe that everyone in this room has five or ten friends they can count on. And each of your five or ten friends has five or ten more friends. If we can grow this thing to include hundreds or even thousands of people that feel like we do, they'll never track us down and they'll never be able to stop us. How about a show of hands? How many of you have at least five people you can count on?"

Every hand in the room was raised.

"How many have at least ten people you can count on?"

Again every hand in the room was raised.

Gus decided to demonstrate his mathematical skills. "So there are around thirty of us. If I multiply thirty times ten, that means we'll have three hundred people joining our cause. And if each of those three hundred has ten friends, we'll have three thousand people. How about that!"

The excitement in the room was palpable. Earl, one of the younger members of the group responded. "What are we waiting for?"

"We're not waiting for anything. We begin right now," answered Gus. "Gather round for a class in the construction of Molotov cocktails. They're best used if thrown from a motorcycle speeding past the target. That way, it's doubtful that anyone would be able to catch you."

The remainder of the session was spent showing how easy it was to make the device using a breakable glass bottle filled with gasoline and a little motor oil. The wick, which is soaked in alcohol or kerosene, is shoved into the bottle's neck and held by the stopper. The wick is lit, the bottle is thrown, and when it shatters, the wick causes the contents to explode. The group was enthralled by the simplicity of the device, and they were further enthralled when Gus demonstrated its use in the parking lot behind the church.

Gus concluded the meeting following the demonstration. "So let's get started. Don't forget to enlist your friends. That's top priority. Then decide what you're going to do, but don't discuss it with anyone else in the group. If someone is arrested, we all want to be able to claim ignorance. I'll watch for your progress on the evening news. Go get 'em!"

This was the beginning of a serious conflict between the Christians and the Muslims. Ironically, the plans of Adam and Gus were working toward similar ends, that of uniting Muslims. The difference was that Adam wanted Muslim unity for the purpose of establishing a worldwide caliphate that could withstand and even defeat the United States. Gus just wanted the Muslims to leave. His thinking, as that of many like-minded individuals, did not encompass all possible outcomes of the movement he had started.

***

But Adam's plans were broader and less parochial than those of Gus. Adam was focused on a worldwide conflict leading to the unity of all Muslims, particularly Sunni Muslims. With 1.6 billion adherents, the extent of the Muslim religion was comparable to that of Christianity, with its 2.2 billion followers. The Muslim religion was also growing more rapidly than Christianity, and Adam felt that Muslims tended to be more devout than Christians. For these reasons, he questioned the validity of the statistics. So it was time to plan for the dominance of Allah worldwide. After all, he reasoned, Christianity's current position of worldwide dominance could be traced to its aggressive nature during the Middle Ages, as represented by the Crusades, the Spanish Inquisition, and many other barbaric activities.

With these thoughts in mind, he composed a coded message to Ali, his ISIS ally, using the encryption system through which he had provided the surface-to-air missile systems.

"We have the Americans on the run. They have massive problems in their country. Now is the time for a big offensive. They will have difficulty fighting wars in the Middle East and containing unrest in America. We can help with money and supplies if needed."

When the message had been sent, Adam sat back and considered other avenues for widening the conflict in a way that would weaken America. He didn't feel that the Palestinians would be much help since Israel would take care of any problems they might create. He had cut his ties with Boko Haram, so they were not an option. No. He would have to rely on ISIS and their Mideast allies to expand the battle.

***

Ali did not disappoint Adam. As soon as he received the message, he requested a meeting with General Hussain. With his status as a hero from the battle of Kirkuk, his success in obtaining SAMs from Bis Saif, and several other battlefield victories, Ali had become a confidant of the mercurial general. He was skilled at staying on the general's good side, and knew how to avoid incurring his wrath.

As he entered Hussain's tent, he gave a token salute and began speaking as soon as the general looked up from his paperwork. "Sir, I just received a significant message from my contact at Bis Saif."

"I thought the Americans had destroyed them," replied the general.

"I had worried that might be true, but he is now somewhere unknown, making more trouble for the Americans."

"Apparently your friend is like a cat with nine lives."

"Sir, let me read you the message."

When Ali finished reading the five-sentence message, the general rocked back in his chair and stared at the canvas top of the tent. After a long silence, he replied, "This might be the opportunity we've been waiting for. I've been feeling that our war is currently at a stalemate. We capture a few cities. The Western pigs bomb us and drive us back. Then we capture a few more cities, and the cycle is repeated. If we do this right, we may be able to change things in our favor."

"That is a brilliant analysis," said Ali, never missing an opportunity to flatter Hussain.

"So I think we should immediately act on this," added Hussain, as if Ali had never spoken. "I want you and Mohammed to bring me the plans for a full-scale offensive by tomorrow morning at this time. The plan should be simple so we can begin the offensive within a few days."

"Yes, sir," answered Ali as he exited the general's tent.

And so a second major front was opened in the conflict between Christians and Muslims.

CHAPTER 28

A STATE OF EMERGENCY

The three calls arrived nearly simultaneously at Jan's desk at the White House. The callers included James Proctor of the FBI, General Elliot Drake of the Joint Chiefs, and Janice DeBeers of Homeland Security. While she was fielding the calls, George Wilson showed up at her desk.

My God, thought Jan. *What on earth is going on? This sure doesn't sound good.*

George tried to preempt the calls. "Jan, I've got to talk to the president immediately. Things are not good in California."

Always in control, Jan decided to get things organized. She buzzed the president. "Mr. President, we've got a bad situation developing in California. I've got Drake, DeBeers, and Proctor on hold and George standing here outside your office. Should I get everyone to join you in the Situation Room ASAP?"

"Go ahead, Jan," was the reply. Jeffers appreciated Jan's ability to get things organized on the spur of the moment. But this didn't sound good. He suspected it was going to require some extreme measures to get things under control.

George loitered outside the Oval Office until the president could wrap things up and head to the Situation Room. He had been discussing needed budget changes in order to deal with the many unpleasant things unfolding both in the United States and the Middle East. The result of this discussion was a splitting headache. Chris didn't often get headaches, but the pressure of the last few weeks had begun taking its toll.

George briefed Jeffers as the two walked to the Situation Room. "It's my understanding that things are rapidly becoming unraveled in California. You already know about the Disneyland attack from yesterday. Well the "good guys" have decided to take matters into their own hands. They appear to be seeking revenge and have begun a program of firebombing, assaults, at least one rape, and two murders. Most of this is concentrated in the LA area, but it's beginning to spread out of control throughout the state. If we don't contain it, I personally don't think it will be long until it spreads nationally. The man who we think is instigating this trouble already is known to have connections in the Washington, DC region, so he can readily begin his evil program on the East Coast, beginning in our backyard."

As was his practice when faced with a knotty problem, Jeffers remained silent. After an extended pause, he asked Wilson, "Has the FBI made any progress tracking down the leaders of these movements?"

"You'll have to ask Proctor when he gets here. The last I heard, they haven't made much progress beyond getting the pictures and background histories of the ringleaders."

"What about the army?"

"Here again, it's best to get it from the horse's mouth. I'm sure Drake will be able to fill you in. That's all anybody has been working on for the past forty-eight hours."

Apologetically, Wilson continued. "I'm sorry I can't be more informative, but this thing has been developing so rapidly that I can barely keep up with all my contacts."

Jeffers wasn't in the mood for blaming anyone. "George, I know you're doing the best you can. I'm also doing the best I can. I'm just afraid that I'm letting the country down. I think we're going to have to take some drastic measures."

With that, the two of them walked in silence along with their Secret Service escorts until they reached the Situation Room.

***

A grim group was gathered in the Situation Room. This group was a subset of the task force that usually assembled to discuss these measures. All members of the President's War Cabinet were present, including George Wilson, the DNI, the president, and the ever-present Jan. It was clear that they had all adapted to the power failure, since all were neatly attired in business suits and uniforms.

Jeffers opened the meeting, as usual. "I'm really getting tired of these gatherings. I don't know about all of you, but I don't feel as if we're making much progress. I guess the best way of beginning this meeting is to get reports from each of you. Please tell us what you know of the present situation as well as your progress in each of your areas. Keep it brief, since I don't think we have much time to act. Jim, why don't you lead off? Tell us about the FBI's progress."

"Mr. President, I've got everyone in the LA office working on this. I've moved Lee Sanders to that office to lead the team. So far, we've got photos and drawings of both Adam al-Zhihri and Gus Waters, as well as backgrounds on both men. We've also been intensively interviewing those who know them best. For Adam, we've been interviewing Udo from Nigeria, Kelly and Jim, the computer experts, and Kelly's parents, who were arrested while we were looking for Bis Saif. We've got a good profile for Adam, including his early life, his parents, siblings, and the creation of Bis Saif. For Gus, we've been in contact with the only individual who seems to know him. A guy that met him in a bar in Silver Spring, Maryland. He doesn't seem to have many friends or relatives, so we're not sure why he's become such a fanatic except for the possibility that either he lost his job to a Muslim, or a Muslim did something bad to someone close to him. We've distributed his picture, including possible variations that might exist on the possibility that he has assumed different disguises. The pictures of both Adam and Gus have been distributed throughout California and posted on the Internet and TV news broadcasts. Every law enforcement official in the state of California is carrying these pictures. It goes without saying that they're both on the FBI's most wanted list." As he finished, James Proctor leaned back in his chair, obviously fatigued from the pressure of the past few days.

"So in other words, some progress, but we've got a way to go," Jeffers said.

Proctor just nodded and added, "By the way, Donald Squlo, our favorite representative, has been in his home district of Orange County, California, stirring up yet more trouble. He's continuing his campaign theme of nuking the Arabs to his fellow Californians, and they're buying his message. Some serious anti-Squlo publicity would sure be helpful."

"Let's discuss that when all of the others have reported. Janice, why don't you go next?" said Jeffers. Then with a nod and a half smile at General Drake, he added sarcastically, "I'm saving the best for last."

"Well I don't have a lot to add to my previous reports. Things are staggering along in California. Our system is strained by the fact that most people don't want to leave their homes in spite of the fact they have no power, no heat, no jobs, and no school. Their stay is made easier by the fact that the weather has been mild. And they're very worried about the security of their property. The army is doing a great job," she said, nodding to General Drake, "but they can't guard every dwelling in California twenty-four hours a day."

"Anything else?" asked Jeffers, anxious to move the meeting along.

"There are some small items of good news. I'd like to update the statistics I'd provided at the last meeting regarding the number of people leaving the blacked-out area. Because of the violence in the area, there has been another surge of families migrating to the facilities we've established in neighboring states. This has somewhat eased the strain on the services we're trying to provide in California. The other good news is that power is beginning to be restored in the Washington, DC region. As that happens, it frees up generators and other items for use in California. So we're making a little progress."

"Thanks, Janice. And now, the long-dreaded report from General Drake," said Jeffers as he swiveled to face the solemn-faced Chairman of the Joint Chiefs.

Drake, who had remained silent up that point, sighed and pulled his chair up to the table. "I've got two reports to make. Neither of them is good. One concerns the situation in California, and the other the Middle East."

380

Jeffers realized that it might have been a mistake to limit the meeting to those present and said, "Do you think that Matt O'Brien should be here to provide the CIA's perspective?"

"No, I think the current group is fine. If we need the CIA, we can talk to him later," opined the general, who was always more comfortable when the CIA was absent. "So let me first talk about the situation in California. As you all know, the situation there is terrible and rapidly deteriorating. While the troops have been able to keep some things under control, the events at the mosque and Disneyland are more the responsibility of the FBI and local law enforcement than ours. They have the ability to conduct criminal investigations, and they have the power to arrest suspects, whereas we don't."

"Good point," interrupted the president as he made a note on the pad in front of him.

"What we are trying to do is prevent vandalism and conflicts between the citizens. Our troops have been somewhat successful at that. Nothing helps like carrying a loaded rifle, although it wasn't much good at the mosque. Listening to Ms. DeBeers describe the concerns of citizens about their property being vandalized, I made a quick calculation using some questionable numbers regarding the troop strength needed to provide one-hundred-percent security. There are about two hundred thousand residences within the City of LA. Assuming one soldier can guard ten residences, we'd need twenty thousand troops in the City of Los Angeles alone. If LA is one tenth of the State of California, we'd need about two hundred thousand troops to achieve the high level of security requested by its residents. Even if half the load is picked up by local law enforcement, we'd need four or five divisions, or more than twice our current troop strength. This would drain our resources worldwide, which is a bad idea, as I will explain in a minute. But before doing so, are there any questions about the California situation?"

James Proctor spoke up. "I've got a question. Admittedly our investigation is going slowly, but in the meantime, we've got to prevent a repeat of any more incidents similar to the two we've had so far. Our intelligence tells us that there are discussions of revenge underway among both groups. But our intelligence isn't good enough to tell us the nature of the revenge. Any ideas about prevention?"

"I've been giving this a lot of thought," answered Drake. "First, recognize that I'm not a law enforcement officer. I'm a soldier. Realize that this is also true of my subordinates. But that having been said, we need to flood the area with peacekeepers, including soldiers, police, FBI, and perhaps deputized police from other states. One other helpful thing would be to provide my soldiers with the authority to arrest perpetrators. We have that authority in foreign countries, but not in the United States. At some point we may have to construct a stockade to house all the arrests that are made once we get the authority. My people are working on that with the Justice Department."

Proctor nodded as if a question had been answered, although he was far from satisfied. "Please continue, general."

"Since there are no more questions, let me now move to the second issue, a possible impending ISIS offensive in the near future. What I am about to tell you is highly classified. The information about its existence is not to leave this room." The general then removed a piece of paper from his locked briefcase, put on his reading glasses, and read the email that Adam had sent to Ali. The email had been decrypted by the NSA, who had been watching for emails of this nature.

The email rocked Jeffers, who was hearing Adam's message for the first time. "Now we've really got our hands full. General, have you discussed this with our allies?"

"Not yet. I just received this on the way here this afternoon."

"Well, this is one that we cannot handle ourselves. Particularly with our domestic situations, which will be placing quite a strain on the military."

"I agree and will get on it as soon as this meeting is concluded."

It was Jeffers turn to speak. "Like the general's email, the subject I am about to raise is not to leave this room. If it does, and we learn of the source, that person will be terminated. I am aware of the general's concern that his troops do not have the authority to arrest individuals involved with the clashes in California. We've got other serious problems there, including too many firearms, the slow court system that puts the perpetrators back on the streets to continue their activities, and the ability of the terrorist leadership to travel throughout the region without restriction. I've been having discussions with the Justice Department, who feels that the appropriate response would be to declare a state of emergency in California, with the possibility of expanding it to include the entire United States if the problems spread. In case you are unfamiliar with the concept of a state of emergency, it is a polite way of describing martial law. It is within my prerogative to make such a declaration. I will be sending a letter to Congress and making a speech to the nation this evening. General, I believe this will solve your problem of lack of arresting authority, since the state of emergency will include those powers. Any questions?"

There were dozens of questions, and the meeting dragged on for another hour while the various participants determined the impact that a state of emergency would have on their various responsibilities. General Drake and James Proctor were delighted, feeling that a declaration of this nature would greatly simplify their jobs. Janice DeBeers was concerned that the Department of Homeland Security would now be responsible for housing the dozens, if not hundreds of people that might be arrested. They all raised the question of where the money was coming from, a question that plagued the president as well. When he felt that all present had a thorough understanding of the situation, he adjourned the meeting, saying, "Watch the news. I'll be speaking to Congress and the American people within the next twenty-four hours. My talks are being prepared as we speak."

***

Much to the annoyance of the viewing public, the prime time TV programs were preempted by a speech from the President of the United States. Most politicians were well aware of the fact

383

that the viewing public had little interest in current events. They rarely watched the evening news or read newspapers, and were annoyed when current events intruded on their favorite forms of entertainment, whether it was reality TV or sports. A common excuse for ignorance of current events was that "The news is so depressing, I don't pay attention to it anymore." Yet many of these people were not embarrassed to vote or express their uninformed opinions on any subject. But this time, the president was determined to grab their attention.

Once again he spoke from the Oval Office in a speech that was carried by all of the national TV and radio networks.

He began with the traditional introduction. "Good evening, my fellow Americans. I am speaking to you this evening about a crisis our country is facing that is more serious than almost any we have encountered in the past. Yes, it's more serious than a stock market crash. It's more serious than most of our past wars. It's more serious than a major natural disaster. I say this because we are faced with a crisis that threatens the very foundation of our democracy. Let me begin with a quote from the Declaration of Independence, which I cited in my last talk with you. It is a quote that defines the moral standard by which this country is governed, and one that is engrained in the beliefs of the great majority of our citizens. It goes as follows: 'We hold these truths to be self-evident, that all men are created equal, that they are endowed by their Creator with certain unalienable rights, that among these are life, liberty and the pursuit of happiness.' Abraham Lincoln considered this statement to be the basis for his political philosophy and a statement of principles through which the United States Constitution should be interpreted. I personally share Lincoln's beliefs on this subject.

"So let's consider what the Declaration of Independence says and what it doesn't say. It says that all men are created equal. It does not say that some are better than others depending on their religious affiliation or country of origin. It also says that all men have equal rights, which include the ability to conduct their lives as they choose in freedom. It does not say that they should be attacked by others who feel they are superior.

"Recently, several situations have occurred in this country in which the principles of the Bill of Rights have been flagrantly violated. They include attacks by American citizens on other American citizens. They include attacks on religious institutions. And they include attacks aimed at members of the US Army. These attacks have not been limited to a single group, nor have they been limited to members of a particular religion. However, in all cases these attacks have been religiously motivated. They have degraded into attacks and counterattacks until it appears that the United States of America, a country founded on the Bill of Rights and our Constitution, appears to be sinking into the abyss of an all-out religious war. This is a contradiction of the very principles on which this country was founded. It contradicts the beliefs of most Americans. And it contradicts the foundation of the US Constitution, a document that I swore to uphold and defend when I was inaugurated into the Office of the President of the United States. These attacks represent a situation that I cannot and will not tolerate. As President of the United States, it is my intent to honor the principles that I swore to uphold with all of the tools at my disposal."

At that point Jeffers paused for a drink of water from the glass on his desk with the intent of letting his introductory remarks sink in.

"It is my intent to put an end to the violence that has occurred. For this reason, I am declaring a state of emergency for all of California. This state of emergency is equivalent to the declaration of martial law. The Army's III Corps, currently headquartered in Fort Hood, Texas, will be relocated to California to enforce the state of emergency. Effective immediately, the following actions will be in effect:

"First, I am suspending a significant element of the First Amendment of the US Constitution. For those of you that are not constitutional scholars, the First Amendment prohibits making any law that prevents the free exercise of religion, freedom of speech, freedom of the press, and peaceful assembly. It also prevents suing the government for compensation of grievances. This amendment is fundamental to our American way of life.

However, during the state of emergency, I am suspending those sections of the amendment related to freedom of speech, the press, and the rights of assembly. In other words, any speeches or printed material intended to incite further religious violence will be treated as illegal acts, subject to the arrest of the offending parties. I am also suspending the First Amendment's assurance of the right of peaceful assembly. During the period that the state of emergency is in effect, there will be no public gatherings held for the purpose of inciting further religious violence. The interpretation of this suspension will be left to the judgment of the military commanders on the scene.

"Second, I am suspending the Second Amendment of the US Constitution, which gives citizens the right to keep and bear arms, in the following manner. Citizens will have the right to continue to own weapons to the extent that they are kept for home security, hunting, and as keepsakes. However, weapons are not to be carried outside of the home or place of business, and they are not to be used to threaten others. Violators of this restriction will be dealt with harshly.

"Third, I am temporarily suspending the writ of habeas corpus for those arrested within the State of California. If you are not familiar with legal terms, this is the provision in the law that prevents the possibility of an individual being detained without reason for an unreasonable length of time. In other words, it requires arresting authorities to present the legal basis for the arrest. The basis for this suspension is Article One, Section Nine of the US Constitution, which states that 'The privileges of the writ of habeas corpus shall not be suspended unless when, in cases of rebellion of invasion, the public safety may require it.' I claim that the public safety is currently at stake, and by suspending the writ, the military commanders on the scene will be able to arrest individuals who threaten this safety without being required to justify the detention.

"Fourth, I am imposing travel restrictions between the state of California and other parts of the United States. Those desiring to enter or leave the state must apply for a pass to do so. Justification for travel may include the following: business purposes, health care, and support of needy relatives. In order to obtain a pass, an individual must present proof of identity and documentation justifying the reasons for their travel.

"Fifth, the military authorities governing under this state of emergency are granted the power to impose curfews throughout California. Curfew times are to be determined based on local conditions, and will be modified periodically on an as-needed basis. You will be subject to arrest if you are outside of a dwelling during the curfew period.

"Sixth, I am exercising the rights granted to me under the New War Powers Act to grant law enforcement and military authorities the right of search, seizure, and confiscation without requiring a court order or search warrant prior to initiating the action. Seizure may include any drugs, arms, and contraband discovered during the search.

"I know that these six measures may appear draconian, but I am forced to impose them due to the severity of the current situation. I am determined to regain control of the situation in California and return it to its rightful place as a major contributor to the prosperity of America. Let me add that it is possible that the conditions in California will spread to other parts of the United States. If that occurs, it is my intent to repeat this process in the future for states that are similarly affected.

"I pray that all Americans will work together to restore this country to its position as a model for the peaceful coexistence of its citizens. Thank you, and good night."

***

The response of the news media reflected that of the general public. Many in California were relieved that the government was going to take some action against the Bis Saif terrorists. Others were relieved that both sides would be brought under control. Californians that reveled in conspiracy theory were convinced that this was a power grab by President Jeffers, who was trying to anoint himself the emperor of the United States. Many speculated about the next region to be declared a state of emergency. Some predicted that it would be the entire country. In fact, no one, not even Jeffers, knew where this was heading.

Although the *Los Angeles Times* is generally considered a liberal newspaper, its headline expressed relief when its banner read: "HELP IS ON THE WAY! THE PRESIDENT RESPONDS TO CALIFORNIA'S CRISIS."

Other liberal newspapers were less enthusiastic. The *Washington Post's* front page read: "JEFFERS TAKES CONTROL OF CALIFORNIA'S GOVERNMENT."

The conservative newspapers provided a unique interpretation of the executive order. The *New York Post* headline was typical. "JEFFERS ACTS TO GET THE MUSLIMS UNDER CONTROL."

The *Wall Street Journal* was more thoughtful. "JEFFERS DECLARES STATE OF EMERGENCY IN CALIFORNIA. WILL THAT ELIMINATE RELIGIOUS CONFRONTATIONS?"

The editorials reflected the sentiments of the headline writers. Most of the editors respected the logic of the executive order. But they raised the same questions that were on the minds of the American public following Jeffers' speech. They wondered where this was going to end. Would the entire nation soon be under a state of emergency? They also wondered if it would do any good. Would stationing 40,000 troops in California actually bring the problem under control?

Some of the more thoughtful editors raised a question that appeared to be the end result of the deteriorating situation. The following paragraph from an editorial printed in *The New York Times* was representative.

> *By declaring a state of emergency in California, the president assumed sweeping powers. Not all of these powers are granted to him by the US Constitution. Admittedly, he is Commander in Chief of the country's armed forces, but this powerful prerogative does not give him the right to assume control over the civilian population of the United States. While we do not question the need for this action, and we pray that it may produce the desired end result,*

we question its legality. A look back into ancient history reveals some parallels between Jeffers' actions and those of Julius Caesar of the Roman Empire. The similarities between Caesar and Jeffers is compelling. Caesar, like Jeffers, was descended from an intellectual family. After his famous crossing of the Rubicon north of Rome, he used his legions to bend the Roman Senate to his will. He was ultimately named dictator for life by the Senate. Will this history be repeated in the United States?"

Editorials of this nature were read with concern by the general public as well as their elected officials.

***

Donald Squlo, a member of the US House of Representatives, was one elected official who was determined not to let this happen. Shortly after Jeffers' speech, Squlo booked a flight from Dulles Airport, in Washington, DC, to John Wayne Airport, in Orange County, California. In the opinion of the soldier enforcing the order, his status as a congressman enabled him to bypass the restriction on travel to California included in the executive order. While the opinion may be divided on the wisdom of the soldier's decision, the end result proved that it was definitely the wrong thing to do.

Before leaving, Squlo instructed his aides to organize a gathering of his supporters at the Honda Center in Anaheim. His choice of location was intentional. Home of the Anaheim Ducks hockey team, and almost within sight of Disneyland where the terrorist event had occurred, the center served as the perfect setting for his rabble-rousing speech.

His staff excelled at organizing gatherings of this nature. During his campaign for Congress, Squlo would frequently decide that some recent event would provide him with an opportunity to arouse the public in his heavily Republican and staunchly right-wing district. The staff's organizational ability was amply demonstrated at this gathering, attended by nearly 2,000 of Squlo's supporters. Although he was well aware that the executive order had forbade demonstrations and speeches of this nature, the gathering was billed as an informational presentation in order to avoid arrest by the army.

Their flight landed at John Wayne Airport on time, shortly before noon. After signing for their rental car, Congressman Squlo with his two aides drove directly to the Honda Center, arriving by 1:00 p.m., comfortably before the scheduled time of his rally. The center was already a beehive of activity, which included early arriving fans, TV cameras, and reporters. It also included a large contingent of heavily armed troops and police, many equipped with riot gear.

"Looks as if we're going to get some good publicity out of this," observed Squlo, not missing the point that he was currently up for reelection.

His aides just nodded as they ushered him into one of the center's waiting rooms. They were accustomed to Squlo's full-time obsession with his reelection.

Promptly at 2:00 p.m., the chairman of the Orange County Republican Committee walked up to the podium on a stage filled with American flags. "It fills me with pride that my countrymen are willing to attend a rally in the middle of the workday, in a state without electric power. As we all know, this situation was caused by ISIS and their allies Bis Saif, a group dedicated to America's downfall. And now I'd like to introduce an individual who is leading the fight against our enemies. An individual who is devoted to putting some backbone into our government so that they will take the appropriate actions to defeat those who are arrayed against us. Please join me in welcoming Congressman Donald Squlo, a man who is not afraid of confronting our enemies."

The introduction was met with deafening applause and a roar of support. Squlo walked onto the stage in the midst of the noise, waving his arms as he walked to the podium.

"My fellow Americans," he began. "It is a privilege to address you at this time of great stress. You have survived a power failure and a terrorist attack, and yet you keep on going. You are all demonstrating the strength and fortitude that makes me proud to be an American."

The crowd had grown silent, looking forward to the fire and brimstone speech for which Squlo was well known.

"Last night, President Jeffers issued an executive order that he called the declaration of a state of emergency. The details of this so-called state of emergency put the US Army in charge of the State of California. They now have the right to arrest any citizen for any reason and place them in custody indefinitely. That's what the suspension of habeas corpus means. It also gives the army the right to search you and your homes for any reason, without requiring a search permit. They can also confiscate any of your possessions for any reason. Maybe most importantly, they have outlawed your right to bear arms. You cannot carry weapons of any sort, either concealed or unconcealed. This means that you will not be able to defend yourselves against the evil forces that are at large.

"While I'm certain that President Jeffers is a well-meaning individual, both he and his advisors suffer from the lack of willingness to take the forceful actions needed to solve our problems in California, the United States, and the world. Instead of enlisting your assistance in rooting out our enemies and eliminating them, our president is preventing you from defending yourselves and taking matters into your own hands. Is our Jeffers a coward? This is unacceptable." With his voice rising, he added, "We the citizens of California need to take our state back!"

With that, a riotous cheer erupted from the crowd. Squlo had cleverly tapped into the fears of those present.

The police and soldiers that had surrounded the hall shifted their positions nervously. Several spoke into their radios, looking for orders from the command post that had been set up in a trailer parked outside the center. Apparently receiving orders to do nothing, they resumed their defensive stances and continued to watch the proceedings.

"So I'm here to ask you to do your part while I do mine. I intend to return to Washington to engage my fellow congressmen and women in a movement to take back the government from our new leader—Emperor Jeffers! In the meantime, it is my hope that you will take all the actions that you feel are appropriate to convince Muslims to leave this state."

As he paused to take another sip of water, someone in the crowd fired a pistol into the air. During the investigations that followed the event, it was never clear how the pistol had been smuggled into the center. The shot galvanized the police and soldiers guarding the entrances to the arena. An army major who appeared to be in charge of the troops immediately picked up a bullhorn and announced, "This meeting is now at an end. If you do not want to be arrested, please file out of the center in an orderly fashion. All people leaving will be searched for weapons. Any weapons found during the search will be confiscated and their owners arrested."

At the same time a phalanx of soldiers lined up in front of the stage from which Squlo had been speaking. Three of the soldiers jumped onto the stage. Two of them held the loudly protesting congressman while the third handcuffed him. He was then led from the stage through a side door to a waiting black Chevrolet SUV, which sped off to points unknown. The entire arrest was completed in less than two minutes.

It took considerably longer to clear the center. Each door was guarded by two soldiers and a policeman. Presumably the police presence ensured the legality of the arrest process, even though the army had already been granted these rights by the state of emergency declared by the president. One by one the audience filed through the door. Everyone was subject to a search of their handbags and backpacks, as well as a pat down. The latter was accompanied by much grumbling and many protests, but the soldiers were in no mood for argument and the process proceeded in a slow but orderly manner. The entire process required more than forty-five minutes until the hall was empty. Three of the attendees were arrested, two for carrying concealed weapons, and one for resisting the inspection process. The three shortly joined Squlo at the Anaheim Detention Facility on Harbor Boulevard, a few blocks from the center.

CHAPTER 29

FEAR IS A POWERFUL MOTIVATOR

Minneapolis's Riverside Plaza is Minnesota's largest public housing development and home to 4,000 mostly Somali Muslims. Originally attracted to Minneapolis by the availability of well-paying jobs and the friendly nature of Minnesotans, the Somali population of Minnesota exceeded 100,000, many of whom were uneducated. More than sixty percent lived below the poverty line. The combination of impoverished families sharing communities with middle-class and wealthy Minnesotans was a toxic mix, offering a breeding ground for the creation of potential jihadists. The number of young people attracted to jihadist organizations was typified by the more than forty young Somalis who left the Minnesota area for Somalia to join al Shabab, the local terrorist organization. Others remained in Minneapolis with dreams of inflicting pain on their current homeland in the name of Muslim supremacy.

The declaration of a state of emergency in California energized Minneapolis's Somali youth. If their brothers in California could disrupt the government to such an extent, shouldn't they support them? Together they might make a difference. One of the many small Somali gangs operating in Minneapolis decided to make just such a difference.

Three days following the arrest of Congressman Squlo in Anaheim, a bomb exploded in a trash can near the entrance to Macy's at the Mall of America, in Bloomington, Minnesota. Located approximately fifteen minutes from downtown Minneapolis, it was one of the largest enclosed malls in the United States, and because of its size, with more than 520 shops and fifty restaurants, it was a popular destination for both tourists

Philip J. Tarnoff

and shoppers. By terrorist standards, the damage caused by
the explosion was relatively minor, killing no one and injur-
ing a dozen passers-by. It also broke a plate glass window and
damaged the store's marble fascia. The event was newsworthy
because of the note that was spray painted on the storefront in
Somali Arabic, indicating that it was part of a worldwide jihad
inspired by ISIS and Bis Saif.

The Minneapolis police and the FBI cooperated in an
investigation intended to arrest the perpetrators. Although he
was very busy with the investigations in California, Lee Sanders flew to Minneapolis for a firsthand look at the crime scene
and for discussions with local investigators. It was a frustrating
investigation that had to be conducted without the cooperation
of the Somalian population because of language barriers, suspicion of enforcement agencies, and fear of gang reprisals. As a
result, the police made little progress, and Sanders returned to
California to continue his search for Adam al-Zhihri and Gus
Waters, a search which was proving to be equally difficult,
although for different reasons.

The Somali gangs did not consider their mall bomb a failure. Rather, they considered it a practice run for bigger and
better things. Anxious not to be overshadowed by the gang
that planted the bomb, rival gangs began planning their own
attacks. Within a period of two weeks, four additional explosions occurred with varying degrees of effectiveness. Targets
included the airport, two shopping malls, and an office building.
At the end of the two weeks, more than thirty people had been
injured and two killed.

Minnesota ranks seventeenth in terms of gun ownership.
Nearly fifty percent of the population owns guns, which is not
surprising in a mostly rural state where hunting is a popular sport.
The gun owners of Minneapolis were not about to take the terrorist attacks lying down. They felt that the various governments
responsible for public safety were too slow to move, and as a
result, they were allowing the Muslim community to literally get
away with murder. A group of vigilantes based in the twin city of
St. Paul decided to take matters into their own hands.

Within two days following the attack at the Mall of America, five Minnesotan vigilantes approached one of the Riverside Plaza buildings that served as public housing for Somalian refugees. This cluster of buildings, looking like construction out of Soviet-era public housing, offered a gray façade, which the city had attempted to make more attractive by using randomly placed colored panels between the windows on the exterior walls. But Riverside Plaza remained an upscale slum.

The five men entered the lobby and took the stairs to the second floor. All were armed with rifles or shotguns, and all were dressed in the camouflage popular with duck hunters. One of the men stationed himself at the fire stairs leading to the exit. The second stood by the elevator. The remaining three marched down the hall and pounded on the door of the first apartment. A young pregnant Somali woman answered the door, looking shocked when she saw the three vigilantes.

"We want to talk to your son."

"I have no son. I don't know what you want," she responded with a heavy African accent.

"You'd better be telling the truth," threatened the leader of the three, turning on his heel to lead the group to the next apartment, where they had better luck.

Their knock on the door was answered by a teenage boy who looked as if he was seventeen or eighteen. He was tall and thin, dressed in ragged jeans and a dirty tee shirt with the Minnesota Twins baseball logo emblazoned on the front.

He was grabbed by two of the men and hustled into the hall. The third man barged into the apartment, which was surprisingly clean and neat, albeit with worn furniture, and conducted a quick search. He exited with what could have been a kitchen knife, a pistol, and wiring and fuses that were clearly intended for bomb-making.

The boy was shoved against the filthy hall wall and his hands were pinned behind his back. "Boy, what were you going to use these for?" asked the leader.

"They're for a science project at school." Was the response, which, in the opinion of the vigilantes, was a boldfaced lie.

395

Philip J. Tarnoff

"I think you and your friends were planning to make a bomb."

"I don't know what you're talking about."

"Well, we're going to help you figure it out. We're going to have our own science experiment. It's called how much pain can you take before you talk?"

And with that introduction, the three of them began punching the boy as if he were one of the heavy boxing bags found in gyms. The pounding continued without stop until he fell to the floor and huddled to protect himself. At that point, the punching was replaced by kicking.

The merciless pounding continued until the boy shouted, "Enough! Enough! I'll tell you what you want to know if you swear that you won't tell where you heard it."

The three men paused, and the bleeding boy spoke in a low voice. "We're going to bomb the bus terminal."

The leader asked, "Who else is in your gang?"

"You'd have to kill me before I told you that. I'd rather die than be looked at as a traitor, tortured and killed in the end."

"Are other members of your gang in this building?"

"Yes. But don't let on that I told you."

The leader snarled. "Get outta here before we kill you."

They released the boy, who fled down the dirty hall and presumably into the area of Riverside Plaza that was intended to be a park to warn his friends.

The armed men continued their search of the second floor, but without any useful results other than upsetting the building's tenants, a result they also considered useful. After a couple of hours of fruitless searching, they abandoned their activity and retired to Johnny Baby's, a bar on University Avenue in St. Paul that they frequented. It was agreed that their morning had been productive. It was also agreed that they should tell the police about the planned bombing, but the tip should be anonymous to avoid revealing their questionable activities. And finally, it was agreed that they should continue their activities. They were in tacit agreement that these activities were an opening salvo in a war between Minnesota's Christian and Muslim communities.

A surprising development in an area that had been known for its welcoming attitudes.

***

The first mosque in the state was established quietly in a private home in Gillette, Wyoming. But the quiet didn't last long. Soon after it was opened, a group known as "Stop Islam in Gillette" was organized, with the objective of ensuring that there were no jihadists in the neighborhood. Clearly an intolerant and ignorant reaction in a state with the highest gun ownership in the nation, where crimes were not committed by Muslims, but by Christians against Christians.

The debate over the mosque's presence raged between the fearful and intolerant members of the community and those who were open to peaceful coexistence between religions.

Things threatened to get out of control as Somali Muslims began moving to Cheyenne, Wyoming, attracted by the availability of housing and lack of overcrowding found in many big cities with Muslim communities. The citizens of Wyoming were not happy.

Developments in Wyoming paralleled those in Minnesota and California, where self-organized groups of vigilantes began a program of harassment, including illegal searches of Muslim homes, beatings, threats, rapes, and other forms of intimidation. All of this conducted with the intent of driving the unwanted refugees out of the state.

***

Meanwhile, in California, the principal actors in the unfolding drama had been quite busy. Both Adam al-Zhihri and Gus Waters continued to elude the efforts of the FBI and local law enforcement to locate them. Although Lee Sanders had lumped them together as gang leaders and criminal instigators, he also recognized the differences between their objectives. Sanders recognized that Adam's goal was to foment violence between

Christians and Muslims, with the objective of uniting the US Muslims with those in the Middle East. He felt this was a necessary step in the formation of a worldwide caliphate. A US-Muslim rebellion was his dream.

On the other hand, Gus was less sophisticated. He just wanted the Muslims to leave. He didn't care whether or not they left the United States, just as long as someone kept an eye on them. His ideal solution would be to round up all the American Muslims and place them in internment camps where they could be guarded. He didn't know or care about the similar treatment of Japanese Americans that had occurred during World War II, much to the embarrassment of the country. He had no particular argument with the federal government, as long as they left him alone. Gus continued to communicate with David Crain, one of the few people he mistakenly thought he could trust.

Once again, Gus's group met at the First Baptist Church to plan their next moves. Gus paced back and forth in front of his followers seated on their metal folding chairs. "Apparently, we haven't yet convinced our Arab friends that we don't want them in California. We've got to make sure they get the message. I believe this means that we've got to make things even more uncomfortable for them. Every time we do something to them, they try to get back at us. They just aren't listening. I think we're being too timid. What do you all think?"

Gus's introductory remarks were met with grunts and nods. Finally Bear spoke up. "I think we've got to make an impression on those people. How about we bomb a mosque while they're bowing on their rugs?"

"Call me a coward, but I think we should stop short of bombing mosques with people inside," said Earl, joining the conversation. "Think about it, if someone dies because of our bombing, we become murders. I don't want to spend the rest of my life in jail. There's got to be a better way."

Gus agreed. "I think we need to be careful about two things. First, making sure no one dies as a result of our work. Second, to make sure that no one in this room rats on this group or anyone in it. If we have a leak, the leaker will face serious consequences."

Then he introduced an idea that he'd been toying with for several weeks. "I have an idea I'd like to try out on you."

***

Friday is a holy day for Muslims. It's a day that they are expected to be at the mosque praying. Their schedule was well known to the group at the First Baptist Church. On Friday, following their planning meeting, four carloads of men left the church headed for selected locations in the Los Angeles region. Each location was the dwelling of an imam at one of the Los Angeles mosques. They had chosen Friday to ensure that its occupants would all be at their respective mosques. The men had become proficient at preparing Molotov cocktails, and they used their skills effectively. Within a period of two hours, twelve houses were set on fire, and most burned to the ground. The message was clear. Muslims, and particularly their religious leaders, were no longer welcome in Los Angeles.

The Christian terrorists, for that's what they were, had not counted on the fact that the army had also decided that Fridays might be good days for anti-Muslim activities, and had increased their patrols throughout the LA region. Several units heard the Molotov cocktails exploding not far from their posts and had alerted the troops on the street to set up roadblocks and to search all suspicious vehicles. As luck would have it, one of the last vehicles was driven by Brian Klenger, the youngest member of the church group. He drove past an imam's residence, and one of the three other men in his car ignited a Molotov cocktail and threw it at the house, where it exploded as planned, igniting its flammable exterior, which created an inferno that soon demolished the building. Black smoke curled up into the blue Los Angeles sky, which attracted the attention of a platoon of soldiers guarding the neighborhood.

As Brian reached the end of the street, he was startled to see that it was blocked by a Humvee and armed, helmeted soldiers standing in the road wearing MP armbands. Without hesitation, he made a quick U-turn and sped down the street in the other direction. The soldiers immediately mounted the Humvee and gave chase. The men in Brian's car were startled to realize that the Humvee had been equipped with flashing lights and a siren. They were also surprised to discover the speed with which the Humvee traveled. It was gradually gaining on Brian's Honda, no matter how fast he drove. The sound of the Humvee's siren accompanied by a message from a bullhorn telling them to pull over or be shot ended the chase. Bear, who was riding shotgun, reminded his fellow occupants: "Remember Gus's instructions. No one is to talk to the cops."

The Humvee swerved around the Honda and stopped at an angle that would prevent further escape attempts. They were immediately surrounded by armed soldiers, ordered out of the car and onto the ground. As their car was searched, there was little doubt of their guilt as the searchers discovered the components of an unused Molotov cocktail.

Brian was shaking with fear as he and his three passengers were handcuffed and shoved roughly into the back of the two LAPD cruisers that had arrived at the scene. No one in either of the cruisers spoke during the twenty-minute trip downtown to the police headquarters. The trip was faster than usual due to the light traffic, the one blessing of the statewide power failure. Their arrival was accompanied by the sound of a police helicopter landing on the roof of the headquarters carrying Lee Sanders, who had been made aware of the chase and subsequent arrest.

Sanders looked the four men over as they were being fingerprinted and photographed. He sensed that his questioning would be most successful if he spoke with Brian first, as soon as the booking process was completed.

As Brian was ushered into the interview room in handcuffs, Lee was already seated. The two sat across the table from each other with Brian facing the one-way glass mirror across from his chair. Lee began the interview. "Let me introduce myself. I am Lee Sanders of the FBI, and I am the Special Agent in Charge of terrorist activities occurring throughout the United States. And who are you?"

Remembering his instructions from Bear, Brian remained silent.

"Well now, that's kind or rude," Lee said. "I've introduced myself, the least you could do is to tell me who you are. It would save both of us a lot of trouble. I'll know who you are from your fingerprints within the hour, so you might at least tell me your name."

"Brian Klenger."

"There now, that wasn't so hard, was it?"

Silence.

"As long as you've told me who you are, why don't you tell me where you live? I'll know that also within the hour."

Silence.

"Look, Brian, to start with, I'm not looking for evidence that will put you away. We've already got all the evidence we need. I'm trying to get some background on your activities so that I can prevent future vandalism and worse. And let me assure you, I'll find the answers either with or without your assistance. Now you've got two choices here. You can either tell me what I want to know, or you can clam up. If you clam up, you go to prison for ten to twenty years on an arson charge and any other crimes we might discover. Don't forget that under the state of emergency we can send you to prison without a trial. Duration of your sentence to be determined by the FBI—that's me. Let's see. I guess you'd be middle aged and have lost the best part of your life when you got out. If you tell me what I want to know, I'm authorized to substitute your relocation to an internment camp we are building for Christian terrorists. It won't be a bad place, plenty of food, entertainment, and company. Freedom to move around instead of occupying a ten-foot by ten-foot jail cell. You can also bring your wife and kids, if you have any. If I were you, I'd pick the latter. I'll give you exactly one minute to decide on your fate for the rest of your life. And don't forget, your sentencing is up to me." As he finished giving Brian his options, Lee made an exaggerated look at his watch.

The room was silent for nearly a minute before Brian spoke. "The problem with me picking the second option is that I'm sure my friends would kill me."

Lee responded without hesitation. "I don't think so. They don't have to know that you told us anything, and it's likely you'll all be sent to the internment camp as a group. I'm going to have a similar session with your other friends, so our discussion will not cause any suspicion. If they wonder where we got our information, they would have to wonder about everyone."

Brian said, "OK."

With that, Lee squeezed every drop of information from Brian that the boy could provide. The name of the church, their other activities, and the names of other members of the group. Brian only knew the men's first names, which included Bear, Earl, and Gus. Lee did not react when Brian mentioned Gus, but a feeling of relief passed through him, realizing he was closing in on his prey. He asked some follow-up questions, but other than the church where they met, Brian could be of no more help.

Lee followed his interview of Brian with the other three occupants of the car. Bear would not cooperate and was shipped off to the LAPD Metropolitan Detention Center until his sentence could be determined, at which time he would be transferred to a federal facility. The other two were as cooperative as Brian but could provide little additional information other than a few last names. The three of them were then sent to holding cells at the LAPD Detention Center, where they would languish until construction of the army's detention center was completed.

Things moved quickly after that. A host of FBI agents were mobilized to search the apartments of the four men in the Honda. Others were dispatched to the Baptist Church, where they obtained membership lists, including names, addresses, and phone numbers. Bear's apartment produced a promising clue. On a message pad by his telephone, they found a phone number with the name Gus written next to it. But Lee quickly realized that it was a number he already had that had been provided by David Crain in Maryland. Further interrogation of their suspects revealed that Gus had planned to move on to other locations in California following the mass firebombing.

Lee remained frustrated in the search for his elusive prey.

***

Adam felt that his time in the United States was limited. He knew he was a wanted man, and sooner or later, the FBI, an organization whose capabilities he respected, would receive a tip that would lead to his arrest. He was determined not to let that happen. But before leaving, he was determined to ensure that the West's fear of Bis Saif did not diminish following his departure. Like Gus, he felt that one final unforgettable act would be needed before his departure. On Friday evening following prayer services, he met at the Hadad-Mahmood Mosque with his followers. He no longer felt it necessary to meet at a member's home, fearing that it would attract the attention of the Christian militia that was already firebombing their residences. The mosque also offered the advantage of having electricity, a luxury that most homes couldn't offer.

The men sat on overstuffed chairs in the imam's office, looking expectantly at Adam. As the meeting was called to order, a TV tuned to a local news station was playing softly in the corner. Everyone's attention was suddenly diverted to a news bulletin announcing the firebombing of the imams' homes. The room turned silent as they watched in horror as their leaders' residences were engulfed in flames.

One of the men in the room muttered "Nauzubillah" under his breath, which the others knew as "I seek refuge in Allah" as they stared transfixed at the TV.

Although Adam shared their shock, inwardly he was overjoyed at the convenient timing of the events. He had planned to try to whip them into a frenzy of revenge, but had no need for an inspiring speech since his goal had been achieved by the acts of the militia. Instead he began on a milder note. "I have warned you about them. They are trying to drive us out of America. These acts are occurring everywhere and should not be tolerated. I think we should plan for immediate revenge."

His words were answered with nods and muttering throughout the room.

"This is what I propose," he said. "We've got to move quickly so that the Christians will recognize our actions are a direct response to the firebombing. Tomorrow, we should park several cars loaded with explosives on Rodeo Drive, one of the most upscale shopping centers in the world. You know how to create car bombs. We need four vehicles, two to be parked on each side of Rodeo Drive, and all to be activated at the same time. We need upscale cars, Mercedes or BMWs, so that they are not considered to be suspicious. Either use your own cars or steal the cars to be detonated. Is everyone in agreement with the plan?"

Once again, the response was nods and mutters of agreement throughout the room. The remainder of the meeting was spent planning the details of the attack. With the exception of the one individual designated to detonate the bombs, everyone would be at home on Saturday, the day of the planned attack.

***

Saturday was a sunny, cloudless day, typical of LA in the springtime. Rodeo Drive was crowded with shoppers and tourists gawking at the overpriced merchandise being sold in the upscale stores. Two black Mercedes, a dark red BMW, and a white Lexus drove onto Rodeo Drive at five-minute intervals and began to circulate, looking for a place to park. Their drivers were in communication with each other using their cellphones. The Lexus driver was lucky. He found a metered parking spot, which he promptly claimed, and carefully fed coins into the meter. At five minutes before noon, the drivers of the remaining three vehicles double-parked and turned on their flashers as if they had run into a store to pick up a package. However, instead of entering the stores, the drivers fled their locked vehicles and dispersed in opposite directions without acknowledging each other. At exactly noon on that beautiful Saturday, there were four gigantic explosions. The damage was horrific. Storefronts were blown out, and the street was littered with dead and dying shoppers and tourists. The noise of the explosion and the smoke from the burning buildings could be seen miles away.

The casualties included more than sixty dead and over 300 injured, many of them seriously. LA hospitals and emergency services were swamped with patients. Police quickly converged on the area, but it was too late. The perpetrators were long gone, and many of them were already at home watching the clean-up on TV. Since the vehicles had been stolen and wiped clean of fingerprints, there were few clues that either the army or their law enforcement counterparts could use to identify the culprits. Lee Sanders had been called to the scene and correctly concluded along with his fellow investigators that this was retribution for the bombing of the imams' residences on the previous day. Sanders was equally certain that Adam al-Zhihri was behind the attack, and felt they should redouble their efforts to locate him.

***

At 9:00 a.m., an elderly woman in a walker exited from a taxi at LAX. She had a small carry-on bag and a larger suitcase, which she checked at the curbside baggage service of the international terminal for Qatar Airways 11:00 a.m. flight to Baghdad, Iraq. The porter at the service dutifully checked her passport, placed a tag on her bag, and accepted her five-dollar tip. He then motioned to an attendant with a wheelchair to take her to her gate. The trip to the gate was uneventful, since security checks of wheelchair-bound individuals were perfunctory. Furthermore, her advanced age of seventy-six allowed her to proceed through the metal detectors without requiring a full body scan. As the attendant neared their destination, she asked if she could stop momentarily at the ladies' room before proceeding to the gate. She asked him to watch her bag while she entered the ladies' room. Once in the ladies' room, she entered a stall where she removed her wig and wiped her face. *That wig is sure hot*, thought Adam as he replaced it and resumed his disguise as a seventy-six-year-old woman. Checking his makeup in the mirror over the sink, he resumed his doddering gait and returned to the wheelchair.

Adam was prepared for a miserable flight to Baghdad, seated in the middle section of a row of seats that were all occu-

405

pied. The twenty-two- hour flight made two stops, in Chicago and Doha Qatar, which was annoying, but at least it gave him a chance to stretch his cramped legs during each stop. He still had a distance to travel when he reached Baghdad. Adam would then have to change planes for the risky part of the trip on Al-Naser Airlines, one of the few flights that would take him from Baghdad to Damascus, Syria. Once he reached Damascus, he was then faced with a long dangerous six-hour ride to Raqqa in an open jeep that was to be provided by Ali, his ISIS contact in that region. The jeep ride would be physically numbing with its poor suspension and lack of protection from the sun, accentuated by the barren desert landscape through which they would pass. Recognizing the arduous trip that he was facing, Adam spent the night he arrived in Baghdad at the Palm Hotel, located on the airport property, enjoying the air conditioning and comfortable bed before leaving for Damascus.

The morning following his stay at the hotel, he left for the airport looking like a visiting newspaper journalist, without his wig, wearing desert army fatigues and sunglasses and carrying a knapsack. He had discarded his wig, makeup, and dress in a dumpster behind the hotel without any regrets. The trip to Raqqa was every bit as wretched as Adam had anticipated, and he was glad he had remained overnight in Baghdad before undertaking this final leg of his journey.

Raqqa Syria was a tired city. It had suffered many years of fighting before Adam's arrival, and it showed. Many buildings were in rubble, with a joyless population, most of whom either lived in improvised shelters at street level or in partially collapsed buildings. Adam surveyed the depressing situation without emotion as the jeep proceeded to the ISIS headquarters in the middle of town. The headquarters was in the basement of a building whose above-ground structure had been demolished and was intentionally left unrepaired to avoid it becoming an obvious target during a bombing run by either the Russians or one of the Western allies.

Although he was operating on the edge of exhaustion, Adam jumped out of the jeep, grabbed his knapsack, and bounded through the entrance that had been indicated by the driver. As he walked from the bright sun outdoors into the dimly lit vestibule of the headquarters, he was grabbed by two burly Arab guards who unceremoniously emptied his knapsack on the floor and held him while he was subjected to a thoroughly embarrassing and intrusive body search. At the end of the search, one of the guards nodded to Adam, indicating that it would be all right for him to proceed into the headquarters area. He was tired and mad and took his time gathering his possessions and repacking his knapsack, much to the annoyance of the guards.

Adam then walked calmly into the reception area, where he was met by a surprisingly attractive and polite young lady with a spectacular figure, jet black hair, and matching eyes. She was wearing military fatigues and seated at a battered green metal desk. "Welcome to Raqqa, home of ISIS."

Taking a deep breath, he replied, "I am glad to be here and look forward to meeting with your leaders."

He was taken aback by her answer. "Do you have an appointment with them?"

Adam was about to introduce himself to her and explain his importance when Ali walked out of one of the offices behind her. "My friend, Adam! I am so glad to see you! I have been telling the general of your organization and your power among the Sunni Muslim faithful."

Ali then scolded the receptionist. "Do you know who you are treating with such indifference? He is the leader of Bis Saif, our powerful allies in the fight against the warmongering Westerners."

The receptionist blushed. "I am so sorry, sir. I will see that it never happens again. Allah be praised."

Ali then draped his arm around Adam's shoulder and led him into a conference room immediately behind the receptionist's desk. "I will tell our glorious leader that you are here. I am certain that he is most anxious to speak with you."

Adam dropped into one of the chairs, happy to relieve his tired body. "Thank you. I would also appreciate a glass of water, if that is possible. The drive through the desert was hot and dry."

"Certainly. I will take care of that as well," said Ali over his shoulder as he left the conference room.

Adam didn't have long to wait before both General Hussain and the glass of water arrived along with a plate of baklava. He realized it had been more than seven hours since he had eaten, and began filling up on the baklava, which was delicious. He looked up to see the general standing by the table watching him. "I'm sorry, but I haven't had food most of the day, and this is delicious."

"No need to apologize. We have an excellent cook on the premises. Life here is better than eating out of a field kitchen." Ali, who had spent the majority of his adult life in the field, nodded in agreement.

Adam began to introduce himself. "I'm not certain what Ali has told you about me, but I'm the leader of Bis Saif. Although we have never met, Bis Saif has provided you with many of your advanced SAM systems that I understand you've been using with great success against the warplanes of the West."

"That is true," replied Hussain as he wondered what Adam wanted in return and why he was there. "We're most grateful. You have made a long and dangerous trip to see me. I would be happy to repay you for your efforts."

Reading the general's mind, Adam replied, "I don't know how much news you receive from the West, but things are going very well for us in America and very poorly for the Americans. We should try to cripple them. I believe that together we can have a great effect."

"What have you done to cause the Americans so many problems?"

"Bis Saif has turned off the electricity to more than thirty million Americans," replied Adam, being careless with his statistics. "That might not seem like such a big thing in Raqqa, Syria, where you have been living without power for many years, but the American society is collapsing without their air conditioning, TV, and movies. Many Americans have moved to other parts of the country to find their critical comforts. Their president is frantically trying to make their lives easier. To

Americans, a difficult life is reason to rebel against the government. I'm trying to encourage that rebellion."

"I can't believe that living without electricity has upset the Americans so much."

"You have to understand the Americans. They're not used to suffering like those of us in the Middle East. Consider the fact that a restaurant serving a leaf of lettuce that makes someone sick leads to national news. The restaurant may be shut down until the source of the bad lettuce is identified. Or think about a baby whose head accidentally gets caught in the bars of a crib and dies. The American government forces the manufacturer to discontinue selling the crib and buy all the other cribs back from the owners and replace them with new cribs. That is one death that was probably caused because the mother wasn't watching her baby. Or one death from a bad piece of lettuce out of a population of three hundred million people. Can you imagine a society that worries about that? In the meantime, that same society is bombing Muslims and killing thousands without any worries. That proves how soft the Americans have become and it proves that Americans don't like Muslims. If you need further proof, Muslims are being attacked by Christians in many regions of America."

Hussain listened intently. "I know Americans don't like Muslims, but I had no idea their society had become so soft. They would never be able to tolerate the conditions that our fellow Arabs are enduring. We're trying to establish a caliphate that will rule the Muslim world in the Middle East, but how do we include the rest of the world within that order?"

"I believe that we need to take one step at a time. Let us continue to focus on the Middle East. This is a good time to solidify our gains because the Americans are weakened and are focusing on their problems at home. I have taken steps to ensure that their problems continue. They may be wealthy, but their wealth is not unlimited. If we strike now, they will have problems responding because they're using their troops and their wealth to control their own populations. Once we have established control over the Middle East, we can move against the West."

"That sounds like a good plan. I believe we have the resources to mount an assault throughout the Middle East. We need some help from you acquiring more SAMs, but aside from that, we're capable of pursuing our mutual goals. In the meantime, Bis Saif should continue to harass the Americans in their own country."

The two paused in their discussion and raised their cups of lemon tea in a toast that served to seal their agreement.

But the general thought there was one more item to discuss. "Adam, I have one more concern. Let's assume we successfully consolidate the Middle East as a caliphate under the ISIS flag. As they say in the West, who will be running the show?"

"But of course ISIS will be in charge." Was the surprising response. "If as you say the caliphate is established under the ISIS flag, it should be obvious that you would be in charge."

The general was relieved by Adam's response but suspicious. In the Arab world, agreements were never reached that easily and without extensive negotiation. So he tried once more to test Adam's commitment to an ISIS-led caliphate. "What role would you like to play in the caliphate?"

"I do not command any troops. But I have the commitments of the Palestinians and others to unite with the Sunni Muslim cause. I also have relationships with weapons suppliers and financiers throughout the world. I would expect to have a high position in the caliphate and to be consulted in all important decisions. My goal is to see the Arab world united."

The general was appeased but remained suspicious. "And that is all you want?"

Adam added, "There is one more thing. If I should succeed in my efforts to weaken the Christian government of America, I would like to be the ruler of that society."

It was the general's private belief that the overthrow of the American government would never occur, a consideration that influenced his response. "I would happily agree to that."

Once again the two raised their tea cups in a toast to the consummation of their agreement.

CHAPTER 30

SOCIETAL CHANGE

The US Army was engaged in a major, high-priority construction project. Two internment camps were being constructed. One for non-Muslims and the second, which Gus would have liked, for Muslims. These camps were not prisons, and were not a re-creation of the prison at Guantanamo for terrorists. They were intended to serve as long-term holding areas for troublemakers. The troublemakers could be accompanied by their families if they chose to join them. Housing was provided in the form of metal pre-fabricated Butler buildings, which were heated and air-conditioned. The buildings were divided into small ten- foot by fifteen-foot compartments that provided occupants with a minimal degree of privacy. Each compartment contained a double bed, a bureau, a desk, and two chairs. The living quarters of each facility could accommodate nearly 1,000 occupants, a population that neither the army nor the White House wanted to achieve.

Other buildings erected at the site contained communal dining areas, exercise facilities, game rooms, a gymnasium, an auditorium-style meeting space, and smaller meeting rooms. The auditorium would be used for movies, shows, and community meetings. Except for the barbed wire and patrolling troops on the perimeter of the internment camps, they were undistinguishable from overseas military bases. The absence of pictures, or any other sort of decorations on their interior walls, further cemented their depressing appearance as that of a military installation.

The camps, designated Camp #1 for non-Muslims and Camp #2 for Muslims, were located in Panamint City, Califor-

411

nia, separated from each other by more than two miles of desert and scrub growth, and more than 100 miles from civilization. Panamint City is near Death Valley and was a boom town, which at its peak had a population of 2,000, resulting from the discovery of silver and copper in nearby deposits in 1872. It was now a ghost town visited occasionally by tourists. It was surrounded by rocky terrain and scattered scrub growth. Escaping from the internment camps to Beatty City, Nevada, the nearest civilization, would require a fifty-eight-mile hike through the rugged wilderness of Death Valley National Park, a challenge to even the most experienced hikers. With minimal natural cover, discovery by helicopter searchers would be guaranteed.

The buses with army MPs who would serve as guards for the camp began arriving shortly after it was completed. They traveled on a newly paved road that was essential for shipping in the supplies required by a population of 3,000 inmates and guards. The inmates began to arrive one day after the guards had settled in and received their duty assignments. Busload after busload appeared carrying Christians and Muslims to their respective camps. The arrivals were individuals that had been discovered in the act of harassing each other and committing various petty crimes and some felonies as well. They were frequently accompanied by their immediate families, which included spouses and in some cases children. The camp designers quickly realized that their plans had not included school rooms, an oversight which required conversion of some of the meeting rooms into classrooms.

The population of the camps rapidly increased until at the end of three months they had each reached their 1,000 internment limit. The army command immediately began planning for the construction of a second set of camps, but, as usual, progress was slowed by availability of funds.

As a result, Camps #1 and #2 became overcrowded, and discipline was a challenge. While most of the arrivals continued to be from California, many were also from Minnesota, Wyoming, and the Washington, DC region. The weeks following the opening of the camps also saw many individuals and families sent to the camps from Arizona and Texas, most of whom were sent to Camp #1.

One unforeseen result of the internment camps was that their facilities became attractive to indigent individuals, many of whom were homeless. As a result, petty crimes were being committed throughout the United States against people of the opposite religion with the hope that the criminal would be sent to one of the relatively comfortable internment camps rather than prison. This further swelled the population of the camps and increased the frequency of crimes within its population. Far from solving any inter-religious conflicts, the camps then confronted the US government with a new set of problems.

Lee Sanders felt that those in the camps could be helpful in his ongoing efforts to locate Gus Waters and Adam al-Zhihri. As a result, he spent several weeks in the heat of Panamint City interviewing their residents. While many exhibited outright distrust and hatred of all law enforcement, including the FBI, some were cooperative. Unfortunately, they had little information to offer Lee as he sat behind a desk in the small office with the noisy window air conditioner the army had given him to conduct his interviews. As he ended his work at the camps, he concluded that he had learned very little. It appeared that Gus had left the Los Angeles area and was on the move up and down the Pacific Coast recruiting additional adherents to his anti-Muslim cause. Occasionally he met someone who had seen Gus, but never in the same city and never for very long. Adam, on the other hand, seemed to have entirely disappeared from the scene. Sanders concluded that he had left the country.

It was rapidly becoming clear that the internment camps were becoming more of a curse than a blessing.

***

The Crain family had grown weary of life in Ohio. Joanna had appreciated David's suggestion that she travel to stay with her sister so that she and the kids didn't have to put up with the inconveniences of the power failure. But enough was enough. It

Philip J. Tarnoff

was only possible to tolerate relatives for so long before people began to tire of each other. As Benjamin Franklin once said, 'guests, like fish, begin to smell after three days.' As soon as she heard rumors of the possible restoration of power at home, she packed up Megan and Steve along with all their belongings, and made the ten-hour drive back to Silver Spring.

The family reunion after months of separation was ecstatic. The kids immediately went to their rooms and luxuriated in the space and access to their personal belongings. After hugging and tears, Joanna and Steve settled down on the sofa in the living room with a glass of wine and some quiet conversation.

"So how was Ohio?" Dave asked as sat with one arm around Joanna, taking a sip of wine with his free hand.

"You know Ohio. The most boring place on the face of the earth. The people are very nice. Warm and welcoming. But there's very little to do. Some local theater, most of the restaurants are franchises, a few mediocre professional sports teams, and that's it. And, oh yes, lots of hay fever. I sneezed constantly for a month."

"Yes. But they had electricity."

"True. We were definitely more comfortable than you were. Although I love my sister, living with her is difficult. She's got more annoying habits than I remembered from when we were growing up. So we're really glad to be home. I hope the power will be turned on soon."

"I've heard that it might only be a few days before we can lose the candles."

Then David changed the subject. "How do people in Ohio feel about Muslims?"

"They hate them and they're afraid of them even though I don't think I met a single person who had ever met a Muslim."

"I sense the same is true in the Washington area. To me it's almost irrational. I'm sure glad I'm not a Muslim."

"What is this country coming to? I always believed that religious tolerance was a hallmark of our society."

David expanded on Joanna's statement. "It's not only the ordinary people. I think they're being stirred up by political

414

opportunists. I don't know how much news you received in Ohio, but there's this guy Donald Squlo, who I think is a representative from California, who managed to get himself arrested near Disneyland for stirring up a crowd. If all you care about is being in Congress, the thing to do is to bad-mouth Muslims."

Joanna had always been a fearful person, and this conversation was adding to her fears. "What are we going to do? I'm not going to live in a country that mimics Nazi Germany during World War II."

Half joking, David responded, "We could always move to Canada."

"I'm not sure I'd like that. I guess we'll have to stay here and tough it out," was Joanna's completely serious response.

David's final statement of the discussion was significant. "Unfortunately, I'm afraid we're in the minority. People are scared, and they're looking for scapegoats."

***

The White House, which had been carefully monitoring the situation, had come to the same conclusion. President Jeffers was rapidly running out of ideas as violence and inter-religious hatred continued to grow. He did not feel that the resources existed to declare a national state of emergency, and he was concerned that if he did so, the growing resistance to his actions by Congress would lead to legislation that would further limit his options. He had federalized the National Guard in states that included Minnesota and Wyoming, which, acting as a branch of the US Army, provided assistance to local law enforcement agencies. This was one step short of the declaration of a state of emergency.

The one bright spot in the situation was that as a result of the round-the-clock efforts of the utilities, power had been restored to the Washington, DC region, much to the relief of its residents as well as the government agencies tasked with their relief. It also provided them with the additional resources needed to send equipment and personnel used in the Washington region to ease the situation in California.

While his actions had kept the lid on the boiling pot, he knew that a long-term solution was needed. The United States could not continue to use the National Guard to police its citizens nationally, and the internment camps were not having their desired effect. If anything, they were creating additional problems. All of this was straining the already stressed federal budget.

The increased activity in the Middle East was a new concern. Jeffers was startled to see Matthew O'Brien, the Director of the CIA, arrive to deliver the morning security briefing, a daily event at the White House.

"Good morning, Mr. President."

"Good morning, Matt. It is a pleasant surprise to see you this morning. I hope that you're not here for unpleasant reasons."

"Unfortunately, I am here for unpleasant reasons."

"I was afraid of that. What've you got?"

"As you know from our previous briefings, we've had some indications of increased military activity in the Middle East." Jeffers nodded, encouraging O'Brien to continue.

"Mr. President, the information we now have is more than an indication. We're positive that a multi-front attack is planned for the near future in Syria, Iraq, Israel, and possibly other countries. We're also confident that this attack will be led by ISIS, but will be coordinated with other Sunni Muslim groups, including the Palestinians. We are seeing vast shipments of equipment being made to these groups, which include SAMs that were manufactured by the Chinese. Our analysts don't believe that the United States and its allies have adequate resources positioned in these locations to resist the attack. I've spoken briefly with General Drake about this, and he agrees that we're in a world of trouble. The Pentagon has begun repositioning troops and ships to the region, but we're limited by the fact that we've pulled some troops out of the Middle East to patrol the streets of California. Quite an irony."

Chris knew he couldn't show weakness, but his one thought while O'Brien was speaking was that he'd sure like to give his job to someone else. Instead he answered impassively. "Matt, what do you and the general recommend?"

"You're not going to like this, but there appears to be only one solution. We've got to redeploy some percentage of the troops we have in Germany, Japan, and South Korea into the Middle East. Currently, we have more than one hundred thousand military personnel in these three locations, including all three branches. According to Drake, we could move approximately half to the Middle East without seriously affecting their mission. We've also got to move our naval resources from the Pacific to the Middle East. And these actions have to be taken immediately. That's the only way that we can respond forcefully without waiting for the bureaucracy to catch up. General Drake wanted to accompany me this morning but couldn't because of everything that's going on at the Pentagon. As you can imagine, he's totally immersed in planning for a redeployment." Then he quickly added, "Assuming you approve it, of course."

Chris knew that delaying the decision would accomplish nothing other than to make the military's job more difficult. So after only a moment's hesitation he answered. "Do it." And then thought, *I only hope we can afford it. I'm sure glad I asked for a hundred billion.*

O'Brien answered with the obvious. "We can't afford not to do it."

With that he picked up his coat, which he had laid over a chair, and left the office.

***

As soon as O'Brien left the Oval Office, Jeffers called Jan on the intercom and asked her to schedule an emergency meeting with the Leadership Group. As luck would have it, Congress was in recess and none of the four had yet departed for their home districts. Two hours later the president and his ad hoc congressional cabinet were settled into one of the small White House meeting rooms.

417

"Well, Mr. President, how are things going?" Asked Bob McIntyre, the Senate Majority Leader, again taking advantage of their long working relationship.

"Not so well. I don't feel that we're making much progress, and I'm not getting much help from your colleagues."

"Yes. I heard about Squlo's arrest. He's now happily ensconced in Panamint City, probably stirring up trouble there too. He may be the worst of the bunch, but he's not alone. People are scared, and don't forget these guys represent our citizens, so their feelings reflect those of their constituents."

"Mr. President, what are friends for? The four of us would like to help you get this situation under control. But you know the limits of our power. As you well know, Congress is divided both along party lines and within parties over the subject of our response to ISIS and Bis Saif. There are as many different thoughts about our possible responses as there are members of Congress." Bob then added, "What can we do to help?"

"Well, gentlemen, here's the problem. In spite of your successful efforts to increase the debt ceiling by a hundred billion, we're out of money again. I'm assuming you've heard about the combined offensives of ISIS and the Palestinians in the Middle East. The CIA believes that other groups will join the show in order to strike under the cover of the ISIS battles. We're pulling troops out of Germany and Asia to supplement the troops that can be made available from units in the Middle East. We're also repositioning the Pacific Fleet to support them. Repositioning is very expensive when the costs of additional bases and supplies are included. Then add to that the cost of combat supplies. I don't have precise numbers, but I'm confident that we're talking about many billions of additional dollars. I just don't want to raise the debt ceiling again, which leaves the possibility of a tax increase or cancellation of some of our more expensive military weapon-development programs. The latter is a problem since cancelling ongoing contracts is a very time-consuming and expensive process that once again requires the concurrence of our dysfunctional Congress. Don't forget we have contracts with the folks doing the weapons-development work, which all have expensive cancellation clauses. So we're back to the tax increase question again."

When Jeffers finished his review of the situation, the room was silent for a long time. He was determined not to speak again until one of the congressmen expressed an opinion.

Finally, Wayne Zyder spoke up. "Mr. President, we've already been over this at least twice, and I thought we made it clear that additional taxes are not a realistic possibility. You and I are both Republicans, and you know that our party has taken a pledge of no new taxes. I understand your situation, but speaking for the House of Representatives, the votes just aren't there. I've had representatives ask me whether dropping a nuke on Syria wouldn't solve the problem in a less costly manner. To tell you the truth, I sometimes wonder about the same thing."

"You're kidding!" Chris said incredulously. "It's really annoying that you called it *my situation*. Isn't this *our* situation?"

Wayne felt obligated to respond, although he did so tersely. "Duly noted."

Paul Greenberg, the philosopher of the group, joined the conversation. "Mr. President, we all know we're in this together, but I'm sure you know that we're all running out of ideas."

Jeffers wasn't willing to be pacified. "I'm glad you realize that we're all in this together. I just hope that Congress recognizes that they're responsible for helping with the solution rather than making grandstanding proposals about nuclear weapons." Then in a calmer but firm voice he added, "What I don't believe you understand is that I'm against putting this country further into debt. While another hundred billion or so is a small addition to the debt, it is still one hell of a lot of money. If I were to ask for an increase in the debt ceiling and Congress were to grant it, we'd be on a path to more inflation. The value of everyone's income and savings would be decreased just a little bit more. I know that the public doesn't understand the effects of government borrowing, but it's a hidden tax that is appealing to your friends in Congress since they can sneak it through without anyone accusing them of raising taxes. It's time we got honest with our constituents."

Sensing the discussion was getting out of hand, Brad Nelson asked, "So what are we going to do? It appears that we're at an impasse."

Jeffers response did little to pacify the four congressmen. "Gentlemen, I've had it with these cute little games. We're confronted with a serious situation. I'm going to cancel every program I can get my hands on, whether it's medical research, foreign aid, military weapons programs, or National Guard call-ups. We'll see how Congress and the general public like my new super-austerity program."

Brad felt that Jeffers was speaking directly to him. So he answered. "That sounds like some pretty serious stuff. In fact, it sounds a little like a threat. Shouldn't we think this through?"

"It's not as draconian as it sounds. We're obviously not going to discontinue any services that will affect public safety. It will also be very difficult to eliminate any programs that are being conducted under contracts with the private sector. We just can't arbitrarily terminate contracts. Many military contracts and medical research will continue until their end date. But unless we have some serious financial relief, they will not be renewed. This is also true of most of our healthcare and Social Security related expenditures."

Brad tried a different tack. "But Mr. President, reducing our foreign aid is going to cause a lot of hardship overseas."

"We're going to have a lot of hardship here as well unless Congress does its part."

Paul Greenberg, Brad's fellow Democrat, joined the conversation. "Brad, we're getting nowhere. This is a typical Republican tactic –starve the country to get your way."

Wayne Zyder, the House Republican of the group, tried to act as the peacemaker. "Come on Paul, you know that's not true. We're all in a tight spot here, without the votes to raise the money needed to combat ISIS and Bis Saif. You know that the president is doing all he can to keep things under control, and the situation is gradually improving."

Brad was also becoming irritated. "I don't think the situation is improving at all. Granted we now have power in DC, but

California is in bad shape, and the internment camps are rapidly filling up as the war between Christians and Muslims escalates. Maybe our president is being too timid."

Jeffers had heard enough. "How can we be anything but timid when there's no money to pay for a world war? You remember the expenses of our two World Wars. Well, this war includes more than just Europe and Japan. This war also includes the continental United States." Then Jeffers tone changed as he ended the meeting. "I don't think we're getting anywhere other than annoying each other. Why don't we give this a few days to think about? But I want to let you know that I intend to speak to the country this evening in order to describe our situation."

No one said another word. The congressmen filed silently out of the meeting room. As they left, Chris couldn't shake the thought that the terrorists had won.

***

That night as they were getting ready for bed, Chris repeated his earlier refrain to Melissa. "I don't know why I ever took this job. I never realized how little power I had to deal with an intransigent Congress. The country is going to hell in a handbag, and I feel powerless to do anything about it."

For once Melissa couldn't find the words to console her husband. "Maybe you feel powerless because you don't have the power to do what is needed."

"What power do you think I should have?"

Melissa thought for a minute before replying. "When we were first married, your dream was a prosperous country in which the president had the ability to ensure that people of all religions lived and worked together in harmony. So far, all your efforts to achieve that have been thwarted by crazy congressmen and their constituents who just wanted to drop a bomb on the Middle East. As if that would solve anything. Do you think any of them have taken the time to study the Muslim religion, which preaches harmony among the various religions?"

"I'm sure none of them have a clue as to the teachings of anything but fundamental Christianity."

"Then if that's the case," concluded Melissa, "it's time to sideline Congress so that you can achieve your goals."

"I hadn't thought of that," replied Chris thoughtfully. "But you're describing a serious step that would require an amendment to the Constitution. And I'm not sure exactly what the amendment would say, nor would I know how to get it approved."

"Maybe that's something we should think about. You've got smart people in your administration. Maybe they can offer some ideas," Melissa concluded.

Then with a hug and a kiss, and the two retired to bed. With the pressure of the past six months, Chris wasn't interested in anything more active than the kiss.

As he lay in bed staring at the ceiling, he reflected on their conversation. Melissa had certainly come up with an interesting idea. He'd have to put someone in the Justice Department on it immediately. Maybe one of those bright attorneys working in the Constitutional Law Division, or CLD, as they refer to it at Justice.

***

Chris was up early the next morning anxious to pursue Melissa's idea. After a quick shower, coffee and toast, he was at his desk by six. Due to the early hour, he was dressed in slacks and a white shirt opened at the neck so he could add a tie at the appropriate moment.

To his surprise, Jan was already there. "Don't you ever sleep?" he asked her.

"I've worked with you long enough to know when a crisis is looming. I like to be here to help you when these things arise."

"Well I'm glad you're here. I'd like you to speak with the Justice Department and have them send their best expert on constitutional law. This is a highly classified activity, so I'd like someone with a top secret security clearance."

Jan gave her usual response. "Will do, boss."

Three hours later she told him that she'd found someone named Sam Papas who could help and had squeezed him into the schedule for 11:00 AM. Jan then emailed Papas's resume to Chris, who spent every spare minute of the intervening time preparing for the meeting, including a quick scan of Papas's impressive resume.

At exactly 11:00 a.m., Jan announced Papas's arrival in the Oval Office reception area. This was his first visit to the White House, and Sam was obviously in awe of his surroundings, not to mention the opportunity of meeting with the President of the United States.

Jan formally announced him to Chris as she ushered him into the Oval Office, saying, "Mr. President, I would like to introduce Sam Papas from the Justice Department." Then turning to the awestruck lawyer, she asked, "Mr. Papas, can I get you some coffee?"

"No thank you, ma'am," Sam managed to gulp.

In spite of the severity of the situation, Jeffers was amused by Papas's awe of the surroundings, which he had begun to take for granted. Papas was young, most likely in his early thirties, but old beyond his years in terms of his experiences both with a private law firm as well as with the Justice Department. He had majored in constitutional law while working for his degree at Georgetown Law School, and had excelled academically. His dissertation had been an analysis of the relationship between historical circumstances and the amendments to the US Constitution, a paper that had won several awards. He was dressed immaculately, obviously having raced home to change when the summons to the White House had arrived. Dark suit, white shirt, solid dark blue tie, and spit-shined shoes. Jeffers was pleased with Jan's selection of Sam for his special assignment.

"Have a seat Sam, and relax. I'm not going to take your head off," Jeffers began in an effort to put his visitor at ease. "I have a very important assignment for you. The subject of this assignment is not to leave this room. Your boss has given you a leave of absence for as long as it takes for you to complete your assignment. You are not to discuss your work with anyone, including friends, relatives, and your spouse if you're married. You will receive full pay from the Justice Department during the assignment, but you've been detailed to the White House and will report only to me. Are you okay with all of that?"

Sam was clearly impressed with and curious about the mysterious assignment. His head was spinning from his sudden elevation as one of dozens of lawyers in the Justice Department to a position in which he reported directly to the President of the United States. He could only nod and answer, "Yes sir."

"One other thing," added the president. "Unless I tell you otherwise, you will not be able to discuss this assignment even after it has been completed. I know this will be frustrating, since it will be important and even historic work. But the cloak of secrecy must be maintained for generations after you finish. Still okay with all of this?"

Sam was frustrated by his sudden inability to speak coherently by answering, so instead he just nodded his head.

"You're an attorney, so you know the importance of written agreements. I've prepared this document for you to sign before you learn of your assignment. It contains all of the terms and conditions we just discussed. There are no surprises, and you will quickly realize when you read it that it was not prepared by an attorney. In fact, I'm the one who prepared it, so feel free to identify any inaccuracies or wording errors that you feel need to be corrected. After all, you're the attorney in the room. I'll give you a minute to read it before signing."

With that, Jeffers pushed a single sheet of paper across his desk to Sam, who, forgetting his awe at the situation, sat back and began to read. After all, this was familiar territory, reviewing a quasi-legal document prepared by a layman. He was unaware that Jeffers's graduate degree was in law, with the result that he was surprised at the quality of the document. Seeing neither surprises nor errors, he nodded, looked up and said, "This looks fine to me, sir."

The president handed him a pen, and with the signing of the document, Sam Papas was about to become part of history.

Then Jeffers explained his needs. "Sam, unless you've been living underground in a coal mine, you know that things are not going well for our country. We've had power failures that have led to strife between Christians and Muslims, and now things are heating up overseas. In addition to the obvious threats to our national well-being, the cost of dealing with these problems is staggering. Yet in spite of my best efforts, Congress is frozen in place due to the deep philosophical divisions that exist regarding taxes and our national budget. Debates are raging over the way in which we should respond to these problems, as well as the manner in which our responses should be financed. We don't have the luxury of waiting for the conclusion of an extended debate while the participants wave the philosophical flag of their particular party. I've exhausted the legal means provided to the presidency to unilaterally combat our enemies from without and within. In short, our Congress has become dysfunctional, and I'm afraid the country won't survive their inaction."

The president paused and Sam started to comment. "Wait, Sam. Let me finish. I'm just getting to the punch line."

Sam lapsed into silence and the president continued. "I've been searching for ways to resolve these problems and have come to a conclusion. I'm glad you're sitting down for this. I believe that the only solution is to amend our Constitution in a way that gives me the ability to act without dragging the ball and chain known as Congress along behind me. So I'm asking you for two things. First, I need an evaluation of the Constitution as it currently stands and how it should be amended to get our government moving again. Second, and possibly more difficult, I need some ideas of an approach that I can use to get a convention organized for a Constitutional Amendment that will move us in a productive direction. On the surface, this might seem as if it's a relatively simple assignment, since the Constitution is a relatively simple document. However, as you know better than I do, all of our actions must be based on strict adherence to the principles of the Constitution at a level that will stand up in court. Undoubtedly, there will be challenges to everything we do that will end up in the Supreme Court."

Jeffers then concluded his explanation by repeating his instructions to Sam. "I know these are tough questions, but now you can see why complete secrecy is needed. If this leaks prematurely, I'll be accused of being power mad and worse. We've got to do our work with the utmost secrecy."

"Whew," said Sam, "how much time have I got?"

"Ideally I'd like answers to these questions yesterday. But realistically, it would be useful if I could have some answers within a week or two. I'd prefer it if we could discuss things as you moved along. I don't need a fancy report on the entire picture when you're completed. I just need your thoughts and some ideas of the options as you progress. Let's meet for twenty or thirty minutes every couple of days so I can have a sense of your direction. Jan will get you set up in an office and introduce you around. Remember, don't share your assignment with anyone, even Jan." With those concluding remarks, Jeffers stood up, indicating the meeting was over.

"Thank you, sir, I won't let you down," answered Sam, not certain whether a thank you was appropriate. But the president didn't notice. He was already focusing on the paperwork on his desk.

CHAPTER 31

MOVING THE BALL FORWARD

Three days had passed since the president had met with Sam Papas to ask him for an analysis of the Constitution when Jan called on the intercom to ask whether this would be a good time to meet.

"Send him in," Jeffers replied eagerly.

Sam was again ushered into the Oval Office where he was offered and again declined a cup of coffee.

"What have you got for me?" asked Jeffers without preamble.

"Well, sir, I've made good progress on both of your questions, although I haven't yet performed a detailed legal analysis of my conclusions. I know you didn't want a fancy report, but I've prepared some briefing material for your review. You're likely to have some follow-up questions in addition to the need for a legal analysis, but I have some useful preliminary answers."

"Let's see them."

"Well, sir, I've prepared two lists. The first contains the powers that are currently given to Congress, and the second contains the powers that have been given to you by the Constitution. I'm sure you know most of it, but the lists provide a useful basis for you to consider which powers should be moved from Congress to the presidency. I'm assuming that is what you had in mind when we discussed this."

"I'll let you know when I see the lists."

"OK then, this first list has the powers that the Constitution gives to Congress," said Sam, handing the president a single sheet of paper with the following information, adding, "I've paraphrased some of the wording in the interest of brevity. But

427

I'd be happy to elaborate on any of the items on the list if you'd like."

With that, Jeffers picked up the sheet of paper that contained the following itemized list:

- Congress has all legislative powers listed in the Constitution, which include:
- The power of impeachment (Senate only)
- Bills for raising revenue (originate in the House of Representatives, amended by the Senate)
- Collect taxes, duties, imposts, and excises
- Borrow money
- Regulate commerce with foreign nations
- Establish laws for naturalization and bankruptcies
- Coin money and fix standard of weights and measures
- Punish counterfeiting of securities and money
- Establish post offices
- Promote science and arts and patents
- Establish tribunals inferior to the Supreme Court
- Define and punish felonies on the high seas and offense against the law of nations
- Declare war
- Raise and support armies and navies
- Call forth the militia to execute the laws of the union, suppress insurrections and repel invasions
- Organize, arm, and discipline the militia
- Exercise legislation over the District of Columbia
- Create all laws needed to carry out these powers

Jeffers studied the list carefully, and when it appeared that he was finished, Sam handed him a second sheet of paper, saying, "This sheet summarizes the powers of the presidency.

- The president has the following powers:
- Commander in chief of the military, including the militia when called into service

- Ability to make treaties providing two-thirds of the Senators concurs
- Nominate ambassadors, officers, and Supreme Court Justices with the approval of the Senate
- Provide state-of-the-union information periodically
- On extraordinary occasions, convene and adjourn both houses of Congress

After scanning the second document and reflecting for a minute, Jeffers looked up and said, "Not much for me to do, according to the Constitution. Why am I so busy all the time?"

Sam didn't think a reply was necessary, so he remained silent for a minute before moving on to the next topic. "Sir, you also asked about the procedures for amending the Constitution. Here again, I believe you know the answer, but let me summarize."

"Go ahead."

"There are two ways to amend the Constitution. The first is for Congress to propose amendments when two-thirds of both houses approve. The second is an application by the legislatures of two-thirds of the states. Both approaches lead to a constitutional convention, which formally develops and proposes the final version of the amendment. When this is completed, the amendments must be ratified by the legislatures of three-fourths of the states. Alternatively, the states can hold their own individual conventions. Here again, three-fourths approval is needed for ratification. So you can see that this is a long and arduous process that would require considerable work."

"You've given me a lot to think about," answered Jeffers. "I would appreciate it if you could summarize all of this in a very brief memo. Have the memo classified top secret."

Sam waited quietly while the president mulled over his next action. Finally he came to a decision. "Sam," he said, "when I gave you this assignment, I asked you for recommendations of the manner in which the Constitution could be amended so that I can do the necessary things to keep the country from flying apart. You've given me an excellent summary of the Constitution as it currently stands, but now we need to move on to the contents of the amendment. After looking at your summaries of the relative authority of Congress and the president, it becomes clear that the early framers of the Constitution tried to maximize the control that was granted to Congress and gave very little to the president. I believe that this is an accurate conclusion since they were trying to avoid making the presidency into a monarchy. I think the amendment should be worded in a manner that ensures the public's support, but it should change the balance of power somewhat between the two branches of government. In short, I think the president must have the ability to finance his initiatives."

Sam nodded his head in apparent agreement, but his answer was noncommittal. "Sir, I sensed that was the direction in which you were headed. It's clear to me that to achieve your objectives, what you need is the power of taxation and borrowing. The trick will be to write an amendment that doesn't look as if you're emasculating Congress."

"You've got it!" exclaimed Jeffers. "Let's talk again in a day or two, but no more than that. I'll work on the problem of getting the states to call for a convention, and you work on the wording of an amendment."

"Yes, sir," replied Sam as he left the Oval Office.

***

Less than twenty-four hours later, Sam returned to the Oval Office with some ideas to offer the president. As before, Jan was able to rearrange Jeffers' schedule so that their meeting could occur without delay.

"What've you got?" asked Chris as Sam entered the office.

"You've given me a tough assignment. Section Eight of Article One states that, 'The Congress shall have power to lay and collect taxes . . .' It would be easy to substitute the words 'The president shall have the power . . .' But I doubt that would sit well with your friends on the Hill. So I've developed a few alternative proposals. One would be to modify the section so that it's a shared responsibility, as in 'Either the president or Congress shall have the power . . .' and optionally to add that the proposals of one body require the approval of the other. Another alternative would be to simply shift the authority to the president and add that it becomes effective with the advice and consent of the Senate. This alternative would be similar to the wording of the appointments of Supreme Court Justices, ambassadors, and cabinet officials." Sam then sat back in his chair and waited for the president's reaction.

Jeffers nodded and sat thoughtfully for a minute before reacting to Sam's analysis. "I don't think that shared responsibility would work. We'd still encounter the same obstacles that currently exist. I kind of like the advice and consent idea since it parallels that of other presidential authorities, and the Senate tends to be a more responsible gathering than the House. Let me think about it."

Then Jeffers continued in a collegial manner. "Sam, I've been giving some thought to the manner in which the amendment process can be initiated. Obviously the only practical approach would be to encourage the states to initiate the process. I'm considering an indirect approach in which the dysfunctional Congress fails to act on my requests for additional funds, and I begin to make some painful decisions that will make the governors unhappy. At an appropriate time, we'll suggest that they initiate the amendment process. I'm hoping that most people realize that we can't continue like this."

"Well, sir, that might work. But three-quarters of the states will have to be on board before it can succeed. Thirty-eight states are a lot of states."

"I'm out of ideas for simpler approaches. Let's assume that our scheme is going to work. So before you return to Justice, I'd like you to prepare a draft of the amendment that would be introduced at a convention. While it may be as simple as a few wording changes, there are other issues to be considered, such as the other financial authorities of Congress for paying debts and borrowing money as well as approval of all these measures. As usual, the devil is in the details. If you have questions regarding the balance to achieve when preparing this amendment, tilt the wording in the favor of the presidency. These will all become negotiating points during the process. As you can imagine, there is not a tight deadline on this, since there are many bridges to cross before we will be dealing with a convention."

"I'll get right on it, sir," Sam said as he left the office.

***

While Jeffers and Papas were studying the Constitution, other wheels were turning. The president's congressional liaison had notified Congress of the need to increase the spending limit by another $50 billion on top of the $100 billion that had already been received. Even though the $150 billion increase was only one percent of the overall national debt, the White House staffers making the request thought it was a staggering amount. Rarely had midyear increases of this magnitude been requested.

The Democrats in Congress used the request as evidence that Jeffers was mismanaging the country's fiscal affairs, while the Republicans, recognizing that the alternative was a significant tax increase, downplayed the significance of a larger national debt. During the hearings on the increased debt ceiling, both sides were able to call on economists who were happy to provide supporting testimony. Both sides were experienced at delivering their arguments, since debates over the national debt had been going on for the entire history of the republic. Multiple proposals were made and rejected to offset some of the borrowing with a tax increase. Americans had little understanding of the inflationary effects of additional debt and were happy with low taxes, particularly the upper class.

It had been evident from the beginning that the Senate with its Republican majority would reluctantly support their president and agree to the increased debt ceiling. But the House of Representatives with its Democratic majority was more problematic. Despite the pleas of the White House liaisons, it appeared that the bill to increase the debt ceiling was going to fail. Toward the end of the debate it was decided that Jeffers would have to address the recalcitrant body himself. His speech was direct and factual. He did not threaten or cajole. He just made it clear that we could not continue to resist ISIS and their collaborators while at the same time protecting the American public within the constraints of available funding. While he recognized their reluctance to raise taxes, increased borrowing was one of two alternatives. The other alternative was reduction or elimination of services and national defense.

Congress was unimpressed. Representative Donald Squlo, from his exile at Internment Camp #1, issued a press release that described a third, less costly option available to the president—nuclear attacks on the Middle East and deportation of American Muslims. The press continued to dismiss him as a nutcase, while many of those in Congress and the White House simply ignored him.

As Jeffers had expected, the requested increase in the debt ceiling failed. It was a bittersweet moment, in that it opened the door for him to execute his plan regarding a state-requested amendment convention, but at the same time it greatly complicated his efforts to keep the nation moving forward on an even keel.

***

It was now time for Jeffers to implement the second phase of his plan. The internment centers were resulting in a slight decrease of the Christian-Muslim violence occurring throughout the country. The National Guard had either been called up by their state governors or nationalized by the Department of Defense. In the former case, the costs of the call-up were the responsibility of the state in which they had been activated. In the latter case, their costs became the responsibility of the federal government. To date, twenty-three guard units had been called up—five by individual states and eighteen by the federal government. In all cases, those arrested by the guard units could either be sent to the internment centers, or, optionally, housed in the local jails. Most opted for the internment centers since here again, the federal government would be paying for their detention.

Fortunately, the National Governors' Conference was scheduled to be held at the convention center in Washington, DC at a time shortly after the unfavorable votes in Congress. So instead of going on national TV, as he had originally intended, Jeffers decided to take his case directly to those that could help him the most—the fifty state governors.

President Jeffers was the featured speaker at the conference, which meant that he was the first speaker of any substance on the program. This was an ideal position, for it provided him with a forum that would set the stage for the remainder of the conference. He was introduced to a standing ovation from the audience. In spite of his difficulties with Bis Saif, ISIS, and the local Muslim-Christian conflicts, he was a popular president, and most politicians as well as the general public gave him high marks for his efforts. In short, the country rallied around its president as it usually does in a time of crisis.

The room was silent as he began his carefully prepared speech. Most of the governors were present. Hawaii and Idaho were represented by senior officials of their state governments, because their governors could not attend in person due to a family wedding and illness, respectively.

Jeffers began in the traditional manner. "Good morning, ladies and gentlemen. It is good to see the real power within the United States assembled to discuss the solutions facing the many serious problems that exist in our country."

Without further preamble, he then launched directly into the subject at hand. "My goal is to work collaboratively with you to address these problems. I want to help you eliminate the violence that has occurred between various religions within our country, most of which is caused by fear and lack of understanding. Both Christianity and Islam are based on principles of peace and understanding. Both religions worship a single God, and both religions have their roots in the Holy Bible's Old Testament. The violence is being perpetuated by fringe groups with limited understanding of their own cultures, much less those of the other side. These folks are expressing their frustrations with society through intolerance. I will not and cannot let this happen."

At that point, Jeffers paused to take a sip of water from the podium while the audience clapped politely. He then continued.

"As you know, we in the federal government have taken a number of actions to restore the peace and prosperity of our nation. We have federalized and deployed the National Guard in several states. We have established internment centers in an effort to contain the troublemakers. We have given the National Guard the power to make warrantless searches and arrests of troublemakers. In short, we have significantly strengthened our ability to support the law enforcement organizations within your states. We have also established retail distribution centers in states affected by the power blackout.

"I believe that as a result of the efforts at both the federal and state levels, we are making some progress. While the violence has not been totally eradicated, it has certainly been reduced. In order to continue this progress, we must maintain these programs at their current levels.

"However, I have some bad news. The programs I have described are very expensive. Their continuation, combined with the need to commit additional resources to combat ISIS and Bis Saif throughout the world, has exceeded the financial resources at our disposal. I have petitioned Congress to increase the debt ceiling by the staggering amount of a hundred and fifty billion, which is a significant amount of money but represents less than a one-percent increase in our overall national debt. As most of you undoubtedly know, Congress has refused to honor my request. I have privately discussed the possibility of a tax increase with senior leaders in Congress. They have told me that it would not be possible to pass such a measure. So if we were to continue on our present course, the United States would soon face bankruptcy. This is an unimaginable situation for the greatest power on earth.

"You might ask why we don't just cut back on other govern-ment programs. I have studied this possibility and concluded that our military budget and entitlement programs, which include Social Security, health care, certain retirement programs, unemployment insurance, and certain Veterans Administration programs, cannot be scaled back. These programs along with payment of interest on the national debt are responsible for two-thirds of our budget. As a result, if we were to eliminate all other discretionary programs, including medical research, funding for education, highway programs, and on and on, we would not have the funds needed to cover our increased costs for combat and domestic law enforcement."

The president paused again, and the room remained eerily silent. It was if his speech had taken the oxygen out of the room.

"You're probably wondering where I'm going with this. My response is that unless additional sources of revenue are found, we will have to review all ongoing federal programs, and triage those that are not of the highest priority. As I said earlier, the magnitude of our problem means that some of the programs that must be significantly reduced includes the assistance that we are providing the states for combatting ongoing violence in the form of both troops and supplemental funding for increased law enforcement. It grieves me to say this, because I'm fearful that this step is likely to result in a resurgence of the religious warfare that we've been trying to combat."

Then Jeffers reached the punchline. "As I'm certain you know, we are staggering from one financial crisis to the next. Even if the spending limit had been increased by Congress, we'd be facing a new crisis next year, and the year after that, and on into the foreseeable future. We can't keep going like this. We need tax reform that includes realistic policies that support the expenses being incurred in support of the American public. Federal taxation is not a Christmas tree on which congressional ornaments are hung. While our Constitution was written by reasonable men who produced a remarkable document, it is doubtful that they anticipated trillion-dollar budgets. Nor did they anticipate the existence of a fundamentalist Islamic organization knocking at our doors with the intent of defeating us. There are many other things they failed to anticipate, including the existence of political action committees with the power to influence the votes of many members of Congress. It has become clear to me that the system is just not working."

Again the audience remained silent as the president paused for emphasis. They were undoubtedly reflecting on the significance of Jeffers' words, and it was even possible that some had extrapolated his statement to mean that there was the need for a constitutional amendment.

"I'm anxious to help you. But I need your help too. I need you to speak with your representatives in Washington and explain the urgency of our financial situation. I'm also asking you to consider ways in which our current political processes may be modified to provide the resources needed to continue to maintain our national security. I may be wrong, but I feel that our citizens have become soft. They enjoy watching their favorite sports on TV, they enjoy the overall luxury of their lives, and they enjoy feeling that state and federal governments will see to their every need. It does not occur to most that in a democracy, they are the government and it is up to them to ensure that it has the resources needed to live up to their expectations. As John F. Kennedy so eloquently stated during his inaugural address: 'Ask not what your country can do for you—ask what you can do for your country.'"

With that, Jeffers concluded his address. After a moment of silence, applause erupted and continued for several minutes. It was clear that the address had been well-received and the governors had understood the message.

Several other speakers followed Jeffers, but none of their words were remembered. At the cocktail hour following the meeting, the discussion focused on his speech. Most were shocked to learn that their federal law enforcement backup was likely to be discontinued and discussed its implications as well as various ways in which the problem could be overcome.

Jeffers had asked members of his staff to attend the cocktail party, with the dual objectives of sampling reactions to his speech, while at the same time encouraging consideration of possible constitutional changes.

The next day, the National Governors Association modified its agenda to include an hour for discussion of the implications of the country's budget deficit and its impact on the states. There was no shortage of opinions offered during the discussion, including possible recall of congressmen such as Don Squlo who had been particularly disruptive, and in the eyes of some, irrational.

Due to pressing commitments at the White House related to an expanded ISIS offensive in Syria, the president was not able to participate in the discussion, nor did he feel it would have been appropriate. Instead, he assigned Sam Papas to attend in order to record the discussion and to provide any insights that might have been requested by the group. No insights were required, but as the discussion neared the end of the hour that had been allotted, Sam was discouraged that no one had raised the possibility of a constitutional amendment, in spite of the president's broad hints regarding its necessity.

As luck would have it, Sam found himself seated in the audience next to the governor of Minnesota, one of the states most affected by the Christian-Muslim friction. While one of the governors was droning on about the dire consequences of reduced federal support, Sam whispered to his neighbor, "Has anyone considered the possibility of a constitutional amendment giving the president greater authority over taxation?"

At first the governor appeared startled, since he had barely paid attention to the young man seated next to him. "That's such a radical idea that I doubt it has occurred to anyone. Let me think about it."

Then the two lapsed into silence. But when the current speaker had completed his monolog, the governor rose, walked to one of the microphones positioned in the aisle of the meeting room, and spoke. "Let me introduce myself. I am Loren Sanderson, Governor of Minnesota. We have suffered with the problems of this conflict more than any of the other states that have not experienced a power failure. I agree with all of the statements made so far, but there is one possibility that none of you appear to have considered. I think we should discuss the possibility of a constitutional amendment that shifts financial power from Congress to the president. That august body seems incapable of meeting its responsibilities. In fact, that has been the case for many years now, and I'm fed up with it. Until now, we've been able to stagger along, ignoring the problem, but the time has come to do something about it. I would like to propose that a committee of governors be established with the objective of assessing the viability of an amendment, considering its contents, and developing a roadmap for its implementation. I would further propose that we include a representative from the White House as an observer."

With the final sentence of Sanderson's proposal, Sam Papas nearly left his seat with excitement. His suggestion had succeeded beyond his wildest expectations. He hoped that the president would nominate him to participate with the committee.As soon as Sanderson sat down, the governors of California and Wyoming rose to support his suggestion as did the governor of Texas, Jeffers' home state. While there were some negative reactions, it was difficult to object to the idea that the committee would deal with the many issues associated with a drastic suggestion such as the one being made by Sanderson. When the committee had completed its work, a discussion with more substance could occur. A straw vote was taken and unanimously passed.

Sam was ecstatic.

CHAPTER 32

IS THIS THE BEGINNING OF THE END?

Over the strong objection of the US Congress, thirty-nine states—one more than required—voted to convene a convention to consider amending the Constitution. Representatives from fifty states participated at the event, which was again held at the Convention Center in Washington, DC, six months following the Governor's Conference. The convention was a raucous affair, with proposals and objections hotly debated. With the state of Minnesota acting as his proxy, Sam was able to introduce the wording of the amendment that he had developed in collaboration with the president. The proposed amendment read:

"In the event that Congress fails to enact a policy to collect the taxes and other revenue needed to support programs that have been lawfully established either by the Congress or the president, the president shall prepare a revenue program to be implemented with the advice and consent of the Senate. The Senate shall have sixty days to either approve the president's program or prepare an alternative program approved by both houses of Congress to be submitted for the president's approval."

As Sam explained to the convention, the amendment gave Congress two opportunities to prepare a tax program responsive to the nation's needs. If they failed at both attempts, the president was authorized to prepare his own proposal, which would then become law with the majority approval of the Senate.

As might be expected, the proposal generated significant discussion. Many alternatives were proposed and rejected. One

440

particular concern was with the phrase *taxes and other revenue*. The debate revealed that this was a reference to other sources of income for the federal government, including Social Security and Medicare payments. Supporters of the amendment argued successfully that without this authority, the president could raise taxes and Congress could make compensating reductions in other payments made by the public, thus nullifying the president's efforts.

The amendment was approved with one modification before the convention was adjourned. The sixty-day approval period was extended to ninety days. When preparing the draft amendment, the president had cleverly suggested to Sam that they use the more aggressive number of sixty days, recognizing it would be extended to give the delegates the impression that their ideas had helped shape the process, rather than rubber stamping the draft.

As required by the Constitution, the proposed amendment was then submitted to the states for ratification. Another year was needed for ratification, a year during which the president lobbied vigorously for the amendment, while those in Congress opposed to its adoption lobbied equally vigorously. Those opposed to the amendment began calling Jeffers the emperor rather than president, a reference to his perceived attempts to increase the power of the presidency to that of a Roman emperor. Their slurs had little impact on the national sentiment to overcome Congress's partisan bickering.

Even more effective than the president's lobbying was the cancellation of federal funding for National Guard units that had been assigned to supplement local law enforcement activities. As these units were withdrawn from the field, violence once again began to escalate in locations susceptible to religious unrest. As the country's financial woes increased, the population of the internment camps was held constant, a factor that aggravated the overcrowding at the local jails, to which recently arrested agitators were sent. These factors combined to increase pressure on Congress as well as the framers of the constitutional amendment to take the needed actions.

Philip J. Tarnoff

The states that had voted to convene the convention voted in its favor, with the result that there was now a twenty-eighth amendment to the US Constitution. The immediate impact of the new amendment was relatively minor, but greater in the longer term. While many in Washington viewed the amendment as a first step of Jeffers' efforts to establish a monarchy, in deed if not in name, they were proven wrong when he refused to support the repeal of the twenty-second amendment to the Constitution, which limits the number of times a president can be elected to office to two. The movement to repeal this amendment was based on his popularity with the public, and the perception that he was acting forcefully to contain the ISIS-Bis Saif menace. Although they did not understand all the details, and in fact few even followed the news from Washington, it was the public's general perception that Jeffers had things under control. They wanted to ensure that power did not revert to Congress, which the public felt had generally been responsible for the current state of affairs, even though no one that professed that feeling could provide concrete reasons to support their opinion.

Whether understood by the public or not, in time the 28th Amendment led to a profound change in the way that the United States was governed. Granting the president the power of the purse strengthened his office to the point at which he could dictate the terms of many different bills that came before Congress. If the president did not like a particular bill, it would not be funded. If the president supported a particular bill, he could readily buy the votes to ensure that it would be passed. Many felt that the impact of the 28th Amendment was to reduce Congress to a rubber stamp organization, with little power or ability to establish the direction of the country. It was recognized by scholars as a significant erosion of the principles on which the country was founded. The more philosophical interpreted the amendment as a victory for ISIS, in that the future of the United States as a democracy was now in doubt.

***

In spite of the new constitutional amendment, things were not going nearly as well in the Middle East. ISIS took advantage of the distractions in the United States as well as their expanded supply of SAMs and fire-control systems to begin several major initiatives in Iraq and Syria as well as a new front in Lebanon. Their efforts led to several near-term successes. In Iraq, ISIS was able to consolidate its control of the northwest area of the country and was advancing to the suburbs of Baghdad. In Syria, ISIS was able to consolidate their control of the areas that they already occupied.

But of particular concern to the West was a new initiative in Lebanon that included attacks on a swath of territory in the central section of the country that included Zahle and Beirut. The attacks resulted in fierce fighting between the Lebanese army and ISIS, with only limited support from the West due to the danger of the new ISIS SAMs. Ultimately, this section of Lebanon came under ISIS control, effectively separating the northern and southern parts of the country.

Hamas, with support from both ISIS and Bis Saif, also became more active. ISIS supporters had been appearing in the Gaza Strip even before the emergence of Bis Saif. Increased aggression against Israel took the form of attacks on Israeli settlements near the Gaza Strip as well as a significant increase in the number of suicide bombings in the major cities. Tel Aviv and Jerusalem were the primary targets. Israel responded to these attacks with increased air raids on the Gaza Strip. The army had been called up, and it appeared that a major assault was being planned.

The United States provided assistance to the defenders in these various regions with increased air attacks and expansion of the number of embedded troops for training and coordination. However, US support was limited due to its domestic needs. Limited supplemental assistance was provided by European allies, although they were also stretched thin.

Adam al-Zhihri seemed to be everywhere during these conflicts. He assumed the role of coordinator, advisor, and financier of the ISIS efforts. One of his many assumed duties was the formal establishment of the caliphate in Raqqa. He was anxious to develop a new fortified compound that offered both the security protection and the grandeur appropriate for the new caliphate. In other words, he wanted to remove General Hussain from his basement quarters so that he could be seen in surroundings appropriate for his stature. Hussain agreed with Adam's objectives and together they planned the new facility. Much of it was underground to protect its occupants from air raids. A small but impressive structure was to be erected above the underground rooms that would demonstrate the power and permanence of the new Sunni Muslim Caliphate. Adam and Hussain agreed to begin construction as soon as the region surrounding Raqqa had been brought under ISIS control. They were both excited with the prospects of achieving the goal that they had worked so hard to accomplish.

***

Adam was determined to maintain the momentum that had been established by the Bis Saif attacks. He had created chaos with the power failures in California and Washington, DC, and didn't want to give the United States an opportunity to recover. It was also his desire to avenge the destruction of his Jakarta headquarters. He admired Al Qaeda's 9/11 attack that had destroyed New York's World Trade Center. The 9/11 attacks had a devastating impact on the US society, forcing the country to spend trillions of dollars for increased security. He had read an article in *The New York Times* which estimated that the total cost in terms of both government and non-government expenditures was a staggering $3.3 trillion, or about $7 million for every dollar Al Qaeda spent executing the attacks. Adam wanted to create an incident with similar consequences. Sooner or later these multiple crippling events would cause US society as it currently exists to begin to crumble. But he realized that the US security services had improved surveillance of airports and pilot training facilities so that replication of the 9/11 attacks would be nearly impossible.

Adam and General Hussein spent weeks conceiving a suitable plan. Adam led these discussions since the war against the West was his responsibility, while Hussein was concentrating on the Middle East and the rest of Asia. Initially they considered additional terror attacks similar to the ones at Union Station and Disneyland. Adam expressed his frustration at the end of a long day while the two of them were relaxing over cups of Turkish coffee. "General, I don't think a repetition of terrorist style attacks will achieve the desired purpose. I sense that the American people are adjusting to these attacks in the same way that people in the Middle East have. We need something bigger."

General Hussein thought for a minute before answering. "It's too bad we can't replicate an attack from the air. Maybe drones ..."

Adam stood up suddenly and began pacing. "What an idea," he exclaimed. "Why didn't I think of it? I've even got the source of the drones. We could use the same model that I purchased for the Palestinians. I think it was a Chinese CH-3 drone, which would more than meet our needs. It can carry a payload of up to 400 pounds. Enough for a lot of damage. They're expensive, but we should probably purchase at least four. Two for training and two for the mission."

Hussain smiled. "I think we're onto something, but a few more details need to be considered. Now all we need is a location, a target, and people to fly it."

Ali thought for a minute before responding. "It seems to me that the Nigerians, Pakistanis, and, of course, the Chinese are using the CH-3. It should be easy to smuggle several of their operators into America if they're not there already. I'm sure the Chinese would be willing to help us smuggle the drones."

After pouring over maps of the Washington, DC, area, Adam concluded that a drone controlled and launched from Virginia could cross the Potomac River and reach a target in Washington, DC, before it could be detected and intercepted. He wished he had his staff from Jakarta to help him with the execution of the plan.

Instead of relying on local staff, Ali reached out to the Chinese manufacturer for ways in which the CH-3s could be smuggled into the United States. The solution they offered was deceptively simple. They could be disassembled and the pieces hidden within shipments of cars manufactured in China and shipped to the US. Volvo, Buick, and Cadillac each have at least one model manufactured there. The two 12-foot wings were to be disguised as the floorboards of the imported vehicles. With these final pieces in place, Bis Saif, with the support of the Caliphate, proceeded with its plan.

***

As Chris and Melissa dressed for his delivery of the State-of-the-Union address to the joint session of Congress, Chris reflected on the past attacks that had been endured by the United States. First 9/11, and then Union Station and Disneyworld, along with massive power failures had been inflicted on the country. He couldn't ship the entire country to Panamint City to prevent ethnic violence, and his efforts to keep Congress under control were slipping. The only bright spot in all of this was the new amendment to the Constitution which provided him with the tools he needed to finance the government's needs.

Returning his attention to the present, Chris turned to Melissa, who, he suddenly noticed, was dressed in a stylish, form-fitting, wine-colored cocktail dress. He loved the look of her with her blond hair accented against the dress. "You look spectacular," he exclaimed. "Maybe you should be addressing the nation instead of me. No one would dare disagree with you."

She laughed at his flirtation. "You'd better keep your mind on your business instead of monkey business. The nation needs your leadership."

"I wish we had more time for recreation," he said regret-fully, folding his speech and placing it inside his suitcoat pocket. "This speech is going to be a doozy. After tonight I'm sure I'll be up to my ears defending it."

A polite knock on the door from the White House valet reminded them that it was time to leave.

Shortly afterward, two motorcades left the White House for the Capitol, where the State of the Union Address would be delivered. One of the motorcades was intended as a decoy; the second carried the president and first lady.

As the armored presidential limousine pulled out of the underground White House garage, Jeffers reviewed the contents of his address. It was a speech that focused on the financial steps that needed to be taken to keep the nation on stable footing following the terrorist attacks. It included a modest tax increase and greatly decreased funding for all civilian agencies. He had increased payments for both Social Security and Medicare while terminating several expensive military weapons programs. He felt it was a balanced approach toward tackling America's problems and was optimistic that this might be a way that the nation could turn a corner toward a more stable society.

As the president was replacing his folded speech in his jacket pocket, two drone aircraft seemed to appear out of nowhere. They had flown from Virginia at treetop height to avoid detection by the defenders of the Washington, DC, airspace. The first drone attacked the decoy convoy which had been proceeding slowly down Pennsylvania Avenue toward the Capital. It exploded, destroying both the intended vehicle and those immediately in front and behind, killing the Secret Service unit included in the procession as well as several pedestrians.

The second drone circled briefly near the Washington Monument before diving at the convoy carrying the president and first lady. This done proved as effective as the first, scoring a direct hit on the limousine in which they were riding. The Jeffers and their Secret Service protectors died instantly in the blinding explosion.

In that tragic instant, both the Jeffers and the United States of America were plunged into darkness.

CHAPTER 33

EPILOG

The principal participants in the ongoing drama met with mixed fates. Kelly Jaffari and Jahmir Al-Saadi, the two who had worked for JCN Enterprises and developed the extraordinary high-powered computer system that ultimately caused the blackouts in Washington, DC and California, cooperated with US intelligence agencies following their capture in Jakarta. In one of the most generous plea bargains on record, they were given a sentence of two years' probation and were allowed to return to their original positions at JCN Enterprises. The two were greatly relieved and felt that their new lives were a dream come true as they rejoined the company that had been their lives until their security clearances had been denied.

JCN Enterprises continued to prosper as the federal government and DARPA in particular gained a better understanding of MOM's potential for good and evil. The development of MOM, the computer system with unprecedented capabilities, was accelerated with increased financial support from DARPA and the return of Jahmir and Kelly. It led to improved weather forecasts, greatly enhanced medical research, and many other benefits to areas of science that could benefit from its super processing capability. The security of the United States was also improved, since MOM's spectacular capabilities permitted monitoring data communications and decrypting secure communications at a level that had never been possible. Security specialists recognized that the computational advantage that MOM gave the United States would be temporary, since, like the atomic bomb, other countries would go to great lengths to steal its secrets and duplicate its capabilities. In an effort to delay the spread of neural computing technology, JCN was asked to assemble multiple versions of MOM on which processing time could be leased by other countries. The leased computer time was closely supervised by the CIA to ensure that these powerful devices would be used exclusively for peaceful purposes.

The surprisingly lenient sentences of Kelly and Jahmir influenced the judge presiding over the case of Kelly's parents, Sami and Lilliane Jaffari. The judge reasoned that the parents could not be punished more severely than Kelly and Jahmir, since their only crime was financing their work and helping them surreptitiously to leave the country. He felt that they never understood the intent of their technology and therefore could not be charged with espionage against the United States. In addition, they had spent the last two years in prison awaiting trial, a punishment that he considered more than ample. They returned to their beloved home in Timonium, where Sami immediately set to work on his gardening while workmen repaired the damage done by the FBI.

With the blessing of James Proctor, the Director of the FBI, Lee Sanders never wavered from his mission to track down Gus Waters and put him away for life. Although his crimes were less odious than Adam's had been, he was responsible for many of the conflicts that had been stirred up in the United States. It was to Lee's benefit that Gus had not been as skillful at disguising his appearance and his moves as Adam had been. With the assistance of an alert airline ticket agent and a well-positioned security camera, Gus was ultimately arrested in the waiting area of the San Francisco International Airport.

Perhaps most important to those who ignore world events and think only of their own personal enjoyment, the Super Bowl was not cancelled. As a result of the efforts of the National Football League, it was moved to Arizona, where it was held at the University of Phoenix stadium in Glendale not long before the unfortunate assassination. Had he survived the drone attack, the president would have attended the Super Bowl to cheer for his beloved Cowboys in their game against the New England Patriots. Instead, a somber mood pervaded the game, which was

449

being played in honor of Christopher and Melissa Jeffers—the president and first lady.

***

The fates of those who had attended the initial Bis Saif meeting in Jakarta varied greatly. Ali, the ISIS representative at the meeting, had done well. He became a commander of the ISIS SAM battalion and distinguished himself by the number of allied aircraft and drones that had been destroyed. The battalion's effectiveness prevented the allies from calling in air support during major battles. Instead, it became necessary to limit the use of air support to surprise attacks on isolated targets. When Adam al-Zhihri arrived to coordinate the activities of Bis Saif with ISIS, Ali's status was further enhanced as he became the primary liaison between the two organizations and ultimately served with distinction in the new caliphate.

Udo's life had improved following his emigration to the United States. His contributions to the search for Bis Saif were well-recognized. He was granted sanctuary in the United States and enrolled in the FBI's witness protection program to ensure his safety from those who might seek revenge. He also received the $1 million reward that had been offered for anyone providing the location of the Bis Saif headquarters. Udo was granted the opportunity to attend high school and then college, where he majored in political science. He continued to work with the CIA, providing them with insights into the Boko Haram operations. He never stopped thinking about the village in Borno that they had destroyed and wondered whether he had any surviving relatives in Nigeria.

The third member of the group, Hasan Jouda, had been captured during the attack on the Bis Saif headquarters. His name was revered in Palestine because of the effectiveness of his Suquur missile. Although revered, his fate was less pleasant than that of Ali or Udo in that he was returned to Israel for trial as a Hamas soldier. In spite of the efforts of a legal team financed by Hamas, he was sentenced to ten years in prison.

General Murtaja remained in Palestine directing the fight against Israel. He felt that recruiting Hasan had been a significant success and began scouring the country for other bright Palestinians that could be employed to advance the army's technical capabilities.

Although Leroy Williamson, Adam's technical guru, had been captured during the Bis Saif headquarters raid, other than his presence in Jakarta, it was never possible to identify any specific crimes with which to charge him. He was returned to the United States, where he settled in his home town of New Haven, Connecticut, where he found work with a computer consulting company.

***

Until his untimely death, President Jeffers had become a frequent face on TV and radio news reports as he argued forcefully against the fear and discrimination produced by the conflicts with Bis Saif and ISIS. Local religious groups had joined in the efforts to convince the public of the need to reunite as a nation against foreign efforts to disrupt the American society. Much of this effort was futile. The country's fears and suspicions were greatly increased with the assassination of their president. It would require decades before these feelings dissipated. Can the United States cure these problems without losing its identity?

The power failures in both the Washington, DC, region and California had been repaired. Those who had been evacuated to neighboring states gradually returned to their homes. Life was gradually returning to normal, although the populations of these regions were coping with memories that would take some time to heal. Antagonism toward Muslim extremists as well as the inability of Congress to provide needed financial support remained particularly strong in these regions. Superficially, life had returned to normal, but fear and hatred remained buried under the surface.

Conditions remained in turmoil in the Middle East. ISIS and its allies scored significant victories in their coordinated attacks against their perceived enemies. Adam al-Zhihri gained prominence within the Arab world as the titular head of the caliphate. He was able to command the attention of the united extremist forces from his hideout in Syria. Although the coalition's effectiveness had been demonstrated through its combined efforts, Adam was kept busy preventing infighting among its members, as well as loss of focus on their enemies in the West. Many of the participating organizations had been organized with the goal of disrupting the governments of their home countries and were anxious to return to fighting their local enemies. As a result, the caliphate had failed to develop into the powerful organization capable of dictating the terms of the West's treatment of the Muslim world that Adam had dreamed of.

Adam was persistent and remained a force to be reckoned with by the United States and its allies. The NATO allies had committed more than 30,000 troops as well as untold numbers of ships and combat aircraft to the ongoing war. As usual, the United States provided nearly three-quarters of these resources.

While the West was making progress militarily, they were losing their battle for the hearts and minds of the indigent and the youth of the Arab world. While areas that had been lost by ISIS and their allies were under the control of the West, they continued to recruit volunteers from these same regions. Governing proved difficult with the need to invest billions of dollars to restore the infrastructure that had been destroyed by the fighting. The United States, usually the primary contributor toward rebuilding war-torn areas, was facing financial difficulties and could not contribute its usual largesse. As usual, new governments installed to replace those that had been defeated proved inadequate to the task of rebuilding and reuniting their countries.

Without strong leadership from either the West or the caliphate, turmoil prevailed throughout the Middle East, and worldwide terrorism prevailed. Many in the West wondered where civilization was headed. Without doubt, it appeared to be headed toward different governments and power structures. The path toward the new world would be lengthy, with uncertain outcomes. The changes occurring in the United States were precursors of an unsettled future.

***

As Edward Gibbon wrote in his masterpiece *The Decline and Fall of the Roman Empire*:

> *The spectator who casts a mournful view over the ruins of ancient Rome is tempted to accuse the memory of the Goths and Vandals for the mischief which they had neither leisure nor power, nor perhaps inclination, to perpetrate . . . the destruction which undermined the foundations of those massy fabrics was prosecuted, slowly and silently . . . The decay of the city had gradually impaired the value of the public works. The circus and theaters might still excite, but they seldom gratified the desires of the people.*

The decline of Rome cannot be traced to a single event nor a single emperor. But as Gibbon observed, it was a gradual process which, in Rome's case, occurred over a period of ten centuries, during which much of the treasure was spent on war and political intrigue.

By comparison, the situation in the United States was somewhat different. The country has been in existence for a mere three centuries, and has been consistently led by a series of elected officials guided by a robust document, the US Constitution. But there are also similarities. The United States has spent much of its wealth on war and corruption. Its infrastructure is in decline, and its citizens are diverted by professional sports and various forms of electronic entertainment. The United States is also besieged by factions bent on its destruction. One must wonder whether the country is on a path similar to that of Rome, leading to its ultimate demise.

.

Review Requested:
If you loved this book, would you please provide a review at Amazon.com?

CPSIA information can be obtained
at www.ICGtesting.com
Printed in the USA
FSOW02n0501091216
28168FS